An Amish Country Christmas

An Amish Country Christmas

Charlotte Hubbard
Naomi King

ZEBRA BOOKS
KENSINGTON PUBLISHING CORP.

http://www.kensingtonbooks.com

ZEBRA BOOKS are published by

Kensington Publishing Corp.
119 West 40th Street
New York, NY 10018

All Kensington titles, imprints, and distributed lines are available at special quantity discounts for bulk purchases for sales promotion, premiums, fund-raising, educational, or institutional use.

Special book excerpts or customized printings can also be created to fit specific needs. For details, write or phone the office of the Kensington Special Sales Manager: Attn. Special Sales Department. Kensington Publishing Corp., 119 West 40th Street, New York, NY 10018. Phone: 1-800-221-2647.

Zebra and the Z logo Reg. U.S. Pat. & TM Off.

ISBN-13: 978-1-4201-3188-8
ISBN-10: 1-4201-3188-5
First Printing: October 2013

33614081348111

eISBN-13: 978-1-4201-3189-5
eISBN-10: 1-4201-3189-3
First Electronic Edition: October 2013

10 9 8 7 6 5 4

Printed in the United States of America

Contents

Dear Reader,

When my editor, Alicia Condon, suggested this Christmas anthology, where the characters from both of my Amish series get to mix and mingle, I was so tickled! What a fun way to celebrate my favorite holiday with characters I love, but who won't take center stage in my regular series books.

I have a confession, however: if you have followed the placement clues in my previous books, you might realize that my imaginary Missouri towns, Cedar Creek and Willow Ridge, are too far apart geographically to make a sleigh ride or a buggy trip feasible. So in the spirit of the one-horse open sleigh fantasy so many of us crave, I'm asking you to hop in, wrap up in a cuddly blanket, and ride along with me and my characters anyway! Let the fun and love and the jingle of sleigh bells carry you away. In this festive season, and in these holiday tales, reality can take a back seat for a while!

And because I have been blessed to have a book in each of my series coming out around the same time as this holiday anthology, here is the chronological order for these stories: AMANDA WEDS A GOOD MAN: ONE BIG HAPPY FAMILY by Naomi King, WINTER OF WISHES by Charlotte Hubbard, and then this book, AN AMISH COUNTRY CHRISTMAS. This order will make sense, especially for Preacher Tom and Vernon Gingerich as they court the Hooley sisters and prepare to get married.

Merry Christmas and Happy New Year!
Charlotte and Naomi

Isaiah 9:6

For unto us a child is born, unto us a son is given,
And the government shall be upon his shoulder,
And his name shall be called Wonderful Counselor,
The mighty God, the everlasting Father,
The Prince of Peace.

Luke 2:10–11

And the angel said unto them, Fear not, for behold I
bring you good tidings of great joy, which shall be to
all people. For unto you is born this day in the city of
David a Savior, which is Christ the Lord.

The Christmas Visitors

Naomi King

Chapter One

"Easy, Clyde. Back up, fella." Nate Kanagy stood aside as his Clydesdale came backwards out of the horse trailer, sensing Clyde was every bit as excited as he was on this fine December twenty-third. The horse whickered and shook his massive head, then waited patiently beside his brother's bay gelding while Bram shut the trailer gates. Nate stepped up to pay the driver who had brought them here from Willow Ridge this morning. "Thanks again, Gregg. And a merry Christmas to you."

"Merry Christmas to you boys and your family, too," Gregg replied as he started his van. "Enjoy your new sleigh and courting buggy!"

"*Jah*, we intend to!" Nate's brother, Bram, piped up from behind them. "If you can't have fun drivin' a new rig, what's the point of gettin' one?"

The two of them waved as Gregg headed back onto the county blacktop, hauling their empty trailer behind him. Then Nate gazed around the little town of Cedar Creek, Missouri. From where they stood in the parking lot of Graber's Custom Carriages, the countryside rolled gently beneath a fresh blanket of snow, dotted with tall white homes, silos, and barns. Deep green cedar trees followed the creek at the bottom of the hill, where cardinals called to each other. Across the snow-packed blacktop, Treva's Greenhouse sported a sign that said CLOSED FOR CHRISTMAS, but beside it the Cedar Creek Mercantile bustled with buggies and cars alike. "We'll get our fill of Aunt Beulah Mae's homemade goodies tonight—"

"Along with a hefty helping of her nosy questions and Uncle Abe's looooong stories," Bram added.

"—but a special occasion like this calls for some serious junk food."

"*Jah*, let's hit the merc." Bram hitched their two horses to the railing on the side of the carriage shop. "No tellin' what else we might find there. Looks to be a place that stocks everything under the sun, including stuff you never knew you needed."

To Nate, Cedar Creek seemed a lot like most Plain communities, in that the businesses were scattered along the roadside, on the farms where their owners lived. Back home in Willow Ridge they didn't have a carriage maker, so this trip was indeed a treat: their parents had given them their choice of new vehicles with the understanding that he and his younger brother wouldn't go running the roads in cars like a lot of Amish fellows did during their *rumspringa* years. At eighteen, Bram had chosen a buggy so he'd be ready for that day when a special girl tempted him to court and marry her.

Nate, however, had a hankering for a sleigh. Nothing else felt so grand on a winter's day as skimming across the snow-covered hills—and what could be more glorious than such a ride on a moonlit night? After they ate their snack, he couldn't wait to hitch Clyde to his new rig and take off. He'd been engaged to a special girl last Christmas, only to learn she'd been seeing other fellows, so at twenty, Nate wasn't out to impress anybody. These days, he was pleasing himself.

When they entered the mercantile, he felt right at home. The scent of bulk grass seed, stored in wooden bins along the wall, filled the warm air and a wide wooden staircase led to an open second level where work boots and clothing were sold. A banner on the railing said ABBY'S STITCH IN TIME, and a young woman—Abby, most likely—smiled down at him from her treadle sewing machine. Mesh bags of oranges and locally grown apples and potatoes were displayed by the check-out counter. Nate exchanged greetings with the gray-bearded fellow who was ringing up an order and then followed Bram toward the aisles of bulk snacks that had been bagged and labeled here in the store.

"Here's those chocolate coconut haystacks you like," Bram said, "not to mention trail mix and sweet potato chips and saltwater taffy and—"

But Nate wasn't listening. Down the aisle a ways, where they sold livestock supplies, a girl was hefting a mineral block into her pull cart. Her auburn hair glimmered beneath her white kapp, and as she straightened to her full height, she caught his gaze. Held it for a few moments. Then she leaned down again.

It seemed only polite to see if she needed help.

As Nate headed her way, he wasn't surprised to hear the tattoo of Bram's boots on the plank floor behind him. "How about if I get that for you?" he asked as the redhead wrapped her arms around a fifty-pound sack of horse feed.

"*Jah*, how many of those do you need?" Bram chimed in. "No sense in strainin' yourself when we toss this stuff around all the time."

Nate had always heard that blue eyes could twinkle, but now he was seeing it for himself. The young woman looked from him to his brother as though she hid a secret behind her smile. "Not from around here, are you?"

He blinked. Had he sprouted a second head? Did he sound so very different from the Amish fellows here in

Cedar Creek? Or was it Bram's lovestruck grin that made her say that? "Just got here from Willow Ridge, truth be told," Nate replied. "I'm fetching the sleigh James Graber's built for me—"

"And he's got a courtin' buggy with my name on it," his younger brother added.

"Well, you couldn't ask for a better rig, then," she remarked. "James has even built special carriages for Disney World and the likes of Miss America, you see."

Nate didn't know a thing about Miss America, but she surely couldn't hold a candle to this girl. Her ivory skin glowed, with just a few freckles on the bridge of her nose—tiny ones, that he had to lean closer to see. And then there was the way her eyes widened as she gazed back at him. He caught himself and grabbed the bag of feed she'd been lifting. "So how many of these bags do you need?"

"Four, please. And what'd you say your name was?"

Bram laughed as he, too, hefted a sack of the oats mixture. "Last name's Kanagy. I'm Bram—the cute one," he teased, "and Mr. Shy here is my brother Nate. He got burnt by a girl he was engaged to, so now he mostly keeps to his horses."

Nate closed his eyes against a wave of irritation as he placed a third sack of the rations in her wooden cart. "If you believe everything my kid brother says, well—but you look to be way ahead of him. And your name would be—?"

The redhead looked him over yet again. "Martha. Coblentz." She pointed to the shelf where the mineral blocks were. "A couple more of those and I've got to get on home. *Denki* ever so much for your help, fellas. Have a *gut* time with your new rigs."

It was on the tip of his tongue to invite her for a sleigh ride, yet Nate hesitated. After all, they were only spending the night with their aunt and uncle before returning to

Willow Ridge tomorrow, in time to celebrate Christmas Eve and Christmas Day with their family. As though she suddenly needed to be someplace else, Martha strode down the aisle toward the check-out counter, pulling her sturdy wagon behind her.

"Well, you blew that one," Bram muttered.

"And you, little brother, have a mouth bigger than your brain," Nate replied under his breath. "We'll have to work on that."

"*Jah*, Mary?" Martha murmured into her cell phone. She looked behind her as she walked down the road, with the wind whipping at her black coat and bonnet. "You've got to come see these two fellas who're heading over to James's carriage shop! I just now met them in the mercantile and, well—you can gawk at both of them all you want, but I've already decided to go for Nate."

"Puh! What makes you think you get first pick?" her twin retorted.

"First come, first served. Be there or be square," Martha quipped. She loved the way her breath came out in a frosty vapor on this brisk December morning. Truth be told, she was enjoying this day a lot more now that she'd met the two Kanagy boys in the mercantile. "Better get a move on, though, or you might miss them. They're here to fetch a sleigh and a courting buggy James built for them, and they might head right on home afterward—unless we give them a *gut* reason to hang around, you know."

"Well, I can't get there any too fast if I'm on the phone with *you* now, can I?" *Click.*

Martha tucked her cell into her coat pocket and continued down the snow-covered road as fast as her heavy pull cart would allow. What with her *dat* and her older brother Owen out working on a house today, the barn chores fell to her, as they often did. It was just as well, because she preferred working outdoors while Mary was happier helping their *mamm* get ready for today's meals as well as Christmas dinner. Martha was perfectly capable of placing those heavy sacks of feeds in their covered bins and then setting out the new mineral blocks for the horses, but wasn't it a fine thing that two *gut*-looking fellows had come to help her in the mercantile? The boys around Cedar Creek seemed to think she was part of the landscape . . . always there, so mostly invisible. Apparently not worth a second look.

By the time Martha was within sight of the house, here came Mary up the road. Oh, but she had a glint of mischief in her eyes, too! "So what's in that sack, Sister?"

Mary laughed. "That's *my* beeswax, ain't so?"

"Now don't go thinking you can have those fellas all to yourself," Martha protested, playfully blocking her sister's path. "I was nice enough to tell you about them—"

"And Mamma's already got her suspicions about me taking out of the house so sudden-like, too. This better be worth my time, Sister!" Mary declared. "After all, it was *your* dinner—your favorite oatmeal bread and goodies I was baking when you called."

"Puh! If you don't think the walk's worth your while, then I'll just have some fun with those fellas myself. Not a problem!"

"We'll see about that, won't we?"

Martha hurried on down the snowy lane to the barn with her cart, which was harder to pull on the clumpy gravel. No doubt her sister would know a fine opportunity when she saw one, so it was best to put these supplies away and feed the animals in short order. The Kanagy boys didn't know it yet, but as thanks for helping her, they were about to receive a Christmas gift they hadn't counted on.

Chapter Two

Mary stopped at the main entry of the carriage shop to catch her breath. Had she ever hurried up that hill so quickly? One look through the frosted glass in the door, however, told her this spur-of-the-moment plan was the best one she could have concocted: James Graber stood in the front room where a new sleigh and courting buggy were parked, and he was chatting with two of the finest-looking fellows she'd seen in a long while. And if they were each buying a new rig, well, they had a little jingle in their pockets, didn't they? And what fun would they have going straight home, each in his own vehicle, by himself?

Taking a deep breath, Mary stepped into the shop. As she paused by the door, she wished she had quizzed her sister more. One of the fellows James was chatting with wore the traditional Amish broadfall pants, suspenders, and black broad-brimmed hat while his brother sported a black leather jacket with a jaunty fedora that showed off an English-style haircut. His red plaid shirt looked anything but Amish. Which one was Nate? Had Martha learned both of their names, or anything more about them?

Mary's cheeks flushed when the boys noticed her

standing there. She would have to keep a sharp ear and
rely on her smile . . .

James Graber spoke first. "Well, now. Is that warm
chocolate I'm getting a whiff of? Come to bring your
brother Noah a treat for his morning break?"

Noah was apprenticed to James—and the carriage
maker, bless him, had just offered her a conversational
handle. "Too bad Noah's in the back room, ain't so?" she
said as she removed the plastic container from her sack.
"Wouldn't be polite to walk past you fellows without
offering you some of these mocha brownies."

She lifted the lid and then handed the goodies to the
younger, flashier brother. Mary couldn't miss the way his
dark eyes lit up as she removed her black bonnet, and she
hoped she didn't trip over her tongue when she talked to him.

"Martha!" he said. "What kind of a Christmas miracle
is this, that we just saw you in the mercantile and now—"

"Don't think for a minute she brought these goodies to
you, Bram," the other young man teased as he stepped
over to grab one. He, too, gave her a dazzling smile and
then gestured at the sleigh behind them. "What do you
think of my new ride, Martha? I've got a horse hitched
outside, just waiting for a pretty girl to join me on its
maiden voyage."

"Oh, but you'd rather christen my new buggy, *jah*?"
Bram chimed in. "I'm thinkin' you could show me where
to buy a string of Christmas lights to give it some sparkle,
Martha. And you'd look a lot prettier riding behind Felix,
my trotter, because once you're sitting behind Nate's
Clydesdale, nobody'll see you for his broad backside!"

Such talk! And all of it aimed to lure her into each
brother's new rig while her sister was at home choring.
This was more fun than she'd had in a long while, but she
had to speak quickly before James spoiled her charade
by revealing that she was a twin. As hot as her face felt,

the carriage maker was bound to notice she was up to something.

"How's a girl to choose?" she mused. Stalling, she ambled over to admire the glossy black buggy with its upholstery of deep green velvet. Then she stood before the sleigh, a sleek two-seater fitted out in muted red leather that would withstand winter weather. "Either way, I'll look like the Queen of Christmas—"

Her cell phone dinged to signal she had a text message. No doubt in her mind where it was coming from, either. "Excuse me," she said demurely. "I'll let you fellows finish your business while I make up my mind."

Mary walked to the corner of the shop, taking the phone from her pocket. Her fingers quivered as she read Martha's message. What's going on? U won't leave me here, will u?

Oh, but she was tempted to make these brothers draw straws to decide who would drive her around Cedar Creek first. Wasn't it a fine, fun feeling to be the object of their compliments while they believed she had somehow baked fresh brownies for them in the past fifteen minutes? But after a lifetime of doing everything, sharing everything with Martha, Mary couldn't leave her twin out in the cold—or out in the barn working, either. Martha was more athletic and outspoken while Mary preferred to spend her time baking or embroidering, yet most folks couldn't tell them apart . . . and she suspected any fellow who might want to ask one of them out hesitated, wondering if he would ever have time alone with the sister of his choice.

But the Kanagy boys each had a vehicle . . . a perfect way to provide some privacy while they all had a good time.

Get ready to ride! Mary tapped out with her thumbs. Then she dropped her phone into her coat pocket and turned toward the front counter, where the brothers were collecting their receipts from James. Her heart played hopscotch when Bram turned to flash her a wink as he took another mocha brownie from the plate. She had to admit Martha was right: traditional Nate was more her sister's type, while Mary had taken an instant shine to wavy-haired Bram in his rakish fedora and black leather jacket. Here was a fellow still enjoying his *rumspringa*, who wanted to help her make the most of her running-around years, as well. Seemed the least she could do was to show him a good time before he had to head for home.

"Why don't both of you hitch up?" Mary suggested. "I know where to find those lights you want, Bram. All of us can have a real *gut* time while you're here in Willow Ridge."

"Glad I took your suggestion and got the harness with the sleigh bells, James," Nate remarked as he grinned at her. "Clyde's going to step lively for sure and for certain, with that extra jingle and a girl riding along."

"We'll see about that," Mary replied. Did she sound too brazen, suggesting she would keep both Kanagy boys company? She gave James a pointed look when he seemed ready to say something about her twin sister.

The carriage maker took the last brownie and raised it in salute. "Stop by any time with treats," he said. "And wish your family a merry Christmas for me."

"I'll do that." Mary slipped on her bonnet, grabbed the container, and preceded the brothers out the wide back door Bram was holding open for her. "Give my best to your parents and sister, too."

The brisk winter air invigorated her as she watched Nate and Bram guide their new rigs from the shop and then hitch them to the horses waiting at the rail. The snow sparkled with sun diamonds and chickadees chirped in the evergreens. Had there ever been a shinier December day? A finer chance to get acquainted with these out-of-town fellows who wanted to spend their time with her?

Their choice of horses said a lot about them, too, and this seemed a safe topic of conversation that wouldn't give away her surprise.

Mary approached slowly as Nate fastened a glossy black harness to his Clydesdale. *What would Martha say? She's the one who knows horses.* "This fellow must stand at least, um—eighteen hands," she remarked as she stroked the majestic horse's neck. "And such a docile boy, too. *Gut* thing, considering the size of those hooves!"

"Nineteen hands," Nate remarked approvingly. He buckled the band that was covered with brass sleigh bells. "*Jah*, Clyde's my first Clydesdale, and I'm sold on the breed now. Got him when that big brewery in St. Louis retired some of their show stock. Guess he's been on some television commercials."

Mary's eyes widened. It wasn't every day that Plain folks acquired draft horses with such a pedigree. She turned toward Bram then, who was murmuring to the glossy bay he'd hitched to his courting buggy. Its black mane and tale shimmered when the horse shifted in place, showing its readiness to be out on the road. "Used to be a race horse, did he?" she asked. "Felix has some mighty fine lines."

"He does, at that," Bram replied. "Found him at one of the auctions I was working over by Kansas City. But I have to give Nate the credit for training him to haul buggies."

Mary blinked. "You're *that* Kanagy?" she blurted as she gazed at Nate. "I know lots of men who won't let anybody else break their draft horses."

Nate's cheeks colored, and he seemed tongue-tied. Mary sensed she shouldn't slight his younger brother by giving him all the attention, however. "And you work at auctions, Bram?"

He bowed slightly, tipping his fedora. "I'll have you know I'm a licensed auctioneer, Martha. Hopin' to have my own sale barn and business someday. And since I'm such a natural at sellin' folks on things, you can't help but ride in *my* rig now, ain't so?"

Mary blushed and stepped forward so he could help her up into his new buggy. "That's not to say your brother's to be left out in the cold, though," she teased. "Let's all of us head down this road for a quick tour of Cedar Creek. I think you'll like what you see."

Nate laughed good-naturedly as he sprang into the seat of his sleigh. "Sounds better than heading to Aunt Beulah Mae's. No need for her and Uncle Abe to know we've arrived just yet, or they'll be wanting us to spend the rest of the day there."

"Abe and Beulah Mae Nissley?" she asked. "I bake for Mrs. Nissley's Kitchen—cookies and bars, mostly, while Beulah Mae keeps up with the pies and running her restaurant. She's closed for a few days over Christmas—"

"With nothin' better to do than entertain her two nephews from Willow Ridge," Bram said as he clapped the reins lightly on Felix's back. "I'm for goin' wherever you can think of, Martha. Plenty of time to park our butts in Beulah Mae's kitchen, ain't so, Nate?"

"You've got that right, little brother. Here we go!"

Grinning with her secret plan—hoping she didn't blow it—Mary gestured for Bram to turn right. Was it too soon to dream of spending more time in this rig beside her handsome driver? Sure, there were a good many miles and several hours' travel between Cedar Creek and Willow Ridge, but that matter of geography didn't seem to bother these Kanagy brothers. And she couldn't wait until Martha—and the rest of her family at home—heard whom she and her sister had latched onto. Since there was no other traffic on the road, Nate pulled his sleigh into the lane beside Bram's buggy to keep up with the conversation.

"Seems like a nice place, Cedar Creek," Bram said as

he looked around. "Well-kept farms hereabouts, and lots of folks seem to have businesses, as well."

"Those are Matt Lambright's sheep," she replied, pointing toward the pasture they were passing. "His *dat* runs the mercantile, and his aunt Abby runs her sewing shop upstairs. And farther down this hill, Rudy Ropp has a dairy farm. One of his boys runs a machine repair business while the other son's gotten into raising cage-free chickens—"

"And what does your *dat* do, Martha?" Nate called over.

Mary leaned forward, tickled that he was beside them rather than behind. "Dat and my brother Owen are carpenters—"

"You're *that* Coblentz?" Bram exclaimed. "Why, everybody knows Amos Coblentz as one of the finest master carpenters in northern Missouri. He's built stables and barns for a lot of breeders, Amish and English alike." He turned toward his brother then. "Didn't Amos put up the bishop's big barn?"

"*Jah*, even though we've got the Brenneman boys' carpentry shop right there in Willow Ridge. Guess we'd best behave ourselves with his daughter," Nate added playfully. Then he sat taller, gazing intently ahead of them as they started down the first hill.

When Bram, too, leaned forward to stare, Mary could barely contain her laughter. Sure enough, her sister was standing at the roadside, waving wildly at them as she chomped her gum. With her bonnet off, Martha's auburn hair shone in the sunshine, beneath her kapp. It was time to come clean, and Mary was glad that both of these boys were in high spirits, more likely to laugh at the little trick she and her twin had pulled than get angry.

"Your eyes aren't fooling you," Mary said as Bram slowed the buggy at the end of their lane. "*This* is Martha, the one you met in the mercantile—"

"*Jah*! I didn't want to leave Mary out of the fun I thought the four of us might have, so I called her from the store," Martha explained with a hearty laugh. "We do everything together, you see."

Mary scampered down from the buggy and slung her arm around Martha's shoulders. "So that explains the miracle of the warm brownies, ain't so? Martha's finished her choring now, so if you boys still want some company while you break in your new rigs, we'd be happy to help out."

Nate and Bram had pulled their sleigh and buggy to the shoulder of the road and fastened their reins. The brothers hopped down to assess the situation, both of them studying eyes . . . noses . . . hair . . . lips. Any details they could find that would set the twins apart. Mary noticed that her sister had stopped chewing her gum, to confound the boys even more.

"Holy Moses," Nate murmured. "Not a shade of difference between them."

"Double trouble," Bram agreed, but then he laughed. "I think we're up for it, though, Nate. Still beats spendin' the rest of this fine day with the aunt and uncle—"

"Beulah Mae and Preacher Abe," Mary remarked to her sister.

"No! Well, see there?" Martha replied with a jovial shrug. "You don't know a stranger when you go from one Plain town to the next. Bound to find folks you've met before, and plenty you're kin to."

"Whether you want to be or not," Mary added.

All four of them laughed loudly, and as Martha grinned at her, Mary felt that this might be the start of something wonderful—a Christmas with something extra to celebrate, if things went the way she was hoping.

"See, the plan was to pick up our new vehicles and then head to Nissleys' for the night," Nate explained. "Then we're to start home tomorrow morning, so we'll arrive in plenty of time for the Christmas Eve program at the schoolhouse—"

"We'll be going to that, too, but here in Cedar Creek," Martha said. "Jacob and Joanna are reciting their Christmas poems. They're ten, so—"

"Another set of twins in your family?" Bram asked, his eyes widening.

"*Jah*, but you won't have any trouble telling those two apart." Martha was already caught up in the easy way the four of them were talking and laughing. But if the Kanagy boys were supposed to return home tomorrow, in time to have a traditional Christmas with their family— and this after spending an endless evening with their bossy, gossipy aunt and her stern old husband, the preacher—it sounded as though their fun had a mighty short time frame. Unless . . .

"You know, Christmas Day is our birthday," Mary said, eyeing her sister purposefully. "Wouldn't it be the nicest way for us to turn eighteen—"

"*Jah*! With you fellows here to celebrate!" Martha went on in a rising voice. "And if you don't want to stay at Preacher Abe's, listening to Beulah Mae's gossip and what-all—"

"—why, we've got a spare bedroom at our place!" Mary continued in a breathless rush. "We'll be going to the schoolhouse program on Christmas Eve, of course, and then spending a quiet day at home on Christmas, like always—"

"—but come Second Christmas, just think of the places we can go! The fun we can have," Martha declared. "And you boys would be keeping the Old Ways, following the traditions, except you'd be in our home instead of yours. What do you say?"

"And it better be *yes*!" Mary's cheeks tingled with

more than the winter's cold. How had they dared to concoct such a bold plan without asking Mamma first?

The Kanagy brothers looked at each other, clearly excited by their idea. "Like you said, Bram, we'll be in double trouble if we go along with the twins' ideas," Nate murmured. "Mamm and Dat won't be one bit happy if we don't show up when we're supposed to."

"But we'll be in all the right places at the right times. Even Uncle Abe can't argue with that," Bram reasoned as he fought a grin. "And we'll be with the *Amos Coblentz* family, rather than runnin' the roads unaccounted for. But if you'd rather be a stick in the mud—"

"Don't go calling *me* names, Bram. I might already be a member of the church, but that doesn't mean I've stopped laughing or looking at pretty girls. I say we do it."

"*Gut.* I'm in, too." Bram flashed them a feisty smile and then focused on his brother again. "And since you're the older, more responsible son, you get to tell the aunt and uncle about our new plan."

Martha grinned, gazing up at the brother in the broad-brimmed hat. "If it makes it any easier, Nate, you can tell them Mary and I tempted you into this. Preacher Abe has said in church that cell phones—ours, namely—can be instruments of the Devil, so we've got a reputation to maintain. We have *not* joined the church yet, after all."

"It's not like we're bad apples," Mary added matter-of-factly. "We just want to try all manner of things before we have to confess them."

Bram bowed to her, gesturing toward his buggy. "Can't argue with that, can I? I'm here to help with whatever you'd like to try, missy. Lead the way."

"Let's get Bram those Christmas lights and then find some lunch," Nate suggested as he offered his arm to Martha. "We'd best not make our Christmas plans on empty stomachs, ain't so?"

Chapter Three

Bram watched Mary wrap a double length of Christmas lights so it lined the buggy's dashboard and then followed the outline of the rig all the way around the back and to the front again. Martha was beside her, securing the strand with pieces of black duct tape. Watching the girls work so closely, completing each other's sentences, made him smile wider than he had in months. All thoughts of inviting Hannah Brenneman to ride in this new buggy, maybe courting her in the New Year, dissipated like the vapor of his breath: with Mary Coblentz, it had been love at first bite of that coffee brownie . . . not to mention the way her sparkly blue eyes had sucked him in, hook, line, and sinker. Oh, but they were in for some fun these next few days! And after all the auctions he'd been working of late, keeping company with this fine, feisty redhead was an unanticipated Christmas gift to himself.

"Okay, hook them up!" she said as she handed him the end of the strand.

Bram reached beneath the buggy seat, to the car battery that supplied power for the headlights and taillights, and plugged the cord into the outlet James had wired to it.

When the girls clapped their hands at the flashing of the multi-colored bulbs, his heart thumped like a rock band's drums. "Now that'll be quite a sight, come evening," he remarked happily. "*Denki* for gettin' them on so they're spaced evenly. Looks way better than I could have done."

"*Jah*, your backside'll be flashing all night long, all over the countryside now, little brother," Nate said as he circled the buggy to admire the lights. "But now that we've had our dinner and decked your rig, we'd best be getting over to the Nissleys'. You know how the aunt will be calling over home, asking where we might be, if we wait much longer."

"Like Mamm would have an answer for that," Bram teased. But he handed Mary up into the buggy and hopped in on the other side. "No need to get Mamm or the aunt stirred up, though, considering the new plans we'll be breakin' to them soon. Geddap, Felix. Let's go, fella."

He unplugged the lights to save them for this evening and then grinned at Mary. "I'll understand if you and your sister need to get home to supper tonight, but if you'd stay with us, it would make the meal go quicker—or at least seem to. If you work in Mrs. Nissley's kitchen, you know what I mean."

"What with all of her kids married off and moved to other places, Beulah Mae's *gut* at yacking the ears off anybody who'll listen," she replied with a shy grin. "Let's see how it goes, shall we?"

Let's see how it goes. Bram had all sorts of visions, all manner of ideas about how he would like it to go tonight . . . especially if he could pry the twins apart. Double dating was all right for an ice breaker, but when it came time for sampling Mary's delicious-looking lips, he wanted her all to himself. And judging by Nate's expression, he was guessing his brother felt the same way about Martha.

Had there ever been a prettier day? On both sides of the road, the snow-covered pastures sparkled and tall evergreens and cedars swayed in the breeze. When they came within sight of his uncle's orchard, Bram slowed down. Rows and rows of apple trees covered the hillside, with their lower branches supported by stout wooden braces. "Can't say I've ever come in from this direction," he remarked. "Uncle Abe's orchard looks to be doing well."

"What with his preaching duties taking up so much time, he hires a bunch of us young folks to do his picking in the fall," Mary replied. "Does so much business, he's gone from a roadside stand to a building with sale tables. Sells the honey from his bees and lets local folks bring in their pumpkins, squash, and what-not to sell there, too."

"Gee, Felix." As the horse turned to enter the long lane, Bram took in the old white house with its fieldstone foundation. Smoke curled out of the chimney and the horses in the barnyard came to the fence to watch them approach, their ears pricked forward

"Why am I not surprised to see Uncle Abe out here, like he's waitin' for us?" Bram remarked. "Stayin' out of the aunt's way while she's cookin', no doubt."

Mary's soft laughter and pink cheeks teased at him. How her eyes sparkled with anticipation . . . promises and secrets to share with him later.

"Seems you boys picked up a lot more than new rigs today," Uncle Abe remarked as he came through the barnyard gate. As he held his broad-brimmed hat in a gust of wind, his beard rippled over his dark blue barn coat. "Not sure who's driving Mary and who's with Martha, but then, life's got its little mysteries, ain't so? How are you, girls?"

"We're *gut*, *denki*," Mary replied as she daintily stepped down.

"*Jah*, mighty glad your nephews came into town," Martha added. "Merry Christmas to you, Preacher Abe."

"And pass the same along to your families." Uncle Abe looked a little heavier than last time Bram had seen him, and his bushy hair had gone from gray to white, but he seemed genuinely pleased to see them. "Guess I should warn you that your aunt's in a stew, figuring you should've been here for dinner this noon. I reminded her that we were young once, too—about a hundred years ago."

"Not every day you run across the likes of the Coblentz twins," Bram said as he shook his uncle's gloved hand. "What do you think of these rigs? Seems to me James Graber did a fine job on them."

Uncle Abe stroked Felix's shoulder before he circled the buggy, nodding, and then gave his attention to Nate's sleigh. "Nobody builds a better ride than our James. Seems you young bucks have outdone yourself with these horses, too. Auctioneering and training must suit you, that you're doing so well."

"Bram found us these geldings while he was working a couple of sales," Nate remarked with a nod. "And then I made quick work of training them to pull our rigs."

Bram was thoroughly enjoying this chat, but when the kitchen door opened and his aunt stepped onto the side porch, he knew it was time to stop stalling. "Merry Christmas to you, Aunt Beulah Mae!" he called over to her.

"*Jah*, late as it's getting, I was wondering if Christmas might be here and gone before you boys showed up," came her reply. "But I see now who might've led your *gut* intentions astray. Mary and Martha are known for distracting the fellows around here. Mary bakes me a lot of cookies, though."

"*Jah*, we've found that out." Bram chuckled, exchanging a knowing smile with the young woman at his side.

"Get yourselves inside now, before you catch your

death in this cold wind," Aunt Beulah Mae instructed. "I'll put on water for some cocoa and we can visit."

"Can't argue with that," Abe said, waving the four of them toward the house. "Or at least we'd better not."

Bram gestured for his brother to lead the way, reminding Nate with a purposeful gaze that it was his job to spell out their new plans. When his hand found Mary's, he wanted to drive off with her right then and there, but that was sure to get him into hot water.

The kitchen felt too warm when they stepped inside. Judging from the pans of bars and fresh dinner rolls—not to mention four pies—on the back counter, the ovens had been fired up all day. When Nate hugged their aunt and snatched up a frosted sugar cookie, Bram followed suit . . . always a good idea to make Beulah Mae happy by eating every chance they got. The four of them exchanged pleasantries with the older couple as they hung their coats on pegs near the door. The long table was laid out with plates and mugs, with platters of coffee cake, sticky buns, and colorful cookies in the center. As his aunt quickly added two more place settings and grabbed the whistling kettle, Bram sighed inwardly. Might be an hour or more before they could even hope to slip away . . .

"We don't want to be any trouble, dirtying up sheets and towels and what-not," Nate said as they took seats at the table, "so we won't be staying the night, like we'd originally figured."

The kitchen got deadly quiet. Aunt Beulah Mae peered over the top of her black-rimmed glasses.

Bram jammed the rest of his gingerbread man into his mouth. He was starting to sweat, and not just because the furnace and ovens were stoked up.

"Abram and Nathaniel, you can't tell me you're starting back to Willow Ridge this late in the day." Their aunt gazed intently at Mary and Martha. "Why am I thinking you girls have something to do with this change of plans?"

Mary concentrated on her cocoa. Beside Nate, however, Martha bit back a grin. "At least give us credit for knowing a couple of worthwhile young fellows when we see them," she replied pertly. "We wouldn't invite just anybody to stay over and celebrate our birthday."

"And of course we'll be seeing you at the schoolhouse tomorrow night for the scholars' program, and then spending a prayerful Christmas Day at home. All fit and proper," Mary added quietly. "Mamma and Dat wouldn't have it any other way."

"And what do *your* parents have to say about this?" Beulah Mae quizzed him and Nate. "Abe, was there a message on the phone from Nell, telling us of this change?"

Uncle Abe, who had known to stay out of this conversation, shook his head. "Not the first time young fellows have gotten acquainted with girls over the holidays—"

"But I've been cooking all day! And we've been looking forward to this visit—"

"—and if you recall, Beulah Mae, you and I started courting at Christmas by giving your family the slip," he continued with a quiet laugh. "*Jah*, that was more than fifty years ago, but things haven't changed between girls and boys since then that I've noticed."

Their aunt's cheeks got very pink. "That's neither here nor there, and you know it!" she spouted. Then she focused again on Bram and Nate. "And why do I suspect you haven't told your folks about this, either?"

Bram whipped his cell phone from the pocket of his plaid flannel shirt. "Matter of fact, I was just about to call them," he said as he rose to grab his jacket.

"And then we'll need to head home to let Mamma

know about our guests," Martha confessed. She snatched a chunk of fudge from the platter as she, too, stood up. "*Denki* so much for these wonderful-*gut* goodies, Beulah Mae."

"But we wouldn't *dream* of missing the dinner you've fixed for us," Nate chimed in. "And we're hoping the girls can join us for that?"

"We'll be a lot better at redding up the kitchen afterward than these boys would," Mary pointed out.

The last thing Bram heard as he stepped outside was Uncle Abe's laughter. "Sounds like a mighty fine evening," he said. "We'll see you kids later."

As the four of them scurried along the snow-packed lane, putting on their coats, Bram shook his head in amazement. "Well, that was slicker than all get-out, but we'll pay for our escape tonight at supper, most likely."

"*Jah*, we cut them pretty short," Martha remarked as she tied her bonnet strings. "But it's not like we were telling stories—"

"Because we do have to break the news to Mamma that you boys're staying over," Mary continued. "But make your call first, Bram, out on the road. Nissley's Ridge is the best place out here to get a *gut* signal."

Once they had gone down the lane and headed up the slight grade of the county blacktop, Bram pulled over to the side. He punched the numbers and waited . . . and, as he'd anticipated, no one was near the phone shanty to pick up. "*Jah*, it's Bram, callin' to tell you we're havin' supper tonight with Abe and Beulah Mae, but we've been invited to celebrate a big birthday with carpenter Amos Coblentz's girls," he said. "So we'll be stayin' with them over Christmas Day and Second Christmas instead of headin' home tomorrow like we thought. Bye now."

Mary was smiling mischievously beside him as he

spoke. His heart was thundering, looking forward to the fun they would have over the next few days. After all, it would likely be hours before his parents heard about their change of plans—and what could they do about it? Willow Ridge was three hours away.

"We're *gut* to go," he called back to his brother. "Let's do it!"

Chapter Four

When the sleigh turned in at Coblentz Lane, Martha sat straighter and watched Nate's face for his reactions. How did her home place compare to his in Willow Ridge? Was his house larger or newer than hers? Did the outbuildings appear well-kept to him, or was Nate making unfavorable comparisons as he took in the barnyard . . . the cluster of deep red barns with stone foundations . . . the silos rising behind them? She had lived on this land, in these buildings, every day of her life, yet now she looked at them with a more critical eye.

"Real pretty place," he murmured as he gazed out over the pastures. "It's hillier here than where we live. More trees and rocks breaking up the tillable land. I've noticed how the homes and barns look to be older in Cedar Creek, with a lot of stonework. Our town's not been on the map as long."

"*Jah*, this farm's been in Dat's family for several generations," Martha replied. "What with him and Owen both being carpenters, hay for the livestock is our only crop—and we have a big garden, of course."

Nate slowed the sleigh, watching ahead to see where Bram was going to park the buggy. "Whoa, Clyde," he

crooned in a low voice. Then he gave her a smile that
seemed almost shy. "Hope your folks won't feel like my
brother and I are intruding on your family's Christmas.
Mighty nice of you, asking us to stay in town for longer
than we'd figured on. If your *mamm* seems put out, we
can always stay with the aunt and—"

"We're pretty *gut* at talking her into things, Mary and
I," Martha assured him as they got out of the sleigh. But
now that they were mere steps away from introducing
their two surprise guests, she realized what a challenge
she and her twin had set themselves up for. Not only
would her *mamm* and *dat* wonder what was really going
on with these out-of-town boys, but there would be plenty
of remarks from their brothers and little sister, as well.

"Are you going to tell Mamma, or shall I?" Mary murmured as the four of them stepped onto the wide porch.
"She'll already figure something's up, after the way I took
out of here with those brownies a while ago."

"Should Nate and I wait out here until you girls break
the news?" Bram placed his hand on Mary's back, looking
sincerely concerned about making the right impression.

*He also looks ready to kiss her. And she wouldn't turn
him away!* Martha reached for the doorknob, thinking she
might be the better one—the less distracted one—to break
their news. "You might as well make your entrance, fellows. We've got nothing to hide, after all," she pointed out.

The sweet scents of orange cake and cherries greeted
them as they all entered the kitchen. Her mother was
taking a pan of orange date bars from the oven while
Joanna drizzled white frosting over a batch of cherry pie
bars. Mamma straightened to her full height, her gaze
running quickly from Nate to Bram as they removed their
hats. "Well, now! What's this we have going on?"

Martha jumped in feet first, hoping all the words came

out right. "This is Nate and Bram Kanagy, from over to Willow Ridge," she said, gesturing to each fellow in turn. "The more Mary and I talked to them, the more we wanted to spend our birthday getting better acquainted—"

"So we invited them to stay over for a few days," Mary chimed in. "They're nephews of the Nissleys, and—"

"They came to pick up the new sleigh and courting buggy James has built for them," Martha added.

Silence rang in the kitchen, until Joanna began to giggle. "Oh, but Dat's gonna love this! Wasn't but a couple days ago he was saying you girls should be gettin' hitched, so—"

"Let's not rush things, missy. These young men don't need anyone giving them ideas." Mamma set her pan of hot bars on a cast iron trivet and then shut the oven door. She found her smile. "It's nice to meet you. Nate and Bram Kanagy, is it?"

"*Jah*," Nate replied, "Our *dat* Daniel keeps sheep and our *mamm* Leah has a truck garden—"

"And we run our own businesses," Bram cut in with a winsome grin. "I'm an auctioneer, and my brother's been trainin' horses for a *gut* long while. We were hopin' to test out our new rigs with Mary and Martha before we head back."

"Were you, now?" Her mother didn't look angry, but she wasn't one to be told what to do, either. "You've no doubt figured out that my girls never lack for ideas and that between the two of them they can cook up some mischief. And what are your intentions, far as joining the church, boys? I don't want to see my daughters jumping the fence, understand."

"I took my vows last year, Mrs. Coblentz," Nate assured her. "And while my brother looks anything but Plain in his red plaid shirt and English haircut, our folks are set on having all of us kids follow the Old Ways, as well."

"That's why I've called to let them know we've been invited to a home with the same strong faith," Bram said with a decisive nod. "If we'll be interrupting your plans for Christmas, we'll head back home tomorrow like we'd originally figured on."

Their mother considered this as she studied the boys for a moment. Then she looked at Martha and Mary straight-on. "And where did you think these boys would be sleeping?" she asked quietly. "They'll not be in *your* room—no matter what some Plain families allow, far as courting practices like bundling in their daughters' beds."

"We thought Jacob might move in with Owen and Noah for a couple nights, so these fellows can sleep in the spare beds in his room," Mary suggested. "Like we do when the cousins come to stay."

"And have you asked Jacob about this?"

As Martha glanced at Mary, their youngest brother replied from the front room. "You're gonna have to do me somethin' special for this big favor you're askin'," he declared. "Who *are* these guys, anyway?"

"And you'll have to set up the beds and get their towels and sheets, too," Mamma added with a sly smile. "And since your sister and brother could use some help learning their recitation pieces for the scholars' program tomorrow night, the four of you are to get them *gut* and ready. The sleigh and the new buggy'll have to bide their time in the yard until all those things are ticked off my list."

"Bram and I will see to our horses," Nate said. "Then we'll be in to help with what you've asked, Mrs. Coblentz."

"And we've told Aunt Beulah Mae and Uncle Abe we'll eat supper with them tonight," Bram added. The dimples flickered in his cheeks. "So you can see we've got all manner of *gut*, honorable things to do and places to be, ain't so?"

Their mother's chuckle made Martha relax. Nate's sense of responsibility and Bram's teasing good nature had won her over—for now. "*Jah*, I reckon we can put up with you boys' company for a few days, long as Amos agrees. He'll have the final word."

"Only right." Nate smiled at the tousle-haired boy who had come to the kitchen doorway. "Jacob, I could use some help with my Clydesdale and sleigh, if you've got a minute. I bet you know right where to stable him, too. Along with Bram's bay."

Jacob rushed to the window and his eyes widened. "That's *your* horse? Why, he's the tallest one I've ever seen!"

"Want to drive him for a bit? Clyde's an easygoing fellow—"

"And you can park my buggy, too, if you like," Bram said as he put his fedora on again. "I don't let just anybody drive my new rig, you know."

The three fellows were out the door quicker than Jacob could get his coat on. Martha's heartbeat had returned to normal, but the look on Mamma's face told her they weren't finished with a little business best tended while their guests were out of earshot.

"And what possessed you to invite boys you don't even know into our home?" she asked quietly. "Lord love us all if you start taking up with just anybody who passes through town."

"Oh, but *please*, Mamma! The Kanagy boys aren't just anybody!" Mary pleaded. She pressed the dough she'd abandoned earlier into a clean nine-by-thirteen pan and stuck it in the oven. "Bram's only eighteen, but he's been working livestock sales—going to auctioneer school—so he can make himself a real *gut* living—"

"And a lot of men hereabouts rely on Nate to train their horses," Martha insisted. "Dat will know of him, for sure and for certain."

"But mostly you just thought they were the cutest things you've ever seen," Joanna piped up from her place at the counter. "I might only be ten, but I've got eyes, ya know."

Martha looked at Mary and burst into a giggling fit. "Well, *jah*, there's that. Not to mention the fact that they had James Graber make their new rigs," she added. "Their folks gave them the sleigh and the courting buggy for Christmas, because the boys promised they'd not get cars or driver's licenses. So does *that* make you feel any better about it, Mamma?"

Their mother began melting the butterscotch chips for the cashew bars Mary was making, a grin twitching at her lips. "Your little sister and I had it figured the same way. I might be your mother, but I've got eyes, too, you know. Keep that in mind these next few days while your guests are here."

"We will, Mamma." Mary removed her crust from the oven and sprinkled cashews all over it. Then she poured on the melted butterscotch chips without spilling a drop. Ever the neat and tidy Amish cook, Mary was.

"For sure and for certain, Mamma," Martha agreed as she gathered the dirty bowls and measuring cups. "And *denki* for letting us celebrate an extra-special eighteenth birthday. We won't cause you a lick of trouble."

Joanna laughed out loud. "I've gotta see how *that* will work. You two were causin' trouble long before I was born."

Martha met her twin's gaze from across the kitchen.

Though they had gotten their way, plenty of folks would be watching them with the Kanagy boys. And they had an afternoon of listening to Jacob and Joanna practice their recitations before they would have to endure supper with Preacher Abe and Beulah Mae. It might well be eight or nine o'clock tonight before she joined Nate in his sleigh . . .

Patience is a virtue, Martha reminded herself. *Too bad it's not one of mine.*

"Better be helping yourself to more of these mashed potatoes and the chicken with noodles," Beulah Mae insisted as she passed the bowls to Bram. "Why, I figured you young fellows would eat a whole lot more than this, or I wouldn't have cooked so much!"

Bram groaned inwardly. His plate was still covered with second helpings of creamed succotash, fried apples, baked chicken, and green bean casserole and they hadn't even looked at the desserts lined up on the counter yet. While his aunt was renowned for her cooking and had a successful restaurant, a fellow could only find room for so many big, fluffy dinner rolls while doing justice to the chickens and apples his aunt and uncle raised here on their farm.

"*Jah*, I can remember how your *dat* would eat us out of house and home at your age," Uncle Abe said with a chuckle. "Your *mamm* probably cooks a lot of lamb, what with him raising them, ain't so?"

"Oh, not so much," Nate replied. The glance he sent to Bram felt as heavy as the meal they were eating. "He sells off everything he raises, as there's a lot of call for mutton amongst foreign folks in the big cities."

"And it's not like lamb's a big favorite at our house," Bram added. "Mamm turns up her nose at the smell of it—"

"Well then, your mother's never learned to eat what the *gut* Lord has provided." Beulah Mae rose stiffly from her chair, achy from spending so many hours on her feet, no doubt. "I recall some years when I was a girl and the cows and hogs died of infections, so we couldn't butcher them. Went months without fresh meat, we did."

Oh, but this conversation was going nowhere . . . just like the four of them. Had his aunt really been so young and fresh and exciting that Abe had slipped away from their families' Christmas rituals to court her? Martha had laid down her fork, as though looking ready for an excuse to leave, while Mary still picked at her food as she stole glances at him from across the table. *Mary, Mary, quite contrary . . . oh, what I'd rather be doing with you right now, perty girl . . .*

"Maybe we'd best hold off on dessert until after our supper settles," Beulah Mae said as she clucked over the four golden-crusted pies. "We can have some coffee in the front room, maybe play a game of—"

"But I've been looking forward to your pie all day, Aunt," Nate cut in. "Your rhubarb has always been my favorite."

"Did you bake a cherry one, or a peach?" Bram said in a rising voice. "Of course, no matter what kinds you made they'll be like none we get at home. Mamm's not the baker you are—but don't tell her I said so!" he teased as he looked at his uncle.

Abe chortled, making his white beard shimmy across the front of his deep green shirt. "You boys have something other than pie on your minds, and I can't say as I blame you. Not every day a fellow gets a fine new rig—

or a girl to ride it with. Let's have that pie now, Beulah Mae. Blackberry for me, please."

The twins rose together to scrape the plates, as eager to move this evening forward as he and Nate were. His aunt planted a fist against her hip, glaring at the way Uncle Abe had overridden her idea, but she took a pie cutter from its peg on the wall. She was probably peeved because while she and Abe had cleared their plates, their four younger guests had stalled out over the second and third helpings she'd pressed upon them. Bram had been taught not to waste food, of course—but then, his parents didn't insist that he reload his plate, either.

He stole a glance at the kitchen clock while his aunt was cutting pie. Eight o'clock already, even if time had felt like it was standing still all afternoon and evening while they did what they had to do. It was such a pain to be polite! Yet as he caught Mary's smile when she moved next to him to clear his place . . . inhaled her fresh scent as her deep red dress brushed his arm . . . Bram sensed she would make all this waiting well worth his while.

"Wonderful-*gut* rhubarb pie, Aunt," Nate said, closing his eyes over his first big bite.

"*Jah*, this cherry's mighty fine, too," Bram said. His aunt made her pies in smallish pans, so it wouldn't take them long to finish their dessert and move along.

The girls were nodding in agreement over their slices of peach pie, forking up the golden filling that had oozed onto their plates, while Abe and Beulah Mae made short work of their dark slices of blackberry.

"See there?" his aunt clucked. "If you boys were staying the night like you'd first told me, you could be having pie again before bed—and for breakfast if you wanted."

Uncle Abe chortled. "We've got plenty enough left to send a few pieces along with them."

"No, that's not how it works. Pie freezes, if need be." The woman at Abe's left took her time catching her last crumbs between the tines of her fork. "I suppose you young folks'll be dashing off now, leaving me with all the—"

"No, no!" Mary insisted. "Matter of fact, Beulah Mae, you deserve some sit-down time in the front room by the fire while Martha and I wash these dishes—"

"Because, *jah*, after you fixed us a fine meal like this one," Martha joined in, "it's our job to redd up. And if the boys think that'll take longer than they want, well, the dishrag and tea towels will fit their hands same as they fit ours, ain't so?"

Abe laughed aloud at that, and Beulah Mae actually cracked a smile. "Best idea I've heard all day, girls," she remarked wearily. "*Denki* for your help, and pass along my best to your folks for me . . . knowing, of course, that it might be tomorrow before you do that."

At last their uncle ushered his wife out to the front room. Nate rolled his shirtsleeves to his elbows and began filling the sink with hot, sudsy water. "I'll wash and you dry, brother, just like when we were kids. Mamm insisted the cleanup wasn't just for girls—since she didn't have any," he added for the twins' benefit.

"*Jah*? That's different," Martha replied as she stacked dirty plates alongside the sink.

Bram snatched up a clean towel, happy to be helping here rather than enduring stories of long ago in the front room. "Our *mamm* grows several acres of vegetables and jack-o-lantern pumpkins to sell at farmers' markets. Our aunt Miriam buys Mamm's produce for her café, too," he explained. "And with keepin' her bees, sellin' the honey at our roadside stand—and watchin' out for Dat's *mamm*, who lives in the *dawdi haus*—she's got her hands full. But don't think for a minute that we've been raised as sissies," he murmured close to Mary's ear.

Her low laughter and flushed cheeks teased at him. "You think we would've invited sissies to stay over?" she murmured.

Her blue eyes sparkled like snowflakes catching the sun. Bram was grateful that his brother washed dishes faster than anyone else he knew, and that Mary helped him dry while Martha wiped the table and stacked all the clean dinnerware there. Half an hour later, he and Nate were slipping out to the stable to hitch up Felix and Clyde before saying their good-byes . . . and riding off into this paradise of a moonlit winter's night . . .

Chapter Five

Mary scooted closer to Bram on the seat of his courting buggy, wishing she'd thought to bring some old quilts. While the colored Christmas lights looked merry and bright, the rig didn't have a top on it, so they were at the mercy of the wind. But what an absolutely beautiful night it was, with the stars twinkling in a navy velvet sky above a countryside that glowed a pale blue in the twilight. Nate's sleigh had taken off in the other direction, so now only the *clip-clop! clip-clop!* of Felix's hooves broke the serene silence as she directed Bram along the back roads of Cedar Creek.

"I've been waitin' all day for this," he murmured as he wrapped his arm around her. "I thought the kids would *never* get their poems memorized—"

Mary smiled. Joanna and Jacob had found all manner of distractions and questions to ask Nate and Bram this afternoon while practicing their Christmas Eve pieces.

"—and then when we couldn't find the footboards for those beds we were puttin' together, I was ready to say we'd sleep on the floor!" he continued with a good-natured shake of his head. He sighed then. "*Denki* for bein' a *gut* sport during supper, too. Hope you didn't get upset when my aunt was actin' so peevish."

"We're all used to that, you know," she remarked. "Every now and again Preacher Abe gets after Beulah Mae for being so testy, because folks expect a minister's wife to rise above what irritates her and show Christ's own patience. Not an easy order to fill when she's got a restaurant to run. Plus she's been catering holiday dinners for most of December."

"*Jah*, I'm surprised he lets her keep workin' that way. Not all preachers allow their wives to be so busy, or away from home so much."

Mary shrugged and it turned into a shiver. "She's helping make ends meet. What with him not being paid as a preacher—since long before I was born and for the rest of his life—Bishop Gingerich doesn't fuss about her outside work, so nobody else does, either."

Bram nodded and then gazed down into her eyes for the longest time. "Why on God's *gut* Earth am I fussin' over my aunt when I've got such a sweet somebody sittin' at my side?" he murmured. "Windy as it is, I'm thinkin' we should find a place to get in out of this cold. Would you like that, Mary?"

Now *there* was a loaded question! She knew good and well the weather wasn't Bram's only reason for wanting to duck inside somewhere . . . and while she would enjoy a bit of snuggling, she sensed this fine-looking fellow was used to getting whatever he wanted from his girl-friends. "Well, I suppose we could warm up for a bit, before we—"

"I know just how to do that, too, honey-girl," he replied with a low laugh. "Unless my eyes and memory are failin', this next road cuts back over toward Nissley's Ridge. Uncle Abe had some clean, sweet-smellin' hay in a back stall. We'll be all cozy and out of sight there."

When Mary shivered again, she inadvertently shifted closer to Bram, no doubt giving him the idea she was ready for whatever he wanted to do in that stall. "Are . . . are you sure it's a *gut* idea to slip into your uncle's stable? What if he—"

"Want to go to your place then?"

Mary gasped. "Oh, no! What with my older brother Owen courting his fiancée tonight, and Jacob probably watching for us to come in, and Dat waiting to meet you—"

"So where else might be *gut*, then?" Bram nuzzled the temple of her bonnet with a kiss.

He had a point. Even though she knew everyone hereabouts, they couldn't just sneak into a neighbor's stable. This fellow's intentions were a little nervy for a first date, but she really did want to see if Bram kissed as good as he looked . . .

"Wherever you think we should go, Mary-girl. I'm all ears . . . and lips and hands needin' to get warm. Know what I mean?"

And how could she answer *that*? A *no* would make her sound like she'd not been out with a boy before, while a *yes* meant she was eager for anything Bram cared to try. Mary chuckled quietly. "If you're sure Nate and Martha won't be thinking the same thing . . ."

Bram's breath shot out in a burst of vapor when he laughed. "My brother's not lookin' to get serious any time soon, not after the way a Willow Ridge gal he was courtin' married another fella. He'll probably head to your place directly, because his sleigh's no warmer than this rig."

A few minutes later they turned onto the road that followed the crest of Nissley's Ridge, and then Bram slowed his horse . . . reached down to unplug the colorful Christmas lights. Very quietly he told Felix where to turn in, and then steered them to the back side of the barn, away from

the house. It appeared that all the lights were out in the
Nissley house, so Mary relaxed. The way they told it,
other Amish kids did this all the time, after all—and it
was better this way than to be sneaking into her bedroom
at home, or taking the chance that any of her family might
walk in on them in the front room. Bram deftly helped
her down, clutching her gloved hand in his as he ever so
quietly slid the barn door to the side.

A couple of horses nickered and the musky scents of
hay and manure greeted them. "Better let our eyes adjust
so we don't step in anything," Bram whispered as he
closed the door. But instead of looking toward that back
stall he'd mentioned, he pulled her close and lifted her
chin. "Mary, kiss me now. Kiss—"

Oh, but he surely did know how to do that. Mary's
breath left her as Bram's lips found hers and lingered
there. With his mouth gently holding her captive he removed his gloves and then her bonnet, to frame her face
with his hands

"Ohhhh," he murmured, "I've got to have more of this.
I knew it would be *gut* between us. Come on."

Was the barn spinning, or was she dizzy from his kiss?
Mary tiptoed along behind Bram, her heartbeat thundering in her ears as she stepped around a pile of horse
apples. If she got any of that on her shoes, it would be no
secret where she'd been. She still felt twitchy, thinking
somebody might walk in on them . . .

"Here we go. I set up a few bales for us to sit on," he
said as they entered the last stall. "And behind them is a
nice clean nest to cuddle in. Let's take off our coats.
Plenty warm enough for that now."

He'd set this up before dinner, figuring to bring her
here after their ride! Mary didn't know whether to break
away and put him in his place or to admire the way he'd
been planning ahead . . . wanting to be alone with her. Her

pulse pounded as she slipped her coat off and he draped it over the stall wall with his. His fedora and her bonnet landed on top, and then he smiled at her in the darkness. "This is more like it, ain't so?"

When Bram sat down on a bale, he kept hold of her hand. She landed beside him and before she could say anything his lips were on hers again . . . not that she wanted to protest. He pulled her closer and her arms slipped around his waist, and somehow they drifted backwards into that nest of hay.

"Mary, think of it," he said as he held her. "With the experience I've gotten—the money I've saved up—I could be runnin' my own auction business. Meetin' you makes me want to jump the fence so those *gut* things could happen sooner, and—"

As he kissed her again, Mary's thoughts raced. She pulled away to gaze at him in the darkness. Bram was so handsome with his black, layered waves framing his face, and his expression beat anything she'd ever seen with the fellows she'd dated in Willow Ridge. "But Bram, you heard what Mamma said about us girls joining the church and—"

"It's a wider world out there than you know, Mary," he insisted. "If we get out and spread our wings now, before we've said our vows, we can always join later. Or if we don't join, we won't be shunned for goin' against the Old Ways."

Mary's mouth dropped open. It was way too soon for Bram to be suggesting—

He seized the opportunity to kiss her again, more urgently. "I don't want to do it by myself, though, honey-girl," he pleaded. He leaned up on his elbow so he was gazing down at her, holding her close. "I knew you were different from anybody I've ever met, soon as I saw you,

Mary. And now that we're talkin' this way, cuddlin' and kissin', I want it to go on and on—"

"*Off* might be the better word for you, nephew. It's one thing for you to be having such thoughts of breaking away from our faith, but another thing altogether to lead Mary down the path to perdition with you."

With a little cry, Mary struggled to sit up as Preacher Abe raised his lantern above them, lighting the entire stall. Her face was on fire. Abe had obviously heard the secret dreams Bram had poured out, but would he tell Bram's parents? Or worse yet, tell hers? Oh, but Mamma would give her and Martha an earful for inviting such wayward boys to stay with them—and then Dat would have his say, too. No doubt in her mind that their parents would send the Kanagy brothers packing, first thing after they heard from Abe. "We—we'd best be getting home, Bram," she rasped as she struggled to her feet.

"Best idea I've heard since I came in to check on my lame mare," the preacher agreed. "Mighty disappointing, to hear a nephew turning his talents—his ambitions— toward worldly ways. You'd do well to follow in your brother's footsteps instead, Bram." Abe watched them brush the hay from their clothing and escorted them to the door. He was still holding the lantern, watching them as Felix trotted down the lane toward the county blacktop.

Mary hugged herself, saying nothing. Her fears were running amok, her thoughts racing ahead to what she would say if her parents challenged them about this incident. Preacher Abe and the bishop had been known to stop at folks' houses at all hours of the night when they learned a soul might be in danger of straying from the fold. This matter was much too serious for Preacher Abe to leave a message on the phone, where it might not be discovered for a day or two. Her pulse pounded dully in her ears as she hunkered down against the brutal midnight wind.

"Mary, I—" Bram exhaled, sending out a cloud of vapor. "It wasn't my intent to get us—to get *you*—in hot water. I just wanted you to know how special you are—"

"Um, we'll soon find out how special your uncle thinks we are," she remarked in a thin voice. "If he goes over home to tell Mamma and Dat—"

"Then I'll sign on for my instruction, soon as I get back to Willow Ridge," Bram insisted. "I don't want to lose you over this, Mary. I meant every word I said. And . . . and I want more of your kisses, too. Soon as I can get them."

Mary was too scared to answer that. When the courting buggy rolled up the lane and stopped a short ways from the front porch, she didn't take the chance that Bram would go after more kisses in the barn. Mary hopped down into the snow, took off her shoes on the porch, and then entered the dark house in her stocking feet. What a relief that no one had waited up. Oh, the things she had to talk about when her twin came in . . .

I sure hope Mary's having a better time than I am, Martha mused as she looked away from her driver. Wasn't Nate cold enough to at least sit against her? Why hadn't she thought to grab some blankets on their way out? And after this frosty, disappointing ride, Clyde's sleigh bells would alert everyone that they were home, too. Jacob and Joanna would get out of bed to pester them. Dat would probably be waiting up, reading the latest issue of *The Budget* so he could meet the Kanagy brothers. After the fun the four of them had shared earlier today, why was Nate being so quiet now that they were alone together?

Was it something I said? Martha wrapped her arms around herself more tightly as the wind passed through her old coat. As she thought back over the day's conversations, she recalled Bram saying his brother had been stiffed by a girl he'd been courting—*but I'm not that girl, am I?*

As she gazed at his profile in the moonlight, she unwrapped a stick of gum in her coat pocket and then slipped it into her mouth. Nate Kanagy was a fine-looking fellow. Maybe not as flashy as his younger brother, but she was okay with that. Her parents would see his joining the church as a sign of maturity, which would be an improvement over their opinions of the boys she'd slipped out with in the past . . . including a few Mennonite fellows and even an English kid who'd picked her up in his sports car down by Cedar Creek where no one would spot them. Traditionally, Plain girls kept their boyfriends a secret and their folks went along with that until time to announce an engagement. Mamma and Dat had gotten word now and again of which fellows had driven her home from Singings, and to say they hadn't always been pleased was an understatement. But if the sweet tingle of peppermint was the most exhilarating thing she'd felt on this sleigh ride, something was wrong here!

Nothing about meeting these boys has been traditional all day. So what's to lose by trying for more, instead of waiting for Nate to take the lead?

Martha's heart pounded. If she slipped her arm along the back of the seat—

"Beautiful night," Nate murmured.

She jerked her arm back into her lap. "*Jah. Jah*, it is."

"Sorry if I've gone quiet on you."

And how did she respond to *that*? Martha bit back a retort, willing him to look at her. Maybe if she could catch his eye, as she'd done several times today, Nate would figure out what she wanted. "Best sometimes to think things through rather than blurting them out."

"*Jah*. Exactly."

Oh, but the steam was about to come out her ears

from exasperation! Martha inhaled the frosty air to settle herself, wondering if she liked Nate's silence better than this conversation that was going nowhere . . . just as their relationship seemed to be. Maybe if she'd chosen Bram instead . . . "Nate, is there something wrong? Did I say something that upset you?" she demanded.

As he gazed at her, the heavy *clip-clop! clip-clop!* of Clyde's hooves, along with the jingle of his harness bells, again filled the space between them. "Nope. Why would you be thinking that?"

"Well—" Martha's breath shot out in a stream of vapor. "You were plenty chatty enough in the mercantile, and while we were putting your beds together and—"

"That was Bram doing most of the talking. I've just been . . . enjoying the way this fine sleigh glides through the snow," he murmured. "Guess I'm more used to spending my time with horses."

"So are you going to kiss your horse *gut*-night, then, instead of me?"

Martha immediately regretted smarting off that way. Yet when Nate's mouth dropped open, she crossed another line—reached up to hold his face so she could give him the kiss that had simmered inside her all day. She sat taller, pressing her lips to his, and for a long, blissful moment Nate kissed her back. Oh, but she longed to reach inside his coat and feel the warmth of his strong, muscular body.

Then he pulled away with a gasp. "If that's what you wanted, Martha—"

"*Jah*, and why wouldn't I?"

"—well, I was just biding my time," Nate continued nervously, "thinking to pass muster with your *dat* before I got my hopes up about you and me—"

"So were you going to kiss Dat *gut*-night, then, too?" she blurted. "I'm feeling a little left out here, Nate, what with you sitting like a bump on a—oh, just take me home. I'm tired and I can't recall ever being this cold in my life."

She shouldn't have snapped at him that way. Nate was being respectful, not rushing into words or actions they might later regret—and he would know about that, and how much it hurt. But what was wrong with having a little fun on such a perfect moonlit night? Joining the church didn't mean you put your happiness away and forgot how to laugh. Or kiss.

Oh, forget it. If he wasn't in the mood before, you've talked him out of cuddling now, for sure and for certain.

Not another word passed between them. Nate's mouth remained in a set line as he gazed at the snowy road and steered Clyde into the lane leading toward the house. When he stopped, Martha jumped down. No sense in waiting with hopeful anticipation in the kitchen or front room while he unhitched his horse and set out some feed. She removed her shoes, got a glass of water, and went on upstairs to get ready for bed. It wasn't even midnight, so Mary and Bram were probably still out in his buggy, laughing and having a fine time.

You should've picked Bram . . .

Everyone was in bed, so Martha ascended the stairs carefully, avoiding the squeaky spots. When she saw dim light shining under the door of the room she shared with Mary, as well as the next bedroom where their guests would sleep, she paused in the hallway. Had Bram lit his lantern and then gone in to be with her sister? Not an uncommon way for Plain kids to date, but it made things awkward when you shared a room.

Martha listened at the door for a moment, and then eased it open. Mary sat cross-legged on her bed. She was in her nightgown, with her auburn hair falling forward like a curtain as she held her head in her hands.

It was a sorrowful sight, and Martha set her water on the nightstand to kneel at her sister's bedside.

"What's wrong, Sister?" she whispered. "I figured you and Bram were still—"

"Oh, but we're in deep trouble." Mary grabbed Martha's hands with trembling fingers. Her face was wet with tears. "We went into Preacher Abe's stable to get warm and, well . . . he caught us rolling in the hay, kissing."

Martha blinked. "Well, it's not fun to get caught. But kissing's not a sin, either."

Mary squeezed her eyes shut. "He heard Bram saying how he wanted to jump the fence—with me—to start his own auction business," she explained in a tiny voice. "I'm just waiting to hear Abe pounding at the door, waking up the parents. Or maybe he'll barge in on our breakfast to tell them what he overheard. I'm on pins and needles, Martha, and I can't seem to settle down."

Martha wrapped her arms around her twin's waist and hugged her hard. "Bram's done enough talking for both brothers then," she murmured. "I couldn't pry three words out of Nate. Finally got so frustrated I kissed him, and now he's not speaking to me at all. Never figured on such a cold, boring sleigh ride, and now things will be *really* chilly around here."

Mary blinked back her tears. "Maybe we should tell them to go home. Maybe right now."

With a sigh, Martha stood up. "*Jah*, and I'm just the one to send them packing, too, if it wouldn't wake everybody up. Maybe they'll have the sense to leave without us saying anything."

A loud creak on the stairway made them stop talking as they listened for Nate to walk past their room. When he had entered the next bedroom and shut the door,

Martha looked purposefully at her sister. She gulped some of her water and poured the rest on the philodendron in the window. Then, with the glass against the wall, she listened for what the boys might be saying. Mary came to stand beside her, and with their heads together they could both hear the conversation.

". . . putty in my hands, I'm tellin' ya," Bram boasted with a low chuckle. "A fine little filly, Mary is, and we're lookin' to have a lot of fun these next couple of days."

Mary's jaw dropped as she gaped at Martha. They kept quiet, though, so as not to miss anything else they needed to know about how their evening had supposedly gone— and what the Kanagy brothers thought would happen next.

"*Jah*, Martha's a feisty one, too," Nate remarked. "She likes it that I'm established in my horse training business, and already a member of the church, too. *Not* that we were talking about church while she was kissing on me."

Martha clapped her hand over her mouth to keep from responding aloud. She and Mary stepped away from the wall, shaking their heads. "Can you believe they were saying—why, that's the same sort of horse hockey I've heard from the boys at our Singings, bragging about their dates."

"Puh!" Mary said with flashing eyes. "If Bram thinks I'm a filly, maybe he needs to step in some you-know-what! Might take him down a peg or two!"

"Right you are, Sister." Martha crossed her arms and glared toward the wall between them and the Kanagy brothers. "They need a lesson in respect and humility, for sure and for certain. And I'm thinking we're just the girls to teach them."

Chapter Six

Nate descended the stairs while it was still dark, partly because he hadn't slept well for recalling last night's fiasco. Mostly, though, the aromas of bacon, coffee, and other heavenly dishes called him to start the day at the table with the Coblentz family. Most mornings, he and his brother ate breakfast at the Sweet Seasons Bakery Café because his Aunt Miriam fed them in exchange for the fresh vegetables and honey his *mamm* provided her. It was nice not to have to walk down a long, snowy lane to eat . . . even though everyone in Martha's family would be eyeballing him, checking him over.

He stopped in the kitchen doorway. What a homey sight, watching Martha and Mary, dressed in identical forest green dresses and white aprons, set plates on the long table. Mrs. Coblentz was stirring a skillet of fried apples while young Joanna placed bacon on a platter. The girl turned, grinning at him.

"I know when *you* got home last night!" she teased. "Heard your sleigh bells."

Nate nodded, almost wishing he'd not indulged himself in such a noisy piece of tack. "And *gut* morning to you, too, missy," he replied evenly. "Still remember your poem for tonight?"

"Got it down perfect. Wanna hear?"

Her mother laughed and elbowed her playfully. "I think we all know it as well as you do, daughter, after listening to it so many times yesterday. Hope you and your brother like breakfast haystacks, Nate. We'll be sitting down soon as Amos and Owen get in from loading their truck."

"*Jah*, saw we had a couple of busted windows in the house we're building," a male voice said from the mudroom. Then a tall, dark-haired man stepped into the kitchen with his shoes in his hand. "Even with it being Christmas Eve, we want to get those fixed so the snow won't get in. Amos Coblentz. Pleased to meet you."

Nate shook the hand he extended. "*Denki* for letting my brother and me stay over. I'm Nate Kanagy, and Bram's coming along behind me."

"*Jah*, that would be me!" His brother entered the kitchen with his hair still wet from a quick shower, buttoning a heavy shirt of pink, purple and black plaid that hung loose over his snug black jeans. "Yesterday was quite a day, pickin' up our new rides at the Graber shop and then meetin' up with your girls. Awfully nice of you folks to put us up—and put up with us."

Within minutes, they had also met Owen, the eldest son, who built houses with his *dat*, and Noah, who was apprenticed at the carriage shop. It was quite a sight to see so many redheads at one table, for he, Bram, and Amos were the only ones with dark hair. But it was the girl sitting across from him that Nate paid particular attention to. When she smiled, her eyes seemed cautious yet hopeful, as though she hoped they could make a fresh start today.

As they passed around bowls of hash browns, fried onions, and chunks of ham, everyone began the "haystack" that would fill his or her plate. Nate piled on the green pepper strips, crumbled bacon, and stewed tomatoes, his stomach rumbling. "Oh, but this looks *gut*," he remarked as he ladled cheese sauce over the top of the small mountain of food he'd taken. There was barely room for a big spoonful of fried apples, which dripped with melted butter and cinnamon, and a fresh biscuit. "And how might Bram and I help you folks today? Need to do something to earn our keep."

"Well, I'll be mucking out the stalls and forking clean straw down from the loft," Mary said, widening her eyes at Bram.

"And we'll need wood chopped and hauled in," Martha continued, "while I'll be helping get our dinner for tomorrow ready—"

"*Jah*, tomorrow might be our birthday but we'll be having the usual quiet, worshipful Christmas Day," Mary explained. "So the cooking and redding up get done today, before we all go to the program at the schoolhouse after supper."

Nate glanced at his brother, whose eyes were half closed in ecstasy as he stuffed another forkful of breakfast into his mouth. While it surprised him a bit that Mary would be choring in the barn while Martha cooked, it seemed only fair that the sisters traded off doing the outside chores while the men were off working.

"Happy to chop that wood for you," Nate said, smiling to himself. Bram had grown up swearing he would find an occupation that didn't require him to shovel manure, the way their *dat* did with the sheep and horses at home, so it would be interesting to see how he handled barn duty today.

Bram, however, nodded good-naturedly. "Count on me to be out in the barn," he said as he reached for another biscuit. His smile for Mary held a secret or two, and she returned it. "It's the least we can do to thank you for feedin' us and our horses."

"That'll be just fine then," Amos said with a satisfied nod. From the head of the table he smiled at Nate and Bram. "Mighty nice having surprise guests for Christmas this year. With all of us getting our work done today, why, the next couple of days off will be a *gut* opportunity to get to know you fellows better."

"And what did your *mamm* say about you staying over?" Nell asked as she started the bowls around again. "You did call her, *jah*?"

"Aunt Beulah Mae saw to that right off," Nate replied, gratified when everyone around the table laughed.

"And *jah*, Mamm called on my cell to let me know it was, um—a bit of a surprise to her, too, our stayin' here," Bram remarked with a roll of his eyes. "But she and Dat send their best wishes to all of you for a wonderful-*gut* Christmas."

Nate glanced across the table at Martha, noting again how she seemed to search his eyes for . . . what? Forgiveness for her snit? A chance to kiss and make up? More than he cared to admit, he'd enjoyed Martha's bold kiss last night . . . the sweet tingle of peppermint on her lips and tongue. He smiled at her, indeed hoping that today they could redeem their new friendship and go forward. "Wouldn't be Christmas without a surprise here and there, ain't so?"

"Do you think Bram suspects he'll be choring with you instead of with me?" Mary whispered. She and Martha had disappeared into the cellar after breakfast, to bring up jars of food for today's meals and tomorrow's Christmas dinner.

Martha's grin turned catlike. "I think we've got them

fooled so far. I'll just explain that you and I take turns at the outdoor chores."

"And don't forget to look outside now and again, watching for Preacher Abe," Mary suggested. "It's *gut* he hasn't come over here, but now we're waiting for the other shoe to drop, ain't so?"

"It'll all work out, Sister. After all, it's not you Abe's peeved at. It's his nephew," Martha pointed out. "Could be he's called Bram's folks, so they're ready to give him a talking-to when he gets home."

Mary placed jars of cherry pie filling, vegetable soup, and sliced peaches in her basket while her sister pulled a ham and a couple of ducks from the deep freeze. "Guess I hadn't thought about it that way." Then she chuckled. "We'll see whether Nate helps me around the house or runs off looking for more *horsey* business after he chops the wood."

"*Jah*, well, they're both in *horsey* up to their knees, far as I'm concerned," Martha replied as she glanced up the cellar steps. "Are you into this switch for the whole day, then?"

"We can't very well change horses in the middle of the stream," Mary quipped. "Can't let them suspect what we're up to, either, or we'll never hear the end of it—from them and the folks, as well."

"We have to be careful in front of the brothers and Joanna, too. She's the one most likely to figure us out." Martha clutched her cold, bulky packages, which were wrapped in butcher's paper. "Better be getting back up there, or they'll be wondering what we're up to. Be a *gut* girl now, *Martha*."

"You, too, *Mary*!"

Chapter Seven

As they followed the crowd into the Cedar Creek schoolhouse, Bram held tightly to Mary's sturdy hand. Back home in Willow Ridge, his family and all the folks in town would be squeezing into a one-room building very much like this one for the annual Christmas program the scholars put on—not that his mind was on recitations about the Christ child. His happiness had a keen edge to it, even after a day of mucking out stalls and scrubbing water troughs. Mary's laughter still rang in his mind from when they'd been horsing around a bit, tossing more clean straw at each other than into the stalls, while the horses had looked on with their ears pricked up.

Oh, but this redhead was keeping him in suspense! He couldn't wait to get her into the courting buggy again, to disappear into the night with the Christmas lights aglow and Mary snuggled against him. She had seemed more spirited today, and Bram was a little surprised that she hadn't been stewing over what Uncle Abe had said last night. He'd thought of ways to comfort her—to convince her he deserved another chance—but then again, life was too short to spend their *rumspringa* fearing the hellfire and damnation the preachers promised to those who turned their backs on the Old Order church.

"There's James Graber," he murmured, waving across the room.

As the carriage maker returned his smile, Mary said, "*Jah*, and that gal beside him is Abby Lambright. We're thinking they'll tie the knot just any day now. High time, too!"

Bram recalled the pretty woman beside James as the one he'd seen sewing in the loft of the mercantile yesterday. He squeezed Mary's hand, thinking how happy James looked . . . how settled and contented. Would he feel that way someday? Maybe with Mary Coblentz?

Waaaay too soon to be thinking about that, his thoughts teased. Yet, considering all the girls he'd dated, he couldn't think that he would've *enjoyed* mucking out stalls with any of them. While Mary hadn't succumbed to his hints about getting cozy in the loft where no one would see them, she had sent him plenty of signals that she was eager to ride with him tonight after the program. Considering how he'd figured her for more of the cooking and sewing type, she had kept up with him every step of the way as they'd shoveled manure, pitched straw for the floors, and hauled fresh hay bales to the stalls.

As though she could read his thoughts, Mary gazed up at him. "Too bad there's such a crowd that we'll have to stand in back, all jammed against each other," she teased.

"*Jah*, I'll be hatin' every minute of this." Bram slipped behind her, allowing Mary to lean back against him as the crowd got quiet. Teacher Frieda motioned to the youngest children, who took their places on the little stage that would make them easier to see this evening. They gave a cheerful welcome and then recited a short poem about Baby Jesus before inviting everyone to sing "Away in a

Manger" with them. It was all Bram could do not to nuzzle Mary's ear as he delighted in her sweet singing voice and a minty essence he hadn't noticed before, but her *mamm* and *dat* were standing nearby, just on the other side of Nate and Martha.

Then a group of middle-grade kids recited their rendition of the Christmas story, standing with solemn, nervous faces and their hands at their sides as they spoke in unison. Bram could remember facing the crowd at that age, wishing the floor would swallow him. He'd been the only boy in his class of five, and try as he might, the words to songs and poems he was to learn went in one ear and out the other no matter how much his *mamm* and the older girls at school had worked with him.

Nowadays, of course, he had figured out that girls didn't give a hoot about recitations. When he stepped into a sale barn and began his auctioneer chant, he could smile out into the crowd and coax the bids higher and higher by pausing at just the right times—gazing into the bidders' eyes until they bought horses, Amish-made quilts, antiques, or whatever was for sale that day. Playing a crowd was a game to him now, a challenge he loved . . . just as Mary was proving to be. As she shifted against him, Bram closed his eyes, wishing the scholars would speak faster.

Up through the grades the presentations went, sometimes combining a class or two for a skit, until finally Jacob and Joanna rose for their poem. Joanna stood with her hands clasped in front of her, resembling a red-haired angel as she spoke her stanzas, while her twin brother looked ready to bolt. But they reached the end without a hitch, and for that Bram felt encouraged. He'd worked with them, after all.

When Mary gazed up at him with mischief twinkling in her blue eyes, however, Bram's thoughts took a different direction. Silently she gripped his hand and led him

between the folks standing in the very back of the room.
The audience was watching up front, where more kids
were preparing to reenact the birth of Jesus in the manger.
As they slipped out into the brisk night air, Bram let out
the chuckle he'd been suppressing.

"Well, *this* is different," he teased. "Just couldn't wait
any longer?" He slipped an arm around Mary's shoulders
and kissed her.

"Too warm in there," she whispered. "Too many people,
to my way of thinking."

"I like your way of thinking, Mary." Was it his imagination, or did her blue eyes seem more intense tonight as
she looked at him? Her face glowed in the moonlight. She
had seemed less chatty today, yet bolder and readier to
play, as though last night's incident with Uncle Abe was
long forgotten. "Let's hook up those Christmas lights and
get ourselves along, shall we?"

"Let's do it," she agreed.

Bram blinked. He sensed Mary had made that remark
in total innocence, yet her tone seemed . . . more knowing than he'd expected. He and other fellows who worked
among English often picked up on phrases more sheltered
Plain kids weren't aware of, so he didn't quiz her about it.
He did, however, return her grins and kisses as Felix
trotted along the snow-packed back roads.

"Are ya happy, Mary?" he whispered as he pulled in
behind a windbreak of huge evergreens. A nice private
spot just off the road, where they'd be out of the breeze
and out of sight to passers-by. He put on the brake and
pulled the quilt she'd brought more closely around them.

Her sly smile teased at him. "*Jah*, Bram, I'm having a
real *gut* time," she replied before scooting closer for a
playful kiss. "Glad to be turning eighteen tomorrow, and
glad you're here to help me celebrate."

"Let me know if you get cold," he hinted, his mind exploring the possibilities of other stables and private places they might hide away. He did *not* want them to be interrupted, now that Mary had recovered from their run-in with Uncle Abe.

"I don't think that's going to happen tonight, Bram."

Once again her response struck him as . . . brassy. Was this the same Mary who had bemoaned her ruined reputation last night? As he pulled her close for a longer, more serious kiss, however, Bram set aside his misgivings . . . forgot all about it being a cold winter's night . . .

Nate bit back a grin as Martha gripped his hand. The scholars had finished their reenactment of Jesus' birth, so now all of the kids were moving to the stage for a final carol sing with their families and guests—and the girl beside him was nodding toward the door with a purposeful smile. He wasn't surprised that she wanted to skip out early, the way her twin had, and he didn't balk. Now was his chance to build upon the rapport they'd reestablished today, and to prove that he wasn't a stick in the mud just because he'd joined the church already. And it was a chance to let go of Roberta Hershberger's betrayal of his affection once and for all.

"Had enough of Christmas tradition for one night?" he teased as they strode toward his sleigh. Clyde whickered and stomped his big feet in greeting as Nate boosted Martha into the seat and then got in on the other side.

"Always nice to see the program the kids have been working so hard on," Martha replied pertly. "And didn't Jacob and Joanna do a really *gut* job on their piece?"

"They did." He clapped the reins lightly across his Clydesdale's back. "Geddap, Clyde."

"But once I got Jacob through it—I was mouthing the words along with him while he watched me, you know," she added with a chuckle, "why, I felt like my job here was finished. I've got a guest to entertain."

Hmm. Martha didn't seem all that caught up in the kids' recitations when we were coaching them, Nate thought as he pulled onto the county highway. But her improved mood was a welcome change from the way their ride had gone last night, so he decided to remain open to whim, to enjoy himself with this pretty redhead. Martha had helped him stack the firewood he'd cut this morning, and as they had filled the built-in bin beside the fireplace, they'd chatted and laughed.

She had baked special breakfast buns with a sweet glaze for Christmas morning, and had insisted he take a break and try one, along with a turtle brownie and a fabulous frosted cookie that had a piece of mint candy baked into its center. He hadn't expected Martha to enjoy baking so much, considering how he'd met her in the horse feed aisle of the mercantile. But what man didn't appreciate good things from the kitchen?

"I'm still recalling how *gut* those cookies were this morning," Nate remarked as Martha scooted closer to him.

"Oh, and we've got plenty more where those came from," she replied. "With Christmas being our birthday, we have all the usual goodies and Mamma makes us a chocolate coconut cake, too. Looks like a regular pan of chocolate cake until you cut it and see the yummy coconut filling in the middle! But then . . . I'm hoping to enjoy another kind of sweetness now that I'm turning eighteen," she added quietly.

When Nate glanced down at her, Martha's eyes were all a-sparkle and her cheeks glowed like roses in the moonlight. He guided Clyde onto the Nissley's Ridge road and stopped the sleigh. Here, it felt like they were on top of the world, surrounded by flawless fields of snow in the pale blue twilight, beneath a velvet canopy studded with stars. Not another soul was in sight. The wind whispered secrets in the silence.

"Might be a little early, but I want to be the first to wish you a happy birthday, Martha," he murmured as he reached for her.

With the slightest twitch of her lips, Martha let her head fall back against his arm. Gone was the insistence, the pushiness she'd kissed him with before she lost her patience last night.

"Mmmm . . ." escaped her. Then, when Nate kissed her again, she opened her mouth to let him explore.

What slow, sweet affection was this? Nate took his time sampling her, nuzzling her cheek before dipping in for another taste of her lips. It was . . . almost like he was kissing a different girl. He kept waiting for Martha to catch fire and press her mouth to his with that same im petuous insistence that had given him a lot to think about last night—that feistiness he'd been gearing up for all day. But even when he deepened his kisses, she seemed content to receive rather than to give back.

When they started off again, Martha sighed and snuggled against him as he put an arm around her. With the jingle of the sleigh bells as an accompaniment, they exchanged an occasional comment . . . more kisses as the mood struck them. Nate was enjoying their relaxed affection, but it wasn't nearly as exciting as having Martha come at him as though she couldn't stop.

"I'm sorry I got so huffy last night, Nate," she murmured. "Don't know what came over me, and I'm glad we've gotten past that. *Denki* for giving me this chance to make up for it."

Nate blinked. Rather than answer her, he listened to his instincts. "Hope you don't mind if we head on back to the house," he said quietly. "It's been a while since I chopped so much wood and I'm starting to droop."

"You worked hard today," she agreed. "Mamma was pleased with how you carried all those big roasting pans and so many jars of food up from the cellar, too."

"Happy to help."

When they got to the Coblentz home, he was glad the rest of the family had already gone to bed in preparation for an early morning of chores and preparing the big Christmas meal. Nate kissed his date goodnight and excused himself to brush and feed Clyde. He stalled in the barn for a while, waiting for Bram, but finally went inside and slipped up to their room.

What was missing? Why did he feel so let down, even though this evening's ride had been a huge success compared to last night's? It seemed as though he'd been settling for an unfrosted sugar cookie instead of exhilarating in—

Peppermint! Martha had reeked of it—had chewed her gum with the same energy she lavished on everything she did, but he hadn't seen or smelled any sign of gum all day. And as Nate replayed his date's interest in the twins' recitation . . . the way she had baked sweet rolls and brownies as though she lived in the kitchen—and then indulged him with samples . . . the passive way she had allowed him to kiss her . . .

Well, all these little differences could mean only one thing.

He was still awake when his younger brother came in, whistling under his breath as though he'd had the time of his life. Nate lit the lantern on the bedside table and crooked his finger for Bram to come to his bunk.

"Now what?" his brother whispered, searching his face. "Don't tell me you struck out two nights in a row."

"We've been had, Bram."

His brother's dark eyebrows rose like question marks.

"And what's that supposed to mean? Mary was her sweet, loveable self and we had ourselves quite a nice—"

"*Jah*, she was," Nate murmured, his heart hammering. "But Mary was with *me*. And the more I've thought about it, the more I believe they switched on us this morning, before you went to the barn and I chopped the wood."

"Get out! What makes you think—"

Nate shushed his brother's outburst with a finger, gesturing toward the wall between their beds and the girls' room. "Martha wouldn't go on and on about how the twins did at the program tonight," he said, "and she wouldn't have been so happy in the kitchen, baking buns and cookies all morning. Didn't you notice any difference in the way your girl was kissing you?" he continued in an urgent whisper. "*That* was the big give-away. Martha went after it with a vengeance—and a wad of peppermint gum in her mouth last night—and tonight it was like you've said. Mary was her sweet, loveable self."

At least his brother had the decency to look sheepish for not noticing. But as Bram reviewed his day choring in the barn, and then his ride tonight, he allowed that *possibly* the twins had pulled a switch on them. "Who's to know, just from looking at them?" he protested in a strained whisper. "They dress alike, and they look identical right down to the freckles on their perky little noses. Even Uncle Abe can't tell them apart, and he's known them all their lives."

"I'm right, little brother," Nate muttered. "You just don't want to admit it."

"So what're you gonna do about it?" Bram challenged. "I sure hope you won't get all bent out of shape while we're havin' such a *gut* time here. If you and I were twins, we'd probably pull the same stunt now and again."

At ten or twelve, maybe. But not at eighteen.

Long after his brother put out the lamp, as the old house creaked and settled in the night, Nate remained awake. He couldn't let go of the way Mary and Martha had behaved, when they could have simply suggested changing partners—especially considering that they had done the choosing from the start. It was Mary who had climbed into Bram's buggy, most likely after consulting with Martha on her cell phone.

How long did the twins intend to continue their charade? Had they no consideration for his and Bram's feelings? Even if this was just meant to be a little Christmas diversion lasting a few days, it galled him that girls from a respected Amish family had played them for fools. It also reminded him of the way Roberta had betrayed him, seeing other fellows after he'd declared his intention to marry her and had joined the church. To the Coblentz girls, their switch had probably seemed like a harmless game, but he had no stomach for such dishonesty in another relationship.

Nate kept his face toward the wall when he heard Bram get up and slip into his clothes, ready for breakfast. Then he dressed, stuck his clothes into his duffel, and went downstairs with a heavy heart but a firm resolve. He didn't change his mind when everyone around the table stopped talking at the sight of his scowl and his luggage.

"I—I thank you for your hospitality," he said, nodding to Amos and Nell, "but I'm going home to spend Christmas with my family. It was *gut* to meet you all."

The twins sprang from their seats. "But Nate, we're just now starting to celebrate our birthday—"

"And it won't be the same without *you* here, when we were counting on the four of us—"

Who had spoken first, and who had followed up? Mary? Martha? He met their gazes briefly but he didn't reply.

Amos cleared his throat. "I hope you haven't gotten

word that someone's ill, or that something's gone wrong in Willow Ridge. It was our pleasure to meet you boys."

Nate pressed his lips together, exchanging a glance with his brother, who looked anything but happy. He had to at least give a reason for his departure, because lame excuses would make him as guilty of duplicity as the twins had been. "No, things are fine at home, far as I know. Sorry to leave on a sour note, but . . . I didn't like it much that while I thought I was with Martha last night, it was really Mary."

He went out the back kitchen door toward the stable then, relieved that none of the Coblentzes followed—and not surprised that Bram didn't join him. This was his own issue to deal with, after all, not his brother's. When he hitched Clyde to his new sleigh, he tossed the harness strap with the bells under his seat, so their merry jingle wouldn't mock him the whole way home. With a last glance at the cozy white house and the smoke curling out of its stone chimney, Nate sighed.

"Let's go, Clyde," he said sadly. "Just you and me, buddy."

Chapter Eight

"So what's this I'm hearing, girls?" Amos asked in a low voice. He looked steadily at his two older daughters as they sat with their heads bowed. "Is it true, what Nate said? Did you mislead your guests about which one of you was Mary and which one was Martha?"

Bram sat silently, not looking at the twins in their moment of truth. It wasn't his place to stick up for them, or to interfere in this conversation. And what would he say? Would he appear stupid if he admitted he hadn't noticed the difference last night? Would these folks—or his brother—think him disloyal if he didn't follow Nate back to Willow Ridge? Owen, Noah, and the younger twins remained quiet as they watched this discussion with interest, but Nell's expression had lost its Christmas morning cheer.

"Answer your *dat*," she said. "We'll not eat until we've gotten the whole story."

The twin across from him cleared her throat. "*Jah*, we did that," she said in a tiny voice.

"But only after we heard Nate and Bram telling each other some mighty tall tales about their dates with us on Friday night," her sister blurted.

Bram's face prickled with heat. He and Nate *had* engaged in some brotherly bragging . . .

"So you're also saying you eavesdropped on their conversation?" Amos asked tersely. "Put a glass against the wall of their room, did you?"

When he peered from beneath his eyelashes, Bram saw how the girls' faces were nearly the same red as their Christmas dresses. Down the table he heard fidgeting and a snicker.

"Oh, but you're gonna get it now," Joanna murmured.

"That'll be enough out of you, missy," Nell declared quietly. "Girls? We need to hear you say it out, what you did, so we'll all know what you'll be asking Bram to forgive you for. You should be ashamed, treating your company that way."

"Thought we had this discussion about your fooling folks enough times when you were wee girls to get that out of your systems," their father went on sternly. "It's not a topic meant for our Savior's birthday, either, but I won't have this cloud hanging over our heads until tomorrow."

The redhead across the table looked at Bram with tear-filled eyes. "I—I'm sorry I pretended to be Mary yesterday," she stammered.

"Switching places on you boys was a low-down trick," her sister agreed woefully, "and listening in on your chat with Nate wasn't one of our finer ideas, either. We're really sorry, Bram—"

"And we feel awful about hurting Nate's feelings."

"—and if you want to go home, too, well, I can't say as I'd blame you. I hope you can—"

"Forgive us?"

"Forgive us?"

Bram let out the breath he'd been holding, not sure he'd kept accurate track of who had said what. "*Jah*, apology accepted. Nate's leery of girls right now, after the way he thought he was gettin' married and Roberta gave him the slip. But, um . . ." He paused, hoping for the right words. "Those tall tales you heard were just a guy thing. Not meant to upset you, see."

"And we didn't swap places to hurt your feelings, either," Mary insisted as she wiped away tears. "We just, well—"

"We each wanted to find out if we were better suited to the other brother, seeing's how neither of us came home real happy Friday night."

Bram glanced at Amos and Nell, but saw no sign that they knew about Uncle Abe's visit to the stable. "I had a hand in the way things turned out that night," he hedged, "and neither of us brothers intended for Friday evening to go sour, believe me. We were both real tickled that you asked us to stay over."

Had he overstated his case? Correctly interpreted the twins' disappointment? It was his experience that girls had their romantic expectations about dates and guys had totally different ones. If a man wanted to make any progress with a special young lady he sometimes had to kiss up. But if he overdid it, he'd be in worse trouble than if he'd not admitted his perceived mistakes. Girls were complicated creatures . . .

But at least their parents seemed to think the issue had been settled for now. Amos bowed his head, a signal that they should begin their meal with silent prayer. Then the food passing began, and Bram filled his plate with an egg casserole loaded with cheese and chunks of sausage, along with baked pineapple and a couple of those glazed buns that Martha—no, *Mary*—had baked yesterday. The table talk still felt strained but everyone was making the best of the situation.

"I'd be happy to do the horse chores for you this morning," Bram offered. "It'll be my Christmas gift, for the way you've fed me and heard me out."

"Well, that'd be a fine thing," Amos replied, and Owen nodded happily as he helped himself to more food.

"We'll help," Mary insisted with a glance at her sister. "It'll go faster with the three of us."

"Can't expect you to do that by yourself," Martha agreed. "Especially not on this special day when we keep the work to a minimum."

Bram grinned, as this was the reaction he'd hoped for. After the twins scraped and stacked the dishes—and declared that Joanna could help their *mamm* wash and dry them because it was their birthday—he and the two girls headed for the barn. When a snowball hit his back, Bram laughed out loud and returned the favor, tossing loosely packed handfuls of snow at Mary and Martha. The way he saw it, Nate had left the party too soon . . . so now it was his mission to keep both Coblentz sisters entertained. There could be worse ways to spend a Christmas morning before they went inside for the traditional Bible reading from Luke, and then quietly pondered the meaning of Jesus' birth in their lives.

"*Denki* for seein' my side of things after my brother left," Bram said as they entered the dim barn. "Glad we got things aired out so as not to spoil your birthday. And I'm hopin' it'll be the happiest one you've ever had, too."

"We're working on that," Martha said as she grabbed a bucket for hauling water.

"*Jah*, I thought we were in for a big lecture and maybe getting sent to our room," Mary added. "Dat would've been a lot tougher on us if you'd left with Nate."

Bram grabbed a shovel and started scooping the piles of manure that had accumulated since yesterday. It seemed like a fine time to discuss another subject that had been on his mind, while it was just the three of them . . . perhaps a topic these girls might consider if they got tired of thinking about religion today. "We can still enjoy each other's company even with my brother gone—if you've a mind to," he said playfully.

Mary and Martha glanced at each other and then back at him, looking hopeful. "What'd you have in mind, Bram?" one of them asked.

"Maybe a ride this afternoon, to get out of the house for a while?" the other twin chimed in. "We could all fit in your buggy."

"Oh, I had something more . . . permanent in mind." He would have to be careful, because he still couldn't tell them apart . . . and he didn't want to ruin his chances for keeping one or both of them interested. They did everything together, it seemed. "I've been wantin' to start up my own auctioneering business, like I've told you. And if I had you girls to help me with the clerkin' and the organizin', we could do a bang-up business, the three of us."

Their eyebrows rose in unison. One stopped raking the soiled hay from the stalls and the other quit filling the water troughs. "You mean, like, moving to Willow Ridge? Finding a place to live and—"

"Are we talking a job that pays? Or just being there to help you out, Bram?"

"Of course I'll pay you!" he assured them. "I've got enough connections with fellows who set up estate sales and livestock auctions to make a *gut* go of it. But I'll need somebody who can make my calls for me, and print up the bills of sale, and run a lunch wagon and—"

Again their eyebrows rose. "So you're talking about a full-time thing? Where we won't be living at home?"

"*Jah*, now's your chance to get out and see something of the world, before you join the church," Bram continued earnestly. "You might even decide the Old Ways aren't your ways. I admit I'm on the verge of jumpin' the fence myself because this religion just isn't feelin' like a *gut* fit for me. If we stick together—"

"You're saying Nate won't be in on this plan?"

Bram suspected it was Martha talking, and she'd brought up another subject he had to handle carefully. But he couldn't help feeling excited. His future seemed to be unfolding even as he was discussing it with these two bright, personable girls. Folks at sales would take to the attractive Coblentz twins immediately. They were hard workers—resourceful—with a good sense of humor. "Nate will always be my brother," he pointed out. "His trainin' business takes him to livestock sales sometimes, and that'll keep us connected. I can't speak for him, understand, but mostly he'll be goin' his way and I'll be goin'—"

"But if you jump the fence, you'll separate yourself from your whole family. They won't be as likely to spend time with us if we've left the Old Order," Martha pointed out.

"And I can't see us causing that sort of split here," Mary said in a rising voice. "We have our tough talks now and again, but I'm not ready to break Mamma's heart by telling her I'm leaving the church—"

"And if she gets wind of this idea that you want to look after both of us, while working mostly amongst English, away from Cedar Creek," Martha went on, "well, that's sounding mighty radical to me."

"Living in sin. That's what Mamma and Dat would call it."

Bram felt his new future—a wonderful opportunity for independence—slipping away with each word they said. "But it wouldn't be that way!" he insisted. "Our families aren't gonna pitch us out like this manure we're shovelin'. I'd be sure you girls had a nice place to stay, and—"

"Oh, that'll be a sticking point, for sure and for certain." Martha gripped her rake, leaning on it as she held his gaze. "If you'd be payin' the rent, that would make it pretty much your place, to come and go as you pleased—"

"And to do whatever else you wanted with us," Mary

said with a firm shake of her head. "You'd best head on back to Willow Ridge, Bram. I'll not ruin our Christmas by breaking this idea to the parents. I'll gather your things together and tell them you've decided to spend the day with your family—"

"And I'll hitch Felix to your buggy," Martha said as she went to the back wall where his tack was hanging.

Bram's jaw dropped. Just that fast these girls had sent him packing. "But—"

"*Jah*, your *butt* is cute and fun to have around," Mary remarked ruefully.

"But your wild ideas will get us in big trouble," her sister finished. "I'm not letting this cat out of the bag and getting another lecture on our birthday." She was already slipping the bridle over Felix's head, while Mary hurried out of the barn, toward the house.

Fifteen minutes later Bram's rig was pointed toward the road. He waved to the twins and they waved back, but the regret he saw on their faces weighed heavily on his heart. He wasn't used to being rejected—especially not by two girls in the same day—and that thought made his resentment simmer as he urged Felix into a trot . . .

Keeping both of those girls happy would've been more work than it was worth, anyway, even if you could've convinced them of your honorable intentions. They're joined at the hip, unable to think for themselves . . . probably would have pulled more of their switching tricks if they'd come to work for you . . .

And yet, as the miles went by, Bram realized he'd acted brashly . . . would have been better off talking up his auctioneering business while Nate was around to soften his sharp edges. It wasn't the first time he'd spoken in all-out excitement and then overstepped some lines. And even if they teased their dates with their sparkly blue eyes and hot kisses, nice girls like Mary and Martha stayed within the lines. He could see that now.

When he got home, Nate was still enduring some stiff talk from their parents. Bram heard their voices in the front room as he came in through the kitchen door, so he paused to get the gist of the conversation.

". . . not the way I'd figured on spending my Christmas, with my family scattered hither and yon," Mamm was saying. "What possessed you boys to take up with girls you'd never seen before?"

"And why would their parents go along with it?" Dat asked sternly. "Seems a sign that their daughters might play fast and loose, inviting you into their home so quick-like."

Bram closed his eyes, waiting for Nate's answer. Some of the blame belonged to him for jumping at the chance to get better acquainted with Mary and Martha, after all.

"It wasn't like we were staying with English," his brother replied with a resigned sigh. "The Coblentz family observes the same traditions we do. We went to the scholars' program on Christmas Eve with them, and—"

"I could tell from the tone of Bram's voice message that he started all of this," Mamm broke in. "And that explains why he stayed behind, too. At least you had the sense to realize those girls were up to no *gut*, and come home."

Oh, but that remark went too far! Bram entered the front room and let his duffel drop. "There's nothing *loose* about Mary and Martha Coblentz," he stated as they all turned his way. "And their family seemed pleased to have Christmas visitors."

"*Jah*, well your aunt and uncle gave me an earful, I can tell you!" Mamm retorted. "Beulah Mae wasn't one bit happy that you boys changed her plans, and I can't say as I blame her."

Bram slipped into his usual seat on the couch, sighing inwardly. His parents and his *dat*'s mother, Mammi Essie, were all seated as though they were ready for the day's reading of the Christmas story, but the big Bible lay open on the table beside Dat, forgotten. Had Uncle Abe called to inform them that he'd been sweet-talking Mary in the stable? Hinting that he'd like to leave the Old Order church? Discussions like this one rubbed him like a starched collar . . . made him even more ready to jump the fence. But this wasn't the time to express such opinions.

"Like I've said already, it wasn't our intention to upset anybody," Nate murmured. "We were just having a little fun, and now we've come home to spend the rest of Christmas Day with you. I'm sorry about this whole thing."

"*Jah*, me, too," Bram added with a sigh. Better to go along with his brother's apology and get their parents out of lecture mode. He saw no sign that Uncle Abe had informed them of what he'd overheard—they would've been quick to bring that up—so it was better not to stir the pot any more.

Bram listened dutifully as his father read the second chapter of Luke from the German Bible. He went through the motions of contemplating the wonder of the Savior's birth, but truth be told, his thoughts had wandered back to Cedar Creek and the Coblentz home. The girls would be helping Nell set the table by now, getting ready to celebrate their eighteenth birthday at dinner. They would be serving up birthday cake and exchanging Christmas gifts and no doubt the ten-year-old twins would keep things lively.

He sighed glumly. Such festivities sounded much more joyful than the rest of the day in the Kanagy home would be. While he knew there was nothing to be done about it, he sometimes wished he and Nate had other brothers and some sisters filling up their table—and distracting their parents—the way most Plain families did.

Bram made his way through a big dinner of meat loaf, mashed potatoes, noodles with caraway seeds, green bean casserole, and fresh rolls, and then topped it off with a slice of his grandmother's coconut pie and some of his *mamm*'s fudge and cookies. While he ate, he thought about the ham and ducks they'd be serving in Cedar Creek . . . saw Mary and Martha's flawless faces and blue-eyed smiles in his mind. Were they making their birthday wishes by now as they blew out their candles? Were they missing him and Nate, or had they been insulted by his invitation to come away and work for him? Maybe they were fed up with Nate's thin-skinned reason for leaving, too.

"Guess I'd better tend to Felix," Bram remarked after they ate. "I came right in, rather than feeding him or brushing him down."

As he shrugged into his barn coat and headed outside, he heard the kitchen door closing behind him. Nate, too, had gotten away from the house, not in the mood to chat with Dat or help Mamm and Mammi with the dishes.

"So why'd you come home?" his brother quizzed him. "And don't tell me it was out of loyalty to *me*."

"It was nothin' like that," Bram assured him, but he didn't want to admit that the twins had shooed him off. "Why couldn't you just play along with Mary and Martha's little game? Or find a more private way of sayin' you were onto them?" he demanded. "We had a *gut* thing going with those girls until you—"

"It's no *gut* when somebody plays games with your heart and your best intentions. I'll stick with training horses, thanks," Nate replied stiffly. "Horses at least listen to me and respect my feelings."

"You're just sore because you joined the church sooner

than you wanted, for a girl who didn't marry you. Get over it!"

"And you've got an *attitude*, Bram. You need to work on that."

He was tired of hearing how many things he needed to work on—as though Nate were Mr. Perfect with all the answers, when it came to girls. Bram entered the barn and dipped out oats for Felix before working him over with the currycomb. It promised to be one of the most disappointing Christmases ever, the way things were shaping up between him and his brother. Maybe he should hitch Felix to his new buggy and look for better company. If those two cute Coblentz sisters wanted nothing to do with him, he might as well scout around . . .

Chapter Nine

"Hold it lower, or we'll not get it through the doorway," Mary grunted. She and Martha were putting Jacob's room back to rights, taking down the spare bed they'd assembled for the Kanagy boys. "And don't be pushing me down the stairs, either — unless *you* want to go first, and go backwards."

"You're already there, Mary. You go, girl," Martha quipped as she gripped her end of the bulky mattress. "This job was a lot easier with Nate and Bram doing the heavy lifting."

"You've got that right. Take it slow, now."

Mary started cautiously down the stairs with her end of the mattress, bearing most of the weight even though Martha was doing her best to hold it back. It would have been *nice* if Owen and Noah had offered to do this, but their brothers had given them so much grief about why their guests had left so suddenly that Mary hadn't asked them to help. It was the fitting end to a birthday that had dragged its feet since their guests had left. At least hefting the pieces of the spare bed gave them something to do besides sitting around, thinking about what they might have been enjoying had Bram and Nate stayed.

In the front room, their *dat* looked up from the magazine he was reading. "Want some help with that?"

"No, thanks!" she replied.

"We've got it," Martha joined in.

"I was looking forward to getting better acquainted with the Kanagy boys today," he remarked. "Nate's made a *gut* name for himself—and a steady income—with his horse training. And Bram might be a little wet behind the ears yet, but he's got a fine future with his auctioneering."

"*Jah*, they've found work that'll make them welcome in Plain settlements anywhere," their mother remarked as she looked up from her quilt frame. "And they come from a respected family, too."

"Bet Bram's already got himself another girlfriend," Joanna remarked as she focused on her embroidery. "You can bet *I* wouldn't have packed his bag for him!"

Mary rolled her eyes at her sister and kept moving through the front room toward the door to the basement. They eased down the stairway, with Martha going first this time. After they leaned the mattress against the storeroom wall, where they'd already placed the box springs, they paused to catch their breath.

"If I hear one more time about how wonderful-*gut* the Kanagy boys are—"

"*Jah*, you'd think we sent away a couple of long-lost sons."

"—and if Joanna makes one more smart remark, I might just smack her!"

Martha heaved a sigh. "You have to admit they were fun while they lasted. And pretty cute, too, each in his own way."

"But we'd be in hot water up to our eyeballs if we went along with Bram's big ideas," Mary whispered. Then her lips curved. "At least he has a plan, though . . . a dream for his future. Can't say that about any of the boys here in Cedar Creek—leastways, not the ones our age."

"*Jah*, and it's too bad about Nate getting the cold shoulder from his fiancée. If we'd had any idea how upset he'd be by us switching around . . ." Martha sighed as she took a piece of gum from her apron pocket.

Mary shrugged, feeling more disappointed with each passing moment. "I was really looking forward to Second Christmas tomorrow . . . spending all day out and around with those boys. But this wishful thinking's not getting the rest of that bed down here."

Together they carried the pieces of the bed frame, and when they'd covered everything with an old sheet to keep it from getting dusty, they returned to Owen and Noah's room. Tearing down the rollaway bed Jacob had bunked in was simpler, because they stored it in a hall closet for when cousins and other kin came to visit.

"It's probably time to help Mamma set the table for supper," Mary remarked as they finished straightening Jacob's room.

"*Jah*, but I'll be thinking about how much food Bram and Nate would've tucked away—"

"And having them there at dinner when we blew out our candles would've been special, ain't so?" Mary asked in a tiny voice. "We're sounding like the folks, going on and on about what nice fellows they were."

"Well, they *are* nice. We all just said and did some things that didn't go over so *gut*," Martha replied. "And who wouldn't get their hopes up, looking forward to some fun with them? I can't think they really *wanted* to head home . . ."

"Puh! Would you listen to us having a pity party instead of celebrating our birthday?" Mary leaned closer to Martha, keeping her voice low as an idea bubbled up inside her. "What's to stop us from going to Willow Ridge? Isn't Second Christmas supposed to be for having fun and visiting?"

"You mean, just drive on over there? To surprise them?"

"Why not?" Mary grinned, grabbing her sister's arm. "I'm thinking Nate and Bram'll be real glad to see us. And if we apologize first thing—"

"*Jah*, it'll be the best chance we have to clear the air," Martha said, her voice rising with excitement. "Really hate to leave things the way they are."

"But not a word about this to anybody else."

"Oh no, I'm not listening to any more remarks about the Kanagy boys leaving—"

"Or about how only loose, wayward girls would go chasing after them," Mary said with a decisive nod. She was grinning from ear to ear, just like her sister. "Let's box up some cookies to take along."

"*Jah*, never hurts to sweeten the deal. And if we pack some clothes tonight, we can get out of here before anybody else is out of bed. It's the best way."

"We can write Mamma a note so she won't worry about us."

Martha let out a short laugh. "She can always call our cells. But by the time she thinks to do that, we'll be having ourselves a *gut* time in Willow Ridge!"

"I like it! We're going!"

When the mantel clock downstairs chimed four, Martha gave up on trying to sleep. As she began to wind her hair into a bun, Mary slipped into the dress she'd laid out last night. They rose so often before the sun that grooming in the dark came as second nature. Their whispered giggles were the only noise they made as they slid their duffels out from under their made-up beds. Down the stairs they went in their stocking feet, missing the squeaky spots from years of practice. Mary laid the note to Mamma on the kitchen counter, and then the two of them slipped into their leather sneakers, coats, and bonnets. Out they went, as silent and light as two snowflakes.

As a team they hitched Taffy to the enclosed buggy they shared with Noah. When they'd loaded the cookie box and their duffels, Martha slid inside and took the reins. "Geddap, Taffy," she said, thankful that their mare seemed as excited about this adventure as they were despite the early hour. After Mary slid the barn door shut she, too, climbed in.

Once they were on the road, they stopped holding their breath. Mary grabbed Martha around the shoulders. "Oh, this is so much fun!"

"*Jah*, we've never tried the likes of *this* before!" Martha replied gleefully. "Bram made a *gut* point when he said we should get out and see something of the world during our *rumspringa*."

"And it's not like the parents don't approve of him and Nate," Mary pointed out. "Not like we're running wild, without a set destination, either."

Martha followed the county road between the Cedar Creek Mercantile and Graber's Custom Carriages, and on beyond the grain elevator at the edge of town. As they passed through LaPlata, the first glimmers of pink glowed along the horizon. She steered Taffy east onto another county blacktop and settled back into the seat. "Now isn't that a pretty sight, seeing the sun rise behind these farms and pastures?" she said. "Most mornings we don't see past our own fences—"

"Or beyond the kitchen sink," Mary remarked.

"—and we have no idea what goes on in the rest of the world. It's all well and *gut* for me to help out around home while you're baking for Beulah Mae—"

"But who knows what we've been missing?" Mary said as she peered eagerly at the farms they were passing in the early morning light. "Sometimes boys get a lot different picture of things before they marry and start families. I'm really glad we're doing this, Sister. It's *gut* to find out we can take care of ourselves beyond Cedar Creek."

Wasn't it wonderful to chitchat this way, just the two of them? Martha had so rarely left home on Second Christmas, except to go visiting with her entire family, that this adventure with only her twin was a real treat. "What do you suppose Nate and Bram will say when we pull into their lane?" she asked. "I can't wait to see their faces when we knock on their door."

"And what do you suppose they'll want to do once we sweeten them up with cookies and convince them we really, truly like them?" Mary gazed through the windshield at the snowy fields now glistening with the sunrise. "Of course, we'll have to stop at a house somewhere when we get to Willow Ridge, to ask where they live. No sense in driving around half the day, trying to guess."

"*Jah*, there's that." Martha laughed. "But we won't be like boys that way. We *will* ask for directions!"

On they drove, through LaPlata and a few other settlements that were too small to be considered towns. Taffy was trotting along, tossing her head and enjoying the brisk morning. The *clip-clop! clip-clop!* of her hooves punctuated their ideas about what they might enjoy doing with Nate and Bram today. When they fell quiet for a moment, however, Martha wondered if they hadn't already passed the farmstead on the left, with its old gray silos and low-slung barns . . . or did a lot of places in central Missouri look much the same as those in Cedar Creek? She didn't think she'd backtracked . . . yet as she saw an intersection coming up, she felt a rumbling in her stomach that had nothing to do with hunger.

"Um . . . which way do you suppose we ought to go at this crossroads?" she asked.

Mary blinked. She studied the horses in the nearest pasture as though they might have the right answer. "I haven't the foggiest idea, Sister," she finally admitted. "Guess we were so excited about this trip, it didn't occur to me we'd never been to Willow Ridge."

"Oh, we've gone through there—I recall seeing the café where the boys said they eat nearly every morning. But I wasn't driving then, so I wasn't paying attention to road signs." Martha drove on for a bit, searching her mind for a logical solution to this problem as she studied the passing countryside. "But we know it's south and west of Cedar Creek, so if we keep heading away from the sun—"

"Or we keep the sun to our left side," Mary continued, gesturing toward the glow in the clear, crystal blue sky.

"—we'll be on a *gut* road. Then when we see somebody out choring or driving, we can ask them."

"Works for me."

They rolled along the snow-packed county highway for another ten minutes . . . or was it twenty? Or only five? Martha shifted in the seat, becoming more aware that they didn't know for sure they were on the best route to Willow Ridge. "How about you grab me a cookie or two out of your box, Mary?"

"I was just thinking the same thing."

"Then maybe you ought to call Bram and ask the best way to get there," Martha said with a sigh. "It'll let our cat out of the bag, but there's no sense wandering lost on roads that won't take us where we want to go."

Mary fumbled in the plastic bin at her feet. She placed a napkin between them on the seat and then chose a couple of turtle brownies and two frosted sugar cookies.

She jammed an angel cookie into her mouth. "*Gut* thing I thought to get Bram's—oh, my stars!"

Martha cried out, too, as the front wheel struck something hard. Their cookies flew to the floor as the buggy lurched toward the ditch. "Whoa, Taffy! Easy now, girl," she called to the mare.

Her heart was pounding frantically now. Here they were, out in the middle of nowhere, with no other vehicles in sight, and when she hopped out of the buggy she saw that the rim and two spokes of the wooden wheel had broken. "Well, we've got to call somebody now, for sure and for certain," she said in a high, tight voice. "Can't go any farther with a wheel like that—and there's the chunk of ice we hit wrong," she said as she pointed to the offending gray lump in the road.

"Oh, Martha . . . Dat's going to be so angry at us."

"Well, we're not calling *him*! Besides, if nobody's in the barn at home or checking the phone by the road, we might sit here forever." Martha fought for reason, determined not to cry.

"I'm not inclined to call Noah's cell, either," Mary remarked as she fished her phone from her coat pocket. "He'll be mad at us for taking the buggy, as it is. Sure hope there's a *gut* cell signal out this way."

With a shaky sigh, Martha got back into the buggy, out of the wind. She watched her twin's fingers dance around the number pad, noting gratefully that she had three strong bars of signal.

"Come on now, Bram," Mary prayed aloud as she listened to his phone ringing. "You always keep your phone close—*jah*, Bram?" she said in a louder, perkier voice. "Well, you'll just never guess who this is, or uh, why I'm calling you."

Martha let out a nervous giggle. She reached for the three cookies that had landed under the dashboard, wishing that the yellow-frosted star could guide them as the star of Bethlehem had led the wise men to the manger. But it was too late to be consulting such heavenly guidance, wasn't it?

"*Jah*, it's Mary! And it's *gut* to hear your voice . . . *jah*, well, we're sorry about how things ended, too. We got pretty put out yesterday and didn't give you much chance to talk us back into a better mood," Mary went on in a hopeful tone, "but right now we need a big favor, Bram."

"A *huge* favor," Martha murmured, shaking her head.

Mary listened for a moment. Her smile indicated that Bram at least hadn't hung up on her so maybe . . . maybe they could get out of this mess without catching any flack from their *dat* or *mamm*.

"Well, we decided to surprise you guys for Second Christmas! Martha and I tossed our duffels in a buggy and started out this morning before anyone else was the wiser," Mary recounted cheerfully. Then she paused. "Trouble is, we've hit a chunk of ice in the road and now a wheel's broken . . . *jah*, just a second."

Mary pressed the phone into her coat. "Sister, do you have any idea where we are?" she murmured.

Martha sighed. "Last town we went through was Cold Stream," she replied, and then she squinted at the signs up ahead of them. "But we're at the intersection of Double A and Highway 3."

Mary repeated their location to Bram . . . chatted with him for another few moments as the sun lit up her relieved expression. "Oh, but I'm so grateful to you for helping us," she said. Then her laughter rang inside the buggy. "*Jah*, we'll owe you for this, for sure and for certain. See you in a little bit, then."

Martha's shoulders relaxed. "So, Bram wasn't still mad at us?"

Mary chuckled as she pressed the End button. "Oh, I figure he's going to get in a few licks about girls who take out on a wild goose chase. But he seemed kind of happy to have something to *do* today."

"Like us, then. Didn't want to hang around the house." Martha reached for the cookie bin, and chose a butterscotch cashew bar. As she bit into its gooey, crunchy richness, relief washed over her. "Did he say how long he might be?"

"Probably twenty minutes. He knew right where this intersection was."

"Maybe we weren't so far off course, after all," she remarked. "I guess whatever he teases us with, or expects us to do in return, well—we've got it coming, ain't so?"

Mary, too, grabbed a butterscotch cashew bar. Then she grinned mischievously. "Bring it on, I say."

Martha laughed out loud. "That's the ticket, Sister! We can handle what's happened to our buggy, and we'll handle Bram and his big ideas along with it."

Chapter Ten

Nate steered Clyde along the road at a brisk clip, trying not to feel too hopeful. While this little diversion with the Coblentz twins was a surprise he couldn't have hoped for on a day that had been dragging by at home, there were still some issues to be cleared away before he allowed himself to fall for their upturned noses and cheerful smiles again. But the bright morning sunshine and the sleigh bells accompanying the steady *clip-clop! clip-clop!* of his draft horse's hooves raised his spirits.

"Did Mary sound upset? Like, will we have to put up with their crying when we get there?" he asked Bram.

Bram, who had been grinning like a little kid ever since Mary had called him, crammed his fedora lower so it wouldn't blow off in the breeze. "She sounded mighty glad I answered the phone, but seemed on top of things, all in all," he replied. "I can't think Martha would be one to weep and wail, either. She impressed me as the more level-headed of the two."

"*Jah*, I caught that about her, too," Nate admitted. "And if she was driving, and they got to that crossroads at

Highway 3 without knowing where they were going, they're neither one helpless."

"*Jah*, and I'm thinking that if I hadn't answered, they'd have called some other fellow." Bram shrugged, obviously delighted at the turn their day had taken. "I hope you can set aside your pity party so we can have a *gut* time today. After all, this was to be their surprise to us. They want to see us again, even after—well, that's not a big deal anymore."

Nate glanced sideways at his younger brother. "So what did you do after I left? I thought it was odd that you weren't that far behind me getting home." Anybody could see Bram was keeping a secret . . . maybe another issue to clear up before they took their relationships with the twins beyond this playful stage.

Sure enough, his younger brother laughed and looked away. "Ohhh, I got the big idea to ask the girls if they'd want to go into business with me, running an auction barn."

"And?" Nate asked pointedly. Things were never the way Bram let on at first. It always paid to dig a little deeper to get to the root of his doings.

"I, um, said I could set them up with a place to stay . . . hinted that I might be up for jumping the fence—"

"And they told you to go fly a kite, ain't so?" Nate let out an exasperated sigh. "And you didn't think you'd upset them by asking them to leave their faith and their family for—"

"*Jah*, I get that now," Bram retorted. "The girls have put it behind them or they wouldn't have started out for Willow Ridge before dawn. So stow it, all right?"

Nate's lips lifted. Somehow, even after Bram had made such an outlandish blunder, the twins had looked beyond his impulsive talk to give him another chance. With any sort of luck, he, too, might get back into their good graces . . .

"And there they are." Bram pointed to a buggy alongside the county road at the intersection they were approaching. When he waved his arms high in the air, a girl in a black bonnet hopped out of each side of the rig to wave back.

Even from here, the Coblentz twins looked bubbly and happy and—well, they were certainly the bright spot in Nate's day. Adventurous and open to getting out of their comfort zone. Unafraid, at least from appearances. Maybe he could take a lesson from the way they were handling this setback in their plans. After all, how many young women had ever asked him to help celebrate their birthday? And now that he was in the driver's seat, in more than one sense, he felt more confident about the direction things might go today.

When Nate pulled the sleigh alongside their buggy, the twins seemed pleased to see that he'd come along with Bram, and that made him return their smiles. "Well now," he teased as he stepped down from the seat. "Imagine meeting the two of *you* out here—"

"And it's mighty *gut* to see you, Nate!" one of the twins remarked.

"Lots more fun with the four of us," her sister chimed in. "But you can see we're going nowhere without your help."

"We did bring a big box of cookies, though."

"And our sunshiny selves, of course."

And didn't they make a sight, smiling up at him? Nate slung an arm around their shoulders and hugged them both briefly. "Let's take a look at this wheel, and we'll decide just how much this personal pickup and repair service is going to cost you."

"Best thing would be to take this wheel to Graber's

carriage shop," Bram said from where he was studying the damage. "We brought a few tools, but this is a pretty bad break. More than we can fix for you."

Both girls' faces fell. "But that's clear back in Cedar Creek—"

"And James has closed his shop until after the holidays."

Nate shrugged. "Not many other carriage makers around here. And it'd be best to leave the buggy close to home so it's easier for you to pick it up when it's fixed, ain't so?" he asked. "We can hitch your buggy behind the sleigh, with your horse tethered behind. Clyde's strong enough to get us there—"

"But we were figuring on spending the rest of the day—"

"Maybe longer, so we brought along a change of clothes."

"—having a *gut* time with you fellows."

"And, truth be told, I'm not wild about Noah finding out what we did to this buggy we share with him. We didn't tell him we'd be taking it, see."

Nate followed the twins' ping-pong ball conversation as he reached into the bin of cookies one of the girls— Mary, he was guessing—offered him. As he bit into a ginger snap that woke up his mouth with its bold spices, he certainly understood why the twins didn't want to be seen at home after they'd ducked out of the house. There was really no need to disappoint them, was there?

Bram had already grabbed a wrench, unfastened the broken wheel, and set it inside the buggy. He came up and snatched a peanut butter and jelly sandwich cookie from the plastic bin, slinging his arm around the girl who held it. "Let's think about all the possibilities over breakfast somewhere. Not a Plain café, though, or we're bound to see folks who know us or know our families."

"They'll all be closed today, anyway," Martha pointed out, and the way she focused on Nate made his heart skitter. "But if we park the buggy behind James's shop and slip Taffy into his stable—"

"That would work!" Mary piped up. "The Grabers won't be home from visiting kin in Queen City until a day or two from now! We'll pay James for a little hay along with fixing the wheel."

"See there? It'll be just that easy to stay out and around for however long you girls would like," Bram said as he chose a frosted sugar cookie. "Me, I'm just real glad you're both willing to spend time with us again, after the wild ideas I was tryin' to sell you on yesterday morning."

Nate, carried along on this wave of good cheer, nodded. "And I hope you two can forgive the way I took your switch-around so seriously. It's not like you were trading places on your wedding day, when the vows would be forever."

The sisters grinned mischievously at each other. "Now there's an idea!"

"*Jah*, I'll keep that idea in mind in case we need it someday!" Martha stood on tiptoe to leave a noisy kiss on Nate's cheek. And didn't that make the morning sun sparkle on the snow in a million shiny-bright diamonds?

"Breakfast!" Bram declared. "I want to save these cookies for when we're sleighing later. Awfully nice of you girls to treat us."

"So breakfast will be Bram's treat," Nate teased. "Let's hitch up your rig and get ourselves along. I know of a place outside of Roanoak that serves up a never-ending stack of pancakes, and we can decide what we want to do after we drop off your buggy. Sound *gut*?"

"Oh, you don't know how *gut*," Martha replied.

"*Jah*, it's like starting our birthday all over again with

a fresh slate. A lot better than yesterday!" Mary answered happily.

Nate smiled at both girls, but especially at Martha. *It is better than yesterday. And you can be the hero if you get past the way Roberta dumped you last spring.*

Roberta? Who's Roberta?

Nate chuckled as he tied the shafts of the buggy to the back of his sleigh. Once Bram had fastened Taffy behind the buggy with a lead rope, they took off like a Plain parade headed back toward Cedar Creek. With Martha beside him and Bram cozying up to Mary in the backseat, it promised to be a Second Christmas such as he'd never imagined when he'd gotten up this morning.

And wasn't it just like the Coblentz twins to make life *fun* again?

As Mary sat beside Bram in a booth at Flo's Down-Home Diner, she closed her eyes over a bite of chocolate chip pancake smothered in warm strawberry syrup. The four of them were talking and laughing as though yesterday's conflicts hadn't happened, and the rest of the day shone bright with promise. Bram and Nate were devouring three eggs apiece alongside their pancakes. A large side order of bacon sat in the center of the table, and as Nate reached for a couple of slices he gazed at her with a . . . curious expression on his face.

"Am I right that you baked most of those fabulous cookies, Mary?" he asked.

She blinked. Nate was studying her very intently, so she squirmed a little and her face got hot, even as she sat close enough to Bram that their thighs brushed. "*Jah*, that would be me."

"And I *like* that about you, Mary. Enough that I want to get to know you better—even though I'm pretty sure it's Martha who makes my clock tick," Nate continued in a low voice. "What say you sit up front in the sleigh with me this afternoon while your sister spends some time with Bram? If we're eventually going to pair up, I'm thinking we brothers and sisters need to understand each other before we make any commitments."

Martha's eyebrows rose. "So, you're saying it'll be like when we girls decided to switch around on you—"

"Except this time everybody knows about it," Nate finished. "Truth be told, I still have trouble telling you apart."

"And this early on, I'm all for keepin' things light." Bram scraped the last of his eggs onto his fork, grinning. "I say let's do it! We all need to be *gut* friends with each other, first and foremost."

Martha rolled her eyes. "This, coming from the fellow who was all set to hire both of us girls yesterday. And rent us an apartment, too."

Mary giggled as she elbowed him. "Don't believe for a minute we couldn't keep your head spinning so fast that you'd never know which one of us was which, Bram. You wouldn't stand a chance, you know."

"I figured that out on the way home yesterday. Had plenty of time to think about what a fix I would've been in, had you two gone along with my ideas." Bram smiled at Martha, his dark eyes sparkling, and then he grinned at Mary. "But when you called me this morning, I was just happy—and relieved—that you'd set that all aside. I thought I'd really messed things up."

"Oh, *jah*, you had! Big time," Martha remarked as she took a slice of bacon.

"But we didn't tell our parents the part about jumping the fence with you," Mary continued, twinkling with this happy chatter. "So all we heard about for the rest of our birthday was how badly *we* had messed up, letting you two hard-working boys from a *gut* family leave us behind."

"But don't let it go to your heads."

"We're just in this for some fun, after all. But we really do appreciate your coming to our rescue—"

"And feeding us this wonderful-*gut* breakfast."

Mary smiled to herself. She and her twin could still make both of these boys strain to keep up with the way they finished each other's sentences and followed the same train of thought with their rapid chatter. Nate's suggestion was indeed a way to keep from getting too attached too soon . . . a way to double date and keep all their options wide open.

So when Nate urged Clyde into a trot again and they headed north to Cedar Creek, Mary felt bubbly and light. She loved the happy sound of the sleigh bells. The same farms they'd passed in the darkness now glowed in the late-morning sunshine and cardinals called from tree to tree. It felt comfortable to sit with Nate, to sense that he was coming out of his shell—maybe setting his misfortune with his former fiancée behind him, at last—even though she knew she'd be happier with his brother. Martha looked contented, too, bundled up in the blanket Bram had brought along. They had about half an hour before they got to the carriage shop.

"I know!" Mary said. "Let's play a game of True Confessions. I'll ask a question we all have to answer, and then it'll be somebody else's turn to ask something."

"Oh, that could get wild in a hurry," Bram remarked.

"*Jah*, but it's only a game. All in fun," Nate said.

"But here's our chance to share our deep, dark secrets—or not!" Martha said. "What's your question, Mary? Make it a *gut* one, now!"

"Hmmm." Mary thought for a moment. "What's something your brother—or sister—does that really sets you off?"

Beside her, Nate laughed loudly. "That one's easy!

Bram gets these hair-brained ideas that he blurts out before he thinks twice. So then he not only steps in it, he puts his foot in his mouth!"

"Ewwww," Martha teased.

"*Jah,* well *you,* brother Nate, take yourself waaay too seriously," Bram retorted. "It's like you were born under a big black cloud and you don't know how to have any fun."

Mary raised her eyebrows as she looked up at their driver. "Maybe it takes spending time with a couple of sisters like us to change all that."

"I like that answer . . . and your attitude," Nate replied quietly.

The way he smiled at her made Mary appreciate his depth. If the brothers were to work closely with each other as they matured, it was good that Bram would have Nate to balance out his impetuous notions—even though she adored Bram's spur-of-the-moment personality. "And what about you, Sister?" she said as she turned toward the backseat.

"Oh," Martha said in a dramatic tone, "it peeves me to no end that Mary always comes across as the sweet, obedient little do-gooder. So any time the parents find fault with something we've done, they always figure it's me who fell short."

"And they're right!" Mary teased. "And you still pout and whine about it just like you did back when Mamma smacked us with her fly swatter, when we were little. You catch more flies with honey than vinegar, you know."

"That's fine, if it's flies you really want to catch!" Martha replied.

When she stuck out her tongue at Mary, all four of them laughed. It was a welcome, jolly sound on a morning that could have gone so much differently. "Who's next with a question?" she asked. "I'm liking this game a lot!"

"How about this one?" Bram offered. "What did you do as a kid that your family thought was odd? For me, it was playing games like Sorry or Yahtzee all by myself," he admitted. "When Nate went off to school or he was out choring, I would roll the dice or draw the cards and move two or three markers around the board to keep myself busy."

Mary blinked. "So there's just the two of you boys? No other kids in your family to play with back then?"

"Nope, just us." Nate smiled as though he had indeed found his little brother an odd duck at times. "Which probably explains why, even today, Bram thinks he can deal all the cards and play all the positions without needing anybody else."

It occurred to Mary then how lucky they were to have Owen, Noah, Joanna, and Jacob in their family. She had never lacked for someone to play with while she was growing up—but then, with a twin, she had spent her life with a constant companion since before she'd been born. Maybe Bram's independent streak was mostly a cover. Maybe he was lonelier than he let on . . .

"For Mary and me," Martha said, "it was the way she and I could communicate without even saying anything—"

"Or we'd finish each other's sentences and keep our own little conversation running." Mary jumped in. Then she laughed. "Like I did just now, without even thinking about it."

Bram and Nate laughed loudly, nodding at each other. "*Jah*, no secret there," Nate remarked. "But then, that's the way of it with twins, they say. Like the two of you are different peas but in the same pod."

"Always have been," Mary agreed.

"Always will be." Martha shrugged. "If you fellows find that peculiar, well—deal with it!"

Beside her, Nate shook with pent-up laughter. "*Jah*, no

doubt in our minds that you girls really don't *need* us to have a *gut* time, or to get by. Between the two of you, you can pretty much handle whatever comes along."

"And we like it that way," Bram said. "We know plenty of clingy, cry-baby girls out there tryin' too hard to latch onto a husband because they can't do much without somebody tellin' them what comes next."

For a moment, only the jingle of the sleigh bells and Clyde's steady footfalls filled the wintry air. This game was bringing out some interesting revelations . . . and just maybe the Kanagy brothers were deeper into this date than they might admit. Mary gazed up at Nate, whose expression told of mysteries he wasn't yet ready to let go of. "How about you?" Mary asked him. "Any little quirks you care to reveal to us?"

"Oh, the parents always thought it odd that I talked more to the horses and sheep than I talked to them when I was wee little." Nate kept his focus on Clyde's backside, thinking back. "I had a couple of imaginary friends who lived in the hay loft, you see, so I went out there a lot to visit with them. Partly to get away from Bram, who was a holy terror and always got me in trouble."

Bram laughed. "*Jah*, I was real *gut* at getting Nate in on my tricks and then leaving him to explain how something got broken, or was done the wrong way. And I was cuter, of course, so Mamm believed me."

"That's how I recall it, *jah*," Nate replied. "Except for the *cute* part. There were some who said that with your curly hair, you were almost too pretty. Like a girl!"

Mary and her sister laughed. As the sleigh went gliding along the county road, familiar scenery was coming into view. It wouldn't be long before they had to figure out how to park the buggy behind Graber's Custom Carriages without anyone—especially Noah—discovering it before they could explain the broken wheel and pay for its repair. "Okay, so what's our next question?"

"I've got one," Martha said. "What's the most un-Amish thing about you?"

The four of them got quiet then, considering their answers. This was a more serious subject than childhood quirks or sibling dynamics.

"Well, I don't believe in hell, or in the eternal damnation Bishop Knepp and the preachers are always throwing up to us in church," Bram replied quietly. "I believe that God is more like the father who welcomes the prodigal home, even after the son in that parable has done a lot of unthinkable things."

Mary's heart stilled and then swelled within her. Bram's statement, made so sincerely and with a lot of forethought, defied the most basic of Old Order beliefs. She sensed his reply indicated that he would rather raise his children knowing the love of the Lord rather than the fear that compelled so many Plain folks to live such tight, stoic lives. When Mary noticed the expression on Nate's handsome face, she saw that he, too, was surprised by his younger brother's reply. Something in his eyes told Mary that he sensed how Bram's statement of faith had touched something deep inside her, and that he understood why she felt closer to Bram in a lot of ways.

"For me," Martha ventured, "it's wanting a houseful of interesting guests instead of filling my rooms with kids. Mary and I have talked of starting up a B and B someday—I've even been taking small business classes online, on a Mennonite friend's computer. But Mamma's not happy about that. And nobody who's Old Order Amish would understand why I want to do more than raise a family."

Nate's grip tightened on the reins and he sat up

straighter. "You know, our *mamm* was only able to have the two of us boys," he remarked quietly, "so she's been tending her bees and raising her vegetables on every spare inch of our property, to sell the honey and produce at farmers' markets. And I think she's happier that way than she would have been raising a raft of kids."

"For sure and for certain," Bram chimed in. "And what with the economy being so tough nowadays, Dat's glad she can help support the family—even if he doesn't come right out and say so."

Isn't that an interesting thing to know? Mary tucked her hand in the crook of Nate's elbow as they came within sight of the Cedar Creek Mercantile and James Graber's shop. Nate's admiration for Martha's idea was evident . . . a sign that he was probably better suited to her sister, if their relationship got that serious. And she sensed it might.

Before they could finish out this round of answers, however, Nate pulled the sleigh behind the carriage shop. From what Mary could see, nobody was watching them from the Lambright place across the road, and the Grabers still appeared to be away, as they had anticipated. While the boys unhitched the buggy from the back of the sleigh, Martha scurried toward the stable behind James's house with Taffy. Mary remained in the seat to write a note on a napkin.

James,

We hope your family had a wonderful-gut Christmas visit in Queen City! Martha and I will be back soon for this buggy, but meanwhile we hope you can repair or replace our wheel. Tell Noah we're paying for it, too, if he raises any ruckus. We also owe you for Taffy's room and board. Denki so much! Mary Coblentz

By the time Mary had set the message on the buggy seat and picked up the bin of cookies on its floor, her sister was returning from the barn.

"I think we did it!" Martha exclaimed as she grabbed their duffels. "I didn't see anybody out and about."

"Most folks are probably finishing their dinner by now," Nate said as he swung up into the front seat of his sleigh again. He seemed as tickled about pulling off this adventure as she and her sister were, so as soon as Bram and Martha had climbed into the back they were headed down the snow-packed blacktop again. "We could stop by Uncle Abe's place," he teased. "Aunt Beulah Mae would be real glad to feed us, and you know her leftovers would be *gut*!"

"Keep on rollin'!" Bram crowed. "They're kin and all, but I'm havin' waaay too much fun today to go there!"

Mary smiled to herself, relishing the feel of the crisp winter air on her cheeks. *Just you wait, Bram. The fun you can have with us—with me—will only get better once you and I are together again.*

Chapter Eleven

Bram's pulse thrummed as they entered the Dutch Country Buffet about half an hour later. He was hungry, yes, but not just for the wide variety of food being served up on the steam tables at the rear of the small restaurant: without a word needing to be exchanged, Mary had taken his hand at the door while Martha had slid into the booth ahead of Nate, across the table from them.

He knew Mary now . . . could feel the subtle differences between her and her twin as the girls talked and laughed. Sure, they both had blue eyes and a sprinkling of freckles and thick, auburn hair but their interests were different. Their views of the world and where they fit into it came from different angles, too. And as his brother slipped an arm around Martha and kissed her temple, Bram was convinced that this day would have a far-reaching effect on their future.

"Get a room!" he teased when Martha returned Nate's affection.

"Or maybe *we* should." Mary winked at him, gesturing toward the window. "Seems there's an old motel right across the road—"

"Oh, don't give him any ideas," Nate warned. "If your

parents believe we're fine, upstanding young fellows, we don't want to blow it by—"

As their waitress approached, they nipped this playful topic in the bud. From the looks of the middle-aged lady dressed in black jeans and a glittery red sweatshirt with Santa Claus on the front, the Plain owners had taken the holiday off. Or perhaps the owners were English, using the "Dutch" part of their name to capitalize on how folks associated Amish and Mennonites with the tastiest home-made food. "Buffet for me, please," Bram told her. "And keep the Coke comin'."

"*Jah*, same here," the other three said.

As he heaped his plate with crispy fried chicken, pot roast, cheesy potatoes, hot mixed vegetables, and then put a sampling of the cold salads on a second plate, Bram felt excited yet amazingly contented. When he and Mary returned to the table first, he took the opportunity to sneak a kiss. "I'm real glad you picked me, honey-girl," he murmured as he drank in her flushed cheeks.

"I wouldn't have it any other way," Mary murmured. "I'm happy that both of you fellows came for us today, and that you're pairing up the same way we feel it should be. Martha decided on Nate from the moment she met you two in the mercantile, you know."

Bram chuckled and dug into his hot food. "Fine by me. You're the cutest."

"No, *you* are. Your *mamm* was right all along, whether or not Nate likes it."

He flashed her a smile, hoping she read his silent message of appreciation . . . of feelings he wasn't yet ready to express. But he couldn't deny that Mary Coblentz was the most exciting, desirable young woman he'd ever met, either.

Martha slid into the booth ahead of Nate, and for a

few moments they all ate as though they'd gone days without food. Was it his imagination, or did this meal taste especially good . . . even if it wasn't nearly as fresh and bountiful as what most Amish families would be enjoying for Second Christmas? He had no doubt that Mary could prepare a wonderful dinner . . . hoped he would get to eat one of her meals soon . . .

"You know, maybe we should rethink spending the rest of the day running the roads," Martha remarked in a pensive tone. "Is it me, or is this chocolate cake too dry?"

"It's not nearly as *gut* as the birthday cake we left at home," Mary agreed. "Mamma's coconut filling and pour-over chocolate glaze tastes a lot more special than what we've got here."

Martha gazed at Nate then, thinking. "And maybe we're missing out on a chance to let the folks visit with you Kanagy brothers. After all, they really liked you—"

"They were just sour on the way *we* behaved, switching places to fool you," Mary said.

"—and considering how early it gets dark on these winter days," Martha went on, "we'll soon have to figure out what to do . . . where to stay."

Nate's face lit up. "I was wondering what we should do for the night, since I'm not nearly ready to head for home," he admitted. "No need to put up that extra bed or shift things all around again. Fine by me if I sleep on a sofa, or stack blankets on the floor."

"We could get rooms at the motel across the street— one for you girls and another for Nate and me," Bram quickly clarified.

As one, the twins wrinkled their noses. Martha shook her head. "No matter how you slice it—"

"Mamma and Dat would see that as the wrong kind of goody to be serving up," Mary finished. "And you know, if we took Taffy on home, and told Noah about the rig's wheel being repaired, it would save poor James a lot of hassle from him. And with you fellows there as guests again, he'd not get into such a snit."

"And our brother Owen wouldn't quiz you about your intentions. Now that he and Phoebe Lambright are taking their instructions to join the church," Martha said with a raised eyebrow, "he's gotten a lot more um, *involved* in who we twins spend our time with."

"Even if it's really none of his beeswax." Mary set her fork down on a plate of food that was only half eaten, and looked from Bram to his brother. "How do you feel about going home with us again? We don't want you to think you always have to do things our way."

"Even if our way is better," Martha teased.

"Works for me," Nate said as he slipped his arm around her. "If you girls want us to spend the evening with your family, I see that as a real *gut* sign of, um . . . things to come."

"Can't argue with that." Bram grasped Mary's hand beneath the table. He was feeling awfully comfortable, even if it was way too soon to be thinking anything they did at the Coblentz home tonight might affect their futures. After all, they'd only met these twins two days ago. "If you want to ask your *mamm* and *dat* first—"

"Nope," Mary insisted.

"They'll be *gut* with it. And I see it as a way to finish celebrating our birthday," Martha went on. "I can tell you that turning eighteen wasn't much fun after you fellows left us yesterday."

Bram liked the sound of that. He pulled his cell phone from his coat pocket and brought up his home phone number on the screen. "I'll let the folks know what we're—*jah*, Dat?" he said when his father picked up out in the sheep barn. "Nate and I rescued the Coblentz girls and towed their buggy to the Graber shop. So now they've asked us to stay over again."

There was a pause, but then his father chuckled. "Gonna get it right this time? I could tell things didn't go well before, but you weren't sayin' who was to blame."

"And it doesn't matter anymore. We're all *gut* friends again, havin' a fine time," Bram replied as he met the three gazes that were focused on him. "I'll give you another ring when we're on the way home—"

"My word, somebody there must be havin' quite an effect on ya, if you'll be keepin' your *mamm* and me updated, son. That's a first."

Bram rolled his eyes. "What can I say? Nate's got his arm around a feisty redhead, lookin' mighty, um— *interested* in her. So I'd best stick around and keep track of him, ain't so? Bye now."

He clicked off his phone, shaking his head. Was it indeed a sign of things to come, that his *dat* sensed he and Nate were more serious about the Coblentz twins than they'd been about other girls? Their parents hadn't known Roberta Hershberger very well, but they'd felt awfully bad for Nate when she'd taken up with a fellow who'd come into a farm with a big house on it. That was behind them, though. Obviously not meant to be.

"Ready?" Bram fished his wallet from his pocket and tossed a twenty at his brother. "Seems I've just made us a few points at home, so you can cover the rest of this bill, Nate. I'm guessin' Dat's already on his way into the house to tell Mamm about how you're finally comin' out of your cave, leavin' Roberta behind. So see, girls? You've done us a big favor, askin' us back to be with your family."

Mary gave him the sweetest smile. "Not that we'll spend every moment at home," she hinted.

"Not by a long shot!" Martha chimed in. "Jacob and Joanna will get nosy—"

"And Noah will have to get in his licks about the broken wheel."

"—so after we stick around for supper and more of that birthday cake—"

"—we'll have to show you around the farm," Mary continued with a mischievous gleam in her eye. "And this time Preacher Abe won't come barging in with his lantern."

"Now there's something to look forward to." Bram took Mary's hand and slid out of the booth ahead of her. "And who knows? Maybe if I tell him you girls are making Nate and me toe the mark now, he won't let on to the folks that I was ready to jump the fence."

As the bell above the café's door jingled when they left, Bram realized that he had just mentioned leaving the Old Order in the past tense . . .

But when Mary took his elbow and gazed up at him, that change of attitude felt pretty good.

Nate drove in a loop, on snow-packed back roads and county highways, allowing the fineness of this day to settle in as they made their way back toward Cedar Creek. While he'd been ready to tromp Bram's toe under the table, for telling their *dat* that he'd taken such a shine to Martha Coblentz, well—now that Martha sat snuggled against him, with her blue eyes shining as they toured this winter wonderland, he knew Bram had been right. After all, hadn't he chosen a sleigh as his Christmas present so he could enjoy just such a picture-perfect day with somebody wonderful? And here it was, his unspoken dream come true.

"What are you thinking?" he whispered. And even

though such a question would have backfired in his face had he asked it of Roberta while they courted, Nate felt easy in his soul . . . confident that Martha wouldn't cut him down or make remarks that seemed hurtful, once he'd thought about them. Until today, he hadn't realized just how negative his relationship with Roberta had been. It had been all about *her*.

Martha eased her head from his shoulder to gaze at him. "We didn't get to finish our game of True Confessions. Bram and I answered, but not you and Mary—about the most un-Amish thing about you," she added as a reminder.

"Ha!" came Mary's response from the backseat. "You know this about me, Sister, for sure and for certain," she began in a playful tone, "but you boys had better listen up. I don't cotton to being told what to do—"

"No surprise there," Bram said with a chuckle.

"—so, where the Scripture talks about wives submitting to their husbands?" she went on. "Well, I'm going to join the church someday, but that total submission thing is *not* how I see my life going. Especially once Martha and I are running our bed and breakfast. That's to be our business, and our men won't figure into it except when we ask them to."

"Like for repair work and heavy lifting we can't do ourselves," Martha clarified.

"And I could see the two of you making a real *gut* go at that, too," Nate said. "Haven't noticed any signs for B and B's hereabouts, so if you get your name out there, and you give your full attention to the little details of servin' your guests, your place will be a big hit."

"*Jah*, you two are naturals at making folks feel welcome," Bram agreed.

For the next few minutes, Nate was content to keep driving, watching Clyde's muscled haunches as the huge horse pulled them effortlessly along. What should he say about his un-Amish traits? He was already a member of the church in the Willow Ridge district, so it was pointless to let on that he didn't fit the mold. Yet he should contribute to the conversation . . . play along, if only to convince the three younger people with him that he, too, had expectations and dreams that might go against some stricture of the Old Order. When he felt Martha silently urging him on, he returned her gaze.

"While I believe that God created the man first, I don't think it's His will that the husband should make all the decisions for his family," Nate murmured. "Just like I don't think He intended for women to take a backseat where education's concerned. I admire you for taking those business classes online, Martha."

He paused, hoping the rest of his thought came out as the compliment he intended it to be. "It means you won't be jumping head-first into a bigger project than you can handle. You'll be ready to keep the books and follow any government regulations, instead of assuming *gut* food and clean rooms will make you an overnight success. And that way, inspectors can't come in and shut you down for not following the proper procedures."

Martha's eyes got so wide that Nate nearly fell into them. "Mary and I haven't told many folks about our dream, on account of how we're afraid they'll think we sound too English, or not devoted to raising families. It's always been a project off in the future somewhere—probably after we marry—but it's definitely not something that'll go away. We're only eighteen, but we *want* this inn to happen."

"Gotta want it," Bram chimed in from the backseat. "That's how Nate and I both got into our businesses so young. We didn't just hang around waiting for the pieces to fall into place. We went to school and went after jobs that'll support us because we know that farmin' won't."

"*Jah*, Dat noticed that about you boys right off." Martha settled back against the seat then, taking in the dazzling late afternoon as they passed evergreen windbreaks dressed in lacy gowns of snow . . . crossed a one-lane bridge over Cedar Creek, which babbled happily between crystal-lined shores.

Nate could have watched her all day.

Chapter Twelve

Martha relaxed, yet her heart was pounding. Had the quiet, conservative Nate Kanagy actually said he admired her for taking some business classes? She hadn't even mentioned this coursework to her *dat*, knowing how he would discourage her—or worse, tell her such classes were altogether wrong for a Plain girl. While Mamma had an inkling that she and Mary would like to run an inn someday, she had dismissed such a dream as something that must come after they became wives and mothers—maybe in the distant future, when they'd finished with wiping noses and packing lunchboxes and guiding the children God had given them.

Martha sat up taller then, paying closer attention to the countryside. "You know, I've lived in Cedar Creek all my life, but I don't recall ever being down this road," she remarked quietly.

"Same here," Mary said from the backseat. "I've not been paying real close attention these past several minutes—"

"Distracted by the company," Bram teased.

"—but I'm not sure where we are."

Nate pointed off into the distance. "If my sense of direction serves me, your place is over that way, maybe twenty minutes from here," he said. "I've been taking the long way home, so to speak. Seems the right thing to do, so my brother and I can hold you girls hostage for a while."

Martha chuckled. She was indeed Nate's willing victim on this winter's afternoon, and the more she talked and listened, the more she felt she was in exactly the right place at the right time. "*Jah*, things have a way of working out if you give them a chance."

She glanced back and saw that Mary hadn't commented because she was caught up in a kiss . . . and Martha knew firsthand that Bram was a fine kisser, just as she sensed the younger Kanagy brother was the better fit for her more traditional sister, even if he had some wild ideas. She leaned her head on Nate's shoulder, gratified by the way he nuzzled her temple.

Then Nate leaned forward. "Now what's this sign say?" He tugged on the reins until Clyde came to a stop beside a large wooden sign posted at the end of a farm lane. "Looks like this acreage is to be auctioned off . . . sealed bids to be accepted through December thirtieth."

"That's next Monday." Martha looked beyond the fencerow, which pitched forward beneath the weight of years and a topping of snow. "Pretty sad, ain't so? The house and the outbuildings need a lot of work."

"But the land has a nice feel to it. And there's space enough for corrals and a horse barn or two," Nate replied as he studied the place.

"And since it's on a paved county road, it would be easily accessible for an auction barn," Bram joined in. "Plenty of room for holding pens and parking—"

"Total of a hundred and five acres . . . about two-thirds of it tillable," Nate summarized from the description on the sign. "Plenty enough to raise hay for our own livestock, and maybe some crops to sell."

"There's most likely a *gut* water source, what with that

creek running down there between the trees. Probably groundwater for wells, too," Bram said as he scooted forward to gaze at the place. "And some big old walnut trees in those hills back there, which could be harvested to bring in some start-up cash."

Once again Martha's heartbeat accelerated. Did these boys stop at every for sale sign they saw, to discuss a potential place to live? Should she allow herself to believe she and Mary might fit into this picture they were painting in their imaginations?

"So, why are they taking sealed bids instead of holding a regular auction? Or just selling the place with a real estate agent?" Mary asked. "That's kind of different, ain't so?"

"Well, by having an auction, the owner will have his place sold by a certain time, instead of having to wait for the right buyer to come along," Bram explained.

"And with a sealed bid auction, you only attract folks ready to put down some money." Nate turned in the sleigh's seat to look at both girls. "Instead of dealing with a couple hundred nosy folks tramping around your buildings and grounds, with maybe a handful of serious bidders, you have those bidders making their best offers. It's a lot simpler."

"If the owner doesn't like any of those offers, he doesn't have to go with them," Bram explained. "And if a few potential buyers go above his acceptable price, he can invite those fellas to bid against each other again."

"Ah." Mary nodded and looked out over the snow-covered fields again. "That makes a lot more sense. And then, this real estate agent on the sign is only showing the really interested folks the house and buildings. Saves a lot of time and effort for everybody."

"But even from here, it's easy to see that the barns and outbuildings need some major renovation—not to mention the house. Might be better to knock them down and start fresh." Nate sighed. "That would take a lot of time. And a major chunk of change."

"*Jah*. Not sure Dat would be so keen on that," came his brother's response.

Nate pulled himself out of his musing then to look at Martha. "Our place in Willow Ridge is mostly pastureland, where Dat's sheep graze, or else it's been cultivated in garden plots for Mamm's vegetable business. We boys have known all along we'll have to find our own places and ways to make our livings," he said. "Dat's offered to pitch in on land for us, when the right place came available."

"It would be a long while before we could live here, though," Bram said sadly. "We'd have to get my auction barn and your stables up and runnin' first, generatin' more income, before we could even think of affordin' houses."

Oh, but her thoughts were thrumming as she drank in this information! Martha turned and shared a long look with her sister. "Just so happens our *dat* and older brother are master carpenters," she reminded the boys.

Mary's secretive grin said she knew exactly what Martha was hinting at. "And while we're not supposed to talk it up amongst the fellows we run with," she continued in a conspiratorial tone, "our *dat* has promised us both new houses as wedding presents. But he and Mamma want us close by—like, in Cedar Creek. Not nearly so far away as Willow Ridge."

"But then, maybe that's neither here nor there, far as the plans you fellows are making for yourselves," Martha added with a nonchalant shrug.

"*Jah*, too much information, no doubt." Mary looked out over the property again, playfully lifting her nose in the air. "Sounds like you boys have things all figured out, without us telling you what to do."

"Like we'll ever figure *you* out," Bram teased.

"*Jah*, if we were to talk up the way we could provide

our husbands with houses, why, we'd have fellows lined
up from here until next Christmas, wanting to court us."
Martha gazed straight-on into Nate's wide eyes, noting
how bottomless and brown they looked . . . liking the way
she saw herself reflected in them.

"Not that either of *you* fellows would fall for a girl just
to get a new house. Ain't so?" Mary, too, was drilling into
Bram's eyes with hers, daring him to reply.

"You're right, Martha. A lot of men would think they
had it made in the shade, hooking up with you." Nate
slung his arm across the sleigh seat. "But I went down
that road with a well-dowried gal before, so I know better
this time."

"And, hey—what's so hard about movin' a house
trailer onto this place?" Bram asked as he bit back a grin.
"A couple of bachelors like Nate and me could get by just
fine, parking a pre-fabricated—"

"House trailer?" Mary cried. "Oh, please."

"Now I get the picture," Martha chimed in. "And I'm
not sketching myself into it as the missus, either. Nope,
what with my plans for a bed and breakfast, I'll be asking
Dat for a lot of bedrooms in my place. He'll be fine with
that, figuring I'll fill them with grandkids." She turned
toward Mary then, as though Nate and Bram had van-
ished into thin air. "And Sister, you've always said you
wanted to cook for our inn if I'd run the business end—"

"So, *jah*, that means we'd have to live across the lane
from each other in our new houses," Mary said with a nod.

"Or even at opposite ends of the same really big house,
with our guest rooms in the middle," Martha continued,
suddenly inspired by this teasing talk. The boys were
playing along, so it seemed a good time to sound out her
ideas . . . to let the Kanagy brothers know where she and
her twin were coming from. "We've always been a package, you and I."

"We've never lived apart and I don't want to start any time soon. So your idea of a double-type house with central guest rooms—and a big area for holding church on the main floor—now, that sounds perfect to me!" Mary clapped her gloved hands together. "And you know, if the right fellows come along, they can have their own shops or—"

"Long as we had space for a big garden—"

"And a few milk cows, and chickens for eggs—"

Nate playfully hooked Martha's neck in the crook of his elbow to muffle her next remark against his coat. His chest vibrated with laughter. "Well, at least we're not short on *gut* ideas. Amongst the four of us, I think we'd figure a way to get by."

"And we'd be close to our families—but not *too* close," Bram added. "I like that part. But meanwhile, I'm for taking down the Realtor's phone number so we can do more than just jaw about our future. Lots of details to consider before any of us set our hearts on havin' this place."

"Might be several other fellows with plans for this acreage, too, considering how land doesn't come up for sale all that often," Nate observed. "It appears to be mostly English in this area, with Amish sprinkled along the back roads until you get into Plain settlements like Cedar Creek or Bloomingdale."

Martha heard her sister opening the cookie bin, and when she glanced back, Bram was writing the phone number on a napkin Mary had handed him. "How about treats all around, to celebrate our . . . interesting talk?" she suggested.

"I'm for that! It'll hold us until we get some of that chocolate coconut cake later." Nate lifted Martha's chin with his finger. His smile looked a little nervous, but he seemed really happy. "And it *is* interesting talk, because you girls shared your plans and listened to ours, too."

Bram chuckled as he finished writing. "*Jah*, gives us a better idea what we have to aim for and what we have to prove, if you twins are to take us seriously. And who ever thought I'd be concerned about such a thing?"

Mary was holding her breath as the four of them stepped onto their back porch about half an hour later. Oh, how the ideas were flying through her mind now! It was too early to think her future was all tucked up as neatly as a crimped piecrust—certainly too soon to mention their ideas about that run-down farm to her family. Yet she felt her face lighting up with a smile like she hadn't known since she was a kid celebrating single-digit birthdays. She didn't let go of Bram's hand as they preceded Nate and Martha into the kitchen, either. "We made it back in time to help set on supper," she announced as the wind blew fresh snowflakes inside with them.

"And look who we ran across!" Martha chimed in. "We told the boys we could scrape up enough leftovers to fill their plates, too, most likely."

Their mother turned toward them as she kept stirring a bowl of biscuit batter, her eyebrows rising. "Well, now. After I found your note this morning, I didn't figure on seeing you girls again for a while. Welcome back, boys," she said. "Why do I suspect you had a hand in corralling these daughters of mine before they got lost or found trouble on the roads? It's not like they've ventured far beyond Cedar Creek—that I know of, anyway."

Mary glanced at Martha and decided to come clean. She could see Noah, Dat, and Jacob in the front room working a jigsaw puzzle, so she spoke loudly enough that their brother could hear. "Truth be told, we did have a little trouble," she admitted, "but Nate and Bram got us—and the buggy—back here in *gut* shape."

"*Jah*, I'll pay James to fix the wheel and we'll be squared away," Martha said. "We'll fetch Taffy after supper."

Noah had come up out of his chair like his backside was afire. "Wheel?" he demanded as he stopped in the kitchen doorway. "And what did you do to my wheel?"

"Ah, but you share that rig with Mary and Martha until you're ready for your own courtin' buggy," Joanna pointed out as she set plates around the table.

"That doesn't mean I like it when they take my ride without tellin' me!" their brother retorted. He raked his hand through his collar-length red hair. "And now they've done enough damage that I might not be drivin' it for *days* yet! Not what I wanted to hear!"

"Could be, if you mind your mouth and your manners, you might have your pick of the other rigs, son." Their *dat* gave Noah a warning look and then stepped past him, extending his hand. "Nate, Bram—*gut* to see you fellows again. Looks like the four of you young folks patched things up, and I'm glad for that."

"Kissed and made up is more like it!" Joanna said with a giggle.

Mary raised an eyebrow at her little sister. "Keep talking like that, and you won't have to worry about any boys kissing *you*."

"Puh! Boys're a nuisance."

"They're not half so bad as know-it-all girls," Jacob stated. He went to the stove to see what his *mamm* was cooking and got his hand smacked for trying to stab a chunk of beef from the stew pot with a fork.

Mary turned toward their guests as the four of them hung their wraps on pegs behind the door. "Welcome back to Coblentz chaos," she remarked wryly. "See what you've missed, not having younger kids at home?"

"Nothing we can't handle," Bram answered.

"We can always hitch them up to Clyde and send them off on a ride—without the sleigh," Nate teased.

"*Jah*! I wanna do that!" Jacob crowed. He came over to gaze up at the Kanagy brothers with a hopeful expression on his face. "I could stand on the snow saucer and off I'd go! Lickety-split, wherever I wanted!"

And wouldn't *that* be a sight, that huge Clydesdale hauling a kid on a snow disc? Mary was glad everyone was laughing . . . and that Noah had backed away from the touchy subject of the broken wheel, too. While Mary spooned the biscuit batter over the bubbling stew to make dumplings, Martha brought some salads out of the fridge and then checked the sideboard.

"We've got about half our birthday cake left," she said as she removed the lid of its pan. "And Mamma made a pumpkin roll, I see. It's a *gut* thing we came back for supper!"

After they all sat down and bowed for a silent prayer, Mary was pleased that the conversation seemed so relaxed. Nate and Bram dipped beef stew and dumplings into their soup bowls and then filled their plates with scalloped corn, fruit-filled green gelatin, stewed tomatoes and other dishes that were ordinary yet made more special because the Kanagys were eating with them. When Bram glanced at Mary, she felt her cheeks heat up.

I could get used to seeing this fellow across my table. But it was best not to let on, so soon after she and Martha had met these fun-loving brothers. Better to let Dat lead the conversation with them, as their parents seemed sincerely pleased that the boys were back for a second visit.

"And what-all did you do while you were out and around?" he asked Nate as he sopped up beef gravy with his slice of bread. "Seeing your fine new sleigh puts me in a mind to have James refurbish the old one out in our shed. Been a while since I took out across snowy pastures just for the fun of it."

"I've already gotten a lot of *gut* out of it, *jah*," Nate replied with a shy smile at Martha. He exchanged a glance with Bram that made Mary's heart skitter, and then looked at Dat again. "Do you know anything about a piece of land for sale out on Double E, about fifteen minutes from here? Looks like they're taking sealed bids on it."

Dat's eyebrows rose as he thought about which property that might be. Or was he reading between Nate's lines, as to why he was interested in that farm? "I seem to recall folks saying the owner's widow couldn't make the payments, and then her heirs haggled over the place for a few years after she passed away. None of them made a go of it, and none of them live there, but that's the last I can recall about it."

"That would explain why the buildings aren't in very *gut* shape. The next big storm might take the barns down, from what I could see." Nate spooned more stewed tomatoes onto his plate and took another slice of bread.

"It was a hobby farm." Dat continued as details came back to him. "And when folks don't know much about making *gut* use of the land—and when nobody lives there for a long while—a place goes downhill mighty quick."

"Probably critters in the house by now." Bram helped himself to more scalloped corn, keeping his expression and voice low-key.

Mary shuddered at the thought of walking in on snakes or raccoons . . . all the more reason to knock the buildings down and start fresh. It was difficult to rid an old place of animals once they'd eaten holes in the walls, and it wouldn't do to have such intruders scurrying across the attic or inside the walls—especially if they were to have paying guests! She met Martha's gaze and then noticed the speculative expression on their mother's face.

"You boys looking to buy a place?" Mamma asked.

Oh, but *that* hammered the nail, didn't it? Their mother didn't dilly-dally around when it came to getting information. Mary took another slice of bread and passed the basket to the kids, noting the looks on Nate and Bram's faces. It told a lot about a fellow when he was faced with a question he hadn't figured on answering yet.

Nate leveled his gaze on Mamma. "If Bram and I are ever to support families, we've got to find property. And what with land not coming up for sale very often—"

"Not to mention gettin' so pricey that a fella can hardly afford a farm on his own," Bram added in a low voice.

"—we brothers have to stick together, have to jump in when we find a place that'll work for us," Nate continued in a quiet, confident voice. "It's not likely that an acreage will be on the market in Willow Ridge any time soon."

"Nor here in Cedar Creek," their *dat* added matter-of-factly. "I wish you boys all the best, if that's what you'd like to do."

"If it's God's will that you have it, then the Lord will guide you toward making the best bid," Mamma affirmed with a nod. "Do your homework on the real estate details. Pray on it. And we'll put in a *gut* word for you, too, while we're praying."

Bram's face took on a glow as he looked at their mother. "*Denki* for that help, Mrs. Coblentz. Means a lot to have you backin' us."

Mary tingled inside, suddenly so excited she had to *move*. As she went to the counter for their desserts, she could practically taste the breads and treats she'd bake when their bed and breakfast was up and running. It seemed a longtime dream was about to leap out of her imagination and into reality, right down the road from home!

Too soon to be counting on that, her thoughts warned, but her heart spoke in a different tone. '*Ask and you shall receive. Knock and the door shall be opened . . .*'

And if *she* didn't believe that someday the door to an inn would open, then who else would make her and Martha's dream come true?

Chapter Thirteen

Bram tucked Mary's gloved hand into the bend of his elbow as the four of them headed to the stable to hitch Clyde to the sleigh. Snowflakes danced in the light from their lantern, just as his thoughts were whirling happily. "Hate to eat and run," he said, "but if we're to make an educated bid on that farm, we've got to set some wheels in motion."

"I'm thinking they already are," Martha replied. "I didn't want to say anything at supper that might back you fellows into a corner where you didn't want to be—"

"But it's obvious Mamma and Dat think you're on the right track," Mary said. "We'll be thinking of you, hoping the pieces fall into place."

As he stepped inside the dark barn, Bram pulled Mary close and kissed her. "We'll do our best," he murmured into her ear. She smelled sweet and clean, and he knew he'd be replaying today's conversations in his mind all week, as inspiration for the enormous project he and Nate were about to take on.

"How about getting together for New Year's Eve?" Nate suggested. He had an arm around Martha, too, and as she hung the lantern on a hook, its glow lit their faces . . .

their intentions. "By then, we should have an idea whether we're in the running for that farm, or if we have to keep looking."

The twins exchanged a happy glance. "*Jah*, that would be fun!" Martha said.

"What a fine way to start a new year, with the four of us together, ain't so? You can catch us up on what's happened with the land auction then, too." When Mary stood on tiptoe to kiss his cheek, Bram knew it was too late to back down—not that he wanted to. He wasn't sure how his attitude, his whole world, had changed in the course of the past few hours, but he suddenly longed to give this pretty young woman everything her heart desired.

He and Nate hitched the sleigh to Clyde and then lit the sleigh's lanterns and the Slow Moving Vehicle sign for their night drive home. As they headed from the lane onto the road, they waved at the two girls who stood on the front porch in the glow of their lantern. Bram memorized the moment, cherishing the energy and excitement of the kisses they blew.

Beside him, Nate settled into the seat and urged the horse into a trot. "Well, little brother, did we just bite off more than we can chew? Will we be sorry we got those girls involved—got their hopes up so high?"

Bram let out a short laugh. "Well, my hopes are flyin' right up there with theirs. It's Dat we've got to convince now," he said. "We'll be askin' him to plunk down a lot of money based on a place we saw by happenstance, with sisters we've only known a couple of days."

"*Jah*, the situation's a stretch for both of us, considering how I walked out on them Christmas morning," Nate remarked. "But I think Mary and Martha are onto something, wanting to run an inn. There's no place like that between Cedar Creek and Willow Ridge, and the two of them together have got the gumption to make it work. But for me . . . it's got to be Martha."

"Hah! You don't think I'm lettin' you have another chance at Mary, do you?" Bram blurted. As a gust of wind whipped around them, he pulled the blanket higher, already missing the warmth his date had created when she'd cuddled with him beneath it. "The big question is, if we don't get that farm . . . will the twins stick with us while we hunt for another place? Do you suppose Amos Coblentz will really put up a double house with extra rooms in the middle, and maybe help us with the barns, too?"

Nate looked at him from across the seat. "We'll have to work on that, won't we?"

The next morning made Nate a firm believer in the power of prayer. As he and Bram sat down to breakfast, their parents' unspoken questions filled the kitchen along with the aromas of the egg casserole Mamm was taking from the oven. Bacon, coffee, and cinnamon sticky buns made him think of how it would smell this good every morning, if he and Bram lived in a bed and breakfast. After they had prayed silently, images of capable, hard-working Martha gave him the confidence to speak up.

"Well, Bram and I had quite a day in Cedar Creek yesterday," he began. "On the way into town, with the Coblentz girls' buggy in tow, we ran across a farm that's up for sale. The sealed bids have to be in by the thirtieth, and we've all four made big plans for the place."

Before their startled *mamm* and *dat* could start firing questions at them, Bram chimed in with more details. "*Jah*, there's a hundred and five acres. Plenty of space for the corrals and barns Nate'll need for his trainin' business, along with *gut* road access and space for an auction barn like I've been wantin' to run."

Mamm's breath came out in a rush. "That's a mighty big project for a fellow your age, Bram," she replied in a tight voice. "And how do these girls figure in?"

"They're going to open a bed and breakfast. The house that's there has to come down," Nate explained. "But Martha and Mary have ideas about how they want family living quarters on either end, with guest rooms and a big space for having church in the center—"

"And their *dat* has promised to build them houses when they get hitched, so that'll be a big advantage, once Nate and I get the land." Bram's grin stretched from ear to ear as he heaped the steaming breakfast casserole onto his plate. "So if it's all right by you, Dat, we'll need to look the place over with the real estate fella in the next day or so and put in our bid."

"Well, now." Their mother set her fork on her plate, staring at them. "This is awfully sudden, boys. You've only just met these girls—and you both came home in a dither yesterday, after something they did or said."

Dat leaned back in his chair to gaze at each of them in turn. "While I've told you I'd put up the money when you boys found places you wanted, I'm not sure I want to throw so much cash at a deal that's blown up out of nowhere— even if these girls' *dat* is known all over Missouri for his fine carpentry."

"That's why we want you to go along with us, to look the place over," Nate replied. His heart was pounding so fast he could hardly think, but he couldn't let these objections get in his way. Not if he was to start the life he'd always wanted. "Bram and I figure if we go in together on a place, it'll save you money in the long run—"

"And we know it's important to you that we keep the family together as much as possible," Bram added.

"Especially since it's not likely we'll find property here in town. Or in Cedar Creek, for that matter."

"Are . . . are you sayin' you're ready to get hitched?" Mamm rasped.

Nate felt a smile flickering all over his face even as he tried to control it. "That wouldn't have to happen in a hurry," he hedged. "After all, it'll take time for Bram and me to get our businesses established. Even so . . . as I think about it, Martha reminds me of *you*, Mamm. She prefers to be outdoors—really knows horses, too, and isn't one bit afraid of hard work. She's been taking some business classes to be sure their inn gets off to a *gut* start."

"And Mary is a lot like Aunt Miriam," Bram murmured, catching the spirit of convincing their doubtful mother. "She's quite the *gut* cook, and has Miriam's same energy about her in the kitchen—and she's patient and caring with her younger brother and sister, too. Loves kids, Mary does."

Their mother's eyes were the size of saucers as she focused intently on her younger son. "Does this mean you're joining the church, Abram Daniel Kanagy?"

Bram didn't miss a beat. "*Jah*, I guess that's about the size of it. The Coblentz girls have made it clear they won't be leavin' the faith, and that they're a package deal. They're a right pretty package, too."

Dat laughed out loud while Mamm smacked the table with her hand. "Glory to God in the highest!" she exclaimed. "I don't want you rushing into anything you'll regret for the rest of your lives, but—"

"I believe we'll visit that place as soon as you boys can set up a time," Dat insisted. "Like you've said, opportunities for land are as scarce as hen's teeth. And if your mother's this excited about you joining the church, Bram, well, I know better than to mess *that* up, ain't so?"

Nate heaved a huge sigh of relief and grinned at his

brother. "See there? Nell Coblentz must be praying for us this very minute. Call that real estate fellow and let's get after it! We've got a lot to accomplish these next couple of days."

When her cell phone vibrated on Wednesday afternoon, Mary wiped the flour from her hands to grab it out of her apron pocket. The number on the little screen made her grin. She rushed out onto the porch so Joanna, who was stirring up a batch of brownies, wouldn't eavesdrop.

"Bram? I was just thinking about you," Mary said in a low rush. But then, when *wasn't* she thinking about him lately? "What's happening? How's it going with the farm we looked at?"

"*Gut* to hear your voice, honey-girl," he replied, and his words sent a tickle of lightning up her spine. "We walked around the place this morning with Dat and the real estate fella, and we just got back from submittin' our bid. Now we have to wait until the end of the day on the thirtieth to see how it all comes out."

Mary saw Martha coming from the chicken house and waved her over excitedly. "So how many people have put in bids?"

"They don't tell you that part. Either they'll call to say our offer was topped by other ones—"

"I hope that won't happen," Mary murmured. "Seems that all Martha and I can talk about is how we want to set up our B and B."

"—or, if a few of the offers are close, they'll ask if we want to increase ours," Bram finished. "I've got to tell you, though, that when Dat saw the place and we did some figurin' to come up with our bid . . . well, it boggled my mind. Even though there's not much tillable land, it's assessed at about two-hundred twenty thousand dollars."

Mary closed her eyes. When her sister came up beside her, they stood with their heads together so Martha could hear the conversation, too. "*Jah*, when we asked Dat about a double house with extra guest rooms, he and Owen figured something like that, finished off real nice, would cost him a bit more than that even with donated labor. The cost of the barns and buildings you fellows will want is added onto that, so *jah*, it's a huge investment, Bram," she agreed in a tiny voice. "And it's not like any of us are as old as most folks who run the businesses we're talking about. Martha just came up to join me."

"Hi, Martha!"

"Bram! So how did the place look?" Martha asked. "Were your parents okay with it, or . . ."

"Let's just say Nate and I took their breath away when we told them what we'd been up to in Cedar Creek," he replied with a chuckle. "But Dat likes the land. Agrees with us that the buildings are better off comin' down, after these past few years of snow and rain and animals gettin' inside."

"So we'll have the answer when we see you for New Year's Eve?" Mary asked.

"That's the plan." Bram paused, as though he might have covered the phone with his hand to talk to Nate. "Um, what would you girls think if we brought you up to Willow Ridge then? The folks are trying not to let on, but they're mighty curious about the girls who've got Nate and me so fired up about . . . settling down."

Mary grabbed Martha's hand, so giddy she couldn't speak for a moment. "That seems only fair, since our folks have met you boys already. Might be the custom for Plain couples to keep their courtin' more of a secret—"

"But sometimes it's best to get everything out in plain sight," Martha said. "After all, both families have a lot riding on this, and, well—it'd be *gut* for us to get acquainted with your family and see where you fellows have grown up. Get things started off on the right foot for all of us."

Bram let out a sigh that ended in a chuckle. "You girls are the best, you know it? We'll fetch you bright and early on Tuesday. I'll ask Mamm to get you a room ready—"

"Tell her we'll bring along some bread and pies and cookies," Mary insisted. "It's the least we can do."

Again Bram let out a little laugh. "She'll be tickled to hear that. I'd never tell her this, but you're way better at bakin' than she is, Mary. And when Nate mentioned how Martha is more like her, preferin' outside work to cookin', he made some *gut* points with her."

Mary and her sister laughed. "It sounds like we're all set, then! We'll look for you boys on Tuesday!"

Chapter Fourteen

"Mary? We're gonna run a little late pickin' you up." Bram paused outside the real estate office Tuesday morning, glad to have Mary's voice in his ear before he joined Nate and Dat inside. "We got called back to make another offer on the farm. Say a little prayer, will ya?"

"Oh, but this is *gut* news! I've been praying ever since you fellows left," she answered. Her giggle did crazy things to his pulse. "If God wants us to have that place, we will, Bram. And if we don't get this one, well . . . Martha and I aren't giving up. In for a penny, in for a pound, we are."

It struck him then just how deeply he cared for the redhead with the sprinkling of freckles across her nose, and how her faith was inspiring his own. Bram suddenly knew he would move heaven and earth to provide a place for Mary's dreams to come true . . . because then his life would be set up for the very best he could hope for, as well. "*Denki* for sayin' it that way, honey-girl," he whispered. "I love ya. Really I do, Mary, and you're the girl I've gotta marry."

"Oh, Bram," she breathed. "I . . . it's all I can think

about now, being your wife someday. It's all going to work out wonderful-*gut*. I—I love you, too, Bram."

"I love hearin' you say that," he murmured. "Gotta go. They're waitin' on me."

When he stepped inside the agent's office, he felt a goofy, lovestruck smile on his face, but he didn't care who saw it. He shook Ken Carnahan's hand and took the chair beside his brother. "*Gut* to see you again," he remarked. "Our havin' to come back means we're still in the runnin' for this place, ain't so?"

Ken smiled from behind his cluttered desk. He was wearing a sweater with elbow patches and an open-necked plaid shirt, and appeared to be slightly younger than Dat. "Indeed it does, and I'm pleased folks like you are interested in the place. I have Amish neighbors and I've always been impressed by their work ethic—their willingness to serve as volunteer firemen and to keep their farms looking nice." The realtor smiled at him and Nate as he shuffled some papers. "What sorts of plans do you have for the property, considering there's so little tillable acreage?"

Behind them, the front door blew open and a tall man in a camel-colored overcoat stepped into the front lobby. As Bram told about the auction barn he envisioned, and his brother mentioned stables and corrals for training horses, Ken got up to close his office door. "Be with you in just a moment, Mr. Dana," he told the fellow who'd just come in.

"And the girls we're courtin' figure to start a bed and breakfast someday," Bram went on. "What with their *dat*, Amos Coblentz, helping out with that project, we hope to support ourselves pretty well once all these businesses get going."

"Fine man, Amos is," Ken remarked. "Watched his crew put up most of a barn in a day, and it's a sight to behold.

Now—if you'll write the amount of your new bid here, and sign on the lines again, we'll be all set. I know this is a big move for you boys, and I appreciate the chance to do business with you."

"Tell the folks who're selling this place we'll pay them cash, too," Dat said as he signed his name.

Once again, the magnitude of this offer . . . his parents' commitment to his and Nate's future, made Bram's throat tighten as he and his brother signed their new, larger offer. He had a good feeling as they rose and shook hands all around, because Ken Carnahan seemed like a down-home sort of fellow who was genuinely interested in their success.

When they stepped into the entryway, however, the man who had come in grabbed his briefcase. "Couldn't help but overhear the cute ideas you boys have for the Westview place," he remarked in a deep Southern accent. His cowboy boots glimmered with fancy toe and heel trim and his tan Stetson was top of the line. "But I'll be bringing in a new tire manufacturing plant, and our business will provide hundreds of jobs—not to mention that the taxes we'll pay will go toward improving area schools and roads," he remarked. "In times like these, such an investment can only benefit everyone in central Missouri, don't you agree?"

Bram was too stunned to say anything. He went on outside, while behind him Nate murmured something like, "*Jah*, whatever." When they reached the enclosed carriages, the three of them sighed.

"Well, that fellow sure knew how to take the wind out of a man's sails," Nate said. "Can't see how our bid will top his."

"*Jah*, I'm wishing I hadn't heard what he had in mind for the place," Bram remarked. "I'm not real crazy for the way he called our ideas *cute*, either."

Dat crammed his broad-brimmed hat farther down on

his head. "You've got your hearts set on that place, I know, but if you don't get it . . . maybe the Lord's got better property in mind for you. We'll keep believing that. And meanwhile, your *mamm* and I are looking forward to meeting Martha and Mary later today. Be careful on the roads, now."

"*Jah*. See you later, Dat. *Denki* for everything you're doin' for us." They waved as their father's rig headed back toward Willow Ridge.

Bram's thoughts tangled like contrary reins as he pointed Felix north on the county highway. Nate sat silently beside him, stewing over the same thing . . . that other fellow's attitude, and the insistence that his tire plant was a worthier use of the land they both wanted so badly. They rode several miles through the snow-covered countryside, keeping to the edge of the road so the occasional car could pass. When Bram's cell phone rang, he handed the lines to Nate.

"*Jah*, this is Bram," he said when he saw the number of the incoming call.

Ken Carnahan sighed. "The heirs of the farm instructed me to accept the highest new offer, and that would be the one Mr. Dana has made. I'm not one bit happy about it, but I wanted you to know so you wouldn't be wondering and waiting over the New Year's holiday."

"Uh—*jah*, thanks," Bram rasped. "I . . . guess we'll keep lookin', then. Let us know if other farms come on the market, will you?"

"I'd be happy to. You can come by for your earnest money check any time it's convenient for you."

As Bram ended the call, his eyes stung and his heart clutched. "Well, now. Mary said she and Martha were in this adventure with us all the way, but I'm not lookin' forward to greetin' them with *this* information."

"Not the way I'd figured on us celebrating the New

Year," Nate agreed glumly. "It's *gut* to keep the faith, like Dat said. But no matter how you slice it, losing this bid changes everything. The more I thought about it these past couple days, the more our businesses seemed so perfectly suited to that piece of property," he continued in a rising voice. "We don't need a lot of tillable land for our hay, so there's no use in paying the higher price for that kind of property."

"But a tire factory?" Bram demanded. "Can you imagine what troubles that'll cause, with heavy construction equipment on this narrow blacktop? And then the car traffic everyday, when the factory workers drive to and from work?" he added. "Truth be told, Mr. Dana doesn't impress me as the type who'll hire many local folks to run that plant, either."

"Well, it's out of our hands now."

"*Jah*," Bram said with another sigh. "And our mistake was figuring it was ever in our hands to begin with."

Through the window of the front room they saw Felix pulling a rig up the lane and then noted the boys' grim faces through the windshield. Martha grabbed Mary's hand. "They're trying to figure out how to tell us the bad news, Sister," she murmured. "If they'd gotten the farm, they'd be jumping out and running to the house."

"*Jah*, let's figure out a way to commiserate without making the whole ride to Willow Ridge feel like a funeral parade. And let's not let on to Mamma just yet." Mary led the way to the kitchen to hug their mother, putting on the same determined smile Martha wore even though they wanted to cry. "We'll see you next year," Mary teased.

"Try to keep the party under control while we're gone, all right?" Martha teased.

"I could say the same for you girls," Mamma replied with a wry smile. "Give the boys and their folks our best. I know you'd like to get on the road again, so I don't expect you to invite them in."

"*Denki*, Mamma. See you in a day or so." Martha slipped into her heavy black coat and bonnet and grabbed the big box of goodies they'd packed, which waited on the porch table along with their suitcases. Mary followed her outside with a pie carrier and a bread basket.

"Let me get this," Nate said as he relieved her of her load.

Martha was careful not to react to his disappointment as she directed Bram to the porch for their luggage. When they were all four settled in the rig, and she sat beneath a blanket with Nate in the backseat, the buggy lurched into motion again.

The silence felt as heavy as wet snow for a few moments.

"You've guessed how the latest bid turned out, *jah*?" Nate murmured.

Martha's hand went to his smooth-shaven face as she blinked back tears. "*Jah*, your expressions told the tale."

"Burns my butt the way it happened, too," Bram remarked. "Some fella in fancy clothes said his company was gonna build a tire factory there! Outbid us big-time, by the looks of him."

"A *tire* factory?" Despite her best effort, Martha choked back a sob. "Why, that's not even—what'll the neighbors think of *that*?"

Nate sighed and clasped her hand. "I get the feeling that man doesn't much care about the neighbors. Even though the place seems like a major investment to the likes of us, it's probably small potatoes to him because land here's so much cheaper than most other places."

"And he's buyin' the place with other people's money."

Bram shook his head as he gazed at Mary, who sat beside him in the front seat. "I'm real sorry, honey-girl. I was hopin' to have all kinds of celebratin' to do these next couple of days."

Mary gazed out over the passing countryside, which was alight with afternoon sunshine. "Maybe this is God's way of telling us we were getting too big for our britches, thinking we could handle two new marriages and three businesses at our age. Maybe—"

"But we at least made your uncle Abe a happy man," Martha piped up with forced cheerfulness. "We told him yesterday we were ready to take our instructions, so we could join the church."

"*Jah*, he won't be reporting our kissing in the barn to Vernon Gingerich, our bishop." Mary muffled a giggle as she hooked her hand around Bram's arm. "That little sin has been forgiven, now that Dat's told him we're courting. Puts me on the higher road, you know."

Nate slung his arm around Martha's shoulders, gazing into her eyes. "And you're still sure about joining the church? Even with this news we got today?"

"*Jah*, we're positive. It's just a matter of sooner rather than later for us," she confirmed. She loved it when Nate thumbed away the tear dribbling down each of her cheeks . . . how he was offering her a way out of the arrangement they had all agreed upon so quickly. "Our folks like it that we've all got plans that make us happy while we start our families. And they're real glad we twins will be in the same house. So if you . . . well, if *you* still want to hitch up with—"

"You're beating me to the punch, but *jah*," Nate rasped as he grabbed her and murmured into her ear. "I want you for my wife, Martha. Will you have me?"

Her body shivered with the thrill of this moment,

dreamed of since she was a girl. Had there ever been a handsomer fellow than Nate Kanagy? Or another man who would respect her desire to work at something besides having a family? "I'm yours," she whispered.

In the front seat, Bram cleared his throat ceremoniously. "You girls aren't the only ones who have taken that step," he announced. "Our Preacher Tom was mighty glad I told him I was ready for my instructions, too. And the parents are acting like a Christmas miracle has taken place."

"They're really eager to meet the two girls who set us along this path to getting hitched—and to getting Bram into the fold," Nate added playfully.

Mary tugged at the lapel of Bram's leather jacket. "Well, would you look at this! I *thought* I saw broadfall pants and suspenders under this English coat— and that's a pretty purple shirt, too. We'll have you looking Amish in no time, ain't so?"

Martha's heart felt lighter and the mood in the buggy lifted. Wasn't it a fine thing, the way the three of them had committed to the Old Order faith, practically on the same day? "This calls for a treat!" she declared as she opened the big box near her feet. "Cookies and candy will sweeten up the news about the farm, too."

"But I've got to tell you, I could already see myself baking in that new kitchen and chatting with guests in our inn," Mary said wistfully. She took the cookie bin from Martha and placed it on the seat so Bram could choose something, and then dug a piece of paper from her apron pocket. "Dat even sat down with us to sketch out a house like we've been talking about—"

"So when the right property comes along," Martha chimed in, "we're ready! There'll be no stopping us then! Show them, Mary."

When Bram had gazed at the drawing, sighing over it, Mary passed it back so Nate could have a look. He traced a finger over the rough lines of a house with two wings on either side of a taller center section.

"You girls are the best," Nate murmured. "We'll just keep believing in this sketch, and in this whole project and the way you've helped us make it even better than Bram and I had imagined." He closed his eyes over his first bite of fudge.

"*Jah*, we were thinkin' we might have to mop a couple buckets of tears during the drive home," Bram remarked. "I'm thankful the two of you can see beyond the clouds to the rainbow. Means a lot."

Martha shared a smile with Nate. Had that remark come from the same Bram Kanagy who had coaxed her and Mary to jump the fence, share an apartment, and live in dubious circumstances?

"You know, if we cut up this next county road, we might make it to the real estate office before Ken closes for the day," Nate suggested, gesturing off to the right. "It'll save somebody a trip to fetch our check."

"*Gut* idea. No need for that much money to be sittin' around with Ken over the holiday. Geddap, Felix!" Bram pulled his cell phone from his jacket pocket and entered a number with one thumb . . . listened as it rang. "*Jah*, Ken—Bram Kanagy here. We've picked up the Coblentz girls and I'm wonderin' if we can swing by your office for our earnest money, say, in half an hour?"

Martha settled against Nate's shoulder, lifting her chocolate chip wreath to share it with him. *We're making the best of this situation, Lord*, she prayed, *so help us accept Your will for us and move on to whatever You've got in mind for our future.* How could she remain downhearted with such a fine man holding her close, his dark eyes shining with the promise of wonderful things to come?

The four of them chatted for the next several minutes as early evening settled over the countryside. The snow-capped silos and barns took on the pale blue shadows of coming nightfall, a reminder that no matter what had happened with the farm they had wanted so badly, their dreams would rise again as surely as the sun would come up tomorrow. Wasn't it a blessing to know that the same God who had set order to the nights and days was watching over them?

It was a comfort, too, when Martha realized that she and Mary no longer needed to play little tricks or trade places to get what—and whom—they wanted. Their lives and loves were playing out just as they were supposed to. Such a thought made her smile in the warmth of Nate's embrace: she'd come a long way in a short time.

Chapter Fifteen

As they pulled into the parking lot, the lights shone in the windows of Ken's office. Nate noticed a black SUV parked close to the door and wondered who else might be conducting end-of-the-year business, but mostly he wanted to duck inside, retrieve their check, and get back on the road. No need to dwell any longer on the fact that this transaction hadn't worked out the way they wanted it to. When Bram pulled the rig around to the side of the building, Nate hopped out. "Be back in a few."

He wasn't expecting Ken Carnahan to open the door just as he got there, wearing a mysterious smile. "Nate, I'm glad you fellows could stop by again—and your girl-friends are with you?"

"*Jah*, they are." He gestured toward where the buggy was parked.

"And is that frosting on the corner of your mouth, by chance?"

Swiping at his face, Nate flushed. "Mary brought along cookies, so we were sweetening up the bad news about not getting the farm—"

"Perfect! How about if all four of you come inside," Ken said quietly, glancing back toward his office. "And if you've got any cookies left, bring them in. It might be worth a few minutes of your time."

What could Ken possibly mean? Nate sensed he shouldn't question the agent's suggestion, so he fetched Bram and the girls from the buggy. "I've got no clue as to what Ken might be cooking up, but what have we got to lose by going along with him?" he said. "Toss the blanket over Felix, just in case it takes a little while."

The realtor held the door, smiling at the four of them as they went inside.

"This is Mary and Martha Coblentz," Nate said, and then he couldn't help but grin. "They've both agreed to be our wives, so it's been a real *gut* day even if we don't yet have a place to live."

"Congratulations! It's a pleasure to meet you girls," Ken replied as he shook their hands. "I'll take your coats and then there's someone I'd like you to meet."

When Bram and the girls questioned him with their glances, Nate shrugged. It felt like the agent might have something up his sleeve, yet he knew better than to get his hopes up. The Amish didn't believe in Santa Claus . . .

And yet, as the twins smoothed their aprons and kapps, Ken Carnahan's expression put a shivery sensation in his stomach. The realtor opened the door and gestured for the four of them to precede him into his office.

"I'd like you kids to meet Carlene and Travis West-view," he said as a middle-aged man and woman rose from their chairs. "The farm you bid on belonged to their parents, and they're settling up the estate now."

After they were all introduced, Ken asked them all to sit down. He gazed first at Mary, Martha, Bram, and Nate before looking at the Westviews. Again, Nate had to wonder why Ken wanted them to meet these folks face-to-face . . . with cookies.

"Bram, after I informed you that I had received a

higher offer—and then heard you were stopping by—I felt I should bring Travis and Carlene here so they could see why I was so . . . unsettled about accepting Mr. Dana's bid."

He sat down at his desk, addressing the Westviews. "While Mr. Dana can probably convince our congressmen to arrange the rezoning required for his factory, as a homeowner who lives down the road, I hate to see the havoc such a plant will create. We'll need a new road to accommodate the construction traffic, not to mention city sewers and other infrastructure that would substantially raise our taxes," he pointed out. "And then there's the disruption of the peace and quiet we came to the country for, and the possible rerouting—or contamination—of the creeks and groundwater we and our livestock depend upon."

Travis smoothed his thinning hair as he glanced at his sister. "As the executor of Mom's will, I've got to follow her wishes—and answer to our other brother and sister about getting the best possible price for the farm, too," he insisted.

Carlene nodded, scooting to the edge of her chair. "While we understand your concerns about how the area would change, we can't let sentiment affect our—"

"And what sorts of businesses did you kids say you wanted to start, if the farm became yours?" Ken prompted, gazing at Nate and Bram.

His younger brother didn't need to be asked twice. "I'm an auctioneer," Bram replied with a smile. "I plan to construct a sale barn—"

"And I'm a horse trainer in Willow Ridge," Nate continued, encouraged by what seemed to be happening. "This place is perfect for us because we can raise the hay we need for our animals and put the rest of the acreage to *gut* use, too."

"And once we marry these fellows," Mary said, fishing the sketch from her apron pocket, "our *dat*, Amos Coblentz the carpenter, plans to build us a double house that'll have a bed and breakfast in the center of it. See?" She walked over to let the Westviews have a look.

"*Jah*," Martha chimed in, "and I've been taking classes to manage the business end of things, while Mary will cook and see to our guests. We've even got some of Mary's goodies along with us. Here—take a taste!"

Carlene and Travis looked like a couple of deer caught in a car's headlights, but Nate understood now what Ken was trying to do—for the four of them, and for the dreams they had shared with him. While Travis bit into a brownie and looked at the house plans with his sister, the girls stood back a bit. They understood that English sometimes couldn't figure out how to react to Amish folks.

After a moment, Carlene glanced up at the twins. "But a house like this must surely cost a fortune. And how will you boys afford this farm?" she asked.

Mary smiled politely. "Ah, but the land's to be a gift from the boys' parents, while our folks have promised us girls homes as our wedding present," she explained. "We Amish are all about families staying together, helping each other out."

Carlene glanced at her brother. She succumbed to a sugar cookie from the bin as she looked at the house plan again.

"Mr. Kanagy has also told me that he plans to pay in cash, so you could settle up with your siblings very quickly, while Mr. Dana's money would have to make its way through corporate channels, out of state," Ken pointed out. "And you'd have nothing to defend to your brother and sister if you accepted the boys' offer, because their latest bid is quite a bit more than the assessed value of the land.

"It's your decision, of course," the realtor went on in a low voice, "but I wanted to offer you a chance to foster local, home-grown businesses that will support two new families."

After a few moments of silence, Ken smiled at Nate. "I expect the Westviews will want a chance to talk this over, so——"

"*Jah*, we'll be on our way, then." Nate offered his hand to Travis. "Thanks for hearing us out. And Happy New Year to both of you."

"It's a big job, settling up amongst your kin," Bram remarked as he, too, shook the land owner's hand. "We hope it all gets worked out with everybody still speakin' to each other."

"You've got *that* right," Travis replied with a short laugh.

The four of them returned to the entryway and started putting on their wraps. Ken joined them, closing his office door behind him with a big smile. "You kids handled this exactly right," he murmured. "I can't guarantee that they'll decide in your favor, but——"

"Well, at least you gave us another shot at it, and that was mighty kind of you." Nate gripped the agent's hand. "Keep us in mind for other places, if the Westviews take Dana's offer."

Mary held out the cookie bin. "We'd like to leave you some of these goodies as our thanks, and——"

"I bet there's paper towels in the restroom to wrap them in," Martha said as she went toward a door in the hallway.

"——we're really grateful for the way you took our side

today, Mr. Carnahan. Come and stay a night with us when we get our inn built, on the house."

It was Ken's turn to look stunned. "What a generous, thoughtful offer. I wish you kids all the best, wherever you make your new home."

While Ken chose some cookies, the girls put on their coats and bonnets. Nate's pulse thrummed with fresh hope even as he reminded himself not to get caught up in how this surprise meeting had gone. He heard two voices on the other side of the office door, but resisted the temptation to listen in. After all, didn't he already have the *yes* that mattered most, from his Martha? With that important piece of his future in place, the rest of the details would surely present themselves when God decided he should have them.

"Happy New Year," Bram said as he opened the outside door. The girls walked out, exclaiming over the fresh snow that was falling, and Nate brought up the rear. They remained quiet as they passed the lighted office windows . . . tugged the blanket from the horse's back . . . tucked the cookie bin under the dashboard . . .

"Kids, wait! The Westviews want to talk to you!"

Nate had never seen Mary and Martha's faces light up so brightly. Bram laughed and clapped the girls' shoulders, steering them toward the office door, where Ken was leaning out, grinning like a kid on Christmas Day.

Inside the lobby, the two Westviews stood side by side, watching them enter. "Mom detested big business," Travis admitted in a raspy voice.

"We'd feel bad every time we drove by, seeing a factory where our home used to be," Carlene joined in. "I have a feeling you kids are going to make the most of this place, so we want you to have it."

Mary and Martha grabbed each other, hopping up and down. "Oh, but this is just the *best* surprise—"

"And we thank you ever so much!"

Nate gripped Travis's hand between his. His eyes were burning and his throat was tight, but he saved his show of emotions for later. "This is a dream come true for us, Mr. Westview."

"*Jah*, it's like we got the twins for Christmas," Bram chimed in, "and now we've got a home forever. How could anything top that?"

Laughter filled the lobby as they shook hands all around. They returned to Ken's office so he could print out the initial sale paperwork, and while Travis was asking Bram about his auction barn, Carlene requested Mary's recipe for sugar cookies. Too excited to sit down, Nate stood in the doorway drinking in the enthusiasm that filled this room. Just as his marriage to Martha had snapped into place like the fastener on Clyde's sleigh bells, the farm that had seemed like a lost cause was suddenly theirs.

Nobody but You could've worked it out this way, God, he mused gratefully. *Denki for helping me keep the faith, and for bringing Martha, Bram, and Mary into the membership, too. From there, everything was a go.*

When they got back to the buggy an hour later, Nate lit the lanterns while his brother brushed the fresh snow from Felix's back.

"Wait till the folks hear this!" Bram crowed. He hadn't stopped grinning the whole time they were inside, and as he reached for Mary she squealed and grabbed him around the neck.

"*Jah*, we should give Mamm and Dat a call, too," Martha agreed. "Might get somebody to answer the phone while they're out doing the horse chores—"

"It can wait." Nate wrapped the redhead in his arms and lost himself in blue eyes that sparkled like crystals on a pond. "Seems like we should seal this deal with a kiss."

Martha smiled up at him, indescribably pretty . . . a face he could gaze at forever. "*Jah*, you're right, Nate," she murmured. "But don't let it go to your head."

As he kissed her, he sensed Martha's words summed up the life that stretched ahead of them like a road winding through the countryside . . . the road home. He and Bram would indeed need to respect the wishes of their energetic young wives, but if there was a happier way to live out their lives, with the four of them working together, he couldn't imagine it. "We'll have to work on that attitude of yours," he teased.

Martha grabbed his hand and led him into the backseat of the rig. "We'll just see about that, won't we?"

Kissing the
Bishop

Charlotte Hubbard

Chapter One

Tom Hostetler opened his mailbox out by the snow-packed road and removed a handful of envelopes. A quick glance revealed a few pieces of junk mail and a letter from an attorney whose name he didn't recognize before the *clip-clop! clip-clop!* of an approaching buggy made him look up.

"Morning to you, Tom. And Happy New Year," Jeremiah Shetler called out as he pulled his Belgian to a halt. "Enos isn't far behind me. Saw him coming up the highway from the other direction as I turned down your road."

"Glad to see you fellows, too," Tom replied as he stepped up into the carriage with the bishop from Morning Star. "Who could've guessed Hiram would disrupt Miriam and Ben's wedding? He's set Willow Ridge on its ear—not to mention throwin' *my* life into a tailspin—now that we've excommunicated him."

"Never seen the likes of it," Jeremiah agreed. He drove down the snowy lane past Tom's house to park beside the barn. "I still feel God's will was done, though. Hiram brought this whole thing on himself when he didn't make his confession. The rumors are flying about that new town he's starting up, too. What's he calling it?"

"Higher Ground," Tom replied with a snort. "But we're pretty sure he's got the lowest of intentions, after his dubious ways of raisin' the money for it. A real sorry situation, this is." He looked up to see Enos Mullet, the bishop from New Haven, turning his buggy down the lane. "Vernon Gingerich is drivin' in from Cedar Creek, too."

"The four of us will figure things out. Wherever two or more gather in the Lord's name, He'll be present." Jeremiah gazed steadily at him as they paused in the dimness of the barn. "I've prayed over this a lot, Tom, and I believe God's ushering in a new Heaven and a new Earth here in Willow Ridge. And He's prepared you to handle whatever comes along, my friend."

Tom raised his eyebrows. As one of the two preachers in the Willow Ridge district, he was a candidate to become its next bishop . . . a huge responsibility for a man who milked a dairy herd twice a day. "Hope you're right, Jeremiah. A lot of fine folks are dependin' on what we decide today."

Tom walked out of the stable, noting the gray clouds that gathered in the distance. When the approaching buggy stopped, the man who stepped down from it looked pale. Enos Mullet seemed to get thinner every time Tom saw him, due to the chemo treatments he was taking after a nasty bout of cancer. "Enos, it's *gut* of ya to come," he said as he shook the bishop's bony hand. "You fellas will be glad to hear the Hooley sisters have been helpin' me get ready for ya. The kitchen smells like they're cookin' up something mighty tasty for our dinner."

"Well then, we certainly won't starve!" Enos remarked. "Seems like they've fit themselves right in amongst you folks. Nice addition to your town."

"That they are." Tom smiled to himself as they led Enos's Morgan into a stall. He didn't let on to folks, but

Nazareth Hooley had been a lot of company to him this winter; it was just too bad she couldn't become more than his friend. His wife Lettie had divorced him last spring, and Old Order Amish couldn't remarry until their former spouses passed on.

But his spirits lightened as they stepped into a kitchen filled with the aromas of the fresh pastries and cookies Nazareth and Jerusalem had baked early this morning. As Jeremiah and Enos greeted the sisters and accepted hot coffee and treats, Tom was glad he'd asked them to host-ess for him today.

"Here comes Vernon," he said, pointing toward the road out front. "And would ya look at that sleigh he's drivin', too! You fellows make yourselves comfortable in the front room, and we'll be right in."

What was it about a sleigh that made him feel like a kid again? Tom hurried outside again, delighting in the merry jingle of the harness bells and the proud way Vernon's Percheron pulled the vehicle.

"Whoa there, Samson," the bishop called out. "And *gut* morning to you, Tom! I've had a fine ride, even if those clouds make me think more snow's on the way."

"*Jah*, I'm glad you've come to visit for a day or so. We'll get right to our business so the other two fellows can be safe on the roads." Tom stroked the horse's black neck, grinning. "This is a fine old sleigh, Vernon. Brings to mind the one my *dat* got from his *dat*, back when we kids prayed for snow so we could ride in it."

"This one's of the same vintage. And thanks to our James Graber's way with restoring old vehicles, it's a beauty again." Vernon patted the cranberry velvet that cov-ered the high-backed seat. "Three of the best pleasures in this life are spirited horses, fine rigs, and a *gut* woman—

not necessarily in that order. Guess I'll be happy with having two of the three."

Tom laughed. "*Jah*, that's how we have to look at it sometimes."

As they stabled Samson and then entered the warm kitchen, Tom felt better about their morning's mission: Vernon Gingerich was known for his down-to-earth faith and simple wisdom, and his sense of humor made even the most difficult tasks easier to accomplish.

"My stars, I must've stepped into Heaven," the bishop from Cedar Creek said as he inhaled appreciatively. "Don't tell me *you* baked the goodies on this sideboard, Tom!"

"The credit for that goes to Nazareth and Jerusalem Hooley," Tom replied as he gestured to each of the women. "Two more generous, kindhearted gals you'll never find, Vernon."

As the women greeted their final guest, Jeremiah and Enos replenished their plates and made Vernon welcome, as well. It did Tom's heart good to hear these voices filling his kitchen, to feel the presence of friends who would put their faith and best intentions to work today on behalf of Willow Ridge. Living alone this past year had taught him to appreciate the company of those who had seen him through some rough months.

As Vernon chose from the array of treats, Tom closed his eyes over a pastry twist that oozed butterscotch filling onto his tongue. When he looked up again, Nazareth was beaming at him, pouring him a mug of coffee. "It's going to be a *gut* morning for all of us, Tom," she assured him. "If you fellows need anything at all, we sisters'll be right here in the kitchen."

"*Denki* for all you've done," he murmured. "Couldn't ask for better help, or a better friend than you, Naz."

Her sweet smile made Tom wish the snow would pile up around the doors so they couldn't get out for days—after Enos and Jeremiah had gotten safely home, of course. But he set such wishful thinking aside and led the way into the front room. It was time to determine who would lead Willow Ridge into the New Year . . . into a future no one but God could foresee.

"Have you ever seen blue eyes that twinkle the way Vernon's do, Sister?" Jerusalem whispered. She peered through the doorway at the four men who sat around the table where Tom usually carved and painted his Nativity sets—except she and Nazareth had cleared the wooden figures from it earlier today. Jerusalem ducked back into the kitchen when the white-bearded bishop from Cedar Creek smiled at her.

Nazareth laughed softly. "Seems like a nice fellow, Vernon does. A far cry from the sort of man Hiram Knepp turned out to be."

"*Jah*, you've got that right. I'm thankful the *gut* Lord opened our eyes to his underhanded ways before I let myself get sucked in." Jerusalem stirred some barley into the pot of vegetable beef soup on the stove. Truth be told, she had been attracted to Hiram Knepp from the moment she'd set foot in Willow Ridge last fall—and he had taken to her right off, too. But as time went by, she'd realized the bishop was more interested in having her keep track of his four younger children than he was in hitching up with an outspoken *maidel* who'd become set in her ways . . .

Is it too late for me, Lord? Jerusalem watched the emotions play across her sister's face as she set places around the kitchen table: it was no secret that Nazareth and Preacher Tom were sweet on each other despite the fact that they couldn't marry. Surely there must be a fellow who would appreciate her own talents for cooking and keeping up a home . . . a man who could tolerate her tendency to speak her mind and do things her way. Was it such a sin to be competent and efficient enough that she'd never needed a husband?

"What do you suppose they'll decide on today?" Nazareth asked as she took six soup bowls from the cabinet. "What with Preacher Gabe havin' poor Wilma to look after while he's gettin' so frail himself—"

"*Jah*, I thought it was the wise thing for him to tell Tom, right out, that he couldn't handle bein' the new bishop," Jerusalem agreed. "That leaves Tom as the only real choice, because I can't see folks wantin' a totally new fella from someplace else to take over. Tom's perfect for the job, too."

Nazareth's brows knit together. "It's a lot to ask of a dairy farmer who's got such a big herd to milk, especially since his kids all live at a distance and he's got no wife. Some districts back East wouldn't even consider a divorced man."

"Everyone knows it's not Tom's doing that he's alone." Jerusalem held her sister's gaze for a moment. "Not that he's really by himself, what with you helpin' him every chance you get."

"Folks might frown on me spendin' so much time here, after he's ordained," Nazareth replied in a shaky voice. "Bishops are expected to walk a higher path. Can't appear to live outside the *Ordnung*—especially after the way Hiram went rotten on us."

Jerusalem set down her long-handled spoon and placed her hands on her younger sister's shoulders. Nazareth was slender and soft-spoken; had chosen a brilliant green cape dress that looked especially festive today. But her quivering chin told the real story. "So you're worried that if Tom's to be the new bishop, he'll have to forget his feelings for you? I don't see him doing that."

"But—but we're to devote ourselves to God first and foremost," Nazareth reminded her. "No matter what Tom and I feel for each other, we're to follow the Old Ways. I'd begun to believe that God had led me here from Lancaster to find him . . . to be his helpmate someday. But now—"

Chairs scooted against the floor in the front room. The men's louder talk made Jerusalem embrace her sister quickly and then step away. "It's in the Lord's hands, Sister. Let's not worry these molehills into mountains before we see what comes of today's meeting."

"*Jah*, you're right." Nazareth swiped at her eyes and began taking food from the fridge. "I'm just being a silly old *maidel*. Until we came to Missouri, I'd been so certain God meant for me to be a teacher rather than a wife, so maybe I'm just confused."

Silly? Confused? Those were hardly words Jerusalem associated with her sweet, hardworking sister, but she certainly understood Nazareth's sentiments. She, too, had spent her adult life believing she had a different mission from most Plain women. If Hiram hadn't upset her emotional apple cart, why, she would still be staunchly convinced that teaching—and then coming to Willow Ridge with their three grown nephews—was what she was meant to do. Now she had a bee in her bonnet and she buzzed with a restlessness she didn't know how to handle. And her longing wouldn't disappear just because Hiram had.

As the four men entered the kitchen, however, Jerusalem set aside her worrisome thoughts. "You fellas ready for some dinner? It's nothing fancy, but we thought soup and hot sandwiches would taste *gut* on a winter's day."

"Ah, but *fancy* isn't our way, is it?" Jeremiah quipped. "You've had my mouth watering all morning."

"The snow's startin' to blow, so we decided Enos and Jeremiah should be gettin' on the road as soon as we eat," Tom said. "We've pretty much settled our business for today."

As the men took places around the table, Jerusalem opened the oven to remove the pan of open-faced ham and cheese sandwiches, which looked like little pizzas. She had picked right up on the fact that Tom hadn't said Vernon was heading back. Although Cedar Creek was a lot farther away than Morning Star or New Haven, he wore an unruffled expression, as though driving home was the least of his concerns. Nazareth dipped up big bowls of the steaming soup, chockful of vegetable chunks and beef, while Jerusalem set butter and jelly alongside a basket of fresh whole-wheat rolls.

"Looks like a feast," Enos said in his raspy voice.

Jerusalem took the empty chair across from her sister, wishing she could feed that poor man enough to fill out all his hollows. They bowed in a silent prayer and then Tom passed the platter in front of him. "You fellas are gettin' a real treat here," he remarked. "Naz and Jerusalem made the cheese on these sandwiches from their goats' milk."

Vernon's face lit up as he took two of them. "So those goats in the stable are yours? They seem right at home among the horses."

"Oh, *jah*," Jerusalem replied, "goats and horses are natural companions. We brought those four from Lancaster with us, well . . . as a gift to the bishop." She paused, wishing she hadn't gone down this conversational path. "But when we informed Hiram we wouldn't be joining him in Higher Ground, we took them back."

"And Preacher Tom's been kind enough to let us keep them here," Nazareth continued. "Our does will be havin' kids this spring, and we couldn't take the chance that they'd not be properly tended."

Jeremiah helped himself to the hot sandwiches. "You folks are in the prayers of all the districts around you," he said in a solemn voice. "Enos and I suspected, back when Hiram confessed to us about his car, that other issues might come to light someday. We can only trust that God has a reason for all the trouble Hiram's caused."

"We also believe, however, that Willow Ridge will be in capable, compassionate hands with Tom as its spiritual leader." Vernon took a big bite of his open-faced sandwich and then closed his eyes. "My goodness, ladies, what a treat you've blessed us with today. I'm ready to buy myself a few goats so I can enjoy more of this marvelous cheese."

Jerusalem's heart fluttered. "Thank you, Vernon. It's been our pleasure to provide you fellas a meal while you've been here on such important business."

"So it's settled then?" Nazareth asked. "Preacher Tom is to become the bishop?"

"It's what our prayers and discussion have led us to, *jah*." Jeremiah smiled at the man who sat at the table's head. "What with you folks needing two new preachers now, we feel Tom will provide the continuity—the leadership and spiritual example—to bind up the wounds Hiram has inflicted. It's not the usual falling of the lot, the way we Amish let God select our bishops, but in your case it's the most practical solution."

Jerusalem noted the way her sister nipped at her lower lip before biting into a roll she'd slathered with butter and jam. Well they knew the blessing Tom Hostetler had been to them and to this entire community, even if it meant Nazareth must put aside her hopes for romance. And while Tom's expression suggested he had his share of doubts and questions about the role he would assume, he was accepting this new wagonload of responsibility as God's will for his life.

Tom's faith—his willingness to serve without complaint or question—will be an inspiration to us all, Jerusalem thought. *Give me the grace to follow where You're leading me, as well, Lord.*

When Jerusalem looked up, Vernon Gingerich was studying her, and he didn't lower his eyes for several seconds. It felt unseemly—downright brazen—to return his gaze, yet she indulged herself in this fascinating man's silent attention anyway. Hadn't Tom mentioned that the bishop of Cedar Creek was a widower?

The conversation continued along the lines of farming, shepherding of human flocks, and other topics of common interest as Jerusalem refilled soup bowls and Nazareth brought the goody trays to the table. What a blessing it was to be surrounded by the wisdom and experience these three bishops had brought with them . . . a balm to her soul, after the way Hiram had condemned them when they hadn't followed him to Higher Ground. It was such a delight to watch the men devour the cookies they'd baked, too. All too soon they were scooting back from the table.

"Can we send goodies home with you fellas?" Jerusalem asked. "It'd be our pleasure, after the help you've given our district today."

Jeremiah's dark eyes flashed with pleasure. "*Jah*, I'll take some! Not that I promise they'll all make it to Morning Star."

Enos laughed until his bony shoulders shook. "You've got a bottomless pit for a stomach, Jeremiah. These days nothin' I eat seems to stick. But I'd be happy to relieve Tom of the burden of having to force the rest of them down."

"None for me, thanks," Vernon said as he slipped into his coat. "Tom invited me to stay over, and by the looks of those huge snowflakes, he's a pretty fine weather forecaster. I'll be back in a few, so don't put those cookies away yet."

A schoolgirl's grin overtook Jerusalem's face. Vernon was staying over! And wasn't that the best news she'd heard in a long, long while?

Chapter Two

As Vernon waved to the two friends who were taking off in their buggies, he felt as light as one of the flakes swirling around his face. While substantial snowfall always caused concern for fellows with livestock and long lanes to plow, today his nephew Abner would cover those responsibilities for him. He felt a child's delight at the prospect of open fields glistening in the sunshine after a winter storm . . . and being snowed in for a day or two suddenly sounded wonderful, too.

"Can't thank you enough for inviting me to visit, Tom." He looked at the tall white house with its snow-covered roof . . . the large red dairy barn and its well-tended fences. "It's a real gift to have time away now and again."

"I don't see nearly enough of ya these days, Vernon. It's been more years than I care to count since the summer you and I worked that fella's ranch in Nebraska." Tom's smile waxed nostalgic. "After all the manure we shoveled, it's a wonder you ended up with a herd of Angus while I'm milkin' all these Holsteins."

Vernon laughed and clapped his friend on the back. "We were mighty full of ourselves at sixteen, weren't we?

But it seems to me we've both come a long way on the same path. And I see God's hand at work here in Willow Ridge, too, with you becoming the bishop. Your patience and dedication will be real gifts to these folks."

Tom sighed, stuffing his hands into his coat pockets. "Hope we're not declarin' our practicality as God's will. The last thing I want is to fall into the same arrogance Hiram had."

"That'll never happen. Hiram's cut from different cloth altogether." Vernon saw movement in the kitchen window . . . a flash of deep red the color of the cardinal that sang in the nearby spruce tree. He took the cooler from behind the seat of his sleigh while Tom grabbed his suitcase. "So tell me how you came to have those two sisters keeping house for you. They're quite a pair."

As they started for the kitchen door, Tom's cheeks took on a blush that had nothing to do with the frosty air. "When they walked out on Hiram—they were lookin' after his youngest four kids, ya see—this seemed the most logical place for them and their goats to land, even though plenty of other folks offered to put them up. If ya have reservations about the way it looks, with me havin' two *maidels* here—"

"The way it looks," Vernon quipped quietly, "is that the situation has worked itself out well for all of you. Maybe more for you and Nazareth than for Jerusalem, eh?"

Tom grinned in spite of his concern. "She's a fine woman, Vernon. And with the two of them being inseparable, I figured it for an honorable way to have a little companionship. This big old house gets lonely of an evening . . ."

They paused outside the door. "I know all about that," Vernon murmured. "Not a day goes by that I don't miss my Dorothea. And I couldn't possibly keep up with my farm or tend to a bishop's business if it weren't for my aunts and my nephew living with me. A man's not meant to do his life's work alone, Tom."

"*Jah*, well, my work was the last thing on Lettie's mind when she left in that fancy fella's car. But I'm tryin' to put that behind me. Movin' forward as best I can."

"God's will be done. It'll all work out."

As his friend opened the door into the kitchen, Vernon's lips twitched. Why was he thinking—hoping—God had brought him to Willow Ridge today for more than counseling his longtime friend? Once again the aromas of beef soup and fresh bread wrapped around him like a blanket as he stepped into the kitchen where the Hooley sisters were redding up. He liked it that Jerusalem wore a holiday shade of red some Plain women would consider too showy, and that her eyes sought his as he stomped the snow from his boots. Dorothea would never have dressed or behaved so boldly . . .

"Unless I miss my guess, we're in for quite a pile-up of that snow," she remarked brightly. "*Gut* thing ya packed to stay over, Vernon."

Was it wishful thinking on his part, or did Jerusalem seem awfully glad he hadn't started for home? He held out the cooler so she could take it while he removed his boots. "I brought along a fresh brisket and some rib-eye steaks. My nephew Abner's a butcher with a fine eye for the best cuts of my Angus, so I'll put these toward my room and board."

"Mighty generous of ya," Tom remarked. "There was no need to cart your own dinner here—"

"But we'll put this meat to real *gut* use, ain't so, Sister?" Jerusalem added.

Nazareth's face crinkled with mirth as she dried the dishes. "Saves us from takin' something from Tom's deep freeze and having to figure out the menu, I'll say. And it'll suit us just fine if ya stay until we've eaten every last bite of it, too, Vernon."

"It's unanimous, then. We're all determined to enjoy the winter weather instead of fretting if the roads become impassable." Vernon nodded, pleased with the way this visit was taking shape. "Let's you and I bring in some firewood and get the hay mangers filled for your cows, Tom."

"*Gut* idea. And we'll park the plow blade in the stable, where it's easy to hitch up after the snow stops." Tom's face reflected his gratitude . . . and maybe he, too, was imagining the potential for spending time sequestered from the rest of the world, with two very pleasant women for company. "We'll be back in after the chorin' and the milkin', girls. Lookin' forward to your company, once the work's all done."

As he and Tom went outside again, Vernon glowed with a special sense that these next days in Willow Ridge would set the tone for the New Year . . . and quite possibly his whole future. He stuck out his tongue to catch some snowflakes, laughing at the quick tingles of coldness. Times like these proved out the wisdom of growing older without fully growing up, didn't they?

"Oh my, but these are wonderful-*gut* steaks, Sister," Nazareth exclaimed as she unwrapped the white butcher paper. "And such a big brisket! Haven't enjoyed fresh beef like this in a long while."

"Awful nice of Vernon to bring it along," Jerusalem agreed. "How about if we pair up some of the corn and lima beans in Tom's freezer—"

"*Jah*, succotash sounds tasty," Nazareth agreed, "and we could bake those last two acorn squashes in the root cellar. Tom's got several jars of beets down there, too."

"And we could cream that head of cabbage we brought. That sounds like enough sides to go with those steaks for tonight and for tomorrow, too, when we can bake that brisket real slow." Jerusalem's face glowed with a girlish flush. "Won't have to spend all of our time in the kitchen that way."

"Cook once and eat twice," Nazareth quipped. "Always a fine plan, in my book."

As she wiped off the countertops, Nazareth glanced at the butterscotch twists and pastries that remained from the men's morning meeting. A batch of cinnamon swirl bread would be a nice addition for their breakfast tomorrow, and it was one of Tom's favorites made up as French toast, too. When she shifted the stack of mail, a long white envelope dropped to the floor.

"Now I wonder what this could be, comin' from an attorney?" she mused aloud. "I suspect Tom forgot all about it, what with the three bishops gettin' here all at once."

"He's got a lot on his mind, for sure and for certain," Jerusalem agreed. "I'm thinkin' a fresh batch of our cinnamon swirl bread would be a nice favor to Tom, as he loves it so."

Nazareth laughed. It had always been one of life's little mysteries, the way she and her sister could pick up on each other's thoughts. "You always know best, Sister," she teased as she restacked the mail and then finished wiping the work surfaces. That letter was Tom's business, not hers, and she didn't want him to think she'd been snooping.

Even after all these years of living with Jerusalem, it was a treat to work in the kitchen with her older sister, for they didn't need to chitchat to pass the time companionably. Jerusalem was paring apples, slicing them into a casserole dish with cinnamon and raisins, for a crisp, most likely. Nazareth tidied the front room then, placing the Nativity figurines Tom had carved on his worktable again. She sensed Vernon would enjoy seeing what his longtime friend did to pass the cold winter days and bring in some extra income.

A pounding on the front door made her scurry to open it. "My word, you fellas have cut quite a load of logs already," she said as Tom and Vernon came inside with their loaded leather carriers.

"They say chopping wood warms you twice—when you cut it, and again when you burn it," Vernon replied as he followed Tom to the storage bin. "I was admiring this stove while we were meeting in here. It's keeping the place toasty even with the wind kicking up."

Tom's smile looked a bit reticent. "Lettie ordered this stove from Lehman's catalog. While I often shook my head over her preference for the most expensive model of everything we bought, I have to admit this soapstone stove holds enough wood to keep us warm all day long." He deftly emptied his carrier so the logs fell into the woodbox without any bark or mess landing on the floor.

"Sometimes an initial investment repays us with long-time quality," Vernon observed. "My Dorothea tended toward making do and erring on the frugal side, so I'll soon have to replace some of the appliances she chose."

As the men trundled back outside in their heavy boots and coats, Nazareth gazed pensively at the wood-burning stove. She had often considered it more elaborate and decorative than something Tom would have chosen himself; now she knew why. *And how will Tom talk of your preferences? Will he think you make expensive requests? Or, since Lettie's things are holding up so well, maybe you won't even be choosing anything new . . .*

And why was she daydreaming as though she would ever have any say over the way Tom's home looked?

Nazareth chuckled at herself and went back to the kitchen to help Jerusalem start their supper. No sense in wishing away her future, considering that Lettie would continue to be a part of Tom's life even though she'd left him for another man.

By the time the two fellows shook the snow from their coats and stood their shovels against the wall of the mud-room, the dusk looked thick with flakes that blew almost horizontally. The kitchen felt cozy, however, as Jerusalem pulled her apple crisp from the oven and Nazareth popped two loaves of cinnamon swirl bread from their pans to finish cooling.

"We've got cocoa on the stove," she said as the men entered the kitchen in their stocking feet. "Looks nasty outside."

"Ah, but we won't have to set foot out again until morning." Vernon approached Jerusalem, inhaling the steam that rose from her pan of crisp. "And what a treat it will be to spend time getting to know you. Both of you," he added with a quick smile at Nazareth. "Rather than get in your way, I'll venture toward that rocking chair in the front room that looked like it might be a perfect fit for my long legs."

"I'm all for that," Tom replied. "We did a *gut* day's work these past few hours, hustlin' about to beat the storm. I appreciate your help with that, Vernon."

"You'd have done the same for me, Tom."

Nazareth was pleased at the way Vernon draped his arm around Tom's shoulders for a moment. This bishop radiated an entirely different attitude than Hiram Knepp had, and if anyone needed a show of confidence and encouragement during these unsettled times in Willow Ridge, it was their gentle, hardworking preacher. "Dinner's all but ready, Jerusalem. Let's sit a spell with the fellas, shall we?"

"Ya don't have to ask me twice." Jerusalem quickly filled four mugs with the hot cocoa and picked up two of them.

Nazareth carried the other two mugs into the front room, secretly hoping she could share the love seat nearest the stove with Tom. Was that a bad idea with a guest in the house? Would Vernon remind them that their next bishop shouldn't be paying attention to a woman who couldn't become his wife? She handed Tom one of her mugs.

"And what have we here?" Vernon had paused beside the table at the window. He picked up a figure of Mary, who wore a shawl painted like a patchwork quilt. "These look like pieces from Nativity sets I've seen in some high-end catalogs, Tom. And you've been carving them?"

Tom sipped his cocoa, blushing a bit. "It's something I do to pass the time. I figure they encourage folks to think more about Jesus' birth instead of all the trim and tinsel so many English focus on."

Vernon turned the figurine over in his hand and then leaned closer to study the other figures. "Can't say as I've ever seen the Wise Men represented as Amish fellows with beards and hats. But I like it that they've brought the gifts of their labors—an ear of corn, a pail of milk, and a lamb—to offer the baby Jesus."

Nazareth smiled at her sister as Jerusalem set a mug of cocoa where Vernon could reach it. It did her heart good to hear someone compliment Tom's talent, even though it wasn't the Plain way to be proud of one's handiwork.

Tom shrugged, not quite comfortable with the bishop's praise. "Truth be told, tourists snap up these sets as fast as I can make them because Amish crafts seem to be all the rage these days. I don't do such a *gut* job of paintin' on the details—"

"Humility suits you, Tom, but there's no need to deny your God-given gift." Vernon's eyes sparkled as he gently ran his finger along the angel above the manger, who also wore a robe in a colorful quilt design. "I've never seen anything that so freshly presents the miracle of God's gift to us. If this set's not spoken for, I'd like to buy it."

"Oh, but I'd be happy for you to have it, Vernon!"

"Nonsense." The bishop held up his hand to stop Tom's protest. "Your work has great worth, my friend. We all know how the extra cash comes in handy, considering that we preachers and bishops spend a great deal of time shepherding our flocks without compensation. Spiritual rewards are a gift from God, of course, but here on Earth we're expected to pay our bills."

Nazareth was grateful to the bishop for saying such a thing to Tom. Her sister was nodding her agreement.

"Nobody else makes sets quite like these," Jerusalem said as she stood beside Vernon. She picked up the cow and the two fluffy, white sheep, smiling at their contented expressions. "Why, if you could carve me a set that included some goats, Tom, I just know the Knepp children would enjoy it. I worry about them," she added softly, "seeing's how Hiram's busy starting up his new town. There's nobody to look after those three little boys and Sara, now that Nazareth and I have walked away from them."

Nazareth's heart constricted with the same regret her sister had just expressed. "*Jah*, we had our differences with Hiram, but his kids are mighty special to us."

"And we can pause for a moment, right here and now, to pray for them."

To Nazareth's surprise, Vernon grasped her hand and took Jerusalem's as he bowed his head. Tom took her other hand, and as the four of them stood in reverent silence, lifting up their petition for Josh, Joey, Sara, and little Timmy, Nazareth felt a subtle power . . . a strength and purpose that was magnified by the way they had joined their hands and hearts.

Lord, I'm ever so grateful for Vernon's presence . . . his guidance as we send our love and prayers to the Knepp kids . . . as we prepare Tom to lead Willow Ridge.

Vernon sighed serenely. "It's a blessing to be here among you folks. A much-needed retreat for me, and a time of discovery, as well." When he smiled at Jerusalem over the top of his cocoa mug, his eyes twinkled with mischief. "Might I suggest a game of Scrabble after dinner? My aunts and nephew aren't as keen for board games as I am, so I rarely get to play."

Nazareth giggled. "Oh, you've opened quite a can of worms there, Bishop, asking two old schoolteachers to play Scrabble!"

"*Jah*, I'll take you on, Vernon," Jerusalem replied without missing a beat. "It's been too long since I enjoyed a game with somebody who plays it the way my sister and I do."

"The perfect way to pass a snowy evening," Tom agreed happily. "I probably haven't had that game out since my kids married and left home."

"We'd better fix that then," Vernon asserted cheerfully. "Who says young people get to have all the fun?"

Chapter Three

Jerusalem felt as if bright, shiny bubbles were bouncing around in her chest. Vernon had indeed opened a fine can of worms by suggesting Scrabble, and she couldn't wait to play. While she reminded herself that winning wasn't the point—that it was an evening well spent if each of them played the best game they could—her fingers itched to arrange wooden letter tiles into long, high-point words.

"This is the best time we've had in a while," Nazareth murmured. They stood side by side at the stove, stirring orange sauce into the sliced beets and adding blended flour, milk, and melted butter to the pan of boiled cabbage. "It's been so long since we played board games!"

"*Jah*, our crochet club's a *gut* way to visit with our female friends, but this!" Jerusalem glanced over her shoulder to be sure neither of the men was within earshot. "This feels like a double date, Sister!"

"Tom's loving it, too. Haven't seen him smile this way, well—since we came here in October." Nazareth turned off the gas burner. "I'll set these beets in the warming oven and start the butter sizzling for the steaks. My word, but we have a feast tonight!"

"In more ways than one." As Jerusalem stirred the cabbage to keep the cream sauce from scorching, she glanced at the table. "I hope Tom won't mind that we got out the better set of dishes and a linen tablecloth. Lettie left some nice things behind and it's a shame not to use them."

She set the lid on the pan of cabbage and took it off the heat. Though she'd been cooking and setting a pretty table since her teens, Jerusalem wanted this evening to stand out . . . wanted everything just so, even if neither of the fellows would care about the cloth napkins folded beside their china plates or the crease in the freshly ironed tablecloth that ran down the exact center of the table.

When she glanced into the front room, she smiled. It was indeed a blessing to see Tom Hostetler looking so relaxed, to hear his laughter as he and Vernon chatted. The past few months of Hiram's duplicity had taken their toll on everyone in Willow Ridge, but Preacher Tom had borne the brunt of it. Some members had whispered of moving to other districts if Bishop Knepp didn't cease his brash, controversial behavior. It was a relief to see the New Year as a fresh slate where they would write the community's next chapter with a calmer, more compassionate leader in charge.

As though he'd felt her gaze, Vernon looked at her. Again his eyes lingered, and Jerusalem wiggled her fingers in a wave. "Won't be but a few more minutes," she announced. "Those are mighty fine steaks you brought us, Vernon."

"And what else smells so delectable?" he asked as he rose from the sofa. "Let's take a look, Tom. The anticipation's making me twitch!"

Jerusalem turned and inhaled deeply. Nothing smelled

as wonderful as beef sizzling in a skillet, with butter, salt, and pepper. As she began setting the vegetables on the table, the two fellows lifted lids of pots and stood a little closer to her and her sister than was the usual way of it. All her life she'd known the men of the house to seat themselves and wait to be served, so it was a treat to have Vernon take the bowl of buttered succotash from her . . . letting his large, warm hands brush hers for a moment.

Oh, but his eyes are so blue and merry! Can it really be me that's making them twinkle so?

"You've outdone yourself," the bishop murmured as she handed him the basket of fresh rolls. "A man couldn't ask for anything finer than this."

"It's a particular pleasure to cook for folks who appreciate it," Jerusalem replied quietly. Then she looked directly into his eyes at close range. "But don't think for a minute that spreadin' such honey will get ya ahead on the Scrabble board, Bishop. I've never been one to *let* anybody win, ya see."

"Oh, I see, all right, Jerusalem," he countered, holding her gaze. "And if for one moment I suspect you're pandering to me, or distracting me with goodies or clever table talk, I'll show you no mercy."

She tingled from the way he'd said that. It was an effort to concentrate on their silent grace instead of letting her imagination gallop away with her. And what a joy it was to watch Vernon and Tom slice off the first bites of their tender steaks and then sigh with utter satisfaction as they chewed.

The meal progressed at a leisurely pace, seasoned with spirited conversation, yet too soon it was over—most likely because they were all ready for the evening's entertainment. Again, Vernon and Tom broke with tradition by washing and drying the dishes so she and Nazareth could put the kitchen to rights faster. Happy talk and laughter filled the room even as the wind whistled outside and snow lodged in the corners of the windows.

"I'll toss on a couple more logs," Tom said. "Something tells me we'll all stay up a little later tonight."

While Jerusalem and Nazareth arranged some cookies on a plate and poured the spiced cider they'd been warming, Vernon laid out the Scrabble board. It was cozy with the four of them at a card table instead of having nieces, nephews, and siblings crowding around a bigger table. With the lamps glowing and the dictionary within reach, they were finally ready to play.

No accident that the two men seated us across from them, Jerusalem mused as she quickly chose her first seven letters. *And no surprise that Vernon's long legs aren't tucked beneath his own chair.*

"I've got a six-letter word to start the game," the bishop announced.

"Well, that's just fine and dandy," Jerusalem replied as she shuffled her tiles. "But I can use all seven of my letters. Shall I proceed?"

Tom chuckled. "You've got me beat."

"Take it away, Sister. Then I'll play something extraordinary from whatever ya lay down," Nazareth remarked as she gazed at her letters. "No sense in letting these fellas think they'll ever have the upper hand."

Jerusalem swiveled the Scrabble board on its lazy susan, considering where she could play to best advantage. "It's not much of a score, because all the letters I drew are only worth a point apiece," she murmured as she formed the word. "But it'll light a firecracker behind the horse, I think."

Beside her, Nazareth gasped. "*Sensual*? We're playin' a respectable game here, Sister!"

As they all laughed, Jerusalem shrugged gleefully. "Just

makin' do. Takin' double the points for usin' all my letters,"
she added as she wrote her score on the scratch pad.

"And it perfectly describes our evening," Vernon observed. "We've tasted outstanding food while savoring
the feel of a fresh linen tablecloth and the sight of fine
china . . . we're inhaling the scent of this spiced cider and
hearing our laughter grow louder by the minute. That kind
of sensuality is indeed a gift from God as we enjoy this
wonderful life He's provided us."

"Amen to that, Vernon," Tom replied.

As Nazareth laid down her tiles, Jerusalem sent Vernon
an appreciative smile. He *had* noticed the trouble she'd
taken with the table, and it touched her that he had woven
his compliments into such an insightful response, too . . .
even as his lips twitched with thoughts he wasn't saying
out loud.

"And who was saying we should keep things respectable?" Tom teased, pointing at Nazareth's word.
"Playin' *liquor* from Jerusalem's L sorta tells us what's on
your mind, ain't so, missy?"

"Or it might suggest what's in this wonderful cider,"
Vernon remarked as he drained his cup. He reached
behind him for the big ceramic teapot, then rose to pour
more of the hot drink for everyone.

Nazareth snickered. "You're just wishin' *you'd* played
the Q on a triple-letter space," she replied saucily. "I've
just scored thirty-five points, Sister."

"*Jah*, and you'd better cover your letters, too, because
Vernon's takin' a peek at them while he plays waiter." Jerusalem placed her hand across her tiles, smiling up at the
white-haired man whose beard shimmied with his laughter. "You think I haven't tried that trick myself, Vernon?"

"I think you've tried every trick known to man, woman."

Jerusalem nearly fainted. The bishop had a low, mellow

voice and such a quick wit with his words. But it was not so much what he said that affected her as the way he said it. And while they weren't in church, by any means, she had never expected to hear a spiritual leader suggest such an . . . earthy topic. Her heart was fluttering so hard she could barely breathe.

"Well, that explains why no man has been able to keep up with my sister, much less catch her," Nazareth remarked pertly. "Jerusalem won't tell ya so herself, but she's been the sharpest pencil in the pack since we were wee girls."

"No doubt in my mind about that." Vernon made a point of looking into Jerusalem's eyes rather than at her letter tiles as he topped off her cider. "I believe Tom's fortunate to have women in his district who speak their mind with grace and intelligence, rather than merely agreeing with whatever the men decide to do."

Somehow Jerusalem resisted the urge to fan herself with her hand. By the time Vernon sat down across the table from her, she could think straight again. She suddenly wondered, had this little exchange been engineered to distract her from her game? Vernon, sly fox that he was, had warned her about doing this very thing with goodies and clever conversation, but she knew when she'd been bested. She studied her letters while Vernon took his turn.

"*Request*," the bishop said as he placed his letters around the Q Nazareth had played. Then he looked purposefully across the table. "Jerusalem, I request the pleasure of your company for a ride in my sleigh after we dig ourselves out tomorrow."

Jerusalem's hands flew to her face, which was growing quite warm. "I—well, it so happens I love nothin' better than glidin' across snow-covered fields behind a fine horse," she replied in a tight voice. "I—I'll join ya, for sure and for certain."

Nazareth clapped her hands. "This is more fun than I've had in a long while, watching my sister get all *ferhoodled*," she laughed. "*Denki* for that, Vernon. You've made my day!"

The game progressed without any long pauses, for they were all adept players who suffered no fools. Every now and again they passed the cookies, and it made Jerusalem's heart sing when their visitor from Cedar Creek tried every variety on the plate and declared each cookie better than the one before. She reminded herself that in a day or two Vernon would be going home . . . so she might be getting way ahead of herself, hoping he would do more than talk a pretty line.

After all, Hiram had been a master at that. Especially when he wanted something.

Jerusalem let herself enjoy the game for what it was, a time for four folks in their middle years to laugh and joke like kids . . . without family or neighborhood gossips picking up on every juicy tidbit. And when had she ever been at a game table where mostly innocent talk could be construed as innuendo?

When the last of the tiles had been taken, they all studied their remaining letters and the spaces available to place them. In a burst of exhilaration, Nazareth played *smooch,* and then Vernon followed it with *kissing*, which used up all of his letters.

Tom looked at Jerusalem with a playful shrug. "*Gut* grief, how can we top those plays? We know what *they're* thinkin' about, ain't so?"

"Thinkin's one thing. Doin's another," Jerusalem quipped—and then she clapped her hand over her mouth. "Didn't mean for that to sound so brazen, Bishop. I've gotten carried away with our fun—"

"What you said wasn't the least bit out of line, dear Jerusalem." Vernon resumed a more serious demeanor, yet his voice remained low and calm. "Kissing has its time and place—to everything there's a season, after all. And as a man who's been without his wife for several years, I pray I still have a season or two of kissing to look forward to. Life's full of unexpected joy, and I try to live so I'm open to every worthwhile surprise that comes my way."

And do you consider me an unexpected joy? A worthwhile surprise?

Jerusalem didn't care to admit how many years had passed since she'd kissed a boy or two, and at this glowing moment, that didn't even matter. No one had ever made her feel so special, so . . . sought after. For a moment they all sat silent, basking in the low glow of the oil lamps and the popping of the fire that was dying down in the stove.

"Well, here it is ten thirty," Tom remarked as his mantel clock chimed the half-hour. "Don't think I've got another game in me this evening, but I can tell ya I'm goin' up to bed with kissin' on my mind." As he smiled at Nazareth, she lowered her eyes in modest delight.

"Tomorrow's another day," Vernon agreed as he rose from the card table. "And I, for one, can't wait to see how it unfolds."

And wasn't that a fine way to look at life? Jerusalem and Nazareth said their goodnights and retired to the bedroom at the far end of the upstairs hallway, gripping each other's hands in their excitement.

"Well, what did ya think of *that*?" Nazareth whispered after they'd closed their door.

Jerusalem chuckled. "I think it's been one of the brightest days in my life. And I doubt I'll get to sleep very fast, for thinkin' back over everything we did and said."

Chapter Four

Tom paused at the top of the stairs to inhale the sweet fragrance of cinnamon as the stronger scent of hot coffee called to him. What a blessing it was to have Nazareth and her sister cooking for him, and to have Vernon here as a friend and an advisor. He couldn't recall the last time he had laughed so often and so loudly as they had last night, and he said a quick prayer of thanksgiving. The sound of Vernon's footsteps made him turn. "*Gut* mornin' to ya, Bishop."

"And you'll soon hear people calling *you* that," Vernon replied as he lightly placed a hand on Tom's shoulder. "I hope you never tire of the blessing and the responsibility that comes with the calling. And meanwhile—for today, anyway—I want to enjoy just being Vernon Gingerich, a man on retreat with three fine friends."

"I can understand that, for sure and for certain."

"And does your armload of winter clothing indicate how many layers you'll be dressed in when we shovel snow?" Vernon teased.

Tom laughed as they started down the stairway. "Wouldn't ya know, I found a note under my door this morning, askin' me for some long johns and work pants because Naz and Jerusalem intend to help us dig out," he said. "And I'll warn ya ahead of time, there'll be no talkin' them out of chorin' with us. They're . . . *determined*, as women go."

"Not the type to shy away from being useful, even if it entails backbreaking labor," Vernon remarked. "I'm not surprised they won't use the deep drifts as reason to stay in the kitchen, although their cooking would certainly justify their remaining in here where it's warm—"

"Don't look for that to happen, Vernon!" Jerusalem called from the kitchen.

"*Jah*, we've got our goats to tend," Nazareth added.

"And besides that, when have we had so much snow to play in? Have you fellas looked outside?"

Tom smiled as he entered the warm, cozy kitchen behind Vernon, who seemed eager for his first glimpse of the Hooley sisters . . . or at least he'd certainly taken a shine to the older one. And wasn't that a happy result of yesterday's conference? Tom wouldn't let on to his long-time friend, but he had secretly hoped Vernon might be attracted to Jerusalem. Living alone was no picnic, and after the happiness and guidance the bishop of Cedar Creek had given to so many, he deserved another woman to share his life.

"We've put out a few things for a first breakfast," Jerusalem remarked as she gestured that they should sit down to eat. "When we come back in, there'll be French toast made with Tom's favorite cinnamon swirl bread—"

"Along with bacon, ham, and fried apples," Nazareth chimed in. When she smiled at Tom, he felt like a kid of sixteen again. "By the looks of those drifts out there, we'll be workin' up an appetite. But what a picture it makes, with the sun just comin' up over the new-fallen snow."

Tom looked out the window at the splendor stretching before him: flawless, rounded drifts for as far as he could see mounded around the barns and nearly as high as the fences in some spots. A rosy pink horizon meant they had all slept later than usual. It was a blessing that his dairy cows were the only creatures who might mind the wait. No one else would care or comment about how the four of them were taking the morning at a more leisurely pace . . . or how he intended to revel in this day with Nazareth while Vernon and Jerusalem provided a measure of propriety. He wished he could express his true feelings, speak his heart to this charming, compassionate companion.

But God was in control of how his life played out, and He had a reason for Tom's living alone, and for the *Ordnung*'s restriction on remarriage.

Patience, he reminded himself as he met Nazareth's eye. *Not your place to know the whys and wherefores of the Almighty.*

After they bowed in prayer, Tom savored another taste of the butterscotch twists they had enjoyed yesterday, along with a thick slice of buttered cinnamon swirl bread immersed in a bowl of warm milk, with sugar sprinkled on top. Nazareth had once teased him about soaking every sort of baked treat in milk or cream, but as a dairy farmer's son, he'd acquired a taste for the simple home-grown foods that had been plentiful when other staples were not.

"You know, that looks tasty," Vernon remarked as he, too, poured warm milk in a bowl and then let a slice of bread sink into it. "Almost like having ice cream for breakfast, but I bet it keeps you warm while working on a winter's day."

The Hooley sisters exchanged a knowing glance as they ate their bread slathered with butter and strawberry jam. "Shovelin' a path from here to the barn'll work up some heat, I'm thinkin'," Jerusalem said.

"And thanks for bringin' us some clothes, Tom." Nazareth patted his wrist in that sweet way she had. "Our *mamm* used to give us fits for dressin' in the boys' pants to help with the chores. We had a slew of older brothers, ya see, so she didn't think Jerusalem and I needed to work outside or in the barns."

Jerusalem let out a short laugh. "But then, Mamm was never one for haulin' out the sleds after the work was done, either. And she didn't know how much fun it was to hitch up the biggest horses and ride the plow blade behind them."

Vernon smiled as though he, too, recalled times from his childhood. "Looking back, I suspect our mothers were too busy raising us to take much time for fun. While I'm sorry God didn't bless Dorothea and me with children, I was grateful that she could enjoy playing with our nieces and nephews all the more because of it."

"Oh, *jah*, we love bein' aunts!" Jerusalem replied with a big grin. "It was our nephews, Ben and Luke and Ira, who brought us out from Lancaster County to help them get settled here in Missouri."

"And I'm glad they did," Vernon replied quickly.

"Hear, hear," Tom chimed in.

They stacked the dishes in the sink, and while the sisters changed into layers of winter clothing, Tom tested the doors to see which one was the easiest to open: deep snow had drifted against the front of the house, so going out through the mudroom was impossible. He and Vernon grabbed the shovels and barely squeezed out the back door from the kitchen because even there, high peaks had formed.

"Must've gotten a foot or more," he grunted as they shoved their blades into the drifts nearest the door.

"Good moisture for the pastures when it melts, though. Dry as it's been out our way, we can use all the water God will bless us with."

"*Jah*, here, too. Lots of fellas ran out of grazing grass before last summer was even half over and had to start feedin' hay to their herds," Tom remarked. "Hard on your pocketbook when that happens. I suspect some of my neighbors are runnin' short on hay by now."

"And with the drought burning out the crops, feed prices are the highest we've seen, too. I won't be surprised if more of my members turn to outside work to make ends meet," Vernon said. "And anything that takes a man away from home every day makes it harder for him to raise his family the way we Plain folks believe is best."

They were making quick, short jabs into the drifts as they spoke, tossing the snow to the sides as they made their way toward the dairy barn. Even though the topic was serious, Tom enjoyed talking with another man who understood the difficulties of maintaining a herd. "I'll have to store today's milk in the big tanks, as it'll be at least tomorrow before the trucks will make it down our roads to—*ach*!"

Tom jumped when a snowball hit the middle of his back, and as they turned toward the house, Vernon's black felt hat flew off his head. Feminine laughter rose up from behind a tall, curling drift and then two more snowballs hit their coats.

"You girls are incorrigible!" Vernon called out.

"*Jah*, we've heard that before," came Jerusalem's reply.

"All work and no play makes Tom a dull boy," Nazareth added.

"Hah! Well, we can't have that." Tom stuck his shovel into the wall of snow they'd been cutting through and grabbed a fistful of snow. "What's *gut* for the goose is *gut* for the gander."

"They won at Scrabble so we can't let them show us up again this morning," Vernon declared as he, too, reached for some snow. "Hmm! Powdery as this is, how in the world did they form—"

Before either of them could pack a solid ball, two thickly padded figures in brown work pants, barn coats, and stocking caps rushed down the path they had cleared to grab their shovels. Jerusalem and Nazareth were laughing as they attacked the snow with the metal blades.

"Time for your break, boys," Nazareth announced. Her breath came through her scarf in wisps of white as she tossed her first shovelful to one side, where the snowbank rose as high as her waist.

"Can't let you old codgers be havin' heart attacks," Jerusalem chimed in. "What with the roads bein' snowed shut, we couldn't get the ambulance here."

"You're calling me *old*? Might be snow on the root," Vernon retorted as he patted his white hair, "but the fire's still burning below." He retrieved his black hat and then playfully whacked it against Jerusalem's backside to get the snow out of it.

"Never doubted it, Bishop. But we can take our turns with the shovels," she said with a laugh. "Keeps the blood pumpin', ya know."

"Yes, I *do* know about that. *Flirt*."

"Not me. I'm a workin' girl, helpin' out every chance I get."

Tom chuckled. While he had watched Vernon in action as a young fellow during their *rumspringa,* he had forgotten how easily this man bantered with women . . . how his blue eyes drew them like magnets. It was food for thought that this esteemed leader of their faith still admitted to his sexuality, as Vernon was a bit older than he and the

Hooley sisters. He kept his language clean, but there was no mistaking the meaning beneath his turn of phrase.

After a few minutes of indulging the women's need to be useful, Tom and Vernon reclaimed the shovels. When they got to the barn doors and could slide them on their tracks, Nazareth and her sister hurried inside. He and Vernon cleared more space around the door to keep the barn from being drifted shut anytime soon. They also shoveled the area around the little shed that housed the diesel generator, which ran Tom's milking machine. By then it felt good to be in the dim, musky building and out of the wind.

As he shut the door, Tom had to smile: the sisters had lit the lanterns and they were baby-talking to the four goats while they scraped the manure from the back stall. In a few moments, the sound of milk hitting a metal bucket echoed in the back of the barn.

"*Jah*, you're a *gut* little girl, Bessie," Nazareth said in a low sing-song. "Givin' us lots of nice milk today."

"And are ya stayin' warm here in Tom's barn, Billy?" Jerusalem asked the buck. She was rubbing his forehead with her knuckles so he wouldn't feel the three females were getting all the attention. "Mighty glad we got ya here ahead of this weather. Can't imagine how you'd be doin' if we'd left ya at Hiram's."

"Ah, but we wouldn't have forgotten ya, Pearl," Nazareth continued as she slipped a rope around the goat's neck and then around a slat of the stall. The bucket scraped the barn floor as she positioned herself for milking. "And you, Matilda, are gettin' to be a chubby thing, ain't so? Won't be long before that baby pops out."

Tom smiled at Vernon. It was a shame Nazareth had never married, as she would have made a wonderful mother. "Guess I'd best get to my cows and stop listenin' in on their goat chatter."

"I won't interrupt your routine, as it's been years since I milked," Vernon replied. "Guess I'll do some mucking."

"We'll be needing a few bales dropped down from the loft, if ya don't mind," Tom said, gesturing to the storage area above them. "Fork down some of the loose stuff, too, to use on the floor."

"I can do that."

Tom smiled as he coaxed his cows into the stanchions. The morning chores went faster because he wasn't doing them alone, and when he saw the devilish grin on Vernon's face as he climbed to the loft, he figured his friend might have something . . . mischievous in mind, and that it probably involved Jerusalem. Sure enough, as he was hooking the milking machine to the last cow in line, a startled squawk rang out.

"Now what on God's *gut* earth—?" Jerusalem cried out. "Vernon Gingerich, that was an ornery thing to do, droppin' straw on my head! Do I look like a cow to you?"

Now how's he gonna get out of that one? Tom glanced up at the figure in the loft as the whole barn got quiet. Every creature there seemed to wait for Vernon's answer.

"Even in Tom's clothes," the bishop began in his low, unruffled voice, "you're as radiant and wondrous as that angel who appeared to the shepherds, telling them the good news of Jesus' birth."

Tom heard a quiet snicker, Nazareth's most likely. Another squirt or two of goat's milk hit her bucket.

"Nice try, Vernon," Jerusalem said as she brushed the loose straw from her shoulders. "But let's don't forget that those shepherds were scared outta their wits by the sight of that angel. That's why all the angels in the Bible go around sayin' 'fear not'."

"And like those shepherds, I stand in awe of a woman so well versed in her faith that she shines . . . and who's kind enough to play along with a prank that probably wasn't my finest idea." Vernon leaned on his pitchfork, gazing down into the stall below him. "Will you forgive me, dear Jerusalem?"

Tom shook his head, wondering how—once again—Vernon had turned a touchy situation to his own advantage by allowing a woman to decide his fate.

"Well . . . since you asked so nicely, I suppose I could. But don't let it happen again," Jerusalem warned.

"I wouldn't dream of upsetting the woman who'll be cooking my breakfast."

Jerusalem's laughter rang around the rafters of the barn. "*Jah*, Hiram never knew how close I came to tinkerin' with his food a time or two. But let's not talk about him anymore. He's history."

"*Gut* idea, Sister," Nazareth replied. "No need to spoil all this fun we're havin'."

Tom had released the first cows and was wiping udders on the next group, hooking them up to the milking machine. Had Vernon set up that little situation to impress Jerusalem? To get her attention? Tom decided not to ask, even when he and Vernon were alone, for what man hadn't put his foot in his mouth a time or two?

When the women finished tending their goats, they insisted he and Vernon come in for breakfast before they plowed the lane—mostly because Jerusalem and Nazareth wanted to ride on the horse-drawn blade. And in snow this deep, their added weight would keep the wide plow bar steadier so fewer trips would be needed.

Tom moved with swift efficiency through the rest of the morning's milking, feeling more lighthearted than he had in years. Lettie had taken no interest in the outdoor chores unless he absolutely needed her assistance, after their sons had married and moved away . . . but there was no need to think about her, either, was there?

She's history. Best to move on, because a whole new future has opened up . . . And even though that future included a lot more responsibility for all the souls in Willow Ridge, Tom felt confident that he could handle whatever came his way. God was always at work in earthly affairs, even when situations didn't appear to be going well. He'd gained even more respect and trust from his district's members these past few months when Hiram was behaving so arrogantly—as well as more experience at dealing with renegade behavior.

Thank you, Lord, for standin' by me whenever I've needed Ya . . . even when I didn't know I needed Ya. This time with Vernon—and with Naz and her sister—has been yet another gut gift from You. I feel so happy, like a man restored . . .

As he entered the kitchen behind Vernon, Tom closed his eyes and inhaled deeply. The aroma of cinnamon, and French toast frying in butter, and maple syrup warming on the stove—and bacon—made him all the more grateful for Nazareth's company. She was still wearing his old work clothes, with his blue bandanna handkerchief tied snugly over her head and coiled hair, yet she looked so at home in his kitchen, as though she'd cooked here for years . . .

And Lord, Your will be done . . . but if there's any way this fine woman and I can be together and still follow Your path . . .

"It'll be on the table in about five minutes, fellas." Jerusalem smiled at them, looking particularly perky in his loose blue sweatshirt with a red kerchief covering her steel-gray hair. "We got enough goat's milk to make another batch of cheese, so be thinkin' about what you'd like us to make from it."

Tom settled into his chair at the table to put his shoes on, thinking he must be the luckiest man on the face of the Earth. His morning chores were done, his home smelled heavenly, he was surrounded by the love and laughter of good friends. He spotted a long white envelope on the countertop nearest the door.

"Guess I'd best solve the mystery of what that attorney sent me," he remarked as he went to fetch it. "Probably another one of those advertisements offering to help me sue somebody—like I'd be interested in such a thing."

"*Jah*, I wonder how my name gets on their mailing lists," Vernon remarked. "It's not like we Amish put any store in the English legal system."

Tom's fingers shook a little as he tore open the envelope. His eyes skimmed past the letterhead. *Dear Mr. Hostetler, It is with sincere sorrow that I must inform you of the death of Lettie Marie Hostetler Redd . . .*

Tom froze as solid as the hydrant pipe on the north side of the barn.

Chapter Five

Nazareth heard Tom suck in his breath. When he didn't let it out again, she quickly shut off the gas burner. "What is it, Tom? You're white as a sheet."

No answer. He was staring right at her, yet didn't seem to see her.

"My word," Jerusalem murmured. "I hope it's not serious-bad news—"

"Oh, my," Tom rasped. The letter fluttered from his hand to the floor. "I—I think I need to sit down—"

"Seems like a fine idea," Vernon said as he gently guided Tom to the nearest chair at the table. "We'll get you a glass of water—"

Nazareth was two steps ahead of the bishop's suggestion and moved the glass from her place to where Tom could reach it. Her mind spun with all sorts of emergencies and disasters that might have happened to his kids, or to kin that he'd mentioned in Indiana. But surely those folks would have called or written the news themselves rather than going through a lawyer. His expression had turned to a blank mask of shock, such a contrast to the joy that had shone in his eyes when he'd entered the kitchen moments ago. She wanted to snatch that letter up off the floor. But it wasn't her place to butt into his business.

"If you'd like a moment alone," Vernon continued with quiet urgency, "we'll wait in the front room."

Tom blinked, exhaling. "No, I . . . maybe you'd better look at that letter, Vernon, to be sure I'm not mistaken. It says . . . it says Lettie has passed on."

Nazareth gasped and looked at her sister, who was gazing right back at her, wide-eyed. All the possibilities—the prayers and dreams she'd dared to imagine—danced in her mind, but this was no time for such girlish folly. Tom had loved his wife deeply and he'd been shattered by Lettie's desertion and the divorce. He'd lived without her for nearly a year now, but that didn't mean his broken heart had hardened against her. Lettie probably hadn't had the faintest idea—hadn't cared—that Tom, true to the Old Ways, had forgiven her even though he hadn't understood why she'd left him.

Nazareth stepped behind his chair, gently placing her hands on his shoulders. "Tom, I'm so sorry," she murmured.

"This is quite a shock," Jerusalem whispered as she, too, stood behind Tom with a hand on his back. "You'd think somebody would've come by the house, or—"

"Do the kids know, Vernon? Does the letter say anything about when, or . . . how?" Tom asked. "It was like I forgot how to read . . . like my eyes couldn't focus once I saw that first line of the letter."

"Understandably so." Vernon pulled a chair closer to Tom and then took a pair of rimless eyeglasses from his shirt pocket.

As the bishop read silently, Nazareth peered at the page but then looked away. Even if she could read the tiny typewritten print from here, it was wrong to look at it unless Tom asked her to. When the sizzling food on the stove began to smell too hot, Jerusalem went to turn off the fire under the fried apples. This was no time to be serving breakfast, but there was no sense in ruining the food, either.

After several moments, Vernon cleared his throat. "Well, my friend, this attorney was carrying out wishes Lettie informed him of a while back—that you and your four children be informed, should anything happen to her," he explained. "She and the English fellow she married were killed instantly when an electric power pole landed on their car in a storm, about a month ago."

"A month?" Nazareth gasped. "You'd think somebody could've gotten word to Tom sooner."

Vernon shrugged. "We don't know all the circumstances. The letter mentioned they were out in Arizona when the accident happened, so it might have taken a while to identify them. Especially if the car caught fire."

Nazareth winced and Tom's body tightened beneath her hands. No matter how cruel Lettie's leaving had been, no one deserved such a horrible death. "Oh, my. This brings pictures to mind I'll be seein' for a while, even though I wasn't there and I never met Lettie."

Beside her, Jerusalem sighed. "Wonder what God was tryin' to say by takin' Lettie in a car, with electricity . . . two of the worldly temptations we Plain folks avoid."

Vernon caught Jerusalem's eye with a silent admonition. "It's not for any of us to speculate about, what the Creator's intentions were."

"*Jah*, you're right about that Bishop. I apologize for bringin' it up." Jerusalem stepped away as though she could hold still no longer. Always a woman who had to be busy at something when bad news came along. "Can I pour anybody some coffee? Or make some tea?"

"So, what's to happen to—does she need buryin', then?" Tom's voice was barely audible, but his question made Nazareth want to weep.

Vernon smiled sadly. "The two of them were cremated and scattered, again as part of Lettie's wishes. Probably her way of sparing you and the kids having to arrange for her funeral."

"Or her way of disappearin' once and for all, without havin' to come amongst us ever again." Tom straightened in his chair, turning toward the stove. "*Jah*, I'll take some of that coffee, Jerusalem. And let me say I'm mighty glad to have my best friends gathered around me at such a . . . time as this. If the kids were here, they'd be scrappin' and fussin' all over again, just like when I had to tell them about their *mamm* takin' off."

"Could be the snow postponed their mail delivery," Nazareth murmured. "Otherwise, you'd think one of them would've called—"

"The only phone message this mornin' was from my milk truck driver, sayin' he'd be here to pick up my tanks as soon as the roads are cleared." Tom looked at Nazareth, smiling wanly. "Truth be told, I can hold off talkin' to the kids. And it's fine by me that the roads out their way are most likely drifted shut like ours are. Gives everybody a chance to think things out . . . to let the old wounds settle down again. If that makes me a thoughtless *dat*, then—"

"Nobody'd believe such a thing about you, Tom," Jerusalem insisted as she brought them cups of coffee. "Lots of things in this life go better if we have a chance to pray over them before we turn our thoughts loose on anyone else."

"Amen to that," Vernon stated quietly. "And a moment of prayer for Tom and his family seems appropriate right now, too. It's the least we can do—and the most powerful thing we can do."

Nazareth bowed her head. *Help me be the kind of friend Tom needs now, Lord, instead of pushin' for what I've so wished could happen between him and me. Your*

*will be done . . . and forgive me for bein' just a wee bit
happy that maybe I'll have the chance to be more than his
friend . . .*

Tom stirred beneath her hands so Nazareth lifted them
from his shoulders. Vernon cleared his throat, and the
powerful silence that had joined the four of them lingered
for a bit as they blinked at each other.

"I feel better already," Tom murmured. "And if Lettie's
affairs are already bein' taken care of, well—there's not a
lot we can accomplish by sittin' around feelin' sorry.
Mopin' won't get the lane cleared out, and there's no
reason not to enjoy that breakfast that smells so wonder-
ful-*gut*, either. While it's nice and hot."

"We'll have it on the table in two shakes of a goat's
tail," Jerusalem said. She bustled to the stove to turn the
burners on again while Nazareth refilled everyone's
coffee.

"It'll be your call as to how we handle this, Tom,"
Vernon suggested as the two of them moved to their
places. "Everyone takes these situations in their own way,
and your circumstances are different from most men's."

"*Jah*, there's that," Tom replied in a pensive tone. "And
to ease my own mind, I think I'll head to the barn after we
eat . . . give all the kids a call. If they haven't gotten their
letters yet, it's only right that they hear of their *mamm*'s
death from me first."

"A wise decision. Take all the time you need with that."
Vernon smiled at Nazareth and Jerusalem as they set out
platters of golden-brown French toast, ham, bacon, and a
big bowl of fried apples. "I'll do my best to keep these
ladies entertained."

"Puh!" Jerusalem teased. "You just want to be in the
kitchen while we put that brisket in the oven and think
toward the rest of our dinner."

"Will this involve cookies?" Vernon teased. "Until I've

sampled every last kind you've baked, I haven't done your handiwork justice."

Their laughter lightened the mood, and Nazareth looked up to find Tom gazing at her with gratitude in his eyes. She smiled back at him, and as they bowed in prayer over the food, she sensed that this difficult day would go much more smoothly because they were all together, bonded now by events that none of them had foreseen. What a difference time and friendship and God's presence among them had made.

"Mmmm . . ." Tom closed his eyes over the first huge bite of French toast he'd soaked in warm maple syrup. "Food for the body, and food for the soul. I'll make it through this day now, for sure and for certain."

Nazareth sighed happily. Wasn't it just the best thing, when her cooking made a difference in someone's life?

Vernon studied the assortment of cookies on the tray before him, enjoying the quandary of having too many choices—all of them good. "And what's in this one?" he asked as he picked up a dark chocolate cookie covered in a swirl of cocoa frosting.

Jerusalem chortled. "You tell *me* what it's made of. Gotta earn your keep in this kitchen, Bishop. We don't suffer slackers here while we're cookin'."

Had there ever been a more delightful, outspoken woman than Jerusalem Hooley? As he bit in, the rich flavors of cocoa and buttercream frosting covered his tongue, along with . . . "Is that a marshmallow in there?"

"You're *gut* at this game, Vernon," Nazareth said, not missing a beat as she peeled carrots at the sink. "Probably had a lot of experience at bein' a cookie tester, I'd guess."

"Tough job, but somebody's got to do it." Vernon sat back in his chair to savor the moist treat in his hand, as well as the joy of watching two women who worked as a seamless team. "How do you suppose folks here in town will react to Lettie's death? How have things been for Tom these past months after she left him?"

"We're the wrong ones to ask about that," Jerusalem replied in a thoughtful tone. "She'd been gone for several months before we came here from Pennsylvania, so we've only known Preacher Tom as a fella livin' alone."

"And he's done fairly well at it, all things considered," Nazareth added. "His girls come by to help with his laundry and cook things for him every now and again. I think it's been a blessing that he's had the Sweet Seasons Café close enough that he can eat a *gut* meal there most mornings, amongst friends."

"*Jah*, everyone in Willow Ridge looks after him." Jerusalem's brows knit together as she scrubbed potatoes. "Had to be a difficult situation for Tom, havin' Lettie up and leave him with an English fellow. The way I've heard it, she took a suitcase and met him out by the road, and they drove off."

Vernon winced. Lettie had obviously been seeing that other man before she ran off . . . had left a marriage and a home—and a faith that didn't fulfill her anymore, after many years of living with Tom and keeping her dissatisfaction to herself. He felt badly that his longtime friend had been dealing with Hiram Knepp's escalating arrogance at the same time. Yet Tom's ability to cope with his loss and to keep serving his district affirmed how well suited he was to becoming a bishop.

Vernon vowed to keep in touch, to visit Tom more often in the future. And didn't he also have another incentive to come to Willow Ridge? He didn't know nearly enough about Jerusalem, but he certainly wanted to. The widows of his district had been trying to capture his fancy with their baking and little gifts for years, but he'd had feelings for none of them.

He groaned with the tangy goodness of a lemon sandwich cookie filled with buttercream and apricot jam. "I was certain that chocolate marshmallow cookie was my favorite, but now I've changed my mind again! This is sheer torture, sampling all these new treats."

Jerusalem grinned at him, looking girlish in her red bandanna. "We're a couple of merciless, wicked temptresses, Nazareth and I. Might as well call us Delilah and Jezebel, ain't so?"

"I like your real names much better. Did your parents catch any criticism for giving you names that drew attention to you?"

Nazareth let out a short laugh. "*Jah*, the bishop mentioned it might be prideful—not keepin' with the Old Ways, to name us for places of the Bible."

"But by the time all ten of us came along, each called Calvary, Canaan, Judea or such," Jerusalem continued, "our names didn't draw any more attention to one of us than to the others. And while I know of five Mary Hooleys, nobody ever mistakes me for another gal named Jerusalem."

Vernon laughed loudly. "That's a fine way to look at it. God created each of us as a unique person, in His own image, so you ladies are yet another example of the Lord's diverse nature."

"We're no doubt a sign He's got a sense of humor, too," Jerusalem said with a firm nod of her head. "Always up to somethin', we are."

"Usually it's somethin' worthwhile," Nazareth chimed in as she placed the blue enamel roaster in the oven. "But every now and again we test people's patience. Mostly when we express opinions and make decisions that wives would probably let their husbands handle."

Vernon considered this as he covered the tray so the

cookies wouldn't dry out. "We who live without a spouse must get by as best we can," he said quietly. "Perhaps that's why God brought the four of us together at this particular time. He knew Tom would need our support when he heard the news that lawyer's letter contained . . . assistance from friends who have dealt with rumors and other people's criticism while we've sincerely tried to follow God's will for our singular lives."

Jerusalem turned, her hands clasped before her as her expression waxed pensive. "I like the way you think, Vernon," she said. "While the *Ordnung* is a *gut* guide for livin' our lives right, we each of us go through times when we answer to God alone . . . and our behavior won't always fit the rules. Or at least other folks won't believe it does."

He held her gaze, his heart beating strongly, steadily, as Jerusalem's words sank in. Here was a woman of amazing faith and intelligence, whose insights went far deeper than most men's. *It is indeed providential that you've met her. Make the most of it.*

Vernon blinked. While he often communicated with God, this particular thought had come to him out of the blue, in a voice that was clearly not his own. It was a message he knew better than to ignore—not that he wanted to.

"The plow blade is parked in the stable, you know, so what if I hitch Samson to it and we three could start clearing the lane?" he suggested. He looked out the kitchen window and smiled. "There! A couple of teams are already clearing the road. Probably other folks as eager to get out in the snow as we are."

He glanced out the back window then, but saw no sign of Tom coming from the dairy barn. "My Percheron loves nothing better than to be pulling a load, and he's young enough to need that sort of exercise every day."

"We're ready whenever you are," Nazareth replied. "Dinner can cook itself now, while we go out and play!"

What a joy it was to step outside into the bright sunshine, where a smooth, flawless blanket of diamonds covered the earth for as far as he could see. Cardinals called to each other from evergreens draped in frills of white. All the world seemed steeped in the season's peace, and Vernon stood still for a moment, taking it all in.

"Doesn't get any pertier than this," Jerusalem remarked as she stopped beside him. Her cheeks glowed with health, rosy from the cold weather, as she raised her face to the sunshine.

Vernon fought the urge to kiss her, startled at this flare of desire. He reminded himself that there was a time and a place for such things . . . and silently rejoiced that he wanted them again. "Are we still taking that sleigh ride later today?" he asked when Nazareth went ahead to the barn.

"Wouldn't miss it." Jerusalem met his eyes with an unwavering gaze.

"Too bad there's only one seat. No room for Tom and Nazareth to join us."

"*Jah*, I'm feelin' real bad about that. We'll just have to make do without them, ain't so?" she teased softly.

Vernon's laughter bounced back from the side of the barn as he hugged her sturdy shoulders. "You're a peach, Jerusalem."

"Would that be a pie, a cobbler, or a crisp?"

He paused to gaze into her deep brown eyes . . . eyes that missed nothing. "Just a peach, sweet and perfect and ripe, the way God alone can create them. And I can't wait for a taste."

She looked ready to cry, but then blinked away the mist. "Oh, Vernon . . . that's the nicest thing any fella's ever said to me."

"High time, too." He let out a long sigh and then cleared his throat purposefully. "Shall we get Samson hooked to that plow? If we loiter out here much longer, your sister will be doing all the work."

Jerusalem chuckled. "No, when she sees we're not comin' right in, she'll either fetch us—or she'll slip out the other door toward the dairy barn where Tom is. Nazareth's not one to go hitchin' up horses she's not familiar with, especially when they're the size of your Samson."

"He's a big boy," Vernon agreed as he slid the barn door on its track. "Spirited, but smart about when to run and when not to."

Jerusalem chuckled. "And wouldn't most of us be better off if we used the same kind of smarts?"

Yes, some of us do indeed want to gallop full speed ahead rather than taking things in their own good time.

They walked through the dim, musky barn past Tom's horses. Then Vernon chatted with Samson, stroking his muscled neck as the tall black Percheron acclimated himself to the two women. The sisters took turns saying admiring things to him, reaching out their palms so the gelding could nuzzle them.

"Ready to take on a big job, Samson?" Vernon asked as he slipped the harness tracings over the horse's head. "I've told these ladies what a fine, dependable fellow you are, so I know you'll rise to the challenge."

Samson nickered, stomping eagerly. Nazareth opened the door so Vernon could let the Percheron step outside into the area he and Tom had cleared earlier. The plow had a platform with wheels, where the driver stood. Behind that, two wooden beams with blades slanted in a vee would throw the snow to either side. When he had hitched the plow to the horse, Vernon stepped up onto the platform and pulled out of the stable. The ladies shut the door and then scrambled to sit sideways on each side of the plow, putting their legs up on the wooden beams. There was barely enough room for their backsides, but he knew better than to mention that.

"Something tells me this kind of ride was easier when you were kids," he teased.

"You're sayin' we're not kids now?" Jerusalem shot back.

"*Jah*, deep as this snow is," Nazareth piped up, "you'll be mighty glad for all our weight back here."

Vernon chuckled. "Let me know if you want to get off. I don't want anybody getting hurt," he said. "Let's *go*, Samson!"

The Percheron stepped proudly into the curve of the lane, where the snow was a foot deep—even taller where the wind had whipped it into peaked drifts. With steady strength, Samson slowly dragged the plow between the banks of higher snow that marked where the lane had been cleared before. Vernon relaxed, letting his fine horse do its job. He smiled at the chatter the sisters passed back and forth behind him. It felt good to be working outdoors on this sparkling day, and he was happy to be moving this snow so they could get out to the road—and so the tanker truck could come for Tom's milk.

They were about two-thirds of the way down the lane when Tom hollered from behind them. "Hey, wait for me! I'm supposed to be helpin' with this job."

"Whoa, Samson." Vernon turned to see Tom jogging to catch up to them. The platform wasn't wide enough for two men to stand on, so he wondered if he should step aside. Maybe Tom would feel better doing some physical work after making those difficult phone calls . . .

"Tom, my backside's tellin' me I've done enough horsin' around," Jerusalem said as she stood up in the cleared lane. "Probably room for you to stand here in the point of this plow while we sisters go shovel out the door-ways of the house."

Tom frowned. "I never intended for you girls to be doin' the heavy liftin' while I just ride around—"

"Preacher Tom!" a male voice called out.

"We've got our lane cleared, and this section of the blacktop, so we'll help with yours now," another fellow added.

The four of them looked toward the road, where two plows similar to Tom's were pulling up at the end of the lane. Each vehicle was being driven by a dark-haired young man in a stocking cap who was waving eagerly, standing closely behind a bonneted girl.

"Bram and Nate Kanagy! *Gut* mornin' to ya," Tom replied. "I see you've got your fiancées along to help."

"*Jah*, can't get them back to Cedar Creek yet, what with all this snow."

Vernon studied their young faces more closely. Women all looked alike with their hair and ears covered by close-fitting black bonnets. "Mary and Martha Coblentz! Happy New Year, girls—and congratulations are in order, too?"

"Bishop?" one of the Coblentz twins exclaimed, while her sister leaned forward to gawk at him. "What're *you* doing in Willow Ridge, Vernon?"

Vernon laughed, as amazed by this coincidental meeting as they were. "Even bishops must stay put when the snow closes the roads," he replied cheerfully. "Awfully nice of you to come over and help Tom with the plowing."

"*Jah*, you kids might as well come on in and warm up with us," Nazareth offered. "I was just ready to make a batch of cocoa—"

"And we've got lots of cookies to share while we hear your *gut* news about gettin' engaged," Jerusalem went on.

One of the Kanagy boys gaped. "Oh, my! I thought you were two other fellas—"

"Jerusalem and Nazareth?" his brother exclaimed. "You got snowed in at Preacher Tom's, too?"

"We were helpin' with a get-together for Tom and three bishops from hereabouts," Nazareth explained.

"And tendin' our goats, because Tom's been nice enough to keep them for us," Jerusalem went on without a moment's pause. "The time and the snowstorm got away from us while we were feedin' everyone yesterday."

Vernon watched the four young people's expressions, almost laughing out loud: they had their own ideas about four single—*old*—people being snowed in at Preacher Tom's. And while the polite thing would be to come inside for a visit, the two boys obviously had other ideas of how to spend this time with Mary and Martha. When he was their age, he'd felt the same way.

"We told our folks we'd be getting on home today," one of the girls began.

"On account of how we've been here since New Year's Eve," her sister finished. "Mamm and Dat are mighty excited about the farm Nate and Bram just bought, between here and Cedar Creek."

"And Dat's drawn up the plans for our house there, too!"

"*Jah*, you boys have been makin' a lot of hay over the holidays," Tom remarked.

"You've got that right," the taller of the two boys replied. Then he looked around. "Do you want us to come on down your lane with a plow? It would mean you'd have to turn that big Percheron around—"

"Oh, Samson's trained to back up with the best of them," Vernon replied. "But he'd rather use that same effort to go forward and finish his job. If you'd like to come on in once we've plowed to the road, though, we'd love to visit. Won't take us but another ten minutes or so."

"And if you've gotta get those girls home," Tom said, "we understand that, too. We've got no place to go, so we're in no hurry to get there."

The four young people laughed, looking politely relieved. "*Denki* for the invite," the younger Kanagy boy said, "but maybe we'd best catch up with you later. Mamm was figurin' on us for dinner before we head out with the twins."

"That's the way it should be then," Jerusalem replied. "Give your folks our best, boys."

"And girls, I look forward to hearing all about your plans when I'm back in Cedar Creek," Vernon added. "Drive safely on the snowy roads, now. I'd much rather preach at your wedding than at your funeral."

Chapter Six

As Tom sat at the table, he savored the succulent beef brisket and vegetables . . . the way Nazareth looked especially pretty in a dress of peacock blue, while her sister's dress brought to mind a butterscotch drop. He thanked God for their laughter, too, for it kept him from thinking too much about Lettie and the conversation he'd had with his son Pete.

"I can just imagine what Leah and Daniel Kanagy must be thinking," Jerusalem said with a chortle. "Their boys were mostly in a hurry to get home so they could tell about Nazareth and me bein' snowed in with you two fellas."

"And wearin' men's clothes, too," Nazareth added. "We gave those kids and their parents quite a lot to talk about!"

Vernon smashed another potato on his plate and then spooned gravy over it. "The romance between my Coblentz girls and your Kanagy boys must've blown up in a hurry. Last I knew, Mary and Martha weren't the least bit inclined to settle down."

"Ah, but then they met up with Bram and Nate." Tom's heart lightened. He took hope from the story that was

unfolding for the young people in their two districts.
"They're doin' well for themselves, too. Nate's trainin'
horses, while Bram plans to start his own auction barn on
that spread they bought a few days ago. *Gut* boys, both of
them," he remarked. "Your Martha and Mary'll be startin'
up a bed and breakfast once their *dat*'s got the house built
with a bunch of extra rooms for guests."

Vernon's eyes widened. "My word, I've fallen behind
even though I've only been away from home a day."

"I heard all about this a couple days ago, when Nate
and Bram said they were ready to take their instruction
for joinin' the church," Tom explained. "And comin' on
the heels of Hiram gettin' the boot, this was the best kind
of news for all of us. It's too bad the kids won't live in
either of our districts, but they're findin' God's way for
their lives. Keepin' the Plain family order instead of
jumpin' the fence."

"A blessing, for sure and for certain." Jerusalem started
the succotash around again. "And it sounds like the
Coblentz family's bein' just as supportive as Leah and
Dan, what with buildin' the kids a house."

"Amos Coblentz will construct a home—and barns for
the boys, most likely—like no other carpenter in these
parts," Vernon affirmed. "Sounds like those young
couples are off to a solid start. I look forward to helping
with Mary and Martha's church instruction. They're spirited little fillies . . . not unlike the ladies gracing this
table."

Tom had to smile at the way two dear faces took on
some color. Nobody who'd ever met the Hooley sisters
doubted for a minute that *spirited* could be their middle
name.

"Fillies kick up their heels a bit more when they've got
playmates," Jerusalem noted with a sparkle in her eye.

Nazareth paused over buttering her bread. When she

looked up at him, Tom wondered how his heart could experience joy and sorrow, regret and hope, all in the same moment. "We can all remember bein' the same age as those kids," she reflected. "Not knowin', at the time, what life might throw at us . . . or how our expectations might not turn out the way we'd planned. I, for one, never figured on remainin' a *maidel.* But it seems that's what God had in mind for me while my friends were gettin' married, back in the day."

Tom closed his eyes against a welling-up of emotion that was surely due to Lettie's passing. But hadn't Nazareth said it just right? Hadn't his marriage taken a turn he'd not foreseen? She was offering a conversational door for him to open, if he cared to. It wasn't his way to carry on about the heartache he'd endured this past year, now compounded by the information in that attorney's letter. He'd been taught by generations of Hostetler men that silent, unquestioning acceptance of God's will was the way to deal with his feelings when the going got rough.

But where had such stoic behavior gotten him?

"*Jah*, when I was courtin' Lettie, she was the prettiest girl I'd ever met. Never had eyes for another," he admitted quietly. "I've tried to make sense of the way she deserted me, but it was easier to just leave it be . . . to figure God had it in His plan all along, and that I was supposed to have enough faith to muddle through it. I suppose bein' whittled down to size by my son's sharp tongue this mornin' fits in there somewhere, too."

Vernon's bushy white eyebrows rose like question marks. "So you reached your kids on the phone, and it didn't go well?"

No way to wiggle out of it now . . . trust these friends to honor feelings you don't know how to handle. Tom cleared his throat. "I called Pete first, and he was chorin' so he answered the phone in his barn. And *jah*, he'd received the lawyer's letter and he was ready for me with quite an earful." He sighed wearily, pressing down the pain that rose with a big lump in his throat. "Pete told me I should've kept better track of Lettie—should've kept her in line—when she was spendin' so many nights away from home."

He paused, considering how to share these details with the trio watching him so closely now. Their gentle but inquisitive expressions encouraged him to continue. "Lettie did a lot of caretakin' for folks who couldn't get out, or who had terminal illnesses. Over the years I suppose she helped more than twenty families," he explained quietly. "That meant she often stayed overnight with a patient so's the spouse and the kids could get their rest."

"An honorable calling," Vernon replied. "Not many of us have the courage to serve those who are so gravely ill."

"You said a mouthful there, Vernon," Jerusalem remarked. "Myself, I wouldn't have the emotional strength for that sort of caretakin'."

Heartened by their support, Tom set down his fork and continued. "Pete was quick to point out that Lettie's new married name, Redd, belonged to the family she was helpin' when she took off. And he reminded me that his *mamm* had told everyone it was the husband who was dyin', and not the wife."

Nazareth's brow furrowed as she thought about this. "So . . . are you sayin' Lettie was really takin' care of Mr. Redd's wife, and that's when she was stayin' over at the house with Mr. Redd?"

Her question pierced him like an ice pick. But he had to answer it, to face the possibility that it was true. "Pete was also quick to point out that if Lettie was lyin' about who the patient was, she might've been goin' to Redd's house when there was no patient at all," he murmured. "That's where he blamed me for not makin' her more accountable—until I pointed out that she was bringin' home pay right up to the day she left."

"Which might point up a different situation altogether, if Mr. Redd was paying her so she could hide their relationship from you." Vernon closed his eyes for a moment, pondering. "Speculating about what happened is a waste of our time and emotional energy, however. We'll never know what went on at the Redd house, so there's no need to accuse Lettie of things she might not have done. I believe your son is speaking out of bitterness . . . the betrayal he still feels about his mother leaving the family."

Tom nodded, clinging to Vernon's quiet wisdom. "*Jah*, the two girls, Lavinia and Sarah, were embarrassed enough about their *mamm*'s sudden departure that they never talked much about it—at least not with me. Pete and Rudy said plenty, though," he added with a scowl. "While they insisted I should be concerned about their mother's soul, they were mostly insinuatin' that I was weak for not chasin' Lettie down and bringin' her back."

"But ya had no idea who she was with until ya opened that letter, did ya?" Jerusalem asked quietly. "Folks who leave that way have made their secret plans and covered their tracks, so's their families won't suspect anything."

"And what *gut* would I have done any of us, haulin' Lettie back here? If she was that unhappy with her Plain life . . . with me, why would she stay?" Tom let out a long sigh, glad to release the details that had burned inside him like hot coals since opening that letter—and since the gutwrenching day last spring when his wife had abandoned him. "Thanks for hearin' me out, and for understandin' my side of things," he said as he gazed at each of them. "I don't know how I'd be endurin' this situation if you *gut* friends weren't here with me."

When Nazareth grabbed his hand, Tom clasped it tightly. It was a balm to his soul that she didn't seem repelled by the dirty laundry he'd aired, just as it was a vote of confidence when Vernon placed a warm hand on his shoulder.

"It's yet another example of how God brought us all here for this moment, Tom," the bishop said. "And this snowstorm has given you the perfect opportunity for dealing with a difficult truth. I suggest you focus on your own needs and feelings, rather than allowing your son's accusations to hurt you further. Pete hasn't forgiven his mother for leaving, and that's a situation he must rectify if he's to follow our faith."

Tom listened closely, gratefully. "I'll have to work at forgivin' Pete for his attitude, as well."

"Everything to its own season," Vernon replied. "You've got plenty on your plate, dealing with Lettie's death."

As Tom released another long sigh, he felt some of his concerns leaving his heart and soul. Though this situation with Lettie and the kids was by no means behind him, he was gaining a valuable new perspective on it. "I appreciate your sayin' that, Vernon. Means a lot, comin' from you," he said with the best smile he could muster. "And now I'd like us to get back to this wonderful-*gut* dinner before it's cold."

His friends were gracious enough, kind enough, to understand that he'd dished up all the troubles he could handle at one sitting. After they had done the main meal justice and devoured the last of Jerusalem's apple crisp, he and Vernon retired to the front room while the sisters cleaned up the dishes.

Over a game of Chinese checkers, Tom allowed his dinner and his whirling thoughts to settle. Vernon focused on strategically moving his green marbles into the dimpled triangle where Tom's white marbles had been. It was another gift from God, the way he and this longtime friend could enjoy each other's company without having to fill every moment with chitchat . . . and their sociable silence allowed him to follow the cleanup noise coming from the kitchen.

"You and Jerusalem gonna take the sleigh out this afternoon?" he asked as he zigzagged a marble over three of Vernon's.

"That's my plan, unless you'd prefer us to chaperone you and Nazareth."

Tom let out a quick laugh. "Oh, we'll behave ourselves. Of course, now that Lettie's gone, Naz and I can be more than just friends," he mused aloud. "And while that's what both of us have been wishin' for, it opens up the possibility of me jumpin' in feet-first before the time's really right. Maybe that's not so *gut*, what with my standin' before the members this Sunday to become the new bishop. Word's gonna get around about her bein' snowed in here—"

"Under perfectly acceptable circumstances, with two other nosy adults present." With quick efficiency, Vernon jumped one of his marbles halfway across the board to position it at the very peak of his target triangle. Then he glanced up, his blue eyes sparkling. "If you'd like me to stay through Sunday, I'll have my preachers cover the Cedar Creek service. Installing the new bishop for your district certainly warrants my presence, after all."

"Would ya do that? It would mean the world to me," Tom replied earnestly. "It might keep the gossips from makin' Naz and me out to be . . . sinful, considerin' how folks'll just be findin' out that Lettie's passed. She's a *gut* woman and I don't wanna do that to her reputation."

"Consider it done, my friend."

Tom felt another rush of relief. Then he chuckled. "For a minute there, I thought you were doin' me a favor, Vernon, but it's really Jerusalem you're stayin' over for, ain't so?"

Vernon's gaze toward the door signaled that the ladies were coming out of the kitchen. "My aunts and my nephew will get along fine without me for another couple of days. A little vacation now and again is good for the soul." With that, he jumped his last green marble over five white ones and into the remaining empty dimple on Tom's side of the board, winning the game.

"Ya didn't answer my question," Tom teased under his breath.

"We'll both win if we play the game fair and square . . . and if we don't lose our marbles!" Vernon quipped. Then he stood up to flash his best blue-eyed smile at Jerusalem, who stood beside her sister, looking at the game board. "Ready for that sleigh ride? Whupping Tom at Chinese checkers has put me in the mood to *play*!"

Chapter Seven

"I could bring us out some cookies, or make cocoa—"

"I'm full as a tick after that fine dinner, Nazareth," Tom replied as he stood beside her. "But thanks for thinkin' of me, as you always do. How about if we just sit by the fire for a spell?"

Nazareth reveled in the way her hand felt so small and protected when Tom wrapped his larger, work-worn fingers around it and led her toward the love seat. Oh, but she'd imagined this scene a dozen times, and she reminded herself not to let her daydreams overrule common sense. She'd been in love with Tom Hostetler for months, but until he'd opened that lawyer's letter, she'd figured her feelings might be filed away for years. He had a lot more to consider right now than her girlish fantasies, however.

As they settled on the small upholstered sofa, Nazareth pointed toward the big picture window. "Off they go!" she murmured as Vernon's sleigh cut through the snow behind his big black horse.

"*Jah*, that's quite a nice rig Vernon's had restored." Tom's smile creased the lines around his eyes and mouth. "He's head over heels for your sister, ya know. Wasn't expectin' to do anything during this visit but catch up with me, yet here he is ready to court again. It's *gut* to see him so happy."

"Jerusalem will put him through some paces, but she's mighty glad he's stayin' over." Nazareth smoothed the folds of her apron, still relishing the way her hand felt in Tom's. "The two of us have been *maidels* for more than half our lives now, so we've got some . . . rethinkin' to do."

Tom nodded, gazing at the fire. His brown hair and beard were shot through with a few strands of silver and his face was chapped from working in the winter wind, but he radiated a kindness . . . a compassion that had drawn her to him from the beginning. "The four of us have that in common," he remarked quietly. "None of us figured on so many possibilities poppin' up these past couple days. But I believe it's a sign that God's not nearly finished with us yet, and that He doesn't want us to get too comfortable or complacent."

A short laugh escaped her. "Well, that letter you and your kids got sure turned a few fiesty horses out of the barn."

"*Jah*, and like that old sayin' goes, there's no gettin' those horses back in after the door's been left open, either." Tom focused intently on her. "While I had to leave a message for my girls and Rudy, tellin' them I was sorry they'd lost their *mamm*, Pete's response tells me I've not heard the last of their accusations about her leavin' the family. Guess that goes with the territory."

"Oh, Tom," Nazareth said with a sigh. "I'm sorry you're goin' through such difficulties all over again. Your kids have no idea what Lettie's leavin' has done to *you*. They're only seein' their own loss . . . and the way it must look to other folks."

"Lucky for me, my friends here in Willow Ridge understand what-all I can't do for myself. Can't tell ya how many meals I've eaten at the Sweet Seasons," he remarked.

"But I get a lot more than *gut* food there. Miriam and her girls, and the other fellas who eat there so often, have gotten me through the tough times. And now that you're sittin' here next to me, Naz, I can't begin to tell ya how . . . peaceful I feel. It's been a long, long time since I felt this happy."

When he grasped her hand between both of his, her heart fluttered like a hummingbird's wings. "It's not right for me to be glad that Lettie has passed on," she whispered. "And I hope that doesn't make me sound like a—"

He shushed her with a gentle finger on her lips. "Don't worry yourself over that, Naz. Ya didn't know Lettie, so why would ya feel any grief over her passin'?" he asked. "You're such a comfort that Lettie's death doesn't bother me near so much as it would've, had I been facin' it alone. And I can finally allow my feelin's for ya to take their natural course."

Oh, but she needed to hear that. For several moments they sat holding hands, treasuring this time together. The flames popped and crackled as logs settled in the wood stove . . . the aromas of brisket and baked vegetables lingered after dinner . . . the steady ticking of the mantel clock became the heartbeat of the entire house as a cozy warmth wrapped around them like an invisible afghan.

Did she dare say the words that tingled on her tongue? Nazareth took a deep breath. She'd lived too much of her life alone to spend even another day—another minute— with her emotions locked away like the linens she'd embroidered for her bride's chest when she was a girl. "I . . . I love ya, Tom."

"Oh, Naz, I—" He embraced her so suddenly, so tightly, she wasn't sure if her arms and hands found the best places. But she held on to his sturdy body as though she'd never let him go. "I've loved ya for so long, but there wasn't the right time to say it. Couldn't leave ya hangin' while I was unable to marry ya, or——"

"We're not past that part yet," she murmured as her head found his shoulder. "Our friends understand that we have feelin's for each other, but you'll still need to be proper about assumin' your duties as bishop."

"*Jah*, now more than ever I have to rise above the low road Hiram took these past several months. Jeremiah, Enos, and Vernon'll advise me about takin' on my new responsibilities," he remarked quietly. "And it's probably best if I follow their guidance, far as how I behave with you, too. If they say you and Jerusalem should be bunkin' elsewhere, that's how it'll have to be."

"We understand that, Tom. We'll do everything ya need us to."

He hugged her close again, sighing as he nuzzled her temple. "Right now, though, it's just you and me, Naz. My heart's hammerin' and my thoughts are whirlin', and I don't wanna do the wrong thing by——"

Nazareth placed her hand alongside his dear face and kissed him on the lips.

Tom sucked in his breath.

She returned his startled gaze. Where on Earth had she gotten such nerve? Wasn't the man supposed to do those things first? Would Tom think she was a loose woman, pushing for physical affection when they'd just agreed that he had to be above moral reproach?

A smile eased over Tom's face. "Well, now. That cuts right to the point, ain't so?" he whispered. "Less talk, more action."

"I couldn't wait," Nazareth whispered. "Couldn't resist."

He pressed his forehead to hers. "Oh, but you've made me feel like a man again, Naz," he murmured. "Maybe . . . maybe ya ought to kiss me again, to be sure I understood your meanin' that first time."

A giggle escaped her as she wrapped her arms around his neck. Tom's lips sought hers, tentative and sweet, before he settled in for an unhurried exploration of her mouth. Nazareth followed his lead, wondering if she would pass out of this world from sheer delight. Years of lonely resignation to her fate as a *maidel* floated away and she was a young girl again, kissing a beau—except this felt so much better. She trusted Tom. Had none of those girlish doubts about his intentions or whether she dared to hope his feelings for her would last beyond this kiss, this moment.

"Oh, Naz." He tucked her head against his shoulder. "I've been waitin' a long time for that. It was even better than I believed it would be."

Her heart thrummed with quiet joy. "*Jah*, it was, Tom."

He gazed at her with eyes as dark and warm as melted chocolate. "Be patient while things unfold these next weeks . . . maybe months," he whispered. "I promise ya, we'll be gettin' back to this lovey-dovey stuff, because it'll bring us a whole new life—better than what came before."

Nazareth flushed. "It's not like I've had much of that, ya know."

"You'll get used to it," he teased. "You're a natural, at bein' a bishop's wife and at bein' my woman, too, Naz. Can ya hang on for me, til the time's right?"

A bishop's wife . . . my woman, too. Oh, but her soul sang as she got warm all over. "It's not like other fellas are bangin' my door down," she said with a laugh.

"Their loss. Lucky for me I spotted ya even though I was lookin' down too much, feelin' the weight of Lettie's leavin' as somethin' I might've brought on."

"Put that behind ya now. I can't understand why any woman would forsake ya, Tom," she replied.

He kissed her again. Then, with a sigh, he glanced at

the clock. "Got some cows in the barn that'll be bawlin' soon, wonderin' where I am. The milkin' sorta sets my schedule—"

"And I want to help with it. Might come a time when ya get called away, a bishop seein' to a member's concerns, and I'll need to see to your chores. Best if the cows get used to me bein' around them, too."

Tom's eyes widened with gratitude. "You're like a miracle come into my life on the coattails of Christmas. Bless ya, Naz."

"Bless ya right back, Tom," she whispered. "I hope to make your life a wonderful-*gut* place every single day, from here on out."

Chapter Eight

"What a glorious day! The other three seasons are fine, but only a snowy winter's afternoon shines this way," Vernon proclaimed. "Geddap, Samson! Let's show this special lady a fine time."

As the sleigh bells jingled to the rhythm of the horse's trot, Jerusalem couldn't quit grinning. The years she'd lived as a *maidel* with her sister, resigned to spending her days in the schoolhouse or with her women friends, faded away. Hiram Knepp's dismissal of her feelings blew off with the *whoosh* of the wind as they pulled past the corner of Tom's stable. For sure and for certain, Vernon Gingerich knew how to make a woman feel special.

Was this bishop as wonderful as he seemed? Was he especially attracted to *her*, or did he enjoy every woman he met? As his huge black Percheron headed across the open pasture, Jerusalem warned herself not to lose her common sense or her heart, for the higher her pie-in-the-sky hopes rose, the farther they might fall.

"Oh, but this is a sight," she murmured, gesturing at the picture-postcard panorama. From this hilltop, they could see miles of glistening whiteness in every direction, punctuated by farmsteads with deep red barns, tall white homes, and their windbreaks of evergreens. Clusters of silos and sheds dotted the distant landscape, with a backdrop of blue sky so brilliant it made her squint. "Haven't taken in such a perty view in a sleigh for more years than I care to count. *Denki* for this ride, Vernon."

"It's my pleasure, dear heart. Anything that makes your eyes shine is worth my time." He gave the horse its head and settled back in the dark red upholstered seat. "This sleigh belonged to my favorite uncle. I didn't know it then, but when I had it refurbished, God must have been planning this outing with you. While I look for any excuse to drive it, occasions like this are meant to be shared, don't you think?"

Truth be told, Jerusalem *couldn't* think. *Dear heart*, he'd called her . . . "You've got that right, Vernon. And it gives Tom and my sister a chance to talk for a while, too," she replied. "My word, but he's had a lot dumped in his lap this past week, what with Hiram gettin' the boot and Lettie's passin'."

"Tom's an exceptional soul. He'll handle whatever life brings his way, and Nazareth's company will be a timely blessing, as well." When Vernon smiled, the lines around his blue eyes crinkled merrily. He scooted closer to her. "But it's *you* I want to hear about, Jerusalem. Dozens of fine women have tried to catch my eye since my Dorothea died six years ago, but the moment I saw you it was spontaneous combustion. I sincerely hope you feel that same sort of . . . heat."

This man's words were warming her, all right. Jerusalem glanced away from his earnest expression, telling herself to breathe—and not to fan her face with her hand. Was Vernon full of himself? Or was he cutting to the chase?

"Think I told ya we sisters came to Missouri from Lancaster County, with nephews lookin' to start fresh where land was affordable. On New Year's Day, Ben married Miriam—the gal who owns the Sweet Seasons Café—and the younger two, Luke and Ira, have been buildin' a gristmill on the riverbank." She met his eyes again. "Nazareth and I like Willow Ridge so much we've not even considered going back East, even though our nephews would get along fine without us."

"Aunts are special people," Vernon replied. "My aunts, Nettie and Florence, came to live with me after their homes washed away in the flood of Ninety-three, along with Florence's son, Abner. I shudder to think how alone I would've been after my wife passed, without their company. We weren't able to have children, you see."

"Ah. That makes it harder when ya get . . . to a certain age."

"Thank you for not calling me *old*," he teased, elbowing her. "Right now I feel about twenty, no matter if my crow's-feet and white hair indicate otherwise."

"Hah! I wouldn't be twenty again," Jerusalem countered. "Too many important life decisions need to be made at that age, when ya don't know spit about anything. And it wasn't like the fellas were poundin' my door down back then."

She nipped her lip. Why had she revealed the fact that no one had been interested in her when she was of courting age?

"Are they now? Pounding your door down, that is?"

Jerusalem blinked and then swatted his arm playfully. "And what if they are? Or what if I'm a nag, or too set in my ways to change? Truth be told, I'm not sure I want to be trainin' a fella to my way of thinkin' at this stage of the game."

Vernon's laughter rang around them, sounding as merry as the sleigh bells. "Maybe I'm just as comfortable in my rut as you are, my dear—not eager to upset my routine. But you know what they say about a rut. If you remain there, entrenching yourself, it eventually becomes your grave."

When he focused on her, unwavering and intense, Jerusalem couldn't look away. "Well," she murmured, "I for one don't intend to die anytime soon."

"If you do, I'll be a sorry . . . lonely man, Jerusalem."

Her mouth dropped open. How did this eloquent fellow keep answering her objections without a moment's hesitation? "I . . . I don't know what to say. And that hardly ever happens—just ask the folks who know me."

Chuckling, Vernon tugged on the reins. When the sleigh stopped, they sat in a hollow of the field, shielded by a row of spruce trees that whispered in the wind. Not a house was in sight. "Maybe you don't need words," he whispered. "Maybe you'd rather say it this way."

When his lips gently found hers, Jerusalem nearly fainted. Vernon eased away to look into her eyes, and then kissed her again with a sweet thoroughness that made her soul sing. She recalled a few neighbor boys sneaking kisses back in the day, but *nothing* had ever made her feel so vibrant . . . so desirable. *So needy*.

With a gasp she backed away. "This feels sinfully delicious. Maybe we shouldn't be—"

"Nonsense," he murmured, cupping her face in his gloved hand. "God created men and women to be together, to please each other and to bless His name by bearing good fruit—whether it be by teaching young scholars or shepherding a flock of church members. Whatever abilities we develop from the gifts He's given us are an offering to Him. Didn't Jesus command us to love one another, after all?"

There was no getting around that one, was there? "*Jah*, that He did. But when things get outta hand—"

"I think we've got things well in hand, Jerusalem." Vernon lightly placed his other palm on her cheek, framing her face as he gazed at her with a tenderness she'd never known. "And while it may be too soon to call this *love*, I hope you'll at least give me the chance to explore that possibility. Life can be short, or life can be long. Either way, it's best when shared with someone who matters. And you *matter* to me, Jerusalem."

Again her mouth dropped open. She'd never had a man render her speechless . . . and it felt better than she had expected. After all, if she insisted on talking, Vernon wouldn't have as much chance to kiss her again, the way he was now. Slowly, mesmerizing her with his mouth, he coaxed her closer . . . entreated her to open her heart and soul to him. Jerusalem let her head fall back against his arm. What would it be like to feel this shimmery, this giddy, every day of her life—every time this man kissed her?

It was too soon to be thinking that way. But what if it might be a long-lost dream about to come true, if she gave it half a chance?

Once again Jerusalem eased her lips from Vernon's, and then she scooted a few inches away from him. "Maybe we'd ought to get on with our ride," she suggested, and then she laughed. "That sounded like an old schoolteacher talkin', ain't so? If you're thinkin' to get serious about me, Vernon, you'll have to deal with my tendency to call things like I see them, and then to . . . suggest improvements."

Vernon clapped the reins lightly on the horse's back. "You can take the teacher away from her class, but you can't take the *class* away from the teacher," he teased as the sleigh began gliding across the snow again. "I knew from the moment we met that you'd be no man's doormat,

Jerusalem. And while I, as a bishop, believe wives should submit to their husbands, I also know that when a husband makes all the decisions—has all the power—a marriage can become badly out of balance."

Well, that sounds reasonable enough. Jerusalem focused on the exquisite beauty of the landscape and the way the black Percheron's gait and strength were making this ride so wonderfully smooth. Better to listen rather than to talk sometimes, as men tended to reveal their true selves when she didn't reply to every little thing . . . allowed them to fill in the blanks of their conversation.

"My Dorothea was a quiet woman, but she had ways of making her wishes known," Vernon continued. "Because we had no children, we were especially close. I adored making her laugh . . . making every day a blessing for her, the way she did for me. I miss doing that," he reflected quietly. "I miss sharing my innermost thoughts as much as I miss sharing . . . my bed."

Jerusalem sat up straighter, her nerves a-jangle. Vernon's voice was mellow and clear, riding the highs and lows of his emotions, which suggested that he was probably a compelling speaker on a Sunday morning. But this talk of sharing a bed . . . *my word, how will I ever be comfortable taking off my clothes for a man, at my age?*

Vernon gazed at her until she figured she'd better look his way.

"Please don't think I'll pressure you into having sex, Jerusalem," he said without blinking an eye. "But it's a pleasure I miss. Something I would dearly love to share with you someday—in the proper circumstances, of course."

Was he suggesting marriage or was he making a very bold pass? Jerusalem's thoughts raced. She'd had such a ready answer for his teasing remarks over the Scrabble board, but being out here alone with him, talking about physical relations . . . private pleasures she knew nothing about while he'd taken them for granted most of his life . . .

"You're very quiet, Jerusalem."

She cleared her throat primly. "I don't make a habit of expressing opinions on topics I know . . . nothing about."

Vernon's eyes widened as he realized what she was saying. "I've offended you," he whispered. "You and I have so many things in common that, well—I've been crass and thoughtless, and I beg your forgiveness, Jerusalem. I'm *sorry*."

She heard true contrition in his voice. A man's admission that he'd been thoughtless came about as often as snow in July, so Vernon Gingerich was indeed a rare fellow. "Apology accepted. You're easy to forgive."

He drove in silence for a few moments, which made Jerusalem fear she'd turned his crank the wrong direction. But then, if it bothered him that she'd lived as an honorable woman, it was better to know that now than later.

"Let me say this," he ventured in his low, steady voice. "If it's a matter of inexperience making you nervous, we can remedy that. If the idea of having sex repels you, or you have no interest in trying it, that's a different story."

Jerusalem sank her fingers into the sleigh's upholstered seat, mostly to get a grip on how she should answer that. Truth be told, having a man want her in that way was making her thrum all over, even if she feared doing something stupid when the time came to try what he was suggesting. "This old dog still has a few tricks in her," she murmured. "Just a matter of how the trainer approaches her and . . . what sort of enticement and reward he offers, once he's got her attention."

For a moment there was only the jingle of the sleigh bells and the *whish* of the sleigh's runners cutting through the snow. Then Vernon's chuckle got louder and the seat vibrated with his mirth.

He slipped his arm around her shoulders. "What a gem you are, Jerusalem. Absolutely priceless. If—*when*—the time comes for your training, I'll be sure to have plenty of treats on hand. Lavish praise works well, too. And repetition."

"Do it again and again until you do it correctly," Jerusalem agreed, fighting a smile. "A school teacher's way to instill knowledge of any topic, ain't so?"

"You're absolutely right, Jerusalem."

She laughed out loud, no longer nervous. "Commit that to memory, Vernon. Ya just said four of the most important words in the English language."

"You're absolutely *right*, Jerusalem!" he proclaimed. When a fellow in the yard they were passing waved at them, they returned the greeting. "There! I've even got a witness."

"*Jah*, that's Henry Zook, the storekeeper. We just gave him somethin' real interesting to report to his wife, Lydia, ain't so?"

As Vernon directed his horse to turn down the next road, Jerusalem felt light and playful. Truth be told, the two of them had covered some important topics . . . and in her *maidel*'s heart, she was pleased—flattered—that Vernon was interested in her as a woman. She'd given up on the dream of becoming a wife, yet that subject shimmered around them like the tiny snowflakes that sparkled in the wind. When the Percheron started down Tom's long lane, two bundled-up figures coming from the dairy barn waved at them.

"See there? We managed to miss the afternoon milking," Vernon teased. He pulled the sleigh to a halt several yards from the house. "What would you say to going home with me, Jerusalem? I'm staying to help Tom with the Sunday service and the Member's Meeting, but I would dearly love your company for the ride back to Cedar Creek . . . and so you could meet my family."

Too soon! her thoughts cried out. And yet, hadn't they been working their way around to this subject all along? Wasn't a visit to his home a logical step in a relationship that had blown them along like a winter wind? "I—I'll certainly consider that, Vernon," she replied. "And you'll be meetin' up with my nephews while you're here, no doubt."

"I'd love to. I passed the mill on my way into town, and I sense your nephews have some interesting things to tell about their new business," he said. His blue eyes sparkled when he gazed into hers. "I won't kiss you right now, because Tom and Nazareth are watching, but when the next opportunity presents itself . . ."

Jerusalem giggled. "I suspect we'll get pretty *gut* at makin' opportunities."

Chapter Nine

When she'd pulled on her flannel nightgown, Nazareth sat on the edge of the double bed beside Jerusalem to brush out her hair. All their lives they had shared a room, and this nightly ritual brought their busy days to a satisfying close before they slipped between the sheets to sleep. Knowing that their voices might carry to where Tom and Vernon still sat chatting downstairs, she leaned close to her sister. "So did ya have a *gut* time on that sleigh ride? Couldn't tell if your cheeks were rosy from the cold or from spoonin' with Vernon."

"Puh! From what I could tell, you and Tom did your share of spoonin', too, Sister," Jerusalem teased as she let her hair spill down over her shoulder. "It's a wonder ya didn't get dinner all over your dress for gawkin' at him instead of payin' attention to your food."

Nazareth chuckled. *Years* had passed since either of them had experienced such romantic opportunities with a man, so she wasn't surprised that her older sister had changed the subject a wee bit. "And what if we did? It's not like Tom and I met just yesterday—or the day before—after all."

Jerusalem raised an eyebrow as she pulled the brush

through her hip-length hair. "Are ya sayin' I'm jumpin' the gun with Vernon? He's the one who started makin' flirty noises the moment he came in the door."

"Not for me to judge," Nazareth replied quietly. It was difficult to keep a schoolgirl grin off her face, recalling her afternoon on the love seat with Tom. "I'm glad to see ya lookin' so happy, is all. Vernon's a mighty nice fella and he seems sincere about his feelin's for ya. Not at all the sort of man Hiram Knepp is."

"Ya got that right," Jerusalem replied with a short laugh. "Truth be told, I can't recall ever havin' such a nice time with any of the fellas we knew as young girls. Maybe this sort of thing gets easier, once ya give up the assumption you'll be a wife all your life."

"*Jah*, there's that." As she drew the brush rhythmically through her hair, Nazareth pondered her options. Part of her wanted to share the exciting highlights of this fine day, yet she also wanted to savor the sweet, private moments she and Tom had shared . . .

"I'm in a bit of a tangle, though," Jerusalem continued. "Of all things, Vernon has asked me to ride back to Cedar Creek with him. Wants me to see his place and meet the two aunts and the nephew who live with him."

"Oh, my! That's a big step."

"Maybe more of a step than these short old legs can make."

Nazareth playfully whacked her sister's flannel-covered arm with her hairbrush. "Since when are ya admittin' to bein' old, Sister? I'd guess Vernon's got ya beat by eight or ten years, but he's prancin' like a stallion who's gotten wind of a mare."

"*Jah*, the old *gray* mare!" Jerusalem protested playfully. Then her expression waxed more serious. "But what if those aunts are set in their way of runnin' things at his place? Or what if he's really just lookin' for somebody to take care of them? And what if his nephew wants no part of havin' another biddy hen cluckin' around the—"

"Since when have ya worried over how other folks'll feel about ya, Sister?"

"Shhh! He'll hear us!" Jerusalem whispered as she pointed toward the floor with her brush.

Nazareth's hand flew to her mouth, but she was ready to laugh. If Jerusalem had such a case of the jitters, it could only mean she was more backside-over-teakettle about the white-haired bishop than she cared to admit. Or was her sister concerned about something else? Something Nazareth had pondered for a while now. "Maybe you're just nervous about sharin' a room with somebody besides me, ain't so? I—I've imagined what it might be like, havin' a man for a roommate . . . but maybe it's time we both found out how that works."

Jerusalem's jaw dropped. "You're gonna start sleepin' with Tom?"

"*No!* I—"

"Shhh!" Jerusalem pressed her finger to Nazareth's lips and leaned closer. "Can't let those fellas get wind that we're talkin' about them, or there'll be no end to the mischief they'll make."

Nazareth swatted her sister's hand away. "Why do ya think that? No doubt in my mind Tom's got the best of intentions, because—well, we talked about that today while you were gone. And . . . and it's only a matter of time before you're gonna have to get yourself a different room." She widened her eyes playfully. "If ya think folks'll talk about how the two of us have been stayin' here after this snowstorm, think what they'll say if you're still sleepin' with me after Tom and I get hitched."

"Nazareth Hooley! Talkin' like that'll lead ya straight to the Devil's—"

"Shhh!" Clapping her hand over Jerusalem's lips,

Nazareth had to hold in her laughter. "I'm teasin' ya, silly goose. But it's gonna happen someday, Sister. And I'm just tickled to pieces about it, even if I'm scared about makin' such a big change at this point of my life."

"*Jah*, I'm with ya there." Jerusalem let out a long breath. "Vernon and I talked about . . . sex today."

"*Ach*, and how did *that* go?" Nazareth's pulse shot up. While she and Tom had only tried kissing, he would expect more intimate relations after he married her . . .

"Well, it seems that's another change comin' my way, if I go along with his wild, romantic plans. Truth be told, I nearly jumped out of the sleigh when he started sayin' how he'd teach me to . . ." Jerusalem cleared her throat nervously. "After all, you and I turn our backs real modest-like when we're puttin' on our clothes and night-gowns. I don't think Vernon'll go along with that."

"Hmmm . . . and if ya move to Cedar Creek, it's not like the two of us can help each other with our jitters, or—"

"Puh! It'd be like the blind leadin' the blind, for all you and I know about bein' with a man!"

Nazareth gripped her hairbrush. She'd imagined this part of being married to Tom, but her sister was right about their lack of knowledge. Sometimes mothers advised their daughters about sexual matters before they became brides, but Mamma was long gone . . . and she'd had no occasion to discuss marital relations with them when they were young. "I'm thinkin' most fellas have eyes that see in the dark. Or they just use their hands to—"

"Something tells me Vernon's gonna have the lamp on. Now *there's* a scary thought!"

Nazareth giggled out loud and then clamped her mouth shut. The bed shook with her mirth.

"It's not all that funny, little sister," Jerusalem warned. "Sounds like you'll be facin' the same situation. And at our age, some of those body parts don't work the way they used to, let alone lookin'—"

"Which explains why Hiram kept marryin' younger women as he went along." Nazareth sat straighter, looking her sister in the eye. "But thank the *gut* Lord we're not dealin' with the likes of Hiram anymore, so why not set aside this talk that's gonna keep us awake all night? For all we know, we're makin' mountains out of molehills."

Jerusalem looked down at the chest beneath her flannel nightgown, shaking her head. "Mountains . . . molehills," she murmured. "Whatever size Vernon'll consider these breasts, they're not used to anybody payin' them any attention. He looks at them when he thinks I'm not watchin', and I . . . I just don't know what to make of it all."

As Nazareth heard the concern in her sister's voice, she tried to think of something to get Jerusalem's mind away from her worrisome thoughts. "Could be, if Vernon wants ya to meet his family, it's time to introduce him to our three nephews. You can bet Bennie, Luke, and Ira will cut him down to size real quick if he's actin' too big for his britches."

Jerusalem's eyes widened and she gave Nazareth a quick hug. "Oh, but that's a fine idea, Sister!" she replied. "And havin' them all over for supper will be a *gut* way to pass an evening between now and Tom's installation at church on Sunday. That way, none of the neighbors'll accuse us of spendin' all this time with two fellas, livin' in sin with only our pajamas on."

Once again Nazareth had to cover her mouth to keep from laughing aloud at the imagery Jerusalem's ideas inspired. "A pajama party! Now *there's* a way to get better acquainted with Tom and Vernon!"

Jerusalem swatted her and then put out the bedside lamp. "You're just full of fine ideas tonight, Sister. Better pray real hard about that."

"Made ya laugh, though, didn't I?"

Jerusalem's quiet chuckle reverberated in the darkness as they settled into the bed. "*Jah*, ya did. And I love ya for it, too, Nazzie."

Nazareth smiled as she turned onto her side to face the wall. *Ya blessed us with a lot of new ideas today, Lord, and we thank Ya for that. Give us the grace and courage to accept Your gifts and make the best of every one of them. Especially the kisses.*

Chapter Ten

Tom stepped into the kitchen and inhaled the warm, wonderful aromas of breakfast . . . sausage and freshly percolated coffee and something sweet and chocolate, he was guessing. "I'm gettin' spoiled, Vernon," he remarked as they stomped the snow from their boots in the mudroom. "Most days I come in from the milking to an empty house that smells like burnt toast. Havin' the girls here has been a real treat."

"I sometimes forget how blessed I am that Aunt Nettie's a willing cook and Aunt Florence can keep a conversation going even when our lives change little from one day to the next." The bishop removed his stocking cap and smoothed his snowy-white hair. "And of course Abner's always on hand to help with the cattle chores, too. Living alone would be a real challenge for me, as I'm sure it's been for you, my friend. But this, too, shall pass."

"Lookin' forward to Naz bein' here full-time," Tom said as he tossed his coat onto the nearest peg by the door. "The trick will be in the timing, so's other folks won't think I'm jumpin' the gun . . . or that I've been hidin' my relations with her."

"It'll all work out, Tom. And nobody's happier for you than I am."

When Vernon clapped him on the back, it was like a benediction, a blessing on the marriage Tom longed for now. But that was putting the cart before the horse, as Nazareth deserved to be courted and given some say about how she wanted the house . . . how she wanted *him*. That thought put a smile on his face as he and Vernon stepped into the kitchen in their stocking feet, shoes in hand.

"And did the cows cooperate with ya this morning?" Jerusalem asked as she turned a loaf of dark, sweet-smelling bread out of its pan.

"Soon as these eggs cook, we'll be ready to eat." Nazareth's smile radiated with contentment. "Might be a *gut* day to venture over to Zook's Market for a few groceries. We've run you low these last couple of days."

"*Jah*, we can do that," Tom replied as he took his place at the table. The eggs were crackling in the skillet and the platter of bread Jerusalem set beside him looked like chocolate with chunks of fruit and nuts. "We can give Vernon a tour of Willow Ridge, if he's up for that much excitement."

"And we were thinking to invite the nephews over some night soon—along with Ben and Miriam, if they're not out collectin' wedding gifts," Jerusalem said.

Tom caught the look that passed between her and Vernon and smiled to himself. Introducing this fellow from Cedar Creek to her family might be the first step toward the altar. "Maybe spendin' some time with the bishop will convince Luke and Ira to join the church, ain't so?"

"We live in hope of that!" Nazareth replied with a shake of her head. "Never seen such holdouts. Most fellas of twenty-eight and thirty would have jumped the fence or committed by now, but our nephews have never followed the path anybody else laid out for them."

"Independent thinking seems to run in the Hooley family," Vernon teased as they all sat down. After they'd bowed in silence for a moment, he reached for the plate of sausage patties in front of him. "With fellows like that, I usually see how the conversation's going before I challenge them about church membership. I suppose I should be more insistent, more direct with folks who drag their feet about declaring their faith. But there's no sense in driving your nephews away by hammering them with Old Order expectations, either. I imagine they've gotten plenty of that from their family."

"You're absolutely *right*, Vernon," Jerusalem said with a teasing wag of her finger.

When Vernon laughed out loud, at a joke they had obviously shared before, Tom laughed, too. It was wonderful to see two of his favorite people having such a good time together. While Tom hadn't invited the bishop to Willow Ridge specifically to get acquainted with Jerusalem Hooley, the match had been in the back of his mind . . . mostly because he sensed Nazareth would feel much freer to fall in love with him if her sister had some romance in her life, as well.

They chatted over breakfast and decided their trip into town should wait until afternoon, when the sun would be warmer. Tom chuckled because it was only six in the morning and they'd already done half a day's work before the market would even open. While the sisters redded up the kitchen, he put more logs on the fire and spent some time carving a figure of Joseph for the Nativity set he'd been working on. Vernon was setting up the Scrabble board . . . probably setting up Jerusalem, too, the way his eyes were twinkling.

"If ya don't mind, I think I'd enjoy sittin' over by the

fire with Naz," Tom said as she came out of the kitchen. "You two can go at it over the game board."

"That sounds nice," Nazareth replied, and as she slipped her hand into his, Tom's heart swelled. "We can figure out our list for the store."

"Puh! Like either one of ya has shoppin' on your mind." Jerusalem took the chair across the table from Vernon. "Ya just can't stand the heat of this game when the bishop and I start layin' down seven-letter words."

"You're absolutely right, Jerusalem," Vernon replied, and their chuckling started up again.

As Tom sank into the love seat, it felt so perfect to stretch his legs over the coffee table . . . to let Nazareth rest her head on his chest as he slipped his arm around her. He closed his eyes in a silent prayer of thanksgiving for such simple pleasures . . . cozy moments in a home that felt lived-in again and smelled heavenly from breakfast. The fire popped and crackled as he and Nazareth talked, vaguely aware that at the other end of the room, Vernon and Jerusalem sparred gleefully over their game. Nazareth smelled like the sausage she'd been frying, and Tom was trying to make an opportunity to kiss her—

A door banged in the kitchen.

"My *gut*ness, would you look at all these cookies!"

"Huh! I can't think our *dat*'s been doin' all this bakin' or cleanin', so who do you suppose—"

"Dat! What are ya doin' with that—that *woman*?"

Tom's mouth went dry. As Nazareth sprang away from him on the love seat, he searched frantically for the right words to stop the storm that was about to cut loose. "Sarah, Lavinia," he began in a strained voice. "Nice of ya to come over and—"

"*Nice* is not my word for it," younger Lavinia retorted as she stalked toward them.

"Here we came over to see how you were doing after

you got that letter about Mamm," Sarah retorted. "And we find you hanging all over this total stranger, as though—"

"As though you've been seeing her for quite some time now!" Lavinia finished. His daughters stood together, crossing their arms exactly the way their mother used to do.

Tom felt his face go six shades of red as he stood up. His girls resembled Lettie to the point that his ex-wife might as well be standing alongside them, joining in their accusations.

"This is Nazareth Hooley," he stammered. "She and her sister came over to—"

"*Jah*, we can see that!"

"And here Sarah and I have been coming all this way each week to cook and keep up with your laundry—"

"Feeling bad about you being here all alone—"

Something inside him snapped: this insolence toward Nazareth was something he refused to tolerate. "Well, you two can stop feelin' sorry now—"

"*Jah*, as of this minute I don't feel much of anything but angry, Dat!"

"And shocked!" Sarah spat. "And ashamed—"

"Ladies, I'm Vernon Gingerich, from Cedar Creek," the bishop said in a quiet but purposeful voice. He came to stand beside Tom while Jerusalem joined her sister. "We had a meeting of the bishops from nearby districts here, and these two sisters, Jerusalem and Nazareth Hooley, made our meals for us. When the snow closed all the roads— "

"Jerusalem? Nazareth?" Lavinia repeated in a voice that rose even higher than her eyebrows. "Those are two made-up names if I ever heard any!"

"*Jah*," Sarah chimed in. "These two—*ladies*—do they keep ya company all the time, Dat? Sounds like what Hiram used to—"

"That's enough. From the both of ya." As Tom took

each of his girls by the shoulder, it required all of his strength not to shake some sense into them. "Your *mamm* and I taught ya to respect your elders, and I'll not have ya lippin' off to the bishop that way. Understand me?"

Sarah and Lavinia shut their mouths in surprise, but it was clear they weren't finished speaking their minds. They shrugged out of his grasp.

"And I'll thank you to take control of your loose talk, too." Vernon gazed sternly at the two younger women, allowing a few moments of silence for his words to sink in. "Nothing sinful or contrary to God's law has gone on here, and you needn't drag these *ladies'* reputations through the gutter simply because your own hearts and minds seem to be there right now. They are indeed ladies in the finest sense of the word."

When had Tom ever felt more embarrassed? His heart ached for Nazareth and her sister even as he wished his daughters hadn't walked in to find him in such a . . . compromising position. But there was nothing to do now except clarify what his daughters had seen—not that he figured they'd keep this juicy information to themselves once they got home.

"As a matter of fact, those other bishops and I have determined that your *dat* should be the next bishop of Willow Ridge," Vernon went on. His voice remained low and deceptively calm as he drove his point home. "You and your brothers are welcome to join us on Sunday as your father takes on his additional responsibilities."

Lavinia, always quicker with a retort, rolled her eyes. "*Jah*, Dat'll be *responsible*, all right."

"Rudy and Pete will see to that when we tell them what we walked in on," Sarah said with a nod.

Nazareth clasped her hands in front of her and stepped

closer. "You—you girls are welcome to join us for some coffee in the kitchen so we can talk about these misunderstandings—"

"Oh, we understand, all right," Lavinia said. "Our *mamm*'s barely dead and buried and here *you* are. Thanks, but I'll be heading home all the same."

"*Jah*, seeing is believing," her sister agreed as they both turned toward the kitchen to go.

"And do you recall how our Lord Jesus reminded Doubting Thomas that it was more blessed to believe without having to see?" Vernon asked quietly. "It would seem a more proper attitude to at least give your father the benefit of the doubt. After all, he forgave you both many times while you were growing up, just as he forgave your mother for divorcing him."

Sarah turned in the doorway for one last glance at them. "Whatever you say, bishop."

"I'll have to think on that for a *gut* long while," her sister replied.

The back door slammed. The house rang with their rancor for several moments.

"I'm mighty sorry for the way those girls came bargin' in here, sayin' such hateful things," Tom murmured. "But I can see why they'd assume the worst about . . . what they saw."

"The timing was unfortunate," Vernon agreed with a sigh. "But it's often this way with adult children. They don't want things to change at home after a parent passes, regardless of how the remaining parent needs comfort and companionship."

"And we sure can't hold ya responsible for what your girls said," Nazareth added as she slipped her hand into

Tom's. "It wasn't what we wanted to hear, but there's no gettin' around what we were doin' when they came in."

Tom let out a long sigh. "Couldn't help but think how much like their *mamm* they are, jumpin' on every little bug to peck at it," he said sadly. "I've always been glad to have my preachin' position as a *gut* reason not to go live with any of my kids after Lettie left."

"And you have your dairy herd, your livelihood," Vernon pointed out. "Not to mention your home and property. You're not nearly decrepit enough to need anyone's assistance getting from one day to the next, Tom!"

"Not by a long shot," Nazareth added with a laugh.

Relief and love washed over Tom as he gripped her slender hand. "Sometimes older eyes and slippin' vision work in our favor, ain't so? We can't see our friends' faults so clearly," he remarked. "Even now that Lettie's dead and gone, the four kids'll have a hard time seein' me as marriage material, so I hope folks around Willow Ridge will be happier that I've found Nazareth."

"Came all the way from Lancaster County to be with ya, Tom," she replied quietly. "There'll be no sendin' me back now, kids or not."

Jerusalem chuckled. "*Jah*, your girls haven't seen faith in action until they've been around us Hooley sisters. We've had a lot of practice at workin' things through. God had His reasons for makin' Willow Ridge look so *gut* to us, just like the nephews put their money toward a mill as soon as Bennie told them to come out here."

"And I, too, believe the Lord has been working out His purpose," Vernon added as he slipped an arm around Jerusalem's shoulders. "Just as I know He'll show us the next best moves to make, and give us the words and the strength of soul to carry them out. The road won't always be straight or smooth, but we'll get where we're supposed to go."

Tom nodded. "Those are *gut* words to see us toward Sunday, when everybody'll hear a *lot* of news during the Members Meeting. Let's hope folks think we've made the right decisions."

"Well, now—what do ya think of that? The sign on the gristmill door says Luke and Ira will return on Monday, or thereabouts." Jerusalem raised her eyebrows at Nazareth. "Where do ya suppose they've gotten themselves off to? Their lane's cleared, so they can't have been outta town very long."

Tom flashed Vernon a knowing look. "No doubt in my mind it involves female companions. These young bucks have been scoutin' around in lots of the nearby settlements, the way I hear it."

"And if they're twenty-eight and thirty, they might be hard-pressed to find many Plain girls to date," Vernon observed. "By that age, most of our young women have husbands and four or five children."

"*Jah*, here in Willow Ridge they've been seein' girls who're a lot younger—one of them bein' Hiram's eldest daughter." Nazareth shrugged. "And Bennie and Miriam went to Bowling Green before the storm hit, to visit some of her brothers' families."

"Makin' the rounds as newlyweds, collectin' their gifts, no doubt." Tom walked past the buggy to look down the county highway. "The Sweet Seasons is closed for another week, I think. Which means the only place open is Zook's Market." He looked at Vernon, biting back a grin. "Looks like ya won't be meetin' any of the Hooley bunch just yet. Guess we might as well stock up on those groceries the girls were wantin' and then figure out a way to entertain ourselves for a few more days."

The bishop scratched his snowy beard, pretending to

think really hard. "Hmm . . . eating, and choring, and keeping these two ladies in line. Sounds like a full schedule to me."

"Can't think of another thing we could possibly fit in," Tom teased as they all climbed into the buggy again.

"Puh!" Jerusalem followed her sister into the backseat, shaking her head at how their dinner plans had fallen through. But there was nothing to be done about the rest of their family being gone, so she and Nazareth would simply have to rely upon schoolteacher ingenuity to maintain a proper sense of decorum until Sunday. "Sounds like a *gut* time to get a couple of thousand-piece jigsaw puzzles, or—"

"It's perfect weather to crochet, Sister," Nazareth remarked cheerfully. "We can get a few new skeins of yarn at Zook's and have our own crochet club meeting. Fast as our fingers fly, we could make Vernon an afghan before he goes home."

Jerusalem cleared her throat, looking at Nazareth over the top of her glasses. "And what do ya suppose those two fellas in front of us will be doin' with *their* fingers while we crochet? Idle hands are the Devil's workshop, ain't so?"

Tom and Vernon laughed loudly as the carriage lurched forward on the snow-packed lane. Then the bishop turned to grin at her, his blue eyes a-twinkle. "Did I hear my name mentioned?" he teased. "While I would love nothing better than to sit beside you and whisper enticements while you crochet, Jerusalem, I have a project in mind, too. Tom can help me find materials for it after we drop you ladies off with the groceries."

"And I figure to be finishin' that Nativity set so's Vernon can take it back to Cedar Creek with him," Tom said.

Both fellows' intentions sounded perfectly honorable, even if she detected an undertone of mischief in their voices. And if Vernon would be working on something . . .

might it possibly be a little gift for *her*? Jerusalem looked out her window, smiling.

Nazareth patted her gloved hand. "Boys will be boys," she murmured. "And we're just the women to handle them. Like the *Gut* Book says, we should pray without ceasing—and they won't dare interrupt us at that, *jah*?"

"'Rejoice evermore. Pray without ceasing,'" Vernon took up the biblical thread. "And the apostle Paul had it right when he also told the Thessalonians to give thanks in everything because that's God's will in Jesus Christ for all of us. And I'm thankful for every moment I'm getting to spend with the three of you. Every moment."

A little thrill went through her, and Jerusalem realized she didn't have to act so prickly . . . so spinsterish. Vernon Gingerich might be a flirt but he was also a devout servant of God. And with Tom becoming the next bishop of Willow Ridge, where could she and her sister find finer men with whom to spend the next few days?

She relaxed then, considering the pattern she'd like to crochet for Vernon's afghan . . . thinking there would be time for a few winks and kisses between now and Sunday, as well. If the four of them kept to their best intentions, what could anyone else say about how they'd been spending their time together?

Chapter Eleven

As Nazareth took her place on the pew bench Sunday morning, she gazed at the familiar faces on the men's side of the big, extended front room in Daniel and Leah Kanagy's home. Leah had mentioned that her sons were surprised to see the Hooley sisters dressed like men, helping to plow out Preacher Tom's lane, but Nazareth had detected no sign of judgment on her face. Truth be told, most of the local gals suspected she and Tom were sweet on each other, and because they faulted Lettie for leaving a hardworking, dedicated man, none of them had ever pointed a finger at her. But the men's reactions might be sharper . . . especially when they learned Tom was the only real candidate for Willow Ridge's next bishop.

"Don't see hide nor hair of Sarah or Lavinia," Jerusalem whispered as the big roomful of folks got quiet. "Maybe they've changed their tune."

"I can't think they're givin' it up that easy. But it would be nice if Tom didn't have to put up with their negative attitudes today," Nazareth replied.

Tom, Vernon, Jeremiah Shetler, and Deacon Reuben Reihl came to the center of the room to sit on their bench, looking serene and ready to worship. The four of them

made an impressive sight as they stood together in their
black *mutze* coats and trousers, wearing crisp white shirts.
As one of the men in the crowd sang out the first note of
the opening hymn, these leaders removed their broad-
brimmed hats in one smooth motion. Nazareth allowed
these rituals and the slow, steady rhythm of the ancient
song to settle her heart . . . prepare her soul for what
would be a momentous day. She'd slept little the night
before, wondering how the details would play out—

As Preacher Tom and the bishops were leaving for an
upstairs room to decide who would deliver the sermons
today, the door behind the men's side swooshed open.
When the two latecomers took their places in the back
row, Nazareth knew right off that they were Tom's sons,
just as she didn't have to look over her shoulder when the
door in the kitchen banged. The shifting and murmuring
behind her meant that Sarah and Lavinia had arrived, as
well, and were already causing a stir.

But it's up to You now, Lord, she prayed while the
others continued singing around her. *Help us all to see
Your light shinin' in this tricky situation. I'm thankful You
already know how it's going to turn out.*

The service proceeded at its usual unhurried pace.
Tom preached the first sermon, about how Joseph
heeded the angel's warning to flee to Egypt so Herod
wouldn't find and kill the baby Jesus. Even though Tom
had admitted to a case of the jitters over breakfast, he
seemed relaxed . . . spoke the words from his heart, about
how all who follow God benefit from truly listening to
Him rather than thinking their own ideas are best.

After a prayer and the scripture reading, Vernon rose
to give the second, longer sermon. Nazareth noticed how
folks sat up straighter to listen to his resonant voice, his
authoritative way with words. While everyone had
greeted him before the service—knew who he was and

why he'd come from Cedar Creek—it was a treat to hear the Word proclaimed in a different style, with the insights this visiting bishop provided.

Beside Nazareth, Jerusalem leaned forward to linger over every word Vernon delivered. Her sister's feelings were written all over her face . . . a face Nazareth might not see much in the future, if Jerusalem took up with this man from partway across the state. But that was for God to decide, as well. Nazareth patted her sister's hand and Jerusalem beamed at her. It was easy to tell yet again, from the tone and sincerity that rang around the room as Vernon spoke, that he was nothing at all like Hiram Knepp. Such a comfort it was, to believe Jerusalem had at last found a man worthy of her . . . just as Nazareth herself had.

Finally, after the last hymn and the benediction, Jeremiah Shetler, the bishop from Morning Star, called a Members Meeting. The children and those who weren't baptized members left the room.

"I think you've all heard this news," Jeremiah began, "but we've received word that Preacher Gabe had to take his Wilma to the emergency room again last night. And while we hold the Glick family up in our prayers, Gabe's situation leads us directly into the discussion about who shall become the next bishop for your congregation."

Kapps bobbed around Nazareth and everyone sat forward to follow this vital line of discussion. The men, too, focused intently on Jeremiah, and when he reminded them that only ordained preachers were eligible for the more elevated post of bishop, Henry Zook raised his hand.

"Most of the talk amongst folks at the store has been about how, with Preacher Gabe not feeling so *gut* and having to constantly watch out for his wife," he said, "it's probably best to figure on Tom being our new bishop, and then choosing two new preachers."

Nazareth exchanged a relieved look with her sister. The storekeeper had just made this whole process a lot easier. It sounded better—stronger—when a mainstay of the Willow Ridge community made such a suggestion. The men were nodding, murmuring among themselves when Vernon raised his hand for silence.

"Selecting a bishop is the most important decision a congregation makes, and we usually rely upon the falling of the lot as God's way of choosing that man for us," he said as he looked around the huge, crowded room. "It's practical—expedient—to select Tom Hostetler and then vote on him, but we shouldn't presume to take this process into our own hands. Does anyone have further discussion? Or objections? Speak now, brothers and sisters."

Whispering filled the room, like the buzz of Leah Kanagy's bees. After a few moments, Miriam Lantz Hooley spoke up. She looked radiant, as a newlywed, and appeared rested after her time away from running her restaurant. "I think everyone agrees that without Tom Hostetler's calm wisdom and solid faith, Willow Ridge might've been torn apart by some of Hiram's finaglin' and—"

"*Jah*, if Hiram hadn't left town, I would have," Reuben Reihl said.

The room got quiet. If their deacon, who managed the church's money and read their scriptures at each service, had been ready to find a new district, this was a serious situation, indeed.

"Tom was the fella who convinced me to stay, saying that God had a bigger plan for Willow Ridge, if I'd just be patient," the burly redhead went on. "And Tom wasn't afraid to put Hiram in his place when he got out of hand, pestering Miriam about marrying him. So Tom's the man I want for my bishop."

Nazareth's heart swelled with a wonderful sense that

everyone here would be in agreement . . . and this was her Tom they were all talking about! Again the women around her nodded and whispered—until a fellow in the back of the men's section stood up.

"I feel it's my Christian duty to let you folks know of some questionable activities we've learned about," he said.

Everyone got quiet. The men turned and the women craned their necks to see who was speaking. Nazareth's insides tightened: it was one of Tom's sons. And then his brother stood up beside him. "*Jah*, we hate to rain on your parade, but—"

"I don't believe we've met," Jeremiah Shetler interrupted. "Do you folks live in this district?"

"Those are my sons, Rudy and Pete," Tom said quietly. "They're carriage makers, over past New Haven."

"I would like to express my sincerest condolences on the passing of your mother," Vernon interjected as he placed a hand on Tom's shoulder. He looked over the roomful of people, who had sucked in a collective breath at this news. "It would be a difficult subject for Tom to bring up, so I will tell you folks that Lettie was killed in a car accident a while back. Tom and his children just got word a few days ago."

An "ohhhh" passed quickly through the crowd, before another voice—this time behind Nazareth—began to speak.

"*Jah*, we no more than got word about our *mamm*'s death, than we went to check on Dat and found him sitting real close and cozy to another woman. Nazareth, her name was."

"Snowed in, they were—with *you*, Vernon Gingerich, and another gal with an outlandish name," her sister chimed in. "So we could pretty much guess what-all had been going on in Dat's house for oh, several days, no doubt!"

Another "ohhhh!" rippled through the room, louder this time. Nazareth felt her cheeks go hot as Jerusalem gripped her hand. Her heart pounded. How would these folks react to that? How would this information influence everyone's opinions of Tom's suitability? Especially considering that she and Jerusalem had just come to Willow Ridge in October.

"These are my daughters, Sarah and Lavinia, and they live over near the boys with their husbands and families," Tom explained to Bishop Shetler. Then he turned to look directly at the young women who had spoken out against him. "I'm glad you've joined us today, girls. It's been a long while since I've seen all four of my kids in the same place at the same time. And it's *gut* to see the four of you in church, even if you didn't bring your families."

Nazareth's eyes widened. Was Tom implying that his children didn't get along? That they didn't always attend services? And why in the world had they come without their spouses and kids? Even so, she sensed that Tom was no longer nervous about this ruckus his children were making . . . as though he had been praying about the possibility of such a scene. And God had surely been listening.

"Let us bow for a moment of prayer," Jeremiah intoned. "We should not only ask the Lord to comfort Tom and his family, but we must pray for Lettie's soul—as we would pray for anyone who has left the church and thereby offended God by breaking the vows they made to Him."

As Nazareth bowed her head, she glanced at Jerusalem, who was holding her fist on her lap with a thumb pointed up. Nazareth nodded. Between Jeremiah and Vernon, the two bishops had indeed let the steam out of a pot that had been ready to boil over. Tom was in good hands, among close friends. After a few moments, while only the shifting of bodies on the pew benches punctuated the silence, Vernon cleared his throat.

"I would be remiss not to address the concerns Preacher Tom's children have come so far to point out to us," he said. As he waited for folks to raise their heads from praying, Cedar Creek's bishop gazed at each of Tom's children in turn. "It was true, what Sarah and Lavinia said. They came to Tom's house a few days ago and found their father seated beside Nazareth Hooley in the front room, while her sister Jerusalem and I were playing Scrabble at the table by the front window," he recounted calmly. "You folks have been to services in Tom's home, so you all understand exactly where we were when his daughters came in through the kitchen and found us this way."

Kapps and beards bobbed around the room.

"This was after the meeting Enos Mullet and I came to Tom's house for? After the big snowstorm hit?" Jeremiah asked.

"Yes, it was. While you and Enos drove home ahead of the snowstorm, I had already decided to remain in Willow Ridge to visit with Tom, who's an old friend from when we were growing up," Vernon replied. Then he smiled, his face radiating his mirth. "You folks who know the Hooley sisters will understand why Tom invited them to be his hostesses, and you can imagine the wonderful meals they prepared while we bishops met with Tom. They also joined us outdoors to clear the snow from the lane to the road, as the Kanagy's sons can attest."

Folks turned their heads to find Leah and Daniel in the crowd.

"*Jah*," said Daniel, "and they invited the boys in for cookies and cocoa, too, but Nate and Bram had to get their fiancées back to Cedar Creek. The Coblentz girls said mighty nice things about ya, Bishop Gingerich."

"This chitty-chat's all fine and dandy," Lavinia Hostetler interrupted in a shrill voice. "But it doesn't change the fact that our *dat* was spooning with Nazareth, and that Vernon and that other woman were looking pretty chummy, too."

"*Jah*," Sarah chimed in, "it's obvious Dat's been seein' this gal since before we knew Mamm was gone. If he's to become a bishop—"

"That other woman's name is Jerusalem," Jeremiah Shetler put in above her strident tone. "And while we understand your concern for your *dat*, I must also say that I've not met two finer, more upright women than the Hooley sisters."

"And I will confess before my children—before all the members here—that yes, I have enjoyed gettin' to know Nazareth," Tom chimed in. He clasped his hands before him, meeting the gazes of several in the crowd. "Matter of fact, I intend to court her now that Lettie's death makes it permissible for me to marry again. If anybody objects to that or needs to ask me any questions, now's the time."

Nazareth blushed, yet a thrill went through her as Tom said these things in front of all their friends. The women around her patted her back and mouthed their congratulations, until Tom's voice silenced their excited whispering.

"I can understand how I've upset you girls, so soon after we learned of your *mamm*'s passin'. And I ask your forgiveness for that part." Tom looked steadily at his two daughters.

The room went quiet again. Nazareth didn't turn around to gauge the expressions on Lavinia and Sarah's faces, but she sensed that as this uncomfortable pause grew longer, any doubts people had about Tom's connections to her were shifting toward his kids instead. When someone asked for forgiveness—especially with witnesses present—an answer was expected.

"And what about us, Dat?" Again Pete Hostetler stood

up behind the rest of the men. "Do you expect Rudy and me to go along with your—*carrying on*—with this other woman? Isn't that a slap in the face of Mamm's memory?"

Tom remained placid, shifting to focus on his two sons. "I seek your forgiveness, as well," he stated quietly. "I don't want this rift betwixt us to grow any wider. Ya haven't had much to do with me since your *mamm* left, and I suspect ya blame me for her leavin' with that other fella."

Eyebrows shot up around her, and Nazareth noted how the older men in the front benches murmured among themselves. Reuben Reihl rose from the center bench, raking his red hair back from his face as he looked at Tom's sons.

"As I recall it, you two boys were mighty eager to leave Willow Ridge rather than help your *dat* with his dairy herd or tend his cropland," the deacon pointed out. Then he turned toward the girls, his scowl deepening. "And you daughters married fellas from outta town, as well, which means your mother had to handle her garden and the house even while she was workin' as a caretaker to help make ends meet. Seems to me you four kids left the family before your mother did. I can't recall many times you've returned to visit Tom or to be in church with us, either."

Reuben's words rang around the room, inspiring another round of nods and murmured "*jah*s" from the members.

"Your *dat* didn't stand in the way of your followin' the paths that would make all of ya happy, either," the deacon continued. "So even if you're not gonna forgive him today, you could at least offer him the same sort of consideration he's showed you, so he can be happy, too."

"Well said, Deacon," Henry Zook spoke up.

"*Jah*, and I'm thinkin' that since Tom's kids aren't members of our district," Ben Hooley added, "they won't be votin' on him becomin' our bishop, anyway. It's time to be gettin' on with that process. My mind's been made up for quite a while now."

"Mine, too," Leah Kanagy added. "This isn't the time or place for airin' Tom's family problems when we've got a bigger issue to decide."

Tom's kids scowled at each other and promptly left. The two doors banged loudly enough to startle folks and make them wince.

As Nazareth dared to sigh with relief, she saw that Tom was gazing right at her. What a fine, upright man he was, never raising his voice or expressing impatience or disgust with the way his children had behaved. She smiled steadily at him, excited that he had publicly stated his intentions toward her . . . ecstatic that he found her worthy to be his wife. She felt sorry that his kids had left the meeting with a cloud still hanging over the Hostetler family's relationships. This situation wouldn't disappear just because Deacon Reihl and Jeremiah Shetler had defended Tom . . .

As Jeremiah called for the vote to begin with the eldest of the men, Nazareth thrilled at every confident "*jah!*" that confirmed the feelings of those in this room: folks were affirming her relationship with Tom as surely as they were deciding that he should be their bishop. As she waited for her turn to vote, she bowed her head.

Lord, I thank Ya for this fine day, and for these gut friends who've stood with Tom and me, seein' our true intentions to be a part of Your plan. Bless Rudy and Pete, Sarah and Lavinia, as they mourn their mamm and deal with their feelings about their dat. Shine Your light on them so they can find the way to bein' right with You.

The vote was unanimous, the meeting was adjourned, and everyone in the room broke into applause as they surged toward Tom. Jerusalem grabbed Nazareth in a hug as the women flocked around her. "Guess it's official now, Sister," she whispered. "And nobody's happier for you and Tom than I am."

"*Denki*, Jerusalem," Nazareth replied as she swiped at sudden tears. "It's your turn now, ain't so?"

Chapter Twelve

Monday morning as Vernon's sleigh took off down the lane behind Samson, Jerusalem waved and waved at Nazareth. Her sister beamed, flanked by their nephews, Ira and Luke. To be proper, they had brought Nazareth back to the apartment above the boys' gristmill to stay, so she and Tom wouldn't be at his home alone. Jerusalem had quickly packed some fresh dresses for the trip to Cedar Creek.

"What a wonderful family you have. Every one of them special," Vernon remarked as he urged his Percheron to turn onto the county highway.

Will I say the same thing about Vernon's aunts and his nephew? But it was too late to worry about that.

"It was clear at yesterday's common meal that folks in Willow Ridge have made your nephews welcome, too," Vernon said. "And as I talked with Ben, I couldn't miss the happiness on his face as he stood with his new bride."

"Miriam's a special woman," Jerusalem agreed. "And we're all real happy that she stood up to Hiram, and that Bennie latched onto her."

"I might miss my guess, but I'd not be surprised if Ben

becomes one of your new preachers. He has that glow of holy purpose about him."

Jerusalem considered this, feeling a glow herself. Even if things didn't work out between her and this bishop, she had to admit Vernon's accuracy when it came to assessing character. "Bennie's a fine fella. Went from bein' a late bloomer to becomin' the biggest blossom on the bush, once he met Miriam," she remarked. "It was just that quick between them. No doubts and no lookin' back."

"The way it was with us."

That remark felt like a pond just waiting for her to jump into it. Was it full of fresh, clear water . . . or would she bang herself up on the rocks at the bottom? And there was no missing the way Vernon gazed at her, expecting some sort of reply.

"I knew ya for a *gut* man the moment ya walked into Tom's," she replied carefully. "And I can't fib to ya, Vernon. I've been mighty happy this past week, havin' ya pay so much attention to me."

Vernon smiled, focusing on the road. "And?"

And? Was he going to keep leading her deeper into that pond, until the bottom dropped out from under her? "And *jah*, I liked the kissin', too," she admitted. "How about you, Vernon? If ya were to change one thing about me, what would it be?"

When his jaw dropped, Jerusalem felt a surge of satisfaction. If this man thought he was the only one who could lead a merry conversational chase, he'd better find out the truth before he got her to Cedar Creek. If he gave a wrong response to her question, it would be best to just turn around now, before—

"Let me ponder that one. It deserves my best effort at an answer. Meanwhile," he said as he reached beneath the seat, "here's that little project I was spending my time on at Tom's. I hope you like it."

"Oh, Vernon, ya really didn't have to—"

"I *wanted* to make this for you, dear heart," he corrected softly. "It's been too long since my fingers itched to work with wood. Too long since I took the time. And it's a trifle, compared to the beautiful afghan you and Nazareth made me."

Jerusalem tore eagerly at the kraft paper wrapping and then sucked in her breath. "Oh, my . . . such a perty little box, and with a J on the top! *Denki*, Vernon, I—I'll cherish it always."

He smiled, almost shyly. "I work best with my own tools in my own shop, but it's a small token of my feelings for you. A keepsake box. Something that, over the years, I hope you'll fill with mementos of our times together."

Jerusalem gazed out over the snowy fields, her heart thrumming as she held the glossy box on her lap. It was made of cherry wood, with an intricate border pattern carved around her initial. Then she smiled. To his credit, Vernon hadn't popped off a clever reply or sidestepped her question by posing another one. But his gift had made for a timely distraction, hadn't it?

"Take your time comin' up with what you'd change about me," she remarked. "I'll just keep enjoyin' the scenery. It's like passin' through a winter wonderland, what with the sun makin' everything sparkle."

She relaxed against the plush seat of the sleigh, admiring the rich red of its upholstery . . . the midnight black of Samson's muscled haunches as he trotted confidently through an open field of snow that shone with fiery sun diamonds . . . the crisp jingle of sleigh bells that made her as giddy as when she'd been a kid.

What a joy the Missouri landscape was, so open and uncomplicated. While they had to be aware of where the ditches and gullies were, and had to watch for the occasional barbed wire fence between one family's place and the next, Vernon and Samson navigated the fields and roads as though they had done it dozens of times. If she hitched up with Vernon . . . would he be willing to visit Willow Ridge often, so she could spend time with Nazareth and her nephews?

"If I could change anything about you, dear Jerusalem," the man beside her began, "I would change your mind. Not your intelligence," he quickly clarified, "because your wit and common sense set you far above most women I know."

Jerusalem let this sink in, sensing the other shoe was about to drop. "I'm with ya so far. Don't stop now."

Vernon's laughter rang out as he squeezed her arm. "What a delight you are, dear heart," he murmured. "But if I'm to truly win you, I must encourage you over that barricade of your second thoughts. I must turn your fear into trust, for while I sense you want to become physically intimate with me someday, you over-think it. And then you get scared."

Scared? Oh, the scary part was how Vernon had hit the nail square on the head, and how he had returned to the topic of sex. Jerusalem nipped her lip, at a loss for a reply.

Vernon sighed as he slipped an arm around her shoulders. "It wasn't my intention to frighten you again just now, and—"

"Not your fault," she said in a shaky whisper. "I just don't have the foggiest notion about what I'm gettin' myself into."

"But you like the kissing."

Her cheeks went hot. "Oh, *jah*, that part's just dandy, but—"

Vernon's lips eased over hers before she knew what had hit her. After a moment's resistance, when he paused to let her catch up with him, Jerusalem relaxed . . . followed his lead down a path that warmed and exhilarated her. For long, lovely moments she luxuriated in his silky lips . . . the softness of his beard against her skin . . . the way her pulse settled into rhythm with his . . .

When Vernon eased away with a satisfied sigh, Jerusalem was surprised to see that they had stopped in the middle of a field, right out in the open. There were no trees to shelter them from whatever eyes might be watching from that farmhouse on the next knoll. "My stars, I just—"

"Shhh," he whispered, and then he kissed her again. "Don't think about it. Let your senses lead you toward whatever feels comfortable, sweetheart, and then push your limit a little farther each time. I'll catch you before you go off the deep end. Although," he said with a wiggle of his white eyebrows, "it's only in the deep end where you truly learn to surrender yourself. I'll be there surrendering, too, you know."

Jerusalem let out the breath she'd been holding. How had Vernon weaved her thoughts about deep water into his reply, anyway? "And I'm supposed to trust ya on that part? That you'll catch me before I go under and don't come back up?"

Vernon smiled gently. His blue eyes twinkled, but there was no sign of derision or impatience in them. "Oh, we'll reach a point of no return, Jerusalem, if you'll give me the chance to take you there." He ran a finger along her cheek, sending tingles down her spine. "If I were a betting man, I'd put my money on you becoming quite an exuberant lover. You approach everything else with such joy, it only follows that you'll bring the same spirit into my bed. As my wife."

Jerusalem's heart flew up into her throat. Here he was, talking so freely about marriage again when only a moment ago he was reassuring her about what husbands did with their wives . . . what he wanted to do with her. "I—I don't wanna disappoint ya, Vernon."

"And you won't, dear Jerusalem. This is fear of the unknown, plain and simple," he whispered as he lightly kissed her again. "Once you allow your fear to become faith, there's no limit to who you can be or how high you can fly. You believe that, don't you?"

Jerusalem hung on his every murmured word, badly wanting to fling herself over the edge . . . wanting, indeed, to fly. She nodded, holding his gaze. For if she had no faith, she had nothing at all.

"Good. Now, kiss me again, and then we'll . . . mulch this subject as though it's your favorite rose bush in the fall," he suggested. "It will gather its strength beneath the winter's snow so it can bloom and flourish in the spring. Love's like that, you know."

Jerusalem lost herself in Vernon's clear blue eyes, seeing herself reflected in them and going deeper . . . down into his soul, just as he was surely permeating hers.

She slipped the keepsake box onto the seat beside her and leaned into the kiss this time, daring to take the lead with subtle pressure and a slight slanting of her mouth. Vernon wrapped his arms around her and held her head, kissing her until she was spinning in dizzy, giddy circles. Her whole being felt as vibrant and shiny as the snow, and she didn't want this moment to end.

"Oh, Jerusalem," he murmured when they finally released each other.

"*Jah*, it's me. But it's me when I was about nineteen— except ever so much finer," she whispered. "Because you're finer than anybody I was kissin' back then."

Vernon chuckled and hugged her again. "I know better than to quibble about that. Shall we get along home? We've only just begun, Jerusalem, and I surely don't want to stop now."

* * *

"Gee, Samson! You've given us a good ride home, boy."

As always, he felt glad to be entering his own lane after a trip away, but today was special. How would Jerusalem see his home place? Would the ancient stone silo make her think he was stuck in the past and hopelessly outmoded? Did the tall stone and brick house, with its single-story wing of white, appear out of proportion? At least the cold weather meant she wouldn't catch the aroma from the cattle that were milling about the barnyard, absently chewing their hay as they peered between the fence slats.

"Doesn't look like we got as much snow here," he remarked as the sleigh slid past the house. "And bless him, Abner has done a fine job of plowing us out."

Jerusalem's smile was a little crooked, but that was to be expected. "Nice to see all those perty black cows gawkin' at us," she said. "Thought I saw somebody peekin' from between the curtains as we passed the house, too. Did ya tell your aunts I was comin' home with ya?"

Vernon pulled the sleigh to a halt. "When I left a phone message that I'd be staying in Willow Ridge through Sunday, I did mention I'd be bringing a friend for a visit, yes."

Jerusalem nailed him with her piercing brown eyes. "A girl-type friend?"

"I confess I was at a loss about what to call you, exactly." He slipped his gloved hand around hers, hoping he hadn't gotten this visit off to an unfortunate start. "Don't let the presence of Aunt Nettie, Aunt Florence, and my nephew worry you, dear heart. This is *my* place," he continued earnestly, "and just as the Lord compelled me to take them in when they lost their homes in a flood, He is now answering my prayers for a woman who is not my aunt! Shall we see where God is leading all of us?"

As he helped Jerusalem from the sleigh and led her up the walk toward the kitchen door, Vernon recalled bringing Dorothea to meet his parents for the first time, about forty years ago. As a young carpenter just getting started, he'd had little to offer a bride—they had lived with Dorothea's family for about a year after they were married, as was the Plain custom—so this presentation of his intended felt a little more comfortable. Still, there was plenty of room for three opinionated women to get crossways . . .

When they stepped into the kitchen, the room was redolent with the rich scents of chicken and vegetables. His aunt Nettie, who stood at the old cookstove stirring a pot of soup, turned to greet him—and then her mouth dropped open.

"Aunt Nettie, this is Jerusalem Hooley. She's come to visit with us for a few days," he said quickly.

"Has she, now?" Nettie chirped. Her long-handled spoon clanked against the stockpot before landing in the hot soup.

"And Jerusalem, I think you have a great many things in common with Nettie," Vernon went on in what he hoped was an encouraging voice. "You both like to cook for me and cluck over me, for instance." *And please, Lord, don't let them start pecking at each other . . .*

Jerusalem put on a smile and ventured toward the stove, sniffing deeply. "Mighty nice to meet ya, Nettie. And I can't tell ya what a treat it is to be welcomed with soup I didn't have to stir up myself."

Aunt Nettie glanced from Jerusalem back to Vernon. She laughed quietly. "I'm fixing everybody's favorite, so I hope you'll like it, too. Just didn't realize who I'd be serving. Kind of took me by surprise."

"I have that effect on folks," Jerusalem replied lightly. "If you'd have told me two weeks ago I'd be visitin' a man's home this way, I would've denied it as sure as that cock crowed three times to condemn Peter, in the Bible."

"And what am I missing out on? Is that you, Vernon?" another voice called from the direction of the front room.

Vernon excused himself to fetch Aunt Florence. As he wheeled her into the kitchen, she checked the oxygen bag strapped to the arm of her chair. "I'm home from a wonderfully productive time in Willow Ridge," he told her, "and along with seeing my old friend Tom Hostetler installed as the new bishop there—"

"I recall Tommy from when you two were running around in your *rumspringa*."

"—I met someone very special," Vernon continued. He stopped her wheelchair as they entered the kitchen. "Aunt Florence, this is Jerusalem Hooley—"

His aunt wheezed loudly, pressing her oxygen nozzle further into her nose.

"—and she loves to talk about as many different subjects as you do," he went on. "I hope you three ladies will get to be good friends."

"She's still got her coat on, like maybe she's not so sure about staying," Florence remarked under her breath. Then she sat straighter in her wheelchair and extended her hand. "You'll have to excuse me, Jerusalem. Vernon likes to bring us little surprises home every now and again, but you take the cake."

"*Jah*, I can see that," Jerusalem murmured.

Vernon cleared his throat, looking from one startled woman to the next. Then he laughed, at himself mostly. "Now that I've upset everybody's apple cart—especially yours, Aunts—let me tell you how much I appreciate the way all three of you love me and take care of me, even when I don't warn you about what I'm going to do," he

said. "Trust the Lord along with me, will you? I believe
He's leading us all to make some changes, and that His will
and purpose are being worked out even during moments
when nobody knows what to think or say."

Bless her, Jerusalem chuckled as she untied her bonnet
and then handed him her coat. "You're a brave man, Vernon,
settin' yourself up amongst three women who could make
ya miserable if we took the notion to—separately, or as a
bunch."

Aunt Nettie grinned as she fished her spoon from the
bubbling soup. "I suspect it won't be long before we *are*
a bunch, hanging together like bananas—"

"Clustered like grapes," Aunt Florence chimed in as
she pointed a playful finger at Vernon. "So you'd best
watch out for yourself, young man. You and Abner are
outnumbered now. Get used to it!"

As the three women laughed, the tension in the kitchen
dissipated like the steam rising from Nettie's soup pot.
Vernon silently gave thanks that they had put their initial
discomfort behind them, because all of them had just
taken an enormous step forward. Jerusalem's presence in
a home where he had gladly let his kinfolk take charge for
these past several years would require a lot of adjustments
for all of them.

*So maybe it's time for you to step into being the head
of this household again.*

That startling thought came at him from out of nowhere,
but as he considered it, Vernon recognized the voice of God
giving him a prod. He'd been all too happy to immerse
himself in leading the people of Cedar Creek . . . perhaps
to avoid the emptiness he'd felt in this home after his wife
had passed on. It occurred to him that he'd been terribly
lonely, even while surrounded by his aunts, Abner, and all
of his friends in town, but he hadn't wanted to give his
feelings a label. Hadn't wanted to face the way his grief

for Dorothea had lingered for so long, in the secret depths of his heart.

Vernon smiled at Jerusalem, at the vulnerable yet willing expression on her dear face. God had given him such a gift this past week by bringing her into his life.

"I'll go on out and tend to Samson," he said. "You ladies can get acquainted while I catch up with Abner—warn the poor boy what he'll be up against, dealing with four of us crotchety old senior citizens now."

"*Jah*, we're mighty disagreeable," Aunt Nettie declared, merrily banging the soup pot with her spoon.

"Puh! Might be just the incentive he needs to get out and court somebody," Abner's mother declared. Then she waved Vernon on. "The sooner you head for the barn, the quicker we girls can start our hen party. If you're lucky, we'll get most of our gossip out of the way before you come back in, so your ears can stop burning."

"*Jah*, the talk'll be all about you, Vernon," Aunt Nettie teased. "You've opened up the hive now, bringing Jerusalem here. We three will be buzzing like bees for a long while. Hope you can handle that."

"I'm a doomed man. I don't stand a chance," he jested.

But as Vernon stepped into the crisp winter's afternoon, he felt truly blessed. The Lord had just handed him a chance at a whole new life, with a woman who would help him enjoy it, much as He had created Eve for Adam. His prayers had been answered, even though—until this past week—he hadn't really known what he was praying for.

Wasn't it just like God to see to his needs before he realized how needy he was?

Chapter Thirteen

After a filling dinner of chicken soup with Nettie's homemade noodles, a relish tray, fresh rye rolls, baked pineapple, and a rich bread pudding studded with raisins and apples, both of Vernon's aunts told Jerusalem to skedaddle.

"We've got the kitchen chores under control," Nettie insisted as she ran hot, soapy water in the sink. "Vernon's itching to show you around the place."

"*Jah*, Nettie washes the dishes and sets them on that drainer so I can dry them and put everything away," Florence explained. "Vernon built that low cabinet with the extra sink and countertop just for me, so I can be as useful as everyone else."

"That's mighty nice, but I feel like I'm slackin' if I don't help ya redd up," Jerusalem protested. It was the cooking and cleaning that made every Plain woman fit in no matter where she visited, because the same jobs had to be done in everyone's home around mealtime.

"Oh, I suspect you'll take over your own set of chores one of these days, and you'll have years and years to clean this kitchen," Nettie remarked with a knowing smile. "So for now, be our guest, Jerusalem. We're real pleased you're here with us."

"And don't think you have to entertain me, either," Abner said as he rose from his seat at the table. He was taller than the rest of them, pudgy from eating his aunts' cooking; a pleasant fellow of about forty, Jerusalem figured. "I'm going to hole up with my accounts for a while, so that means you're stuck with Uncle Vernon for company. *Gut* luck with that!"

"Better with me than with you, Abner," the bishop teased. His blue eyes twinkled as he gestured toward the door of the front room. "Shall we take their hints and disappear into the nooks and crannies of this old home? If it's all right with you, aunts, we'll peek at your rooms first and be out of your way in case you'd like a nap."

"Nap?!" Nettie replied with a hoot.

"Far as I can tell, it's *you* who snoozes in your office after dinner," Florence teased as she wheeled over to grab a dish towel. "You'd have us believe you're praying in there or studying your scriptures for Sunday service, but you don't fool me for a minute, young man."

Vernon tucked Jerusalem's hand into the crook of his elbow as they began their tour. "I can't win with those three," he murmured, "so I pretend to go along with them. You can see how I need someone to take my side, can't you?"

"Puh! I don't feel one bit sorry for ya," Jerusalem said as they entered the large, cozily furnished front room. "Most of us get what we ask for in this life, ya know."

"You're absolutely right, Jerusalem." Vernon's secretive whisper made her skin shimmer as they chuckled over their private joke. He nuzzled her cheek with a quick kiss before steering her down a hallway to their right. "When we rode in, you probably noticed how this newer wing of the house is just one level. I added it when the aunts and Abner lost their homes in the flood of Nineteen Ninety-Three—three rooms with doorways and a bathroom that will accommodate Aunt Florence's chair."

Jerusalem nodded as she gazed at the glossy wood frames around the wider doors . . . a tidy bedroom with yellow walls, and then a similar room painted pale lavender, and a larger room at the end of the hall, which served as Abner's bedroom and office. "And ya built this wing yourself, Vernon? Do I recall ya sayin' that ya worked as a master carpenter before ya took on your duties as the bishop?"

"I had help from some wonderful neighbors, getting this wing framed in and the roof put on," he replied as they headed back down the hallway. "But I did all the interior finishing, yes. Back in the day, I loved nothing better than spending time in my shop, making pieces of furniture Dorothea wanted, but . . ."

He paused, shrugging. "It's not like we need any more furniture."

Jerusalem nodded, understanding how Vernon's wife had taken some of his enthusiasm about working with wood to the grave with her. The large front room was filled with lovely pieces: a china cabinet made of burled walnut displayed a set of old china behind its glass doors, and a matching sideboard served as a place for a swiveling stand where a family Bible rested, open to the second chapter of Luke. Vernon fingered the dresser scarf, which was embroidered on each end with a manger scene.

"Dorothea made this the first Christmas we were married," he murmured, "and Aunt Nettie likes to get it out each year. And the quilting frame," he continued, pointing to the work in progress near the big picture window, "is where Aunt Florence spends most of her time. Her eyesight is still quite keen, thank goodness, as she finds great joy in finishing quilts after other ladies have made the tops."

Jerusalem leaned closer to the framed quilt, an appliqued snowflake design worked in several shades of blue calico. "My word, but that's a lot of loops and swirls she's stitchin' on there," she remarked. "Never had the patience to do such intricate quilting. I'm better with a crochet hook—or a snow shovel," she added with a laugh.

Vernon led her by the hand into an alcove built around the home's front door. "You have more than your share of talents, Jerusalem," he whispered. "And this happens to be my favorite—so far."

When he kissed her, Jerusalem nearly squirmed out of his embrace, thinking that any of the three other folks in this home might catch them. Vernon sensed her skittishness and gently tightened his arms around her.

"Nobody uses this door, dear heart," he said softly, nuzzling her ear. "Even back when the house was built for my grandparents, people usually came in through the kitchen."

"True of most places," Jerusalem replied in a tight voice. "But I feel like my backside's exposed—"

"Now there's a picture," the bishop interrupted with a wink.

Jerusalem's jaw dropped and then she swatted him playfully. "You know what I'm sayin', so stop makin' fun of me," she whispered, fearing her voice might carry out to where Florence would soon resume her quilting. "I'm not used to spoonin', especially where folks might see —"

"Another little adjustment in everyone's attitude," Vernon suggested, his eyes a-twinkle. "I refuse to hide my affection for you, Jerusalem. If that bothers my aunts and Abner, then *they* are the ones who'll have to look the other way. It's my home. And you're to be my wife . . . I hope."

"I'm still thinkin' that over."

"That's why I brought you here. Take your time, my dear." He ran a finger tenderly along the side of her cheek. "Ask me anything that comes to your mind, Jerusalem, for a man and his wife should have no secrets . . . no reservations or unexpressed desires."

Jerusalem swallowed hard, nodding despite her nervousness. It was one thing to enjoy this man's sensual suggestions at Tom Hostetler's place, which was like home turf, but here she was still the guest . . . the young girl looking into the furniture store, daring to dream of the home she would have someday. This opportunity to marry a fine man had come to her unexpectedly, years after she'd given up on the possibility of becoming a wife, and it still scared her if she examined the ramifications of marriage too closely. Holy matrimony wasn't a state to be entered into lightly . . . especially since she'd thrived for so many years as a *maidel*.

Once more Vernon kissed her and then he led her past the old stone fireplace, flanked with shelves that were crammed with almanacs and National Geographic books about every place under the sun.

"Dorothea and I spent many a winter's evening looking at the photographs in those volumes," he remarked as they went toward another hallway on this end of the house's older section. "It wasn't as good as traveling to those places, but we at least got to visit those countries from the comfort of our couch."

"My family had a lot of those same titles," she replied, gazing at the parquet oak floors that led to another secluded room. All over this home, fine craftsmanship showed off the love and skill that had gone into building it many generations ago. "So this is your office, where ya take your naps, then?"

Vernon laughed and then winked at her. "All right, I

confess. After some of Nettie's comfort-food dinners, I catch myself dozing off at this rolltop desk, which my grandfather made. But I feel as though I'm in the company of good, solid men who sat here as preachers and bishops before me," he said in a reverent voice.

"As well ya should, if God chose so many fellas in your family to serve."

Jerusalem wondered if she dared express the misgivings that had simmered on the back burner in her mind. Would Vernon think she was nit-picking? Making excuses not to give him an answer? "I suppose that's one thing givin' me pause," she murmured. "I'm wonderin' if I'm cut out to be a bishop's wife. It's not like I'm always the biddable, submittin' type who'll say and do what I'm supposed to."

Vernon shook his head good-naturedly. "Not once have I doubted your faith or your integrity, Jerusalem. Nor have I questioned your suitability . . . your willingness to attain the higher level of behavior expected of a bishop's family. Honesty is a must in a marriage—in a community of faith—even when the truth you speak isn't what others want to hear."

Jerusalem's lips quirked. "*Jah*, that's exactly why Hiram Knepp's no longer in Willow Ridge. And . . . maybe it's because I believed *he* might want me for his wife that I'm feelin' like a long-tailed cat in a room full of rockin' chairs. Waitin' to get hurt again. Wonderin' what time will tell about *you*, after this first big bubble of excitement bursts."

"Who says it has to?" Vernon stood in front of her, taking her hands in his. "When a man and a woman are meant for each other, they find ways to sustain the excitement and to never tire of each other's company. That's how it was between Dorothea and me, so that's why I believe you and I will share the same sort of love and devotion. It won't happen overnight, understand. But it will happen if you believe it will."

Oh, but this man had an eloquence about him, a convincing confidence Jerusalem wanted to embrace. As he lifted her chin for another kiss, she closed her eyes and allowed herself to venture into that deeper water they'd discussed . . . telling herself this man was nothing at all like the banished bishop of Willow Ridge. After all, Hiram had talked a good line but he'd never once kissed her. And these kisses were the stuff dreams were made of . . .

Jerusalem eased away. Took a deep breath to get her bearings again. She focused on a particularly pretty library table and its four matching chairs, in the center of the room. "My word, you've got such wonderful pieces all through your house, but this one's like nothin' I've ever seen, with these carved curlicues along the border and corners."

"Thank you, my dear," he murmured as he fondly followed the pattern with his finger. "When Dorothea learned she couldn't have children, I made this table for the two of us to eat on. We used the larger table, which is now in the kitchen, when we had family and friends here—and after the aunts and Abner moved in."

"*Jah*, that would make sense," she murmured. So many things to know about this man . . . the life he'd lived with his wife. But she set aside her thoughts to find a smile. "It was a relief to see that Nettie and Florence and I get along well. Of course, we were chattin' about you, mostly, and how I came to Missouri last fall with my nephews. We aunts have a lot in common."

"I knew you would." He took her hand, lifted it to his lips, and then led her toward the door. "Ready to see the upstairs? I'll let you choose your guest room—back in the day, this place was built to house a lot of children, so now we have ample space for visitors."

The stairs creaked comfortably beneath their weight as they ascended, and again Jerusalem noted tidy rooms where the furnishings and quilts were old but well tended. Vernon's bedroom set was another marvel carved from walnut, and she didn't have to ask if he had fashioned it himself. She chose the room farthest down the hall from his, even though it was the smallest, knowing Abner and the aunts would be well aware of where she slept. The bright-colored crazy quilt on the twin bed appealed to her, as did the dormer ceilings and the trio of windows with simple valances made of calico that coordinated with the quilt.

"Feels real homey in here," she remarked as Vernon brought in her suitcase.

He chuckled under his breath. "If I took the notion to come calling in the night, a twin bed would still be large enough, you know. You could sleep out in the loft of the barn, and I'd be there if I thought you'd welcome me. In our youth, bundling was still an accepted practice, after all."

Her eyes widened. Bundling was a form of courtship where young folks slipped between the sheets fully clothed, usually in the girl's bedroom. "Not in *our* house it wasn't!" she clarified. "But then, with so many of us kids at home, we doubled and tripled up on bedrooms. Come time we were old enough to court, we found other places to go."

"And I can imagine you were driven home from many a Singing by many an eager young man," Vernon said. "You and Nazareth probably had a lot of secrets to keep for each other when you were girls growing up."

Jerusalem let out a short laugh. "We attended the Singings, for sure and for certain, because all of us Hooley kids loved to sing and socialize. But more often than not, Nazareth and I went with older sisters and then drove home by ourselves when they got rides with their fellas." She paused, choosing words she hoped wouldn't sound prideful or vain. "Nazareth and I were the sharpest pencils in the pack, ya see . . . and we've always figured the boys couldn't handle the way we ciphered so fast and won the spelling bees and took over classes on days the teacher was sick."

Vernon considered this, his eyes sparkling with mischief. "Since I didn't know you then—and since it's been oh, at least forty years since you and I were scholars—I'm not intimidated by your intelligence, Jerusalem. The older I get, the more I value companions of either gender who converse well and who feel confident about their places in God's creation. It's all about attitude."

"And I've got plenty of that, for sure and for certain!"

"What do you say I take you down a peg or two over the Scrabble board?" he teased. "Aunt Nettie and Aunt Florence would love to watch you challenge me, because they get tired of losing."

"Bring it on!" Jerusalem replied. "We three hens can keep a rooster in his place, no doubt about that. And humility's something everybody—especially bishops—need to work on."

Chapter Fourteen

As Vernon hitched his Percheron to an enclosed buggy, his whistled tune echoed in the dim barn. Even though the early-morning clouds hung low in the sky, promising snow by afternoon, he felt lighthearted and extremely optimistic. For the past couple of days, Jerusalem had regaled his aunts with tales of her family in Lancaster County and her nephews in Willow Ridge. Abner had even told him, privately, that this woman would make a wonderful wife for him and a welcome addition to their family.

Jerusalem said her goodbyes and thank-you's to Nettie, Florence, and his nephew, and then the two of them were headed back to Willow Ridge as the sun painted a pale pink line at the far horizon. The north wind whipped at the buggy, but even so Vernon felt a cozy glow as they started down the road. While the sleigh was a wonderful vehicle for dashing through the snow, with bells jingling merrily, this enclosed vehicle was warmer and felt more conducive to the conversation he hoped to have while they spent a couple of hours on the road.

"We'll take a different route, so you can get a look at our little town," he remarked as Samson clip-clopped along the cleared county blacktop. "Up here on the left, you'll see the Cedar Creek Mercantile, where Sam Lambright keeps us supplied with everything you could possibly want," he remarked. "Sam's mother runs the greenhouse beside his store, and his sister Abby has her sewing business in the mercantile's loft. Across the road is Graber's Custom Carriages, where James refurbished my sleigh."

"Nice-lookin' places," Jerusalem said as she peered out her window. "Looks like we've got sheep in these barns, and a dairy herd over yonder."

"That's the Ropp place. One of Rudy's boys has a machinery repair business, and the other one's getting into cage-free chickens and eggs that sell to some of the more upscale English markets hereabouts."

"*Jah*, seems like folks can't be satisfied with plain old white eggs and white chickens these days. Just like Ira and Luke are havin' the farmers around Willow Ridge grow specialty grains for their new mill."

As they turned onto the main highway, Vernon eased Samson closer to the shoulder and let the horse settle into his own pace. His thoughts whirled like dry leaves caught in the wind . . . should he propose during this ride? He'd told Jerusalem many times he wanted her for his wife, but he'd held off popping the question . . . had kept the words "I love you" reserved for just the right moment, so she wouldn't think he was careless about tossing such an important phrase around.

Vernon considered how best to bring up the subject . . . ran various lead-ins through his mind, rearranging the words and turns of phrase as he did when he was planning key points for a Sunday sermon. Words had always come easily to him, yet he recalled going through this same agitation, this same sense of urgency, so many years ago when Dorothea had been seated beside him in a courting buggy. He thanked God that he'd gained some experience and a keener understanding of females over time, because Jerusalem wouldn't jump as eagerly at the chance to marry as young girls did. She, too, had lived a full life and he sensed she could continue quite contentedly as a single woman . . . except that with her sister planning to marry Tom Hostetler, her world was about to undergo a major change. Vernon smiled. His longtime friend had unwittingly done him a huge favor, falling for Nazareth Hooley!

Finally he felt confident that God would give him the right words, and that the Lord would also open Jerusalem's mind and heart to love him as much as he adored her. He ran his thumbs over the smooth leather traces, getting his nerve up . . .

But when he noticed that Jerusalem was still gazing out her side window, with her jaw tight and her lips pressed into a thin line, Vernon swallowed his big question. Was that a tear trickling down her cheek?

He'd never learned how best to handle a crying woman. So many things could be going through Jerusalem's mind . . . something he'd said or done—or *not* said or done. Or she could be worried about something totally unrelated to these past several days he'd spent with her. She'd seemed to enjoy his aunts' company . . . had fit into the family dynamic better than he'd dared to hope.

So he would tread carefully, delicately. Just the sight of that single tear on this special woman's face tore Vernon up inside, and he reminded himself to remain as calm and observant and patient as he'd ever been with Dorothea, Nettie, or Florence. Older women cried for different reasons than young girls did, if indeed they could pinpoint a reason.

He reached for Jerusalem's hand, realizing that she'd remained beside the door rather than scooting toward the center of the seat, where she'd ridden during their sleigh rides. Not a good sign. "I've been lost in my own thoughts, and it seems you've become upset," he whispered. "How may I help you, dear heart? What's on your mind?"

Jerusalem let out a shuddery sigh.

Vernon shifted slightly closer to her, holding the reins in one hand while he kept his other one on hers. He hoped to clear up this situation quickly, or it would be a very long ride to Willow Ridge. But he remained quiet, sensing that her sniffles . . . the loud blowing of her nose, were her ways of gathering her thoughts. Jerusalem wasn't the type to cry over piddling matters, so she deserved his patience.

"I . . . I had a wonderful-*gut* visit at your place, Vernon," she began in an unsteady voice.

He nodded, knowing the other shoe would only drop if he didn't force it to. "I'm glad you came, too. That took some courage, knowing what my intentions were . . . what they are."

Jerusalem cleared her throat. She was still looking away from him but not moving her hand from under his. "You've got a couple of dear aunts, Vernon. I admire the way ya gave them and Abner a home . . ."

Again Vernon waited, refraining from a reply. Her sigh sounded so despondent that he closed his eyes, hoping the rosy future he'd been dreaming of wasn't about to vanish like the wisps of breath coming from Samson's nostrils.

". . . but you've got so much stuff—so many memories of Dorothea—in your house, I'm not sure there's room for me."

She might as well have pitched a brick at him. Vernon's chest felt like it was caving in, and he exhaled quickly. While he admired Jerusalem for her wit, her way with putting words together, he was now wishing she wasn't quite so succinct. "I—I don't know what to say."

Jerusalem laughed sadly. "*Jah*, I do that to people sometimes. And I hate to burst your perty bubble, Vernon, because I was caught up in it, too," she admitted. "Took me a while to figure out what wasn't settin' just right during my visit, but there it is. Your wife was a blessed woman, no doubt in my mind. But she might as well still be livin' there in all those rooms. I—I'm sorry."

Vernon sighed, very near tears himself. "I . . . hadn't thought about that, Jerusalem. But once again, you're absolutely right about—"

"Don't be playin' that little word game to humor me," she murmured. "It's gonna take more than words and *gut* intentions to fix this."

Jerusalem looked at him, then dabbed her eyes with a handkerchief. "I can't expect ya to change your home or get rid of all those fine pieces ya made for Dorothea, on account of how ya poured so much love into them," she continued in a rueful voice. "Wouldn't be fair of me to ask that of any man, but . . . at our stage of the game, that's how it'll be with anybody we'll meet, most likely."

Bless her, this woman had pointed up something that must be so obvious to everyone who entered his home, and yet he hadn't seen it. Nettie, Florence, and Abner had moved into brand new rooms and they'd chosen new furnishings made new quilts for their beds. Because they had lost everything they'd held dear in the flood, they were thankful to have a roof over their heads and grateful that he and Dorothea had made them welcome. While he knew widowers who had insisted their new wives accept the home and furnishings they provided, Vernon couldn't expect Jerusalem to feel comfortable while surrounded by the mementos of his previous marriage . . . no matter how much he treasured them.

"You've given me a lot to think about," he said quietly. "And no matter how disheartened I am, I truly appreciate your candor, Jerusalem."

She sighed. "Better to spell it all out now, rather than get hitched and have both of us be miserable."

Vernon patted her hand and then let go of it. Squeezed the reins as a way to deal with an anguish that took his breath away. Anything he might say at this point would sound like an excuse or a desperate plea for Jerusalem's love, and that wasn't a good foundation on which to build a lasting relationship.

The next couple of hours went slowly, with only an occasional remark about the passing scenery, yet Vernon was grateful that Jerusalem didn't fill the time with aimless chitchat. Her admission of discomfort further proved what a direct, solid woman she was. Far better that she had aired her true feelings rather than letting them fester. As various solutions to his problem whirled through his mind, Vernon came to terms with the fact that he would have to make some major changes if he wanted to marry this woman who had so quickly woven herself into his dreams, his heart . . . his soul.

When they came within sight of the mill and its big wheel, he crossed the river bridge and pulled the rig to a stop on the side of the road. "I hope you'll give Tom and Nazareth my best?"

"*Jah*, I can do that." She smiled at him. Her eyes were clear now, but sadness lingered on her face. "I won't go on and on about why you're not droppin' in at Tom's now, either."

Vernon shrugged. "I know good and well you'll tell your sister everything—"

"Not everything." Jerusalem reached for his hand, reminding him yet again of how firm her grip was and what a hold she had on his heart. "Some things I keep to myself, to think about in quiet times. To smile about when nobody's lookin'."

"May I stay in touch? I don't intend to pester you, or—"

"When have I ever had so many friends that I could turn one away?" she murmured. "I'd feel real bad if ya wanted nothin' more to do with me, Vernon. But I'd understand that, too, after the way I've let ya down."

Quickly Vernon embraced her, overcome by her simple, heartfelt goodness. "You've not heard the last of me, Jerusalem. I don't give up easily."

He kissed her soft cheek. Then he drove her to the mill entrance, carried her suitcase to the stoop, and felt extremely grateful that her tears had dried. He memorized Jerusalem's kind smile, the sight of her waving from the door.

And then Vernon drove home to Cedar Creek, a man facing a major mission, indeed.

Two days later, as Jerusalem helped Nazareth remove the evergreen and candles that had adorned Tom's mantel and windowsills for the holidays, her sister was still pecking at her. "Jerusalem, ya can't tell me Vernon just up and decided he wasn't crazy about ya," Nazareth remarked. "It's not like ya to be so quiet. Tom's curious about it, too."

Jerusalem smiled to herself. It had taken great restraint, but she had kept the juicy details about her Cedar Creek visit to herself. And indeed, she had mentally replayed many of the lovely moments she'd spent with Vernon, and she could smile now instead of weeping about what she'd walked away from. "Not much to tell," she hedged. "I figured out—"

"Puh! This is *me* you're talkin' to, and Tom'll be muckin' out the barn for a while," her sister insisted. "I'm keepin' after ya for my own reasons, ya know. If you're seein' things, about why gettin' hitched at our age isn't a *gut* idea, maybe you'd better point them out to me. Maybe

I've leaped before I looked, when it comes to fallin' for Tom."

Jerusalem paused with the dust rag halfway across the windowsill they'd just cleared. "Well, since ya put it that way . . . I, um, told Vernon I couldn't move into a house that was full of furniture he'd made for his first wife," she stated. "Don't get me wrong, it was all beautiful and any woman would be glad to have it, I suppose. But to me, it felt like his Dorothea still lived there, and she'd always be lookin' over my shoulder."

Nazareth's eyebrows flew up. She gazed around Tom's front room, a pensive expression on her face. "Well, isn't that the way of it, when ya hitch up with a fella who's been married?" she asked quietly. "It's not like we've got roomfuls of our own things to move into a man's home, after all. Just the linens and what-not we packed into our bride's chests as girls."

Sighing, Jerusalem wiped down the rest of the windowsill. "Maybe most gals could accept that—and if you're happy here in Tom's home, that's what matters," she added emphatically. "But it just wasn't workin' for me. I hurt Vernon's feelings, tellin' him my concerns, but at least I didn't keep him guessin' about why I was so uncomfortable."

She paused, figuring she might as well get the rest of it off her chest and be done with it. "You and I have spent all our lives under somebody else's roof, Nazareth. After the folks passed, when Jericho took us into his *dawdi haus*, that's what we expected, as *maidel* sisters. And here in Willow Ridge," she went on in a rising voice, "the nephews and the Lantz family have looked after us whenever we weren't stayin' at Hiram's, helpin' with his youngest kids."

"And we've been ever grateful—and helpful—to all those who've welcomed us," Nazareth pointed out.

"*Jah*, that's true. But if I'm finally gonna get a home of my own . . . I want it to feel like my place, with my man," she murmured. "Am I makin' sense? Or did I throw a horse-apple pie in Vernon's face for selfish, petty reasons?"

Nazareth gazed at Jerusalem as though seeing her for the first time. "Ya know, I never thought of it that way," she finally admitted. "And I want ya to be happy, Sister. I'll stop gnawin' on this bone now. I'll let you and Vernon figure it out."

Jerusalem grabbed her in a hug. "*Denki* for understandin', Nazareth. I wish you and Tom all the best, too, ya know."

For a moment they held each other, realizing how their lives would change momentously when one or both of them married. Then Nazareth cleared her throat. "Looks like we've got company. Better brace yourself for whatever Sarah and Lavinia have to say."

Glancing out the window at the approaching rig, Jerusalem shrugged. "We're just here helpin' Tom. What are they gonna do about that?" she asked. "It's not like they've come over to take down the greenery and candles they didn't care enough to put out for their *dat*."

Chapter Fifteen

Nazareth squared her shoulders. Carefully, lovingly, she wrapped the old newspaper pieces around the glass candle holders before packing them back into the box they'd probably been stored in for twenty years. While she didn't relish having words with Tom's daughters, Sarah and Lavinia were a part of his life, and they wouldn't disappear . . . the way his wife had. That thought made her determined to be a peacemaker, to smooth the girls' ruffled feathers for Tom's sake. He didn't let on, but he didn't like being at odds with his children. Even if he hadn't become the new bishop of Willow Ridge, concerned about living as an example to his district, he would want to be a good *dat*. A loving father, the way God was.

At the bang of the back kitchen door, she exchanged a glance with her sister. Then she stood tall, watching for the young women to enter the front room. A few moments later she could hear cabinets and drawers being opened.

"It's these dishes I'm wanting," one of them said. "And the towels I embroidered for Mamm's birthday when I was thirteen."

"And what about these *gut* tablecloths?" the other one asked. "And these bone china cups and saucers? Mamm told us those were tucked away in her bride's chest, so she surely intended for us to have them."

"*Jah*, it's a sure thing Dat won't be using them."

"He's probably forgotten she had them. And why should his *girlfriend* get them?"

When Nazareth saw sharp words puckering Jerusalem's face, she signaled for silence with a finger atop her lips. Apparently Tom's daughters didn't realize anyone was in the house, and she could use that to her advantage. Very quietly Nazareth crossed the front room, praying for God's guidance. It wasn't as if the girls were stealing, but she thought Tom ought to know about their intentions.

When she got to the doorway, she leaned against it. Jerusalem remained a few steps behind her, attuned to her thought process as she had always been, at home and in the schoolrooms where they'd taught. "*Gut* morning, girls," she said sweetly. "What a nice surprise, that you've come to see your *dat*. Shall I fetch him from the barn?"

As Tom's daughters whirled around, a glass pitcher flew from Sarah's hands and shattered on the floor. "*Ach*! We just stopped by to—"

"You're still here, are you?" Lavinia challenged. "Now that Dat's the bishop, I'd think you would be more mindful of appearances than to—"

"And speakin' of appearances," came Tom's voice from the mudroom. He stopped in the doorway rather than dirty the kitchen floor with his wet, mucky boots. "It would appear to *me* that ya came to ransack the place. Without so much as a how-do-ya-do for your *dat*. Do ya know how low that makes me feel? Your *mamm* raised ya better than that."

While Nazareth's heart ached for this man in his smeared barn coat and careworn stocking cap, he was an answer to her prayers. Better for Tom to handle this situation. His daughters would only resent her more if she presumed to put them in their place, in the home where they had grown up.

Sarah clasped her hands in front of her. "We . . . well, now that Mamm's passed, we wanted a few of her things. To remember her by."

"Girl things," Lavinia clarified. "Dishes and what-not that don't mean anything to you."

Tom's eyebrows rose. "Ya think I see it that way? Ya think I don't have some memories worth hangin' onto?"

The silence made Nazareth aware of how fast her pulse was pounding. This wasn't a place she enjoyed, being caught in the crossfire of hurt feelings. But these emotions were going to boil over sooner or later, so it was best that they all address the situation now, while everyone was in the same room.

Sarah bowed her head. "We didn't mean to get grabby, or—"

"We didn't figure your new *friend*—or whatever you call her—would want Mamm's stuff, anyway," Lavinia retorted.

"I call her *Nazareth*," Tom replied in a low voice. Slowly, deliberately, he removed his stocking cap and then hung his coat on the nearest wall peg. Bracing himself against the doorframe, he carefully removed his boots so they would drip in the mudroom. "And if ya can't show Nazareth the respect she deserves, leave now. And don't come back."

Oh, but that statement made the whole house hold its breath. While Nazareth felt gratified by Tom's loyalty to her, it wasn't a victory that would encourage his daughters to befriend her. But it was his house. And she understood that he was drawing a line, as far as what he would tolerate from his kids.

Sarah glanced at Nazareth and then murmured, "We

should've asked you before we started taking things from the cupboards. I'm sorry, Dat. Lavinia wanted to come—"

"*Me*?" her younger sister demanded. "You're the one who started talking about all the dinners we used to have, and the special dishes Mamm used then, and—"

"And I understand why ya feel that way," Nazareth interrupted quietly. "When our *mamm* passed, the five of us girls each got to choose something we wanted from the house before our oldest brother moved into it with his wife. To this day, I cherish her sewing basket, thimbles, and the scissors she used to make our clothes."

"And I got the clock our *dat* gave Mamm when they got engaged," Jerusalem said reverently. "It's been in every bedroom I've slept in since she passed, even though I've moved hundreds of miles and several times these past few months."

Sarah smiled a little. Lavinia's shoulders relaxed. They both sighed and looked at their father again.

Tom cleared his throat. "What was it Jesus said? 'Ask and you shall receive? Knock, and the door shall be opened?'" he remarked. "And me, I'm just askin' for a little consideration. I hate to think that your resentment towards Naz . . . your grief over your *mamm*'s passing, has driven ya to come bargin' in like thieves."

Sarah sighed. "*Jah*, we know better, Dat. I'm sorry for the way we've upset you."

"Me, too," Lavinia echoed. Then she cleared her throat. "May we please have a few of our mother's things?"

Tom looked around at the opened cabinets and drawers before letting his gaze settle on Nazareth. "I'd be pleased if we could all have our dinner together, around this table I gave your *mamm* when we married. And then, whatever either of ya cares to have, I'll help ya pack it up real *gut* so nothing breaks."

"Anything?" Lavinia blurted. "As much as we want?"

Tom's lips quirked. "That's the offer, *jah*. If ya fill up your rig, or ya want furniture, we'll load up my wagon. As many times as it takes."

"Oh, Dat, *denki* for understanding!" Lavinia grinned and then swiped at a tear.

"We really didn't mean to come on like a couple of prickly pears," Sarah said. Then she gazed at Nazareth and held out her hand. "It'll take us a while to get used to somebody else living in this house with Dat, but . . . well, we hope you can be patient with us, Nazareth."

Nazareth's heart slipped up into her throat as she gripped Sarah's hand. "Patience is somethin' we can all use more of. We've all got changes to make and habits that'll take some gettin' used to," she murmured. "Jerusalem and I would be pleased to put dinner on while you girls and your *dat* figure out what you'll be takin'."

"Something smells really *gut*," Lavinia admitted with a grin. "For a minute I thought we must be in the wrong house, finding fresh bread on the counter and a ham in the oven. It's a relief to know Dat doesn't have to cook anymore."

Tom laughed out loud. "I know what you're really meanin' to say, Vinny. You're amazed I haven't burned down the house or gotten food poisoning."

As the girls chuckled and turned back toward a cabinet they had opened, Tom stepped over to slip his arm around Nazareth's shoulders. "See there? You're a lifesaver in more ways than I can count, Naz," he whispered. "*Denki* for takin' this so well. I think we're over the hump now."

"I hope so," she replied. As she steered him playfully into the front room to have a word, Jerusalem took the hint and went to the oven to check the ham.

"Are ya really so ready to give up whatever your girls

want to take, Tom?" Nazareth asked quietly. "You have your memories, too. And if they clear out all your dishes, or big pieces of furniture, or—"

He kissed her quickly. "It's only *stuff*, Naz. If havin' their *mamm*'s things makes them happy—makes them feel better about me gettin' hitched again—they can clean out the whole place."

"*Jah*?" Nazareth considered this for a moment. "After the way your kids have acted, and the way they've talked to ya recently, I'm a little surprised at your . . . generosity."

Shrugging, he glanced into the kitchen. When he saw that everyone there was occupied, he kissed her again. "Maybe a little bird's been talkin' to me. Maybe I have a houseful of things I don't really *see* anymore, and if I clear them away, why—you and I can pick out new pieces to start our new life."

Oh, but she knew that little bird's name! Nazareth kept her remarks to herself, however, because once again she was amazed at how the pieces of her future seemed to be falling into place like a jigsaw puzzle . . . God's plan working out even more beautifully than she'd anticipated.

"You're a wonderful-*gut* man, Tom. And I love ya," she whispered.

"That's what I'm livin' for, Naz. You're the best."

Chapter Sixteen

"That went better than I expected," Jerusalem remarked as she and her sister looked out the window in the front room. Sarah and Lavinia's rig was heading down the lane ahead of Tom, who drove a wagonload of bedroom furniture and other pieces his daughters wanted.

"*Jah*, I was glad to see the girls loosenin' up, invitin' their *dat* to supper for his efforts today," Nazareth replied. "It means he'll be gettin' back pretty late tonight, but I think he's real pleased with how things turned out."

"Could be one of the girls will ask him to stay over. Would be *gut* for the whole family to talk about Lettie's passin', without us around. And I don't think Tom sees as much of his grandkids as he'd like." Jerusalem returned Tom's wave as he passed in front of the house, and then she turned to look around the front room. "They left a few gaps along the walls, ain't so?"

Nazareth chuckled. "The way Tom was talkin', he'd have let them have it *all*—lock, stock, and barrel. Told me he was fine with gettin' everything new, to start fresh when I married him."

"Not many fellas would agree to that. You're a lucky woman, Sister."

"*Jah*, and I know it, too." She had a kitty-cat grin on her face, as though she knew something and wasn't about to share it, either.

This information put Jerusalem in a speculative mood: three days had gone by since she'd told Vernon her concerns about his house being full of Dorothea's things . . . and maybe he'd decided he liked his life just as it was. If that was the way he wanted it, well, God had figured that into His plan for her and she'd go right on being a busy, useful woman, wouldn't she?

"So, you're sure about milkin' the cows while Tom's away?" she asked Nazareth as the mantel clock chimed three times.

"I'm *gut* with it, *jah*! Ya should've seen me learning how to do that, while ya were at Vernon's place." Nazareth's grin showed her excitement about taking over Tom's chores. "It's been a long time since you and I did the milkin', and we only had the four cows back then. Things are different when ya have to be ready for the truck to haul off all the milk."

Jerusalem chuckled as they put on barn coats and stocking caps. Her sister looked years younger and ever so happy . . . Jerusalem could only hope her own life would take such a turn with Vernon. But it was up to him. She'd said her piece.

When the two of them stepped inside the dim barn, Jerusalem lit the lanterns while Nazareth went to the stanchions to set up for milking the cows. Jerusalem headed back to the corner where the goats were nestled in their straw, laughing when the four of them hurried toward her with excited bleats.

Wasn't it nice to know these dear creatures appreciated her? Jerusalem glanced over her shoulder. "So once ya hitch up with Tom, what's to happen with our little buddies here?" she called out over the goats' racket.

Nazareth's eyebrows rose. "I hadn't thought about that. Seems a shame to split them up, especially since we've only got the one buck."

Jerusalem gave in to Pearl and Bessie's demand, briskly rubbing their foreheads with her knuckles. "With three kids on the way, it might be best to wait and see what we end up with. We'll figure it out."

She fetched a galvanized bucket and her little stool before tethering Pearl to begin her milking. It was a soothing job, sitting close to the warm goat, hearing the rhythmic splash of the milk as it hit the pail. By the time Jerusalem finished with Bessie and Matilda, she had enough to make a batch of goat cheese, which Tom loved—as did Vernon. Oh, how he'd raved over the grilled goat cheese sandwiches and macaroni and cheese casserole they'd made during his visit.

Best to leave that subject alone. It's his call as to how things go from here, she reminded herself. She saw that Nazareth was doing nicely at handling the cows, and because they were familiar with her sister, Jerusalem didn't interrupt the flow by offering to help.

"I'll go in and put this milk on the stove. And I'll start us some soup for supper," she called across the barn.

"Get the mail, why don't ya? I suspect Tom forgot all about it, what with the girls showin' up."

Jerusalem knuckle-rubbed the goats' four heads one last time and then headed toward the road. She lifted her face to the last rays of sunlight, invigorated by the chill in the air . . . enjoying yet again the splendor of the surrounding pastureland blanketed in pristine white snow. Vernon's place looked pretty in the winter, too, with the old white house, its stone chimney, and the sturdy red barns behind it. If nothing else, she'd made some scenic memories while she'd visited Cedar Creek.

When she opened the mailbox, she gaped. The lone

envelope was addressed to her—and the familiar, precise handwriting made her heart skip into triple time. "Vernon," she whispered as she snatched up the letter.

As Jerusalem hurried toward the house, it was all she could do not to slosh the milk from her pail. She stepped into the mudroom, set the bucket on the floor, and then held the letter to her heart. Would this be the bishop's farewell? Or had Vernon Gingerich found a way to accommodate her concerns? She closed her eyes . . . took a couple of deep breaths before carefully peeling away the envelope's triangular flap.

My dearest Jerusalem,
I hope this finds you well, and I hope Tom hasn't taken too long to deliver this to you. I thought you'd rather receive this privately than have your rambunctious nephews find it in their mailbox.

Jerusalem laughed out loud. For sure and for certain, Ira and Luke would be teasing her to high Heaven if they saw her face right now. She breathed easier and continued reading.

My aunts and Abner send you their best, and I'll have you know they took your side completely when I mentioned your reservations about coming to live among Dorothea's belongings. Please accept my apologies for being oblivious to the obvious: you are absolutely right, Jerusalem. Every room of this home reflects my wife's tastes and probably felt like a shrine to her memory, the way you perceived it.

Oh, but her pulse was pounding. Vernon was a kind and gentle man, but he didn't say things unless he sincerely meant them. He knew better than to pander to her, too.

I have devised a couple of options for you, if
you would still consent to my courting you with
matrimony in mind. I'm sure you'll understand my
desire to keep this home, which has been in my
family for three generations, but I would consider
building on a wing for the two of us—a love nest,
if you will—so we could enjoy our privacy while
sharing the main house with my family.

Jerusalem paused, imagining how the picturesque old
Gingerich home would look with a second extension,
probably on the opposite end from where Abner and the
aunts lived. Truth be told, she had thought their wing
looked . . . patched on. Another extension would only de-
tract further from the overall appearance of the place. But
wasn't it wonderful that Vernon would add on rooms just
for the two of them?

My other idea would be to completely empty the
main rooms of the house, paint the walls whatever
colors you prefer, put down new rugs, and begin
our life together with furnishings of your own
choosing. As Nettie and Florence have pointed out
to me, the upholstered chairs and sofas are nearly
threadbare, while the rugs and curtains are faded,
as well. This idea has already inspired me to begin
another project for you—and my mind and hands
are truly delighted to be crafting something else
from fine wood. Thank you for being my
inspiration, Jerusalem!

I eagerly await your response, and you may
call to discuss these ideas or to suggest your
own, rather than write them to me, if you'd prefer.
Whatever you decide, know that you are already
a blessing from our dear Lord, and that the piece

I'm making for you is intended as another gift
rather than an enticement to marry me.
                    Ever yours, dear Jerusalem,
                    Vernon

Oh, how her pulse raced—but her curiosity ran faster.
The milk would be fine in the mudroom for a while
longer, so she hurried outside again. Tom had a phone in
the barn, for reaching his milk truck driver, and wasn't
this a situation of appropriate magnitude to warrant its
use? After all, her very future had been dangled before
her like a carrot in front of the proverbial donkey. Who
was she to keep the bishop of Cedar Creek waiting?

"What's happened, Sister?" Nazareth called as she was
leaving the barn. "Ya look like there's an emergency—or
a fire!"

"Ya might say that, *jah*. Didn't get our soup started.
Sorry!"

Jerusalem felt anything but sorry, however. She said a
prayer of gratitude that Nazareth was heading for the
house, still smiling as though she *knew* things. Once
inside the barn, Jerusalem lit the lantern again and lifted
the receiver of the old rotary phone. Vernon, too, had a
phone in his barn, to help with Abner's butchering business and to keep in touch with his preachers and church
members . . . but what if he wasn't there? Or what if
Abner answered? She couldn't blurt her questions into the
answering machine—

But her fingers had already dialed the numbers.
Vernon's phone was ringing . . . ringing . . .

"Good afternoon. You've reached Gingerich Custom
Butchering. This is Vernon."

Jerusalem's words stuck in her throat. Was this a
recording, or—but it had to be Vernon, talking directly to
her, didn't it? She had already forgotten how low and

melodic the bishop's voice was, and it made something flutter deep down inside her. "Uh—"

"Hello? Can you hear me?"

"*Jah*! Vernon, it's—"

"Jerusalem! It's wonderful to hear your voice again, dear heart." He let out a sigh that sounded satisfied without being smug. "You've received my letter, I take it?"

"*Jah*, and—well, what on Earth will ya do with all those perty pieces ya made for Dorothea, if ya empty out your house?" she said in a rush. "It wasn't my intention for ya to throw away such wonderful-*gut* work, when—"

"Nothing will be destroyed or wasted, my dear. It's not the Plain way to dispose of perfectly serviceable items."

"*Serviceable*? Those hutches and tables and such are too beautiful to be cast aside," she protested. "If that's what's to happen to them—"

"Relax, sweetheart. Take a deep breath."

Jerusalem exhaled. Vernon wasn't laughing at her, exactly, but he was clearly enjoying the state she had whipped herself into. She managed a chuckle. "Guess I got a little excited there."

"And I love to excite you, Jerusalem. I hope to do much more of that, in time," he remarked with a low laugh. Then he cleared his throat. "There's an auction every spring to benefit the local school. I would like to believe Dorothea's pieces would bring in a fair amount of cash for such a good cause. And because you've been a schoolteacher, I thought you might appreciate that suggestion."

Her jaw dropped. "Oh, Vernon. That's a wonderful-*gut* idea, but I can't think you'd do all of this for . . . for *me*."

His sigh sounded a bit nostalgic. "Actually, I believe Dorothea herself inspired me. She was a schoolteacher when I met her, you see, and up until the time when she became too ill, she was involved with the school's Christmas programs and their picnics and the fundraising events," he explained. "In her quiet way, my wife was every bit as persuasive and influential as you are, Jerusalem."

"Oh, my. What a lovely thing to say, Vernon," she replied. She could hardly breathe, for hanging on to the thrilling timbre of his voice . . .

"And I meant every word. You believe that, don't you?"

She let out the breath she'd been holding. "You're not a fella who talks just to hear himself, or to lead folks along for his own benefit."

"Thank you. Coming from you, that's a high compliment."

Jerusalem paused. So many ideas and emotions were whirling in her head . . . in her heart. There was no doubt in her mind that Vernon's handcrafted furniture would bring top dollar, and he'd made so many pieces over the years that the auctioneer could practically devote an entire sale to the bishop's handiwork.

"Are you still there? You've become very quiet."

She let out a laugh. "I think I'm speechless. *That* doesn't happen often."

Vernon's laughter made her heart take wing. Wasn't it a fine feeling, to have a man talking with her this way, willing to give up so much for the sake of her happiness?

"As I said in my letter, I'm making you another, larger piece even if you decide becoming my wife isn't what God wants for you."

"Puh! You bein' a bishop and all, why would God pay more mind to *my* way of thinkin' than to yours?"

"Because you're His child and He loves you, Jerusalem. And I love you, too. With all my heart."

A little "*oh*" escaped her. Just that easily, he'd told her he loved her . . . and never in her life had a fellow said that. Tears ran down her cheeks. Oh, but she could indeed believe that God loved her very, very much if He had led her to this eloquent, decent man. "I . . . I'm tryin' to take all this in," she rasped. "Ya must think I'm a dunderhead, not to—"

"I'm gratified that you will consider my ideas," he replied quietly. "And I don't want you to feel obligated to repeat those three little words just because I said them to you, Jerusalem. They're not to be taken lightly."

"Ya said a mouthful there, Vernon. *Denki* for . . . for understandin' me like nobody else ever has," she whispered. "I probably sound all *ferhoodled* and a couple pencils short of a pack, but I truly appreciate what-all you're willin' to change to make your home feel like *my* home."

There was a brief pause. "Well, then, I've accomplished what I set out to do, dear lady."

"May . . . may I come for another visit sometime, so's we can talk about this face to face?"

Vernon's low laughter made her tingle all over. "Face to face is precisely the way I'd like to be with you, Jerusalem. Right now," he added. "But I can settle for picking you up tomorrow morning, if that suits you."

"*Jah*! I can be ready by—oh, but I'm soundin' like a silly schoolgirl—"

"You sound delightful. And delighted. Just the way I hope to keep you feeling for a long, long time," he replied. "See you tomorrow, then?"

"For sure and for certain. And Vernon?"

"Yes, dear heart?"

Jerusalem squeezed her eyes shut. *If this is what love*

feels like, what are you afraid of? Why waste another minute? "I—I love ya right back. Truly I do."

"Oh, my." There was another pause, when Vernon's breath drifted through the receiver to wrap her in his steadfast, heartfelt warmth. "I shouldn't admit this," he said with a soft chuckle, "as we Amish husbands have our appearances—our stern, stoic reputations to maintain—you know. But you melted me like butter just now, telling me you love me, Jerusalem. Whatever you want—whatever I have—it's yours."

Well, now! Better not argue with that, or give him a chance to change his mind.

Jerusalem laughed, overjoyed. "See ya tomorrow then. I can't wait, Vernon."

He made kissing noises, and she giggled as though his lips had teased at hers. After she hung up, Jerusalem hugged herself, barely believing the conversation she'd just had. When she finally started toward the house, darkness had fallen and four sections of yellow light from the kitchen windows made a quilt square on the snow.

When Jerusalem entered Tom's kitchen, she cherished the sight of her sister standing at the stove, humming a hymn tune as she stirred a pot of soup. A time would come when she and Nazareth wouldn't cook together or share their thoughts every waking moment . . . but she could handle that now.

Nazareth looked up. Then a slow, sweet smile spread over her dear face. "Well, now. I was gonna ask if everything was goin' okay with Vernon, but the answer to that's written all over ya, Sister. Ya look as perty as a pink poinsettia in full bloom."

Would these compliments ever end? Would these fine, shiny feelings fade like curtains that had hung too long in the sun?

Not if you've got anything to say about it, they won't!

"Nazareth." Jerusalem crossed the kitchen, her feet barely touching the floor, it seemed. She slung her arm around her younger sister and leaned her head so they stood kapp to kapp. "Back when we were girls, watchin' all our friends get married, who would've believed the two of us would be hitchin' up with bishops, in our fifties? Guess God knew what He was doin' all along, ain't so?"

Nazareth slipped her arm around Jerusalem's waist and squeezed her tight. "Amen, Sister. Ya said a mouthful."

Sugar and Spice!

For me, it wouldn't be Christmas without cookies. I've often baked more than 150 dozen in a season and made tubs of candy besides! I give them to family and friends, or take pretty trays of them to holiday events, because a lot of folks are just too busy to bake these days. I wanted to share some of my favorite recipes here, and while they aren't necessarily Amish recipes I've found that home-made treats cross all sorts of cultural lines. Nothing brings folks together like good food!

All of these recipes freeze well, especially if layered between pieces of wax paper. Most of these are also firm enough to pack and mail. The best defense against dry, brittle cookies is to keep the cookie tray covered in plastic wrap—and don't overbake them!

You'll find these recipes plus recipes from my previous books on my website, www.CharlotteHubbard.com, and I hope you'll try those, as well. You can also read excerpts of my books there and sign up for my newsletter. You can email me at NaomiCKing@gmail.com, and you can Friend me on Facebook as Charlotte Hubbard and Like my Naomi C. King author page. Meanwhile, I wish you all the peace, joy, love—and goodies—of the season!

Cookies and Bars

Williamsburg Gingerbread Cut-Outs

I found this recipe in a historical cookbook more than twenty years ago and I've never bothered trying another one: the cookies are spicy and soft and they keep well. The dough is sticky, however, so you need to roll it out on a day when you're feeling patient!

½ C. softened butter (no substitutes)
1 C. sugar
2 T. cinnamon
2 tsp. ground cloves
2 T. ground ginger
1 T. lemon flavoring
¾ C. evaporated milk
1 C. molasses
5 C. flour
1½ tsp. baking powder
1 tsp. salt

Cream the butter and sugar. Add the flavorings and evaporated milk and blend well. Add the molasses, and then the dry ingredients until the dough is thoroughly mixed. Wrap in wax paper and chill overnight (or it'll keep in the fridge for a few days).

Preheat the oven to 350°. Working with about a fourth of the dough at a time, roll out to ¼" thickness on a well-floured surface, rubbing flour on the rolling pin as needed (patience, remember!) and cut out with cookie cutters. Bake 7–8 minutes on pans lined with parchment paper—don't let them brown!—and allow to cool for a minute on the pan before removing them to a wire rack.

Frost/decorate with the buttercream recipe included here for Sugar Cookies, and allow the frosting to dry/set up. Store between sheets of wax paper. Freezes well. 7–8 dozen.

Sugar Cookies

I used this recipe in WINTER OF WISHES, but it bears repeating here: this is the cookie that turns an ordinary cookie tray into a fabulous display of Christmas cookies! I usually make five to six batches of this dough, adding paste coloring and flavored gelatin (see note below). I make and chill the dough one day, bake the cookies another day and store them in a covered container, and then decorate them the next day because it takes that long to finish about 13 dozen of these!

½ C. butter, softened (no substitutes)
1 C. sugar
1 egg
1 T. lemon juice
1 tsp. vanilla
2 C. flour
½ tsp. salt
½ tsp. baking soda

Cream the butter and sugar, then beat in the egg, lemon juice, and vanilla. Combine the dry ingredients and gradually add them to the dough until it's well blended. Tint with paste food coloring, if desired. Wrap dough in wax paper or plastic wrap and refrigerate it for at least 3 hours (it will keep for several days, until you have time to bake). Preheat oven to 350°. Work with half a batch at a time: roll to about ¼" thickness on a floured surface, then cut with cookie cutters. Place 1" apart on a cookie sheet covered with parchment paper, and bake 7–8 minutes for softer, chewier cookies and 9–10 minutes or until lightly browned for crisp cookies. Cool on the pan for a minute and then remove with a spatula to a cooling rack. Makes 2–3 dozen.

<u>Kitchen Hint</u>: For flavored sugar cookies, add a 3 oz. package of sugar free gelatin to the dough! I make green dough with lime, yellow dough with peach or orange, and dark pink dough with cherry gelatin. If you use regular sugar gelatin, reduce the sugar in your recipe by a couple of tablespoons.

Buttercream Frosting

This is the recipe I learned long ago in a cake decorating class. I love it because it doesn't taste like shortening, and it dries firmly when you decorate cookies or cake. It also freezes well in a covered container if you have any left over.

½ C. milk
½ C. softened butter (no substitutes)
½ C. shortening
½ tsp. salt
1 tsp. vanilla
1 tsp. lemon flavoring
6–8 C. (about a pound) confectioners' sugar

In a mixing bowl, blend the milk, butter, shortening, and flavorings. Blend in the sugar a cup or two at a time, scraping the bowl, until the frosting is thick and forms peaks.

For colored frosting, use paste coloring to maintain a thickness that will hold its shape during decorating. Makes enough to decorate/frost 6 batches of sugar cookies, or a cake.

<u>Kitchen Hint</u>: I divide my frosting into 4 or 5 plastic containers and color one batch with deep pink, one batch with yellow, one with green, one with sky blue and I leave some white. Then I get out my pastry bag and decorating tips, the sanding sugars, jimmies, and miniature M&Ms, and I *play*! Let the decorated cookies dry/set up before you store or freeze them.

Mini-Chip Cut-Outs

Here's the perfect Christmas combination: a chocolate chip cookie you roll and cut into shapes! This came from a Nestle's ad, years ago, and is still one of my favorites.

1 C. butter, softened
½ C. brown sugar
½ C. sugar
2 tsp. vanilla
1 egg yolk
2½ C. flour
2 C./one bag mini chocolate chips, divided

Cream butter, the sugars, and the vanilla. Beat in the egg yolk and gradually add the flour. Stir in 1½ C. of the mini chips. Wrap dough in wax paper and chill at least a couple of hours (overnight or longer is fine, too).

Preheat oven to 350°. Allow the dough to warm for a few minutes. On a floured surface, working with one chunk of dough at a time, carefully roll to ¼" thickness and cut into shapes, pressing the dough together again if it separates around the chips. Use a metal spatula to transfer cookies to a cookie sheet lined with parchment paper. Bake about

9 minutes, until just beginning to brown. Cool on pan for a couple of minutes before transferring to a wire rack.

Frost/decorate with chocolate buttercream: melt the remaining ½ C. chips in a microwave safe bowl and stir in 1 C. of already-made buttercream (or store-bought) frosting. Pipe it on with a pastry bag.

<u>Kitchen Hint</u>: I have dumped the entire bag of mini chips into the dough, but discovered that more is *not* better! You can have too many chips in this dough!

Mocha Brownies

Wow, but these are the most fabulous, dense brownies! And who can refuse that extra little jolt of java? No frosting required, but if you want to dust them with powdered sugar while they're still warm, it'll add a snowy effect.

1⅓ C. butter (no substitutes)
⅔ C. unsweetened cocoa powder
2 T. instant coffee crystals or espresso powder
2 C. sugar
4 eggs
2 tsp. vanilla
1½ C. flour
1 C. semisweet or dark chocolate chips
2 tsp. cinnamon

Preheat oven to 350° and spray a 9 x 13" pan. Melt/ microwave butter and stir in cocoa powder and coffee. Stir in the sugar, then stir in the eggs one at a time and add vanilla—stir this mixture until well blended. Stir in the flour and then the chocolate chips and cinnamon. Spread the batter in the pan and bake for about 25 minutes or just until a pick inserted in the center comes out clean. Cool completely in the pan. Cut into bars or triangles. 4 dozen.

<u>Kitchen Hint</u>: Use a mixer on low speed if you don't want to do all this hand stirring.

Orange Date Bars

Light, fruity, and very easy to make!

2 orange cake mixes
1 box (3.4 oz.) of orange or lemon instant pudding
1 C. oil
4 eggs
1 8 oz. box of chopped dates
1½ C. chopped pecans or sliced almonds

Preheat the oven to 350°. Mix the above ingredients, except for the nuts, and spread the dough in two 9 x 13" pans or in a 10 x 17" pan that have been sprayed. Sprinkle nuts over the batter and lightly press them in. Bake for about 20 minutes, just until the center is firm. Cool in the pans.

<u>Drizzle</u>: Mix 1 C. powdered sugar with enough milk to make it pourable, and add a shake of salt, and vanilla, lemon extract or almond extract to taste. Drizzle over top of the cooled cookies and cut into bars.

Turtle Brownies

Who can resist the classic combination of moist chocolate, gooey caramel, and pecans?

1 brownie mix (9 x 13" size)
1 pkg. of caramel bits (Kraft makes them)
⅓ C. whipping cream
2 C. coarsely chopped pecans, divided

Preheat the oven to 350°. Line the pan with foil so it extends up the sides and over the ends, then spray the foil. Mix the brownies according to package directions, then spread half of it in the prepared pan and bake it for 20 minutes or until just firm to the touch.

Meanwhile, microwave the caramel bits and whipping cream in a microwavable bowl on high for 2 minutes, stirring after the first minute. When bits are mostly melted, keep stirring until the mixture is smooth. Stir in 1 C. of the pecans. Spread this mixture evenly over the partly baked brownie crust, then crumble the remaining brownie dough evenly over this (caramel mixture will show through) and sprinkle on the remaining pecans. Press lightly. Return to the oven for an additional 25 minutes or until the top is firm. Cool completely in the pan. Lift the brownies by the foil "handles" and then peel away the foil before cutting to serve. 2 dozen large or 4 dozen smaller brownies.

Jumbles
These drop cookies are best described as a lot of "stuff" held together with a little dough. I bake them year-round, but for Christmas I use red and green M&Ms.

1 stick butter or margarine
½ C. sugar
¼ C. packed brown sugar
1 egg
1¼ C. flour

½ tsp. baking soda
2 C. M&Ms (mini baking chips OR regular-size candies)
1 C. raisins
1 C. chopped peanuts

Preheat the oven to 350°. Cover cookie sheets with parchment paper. Cream the butter and sugars until fluffy, then mix in the egg. Add the dry ingredients and then stir in the candies, raisins, and peanuts. Drop by rounded tablespoons, about 2 inches apart. Bake 10–12 minutes, or until firm. Cool for a couple minutes on the baking sheet before transferring to a wire rack. Makes about 30.

Hidden Treasure Cookies
This has become one of my favorite recipes over the years because I never tire of biting into one of these frosted cookies to discover that hidden chocolate mintiness inside. I triple the ingredients to make about 8 dozen, so I don't run short. If you tint the frosting bright pink, yellow, or green before pressing them into jimmies or sanding sugar, they'll really stand out on a cookie tray.

½ C. sugar
¼ C. packed brown sugar
¼ C. shortening (Crisco, for instance)
¼ C. butter or margarine, softened
½ tsp. vanilla
1 egg
1⅔ C. flour
½ tsp. baking soda
About 2½ doz. Andes mints, unwrapped

Preheat oven to 350°. Mix the sugars, shortening, butter, vanilla and egg in large bowl. Add the flour and soda.

Shape a tablespoon of dough around each mint, covering the corners and pressing together any cracks in the dough. (Be patient! It's worth it!) Place the cookies about 2" apart on baking sheets covered with parchment paper. Bake 8–9 minutes or until barely golden brown. Cool on wire rack.

Frosting: 1 C. powdered sugar, 1 T. plus 1 or 2 tsp. milk, ¼ tsp. vanilla or almond extract, plus food color, if you want. (You can also use the buttercream recipe included in this section.) Frost the centers of the cookies and press into jimmies, sanding sugar, etc. to decorate them. 1 batch makes about 2 dozen.

Gingersnaps

I love to bite into a cookie and have it bite me back, spice-wise! These soft, chewy molasses cookies are easy to mix ahead and then chill until you have time to bake.

¾ C. butter
1 C. sugar
1 egg
¼ C. molasses
2 C. flour
2 tsp. baking soda
1 T. cinnamon
½ tsp. ground cloves
1 tsp. ginger
extra sugar

Cream the butter and sugar, then add the egg and molasses. Mix in the dry ingredients and spices until well blended, wrap the dough in wax paper, and chill until you're ready to bake. Preheat the oven to 375°. Roll the dough into 1¼-inch balls and then roll in sugar. Place 2" apart on the cookie sheet and bake for about 10 minutes for a soft cookie, slightly longer for a crisp cookie. Makes about 3½ dozen.

<u>Kitchen Hint</u>: For a sophisticated presentation, I like to roll one edge of a cooled cookie in melted white chocolate and then quickly roll it in raw sugar or holly-berry jimmies. Let dry on wax paper.

Cream Cheese Macaroons
My mother *loved* coconut, and these were her favorite cookies. If cream cheese and coconut isn't enough yumminess for you, add a cup of M&M mini baking chips for variety.

⅓ C. butter
1 3-oz. pkg. cream cheese (full fat), softened
¾ C. sugar
1 egg yolk
2 tsp. almond extract
2 tsp. Triple Sec, other liqueur, or rum flavoring
1¼. C. flour
2 tsp. baking powder
14-oz. pkg. of coconut, divided

Cream the butter, cream cheese, sugar, egg yolk, and flavorings. Mix in the flour and baking powder, and then 3 C. of the coconut. Chill dough at least an hour (or, it will keep for a few days in the fridge).

Preheat oven to 325°. Shape dough into 1" balls and roll them in remaining coconut, pressing it in. Bake on cookie sheets lined with parchment paper for 15 minutes, or until barely starting to brown. Cool on the sheet for a minute, and carefully remove to a wire rack.

<u>Kitchen Hint</u>: Use good-quality, moist coconut for this, and use full-fat cream cheese or the cookies won't hold together right. If you don't find bags of the mini M&M baking chips in the baking aisle, look for tubes of them at the check-out counter.

Peanut Butter and Jelly Sandwiches
I made the mistake of not baking these one Christmas, and when my niece searched her cookie bucket and found none, Aunt Charlotte heard about it! A soft, yummy cookie beloved by those who can't have chocolate.

1 C. butter-flavored Crisco
1 C. peanut butter (creamy or chunky)
1 C. sugar
1 C. brown sugar
3 eggs
1 tsp. vanilla
3 C. flour
2 tsp. baking soda
extra sugar
18 oz. jar of jelly/jam (see hint)

Preheat the oven to 350°. Cream the Crisco, peanut butter and the sugars, then mix in the eggs and vanilla until well blended. Add the flour and baking soda. Roll dough into 1" balls and then roll in the extra sugar to coat them. Place balls on cookie sheets lined with parchment paper, and bake about 7–8 minutes (don't overbake!). Cool. Match pairs of cookies so they fit, then spread the flat side of one with jelly and press the flat side of the other cookie to form a sandwich. Allow jelly to dry before stacking in a storage container. Freezes well.

Kitchen Hint: I've used a lot of red jams/jellies and they each add their own special tartness or sweetness. Red plum is my favorite, but cherry is tasty and so is raspberry. Be aware that with strawberry jam, the chunks make the sandwiches harder to press together.

Brown Sugar Date Drops

Mom used to stir these up, and the aroma of the brown sugar and cooked dates made the house smell divine. A really moist, chewy cookie.

1 C. margarine or butter, softened
2 C. brown sugar
½ C. buttermilk
1 tsp vanilla
3½ C. flour
1 tsp. baking soda
1 tsp. cinnamon

Filling
2 C. chopped dates
¼ C. sugar
¾ C. water

Preheat the oven to 375°. For the dough, cream the margarine/butter with the sugar, then add the buttermilk and the dry ingredients. Set aside and make the filling: place the dates, sugar and water in a medium pan on the stove and cook, stirring constantly, until thickened.

Line cookie sheets with parchment paper. To form each cookie, drop 1 T. dough, spread slightly with the back of the spoon, then drop on a tsp. of the filling and top with another tsp. of dough. Bake 10 minutes, or until firm. Cool a minute or so on the pan before transferring to a rack to cool completely. About 4 dozen.

<u>Kitchen Hint</u>: Don't have buttermilk? Measure 1 T. vinegar or lemon juice into a measuring cup and then pour the milk to the ½ C. mark. Stir and let it sit until it thickens.

Shortbread Jelly Bites

Here's a versatile shortbread cookie you can fill with any flavor of jelly or jam you prefer. I like this recipe because by baking the jelly filling (rather than adding it after you bake), you make the cookie much easier to freeze, ship, etc. I've nicknamed these "jelly eyes" because they're so perfect and round with shiny centers!

1 C. softened butter (no substitutions)
⅔ C. sugar
½ tsp. almond extract
2 C. flour
⅓ to ½ C. jelly or seedless jam

Cream the butter and sugar. Beat in the extract and gradually add the flour until the dough forms a ball. Wrap the dough in wax paper and chill at least an hour, or up to 3 or 4 days, if that's more convenient.

Preheat oven to 350°. Roll dough into 1" balls. Place balls on a baking sheet covered with parchment paper and carefully make an indentation in the centers with the end of a wooden spoon. Fill with jelly, and bake 12–14 minutes or until firm (I don't let mine get even slightly brown). Cool on a rack.

For a decorative variation, make a glaze of 1 C. powdered sugar, 2–3 tsp. milk, and ½ tsp. almond extract. Tint with paste coloring, if you like. Carefully spoon the glaze into a pastry bag with a small round tip and then zigzag the glaze over the tops of the cooled cookies.

<u>Kitchen Hint</u>: When I'm making the indentations in the dough balls, I "wiggle" the wooden spoon a bit so the top of the indention is wider—but don't let the dough crack. Then I spoon the jelly into a pastry bag with a large round tip and squeeze it into the holes before baking, to keep the jelly nice and neat.

Lemon Cheesecake Bars

Here's another great bar that starts with a cake mix—which means the flavor variations on this recipe are endless! The cream cheese filling keeps them moist and chewy.

1 lemon cake mix
2 eggs
⅓ C. oil
8 oz. bar of cream cheese, softened
⅓ C. sugar
1 tsp. lemon juice or ReaLemon
Colored sugars, jimmies, etc. if desired

Preheat the oven to 350°. Mix the dry cake mix, *one* of the eggs and the oil until the mixture's crumbly. Reserve a cup for topping, and firmly pat the rest of the dough into a sprayed 9 x 13" pan. Bake for 15 minutes. Meanwhile beat the cream cheese, sugar, the remaining egg and the lemon juice until smooth. Spread over the baked layer, and then sprinkle with the reserved crumb mixture. Sprinkle with colored sugar or jimmies, if desired, and bake 15 minutes longer. Cool in the pan before cutting.

<u>Kitchen Hint:</u> I have also used a chocolate cake mix and sprinkled on nuts; strawberry cake mix and sprinkled with mini M&Ms; coconut cake mix and sprinkled it with chopped macadamia nuts. The possibilities are only limited by your taste and imagination!

Chocolate Mint Drop Sugar Cookies
Here's a minty surprise in a firm, sweet cookie. I'm disappointed some years when I can't find mint chocolate chips, but butterscotch chips (or Hershey Special Dark chips) make a tasty replacement.

1 C. sugar
¾ C. oil
2 eggs
1 tsp. vanilla
2½ C. flour
1½ tsp. baking powder
1 10-oz. bag of mint chocolate chips
Extra sugar

Preheat the oven to 350°. In the mixer bowl, blend the sugar with the oil, eggs, and vanilla. Add in the flour and baking powder, then stir in the chips. Shape rounded spoonfuls into balls and roll in the extra sugar. Place balls on cookie sheets that have been covered with parchment paper and bake 8–10 minutes. Cool for a minute on the pan before removing to a wire rack to cool completely. About 5 dozen.

Chocolate Marshmallow Cookies
This recipe comes from Lovina Eicher's "The Amish Cook" column (now featured on a Facebook page called "The Amish Cook from Oasis Newsfeatures") and it's indescribably soft and chocolate and wonderful with a marshmallow surprise beneath the rich cocoa frosting.

1 C. shortening (Crisco, for instance)
2 C. sugar
2 eggs
2 tsp. vanilla
4 C. flour
1 tsp. each baking soda and salt
⅔ C. cocoa powder
1 C. thick sour milk or buttermilk
36 big marshmallows, cut in half

In a medium bowl, stir together the flour, baking soda, salt and cocoa powder. Set aside. Beat together the shortening, sugar, eggs and vanilla until fluffy. Add flour mixture alternately with the sour milk. Drop batter by spoonful onto greased baking sheet. Bake at 350° for 8 minutes. Top each cookie with a marshmallow half and return to oven for 2 minutes to soften. Cool completely.

<u>Frosting</u>
6 T. butter or margarine, melted
¼ C. cocoa powder
1 tsp. vanilla
3½ C. powdered sugar
5–6 T. milk

Combine all ingredients and beat together until smooth. Spread over tops of cooled cookies, covering marshmallows.

<u>Kitchen Hint</u>: To make sour milk, place 1 T. lemon juice or vinegar in measuring cup. Fill with milk to make one cup. Let sit at room temperature for 15 minutes until thick and lumpy.

Lemon Apricot Sandwiches

Soft, chewy, creamy, fruity . . . this cookie has it all! And because it begins with a cake mix, you can create lots of different flavor combinations.

1 lemon cake mix
½ C. oil
2 eggs
Sugar
Jar of apricot fruit spread or jelly
Buttercream frosting (recipe included earlier)

Preheat the oven to 350° and cover cookie sheets with parchment paper. Mix the cake mix with the oil and eggs until well blended. Roll the dough into 1" balls and then roll the balls in sugar. Place about an inch apart and flatten slightly with the bottom of a glass. Bake about 8 minutes, until just firm, and then cool for a minute on the cookie sheet before transferring to a wire rack.

To make the sandwiches, match up cookies by size and spread the flat side of one with the apricot spread, the flat side of the other with buttercream. Press together. Let set for a while before storing. Freezes well.

Cherry Coconut Drops

Sometimes the simplest cookies can be the best! Here's a moist, chewy macaroon made with colorful candied cherries and only five ingredients. No mixer needed.

2 7-oz. bags of flaked coconut
4 T. cornstarch
1 can sweetened condensed milk
2 tsp. vanilla
1 C. chopped candied cherries (mix red and green for the prettiest cookie!)

Preheat the oven to 325° and line baking sheets with parchment paper. In a large mixing bowl, stir the coconut and cornstarch together, then stir in the sweetened condensed milk and vanilla, and stir in the cherries last. Drop dough onto the prepared baking sheets by rounded spoonfuls, about an inch apart. Bake for 12–14 minutes, until just starting to brown on the bottom and edges. Cool on the baking sheets for at least a minute before transferring to wire racks. Store/freeze in layers separated by waxed paper. 4 dozen.

Candy and Fudge

Peanut Clusters
A Christmas classic at our house. This is my mom's recipe.

1 package almond bark
1 12-oz bag of semi-sweet or dark chocolate chips
1 oz. unsweetened chocolate (a square, chopped, or a
    pre-melted pkg.)
24 oz. (or larger!) container of dry roasted peanuts

Coarsely chop the almond bark into chunks and melt in a microwave or crockery pot with the chocolate chips and the unsweetened chocolate, stirring until smooth. Stir in the peanuts. Drop by spoonfuls onto wax-paper-lined cookie sheets, allowing space for the clusters to spread. Cool completely. Devour.

<u>Kitchen Hint</u>: For a variation, use mixed nuts. This is one recipe you don't want to make "healthier" by using un-salted nuts. The salt cuts the sweetness and makes them irresistible.

Peppermint Bark
This is the easiest candy on the face of the earth, and a re-freshing, crunchy addition to a goody tray.

1 package almond bark
1½ pounds of unwrapped peppermint starlight mints OR
    ¾ lb. each of peppermint and spearmint starlights

Melt the chunked-up almond bark in a microwave or crockery cooker, stirring now and again until smooth. Meanwhile, place the unwrapped candies in a large reseal-able plastic bag, lay on top of a towel, and pound carefully with a hammer until all the mints are broken into coarse chunks. (Yes, the bag will get little holes in it. Helps to turn the bag over now and again.). Stir the crushed candies into the melted bark. Line a 10 x 17" pan with wax paper, then pour the hot candy into it and quickly spread it into a fairly even layer. Cool completely. Break into serving pieces. Store covered, in a plastic or wax-paper-lined container, in a cool, dry place. No need to refrigerate, but you can.

Pistachio Cranberry Bark
This is a close cousin to the peppermint bark, but in a salty-sweet-crunchy league by itself.
1 package almond bark

1 bag dried cranberries
1 C. semi-sweet or dark chocolate chips
2 C. shelled, salted pistachios

Chop the bark into chunks and melt in the microwave or
a crockery cooker, stirring until smooth. Line a 10 x 17"
baking pan with waxed paper. Stir the cranberries and pistachios into the bark and pour the hot mixture onto the
wax paper. Sprinkle on the chocolate chips and swirl the
chocolate as you spread the candy into an even layer (use
a cake spatula). Cool completely, then break into chunks.
Store in a plastic- or wax-paper-lined container in a cool,
dry place.

<u>Kitchen Hint</u>: Depending on how much crunch you prefer,
you can add more berries and nuts.

Other Goodies

Chocolate Coconut Cake
When the Coblentz twins request this cake for their birthday, they're girls after my own heart! This looks like an
ordinary cake until you cut in and discover a layer of
moist, chewy coconut filling.

1 chocolate cake mix (pudding in the mix)
1 C. sugar
1 C. milk
24 large marshmallows
1 14-oz. bag of coconut

Preheat oven to 350°. Spray two 9 x 13" pans and cut wax paper
to line the bottom and both ends of one pan. Mix the cake

according to package directions and divide batter into both pans. Bake for 15–20 minutes, until firm. Cool in the pans.

<u>Filling</u>: Bring the milk and sugar to a boil in a medium pan. Reduce heat and stir in the marshmallows to melt them. Stir in the coconut and cool. Spread this filling on the cake without the waxed paper. Run a knife along the edges of the papered cake, invert onto the coconut filling, and peel off the wax paper. Press down lightly.

<u>Frosting</u>: Place 1½ c. sugar, 1 C. evaporated milk, and one stick of butter or margarine in a medium pan on the stove and bring to a boil. Add an 11-oz. bag of chocolate chips, stirring to melt them, and stir in 1 C. chopped nuts. Pour this over the cake and spread evenly. Cool. Chill for several hours and store in the fridge.

<u>Kitchen Hint</u>: You can use any flavor of cake mix with this coconut filling, and simply frost it with a tub of coordinating frosting. Strawberry and lemon are especially good!

Butterscotch Twist Rolls
Leave it to Nazareth and Jerusalem Hooley to tempt us with a breakfast treat that makes the house smell like butterscotch and looks especially pretty in its unique round shape (before you break away one twist after another, that is!) You can substitute maple flavoring for the butterscotch, too.

1 T./1 pkg. yeast
¼ C. water
¾ C. milk
¼ C. butter
1 egg
1 tsp. butterscotch flavoring

½ tsp. salt
3 T. sugar
3 C. flour

Filling
¼ C. butter, softened
½ C. brown sugar
⅓ C. chopped nuts
1 tsp. cinnamon

Glaze
1 C. powdered sugar
1 T. melted butter
1 to 2 T. milk (or enough to make drizzly)
½ tsp. butterscotch flavoring

Dissolve yeast in water. Heat milk and butter until scalded (steaming but not boiling). Cool and add yeast. Beat egg, butterscotch flavoring, salt, and sugar. Add flour and mix well with the liquid. Cover and let rise for 1 hour. Divide into 2 equal parts. Roll out 1 part and put on a greased round pizza pan. Put filling ingredients on top. Roll out second part of dough and lay over filling. Use a greased pizza cutter and slice toward the middle, leaving 2" in the middle not cut. Continue cutting, making 12–14 slices. Twist each slice 2 times. Let rise and bake at 350° for 20 minutes. Drizzle with glaze. Devour.

Old-Fashioned Bread Pudding
A reader asked me for this recipe, so I've included it here—you can make this basic bread pudding to suit any occasion with just a change of add-ins! It's also a great way to use up leftover bread, heels, or slices that have

gone dry. I've even crumbled in a few stale biscuits, and it still comes out great!

2 C. milk
4 C. bread cubes
¼ C. butter or margarine
½ C. sugar
2 eggs
½ C. raisins
1 T. cinnamon
2 tsp. vanilla

Preheat oven to 350°. Spray or grease a 2-qt. baking dish.

Scald the milk (on the stove, or in the microwave for about 3 minutes, until it's steaming), stir in the butter/margarine until it melts, and then pour it over the bread cubes in a large bowl. Cool slightly, then mix the sugar, eggs, raisins and cinnamon. Stir into the bread mixture. Pour into prepared baking dish and bake about 40 minutes, until a knife inserted in the center comes out clean. Serves 6.

<u>Add-ins:</u> Along with, or instead of, the raisins, you can stir in 1 C. chocolate chips, or 1 C. butterscotch chips, and/or some chopped nuts, or 1 C. chopped apple. You can substitute dried cranberries or other dried fruits, as well. Adding flavorings like buttered rum, almond, or lemon extract makes a nice variation, too. You can also drizzle ice cream toppings or maple syrup over it before serving.

Read more heartwarming Christmas
romance from Charlotte Hubbard in her third
Seasons of the Heart novel,
Winter of Wishes,
available now.

As Rhoda Lantz stood gazing out the window of the Sweet Seasons Bakery Café, her mood matched the ominous gray clouds that shrouded the dark, pre-dawn sky. Here it was the day after Thanksgiving and she felt anything but thankful. Oh, she'd eaten Mamma's wonderful dinner yesterday and smiled at all the right times during the gathering of family and friends around their extended kitchen table, but she'd been going through the motions. Feeling distanced . . . not liking it, but not knowing what to do about it, either.

"You all right, honey bug? Ya seem a million miles away."

Rhoda jumped. Mamma had slipped up behind her while she'd been lost in her thoughts. "*Jah, jah.* Fine and dandy," she fibbed. "Just thinkin' how it looks like we're in for a winter storm, which most likely means we won't have as many folks come to eat today and tomorrow. It's just . . . well, things got really slow last year at this time."

Her mother's concerned gaze told Rhoda her little white lie hadn't sounded very convincing. Mamma glanced toward the kitchen, where her partner, Naomi Brenneman, and Naomi's daughter, Hannah, were frying sausage and bacon for the day's breakfast buffet. "Tell ya what," she said gently. "Lydia Zook left a phone message about a couple of fresh turkeys left in their meat case. Why not go to the market and fetch those, along with a case of eggs—and I'm thinkin' it's a perfect day for that wonderful-*gut* cream soup we make with the potatoes and carrots and cheese in the sauce. I'll call in the order, and by the time ya get over there they'll have everything all gathered up."

"*Jah*, Mamma, I can do that," Rhoda murmured. It meant walking down the long lane with the wind whipping at her coat, and then hitching up a carriage, but it was something useful to do.

Useful. Why is it such a struggle lately to feel useful?

Rhoda slipped her coat from the peg at the door, tied on her heavy black bonnet, and stepped outside with a gasp. The temperature had dropped several degrees since she'd come to the café an hour ago. The chill bit through her woolen stockings as she walked briskly along the gravel lane with her head lowered against the wind.

"Hey there, Rhoda! *Gut* mornin' to ya!" a voice sang out as she passed the smithy behind the Sweet Seasons.

Rhoda waved to Ben Hooley but didn't stop to chat. Why did the farrier's cheerfulness irritate her lately? She had gotten over her schoolgirl crush on him and was happy for Ben and Mamma both, but as their New Year's Day wedding approached they seemed more public about their affections—their *joy*—and well, that irritated her, too! Across the road from the Sweet Seasons a new home was going up in record time, as Ben's gift to her mother . . . yet another reminder of how Rhoda's life would change when Mamma moved out of the apartment above the blacksmith shop, and she would be living there alone.

As she reached the white house she'd grown up in,

Rhoda sighed. No lights glowed in the kitchen window and no one ate breakfast at the table: this holiday weekend, her twin sister Rachel and her new groom, Micah Brenneman, were on an extended trip around central Missouri to collect wedding presents as they visited aunts, uncles, and cousins of their two families. Rhoda missed working alongside Rachel at the café more than she could bear to admit, yet here again, she was happy for her sister. The newlyweds radiated a love and sense of satisfaction she could only dream of.

Rhoda hitched up the enclosed carriage and clapped the reins across the mare's broad back. If Thanksgiving had been so difficult yesterday, with so many signposts of the radical changes in all their lives, what would the upcoming Christmas season be like? Ordinarily she loved baking cookies, setting out the Nativity scene, and arranging evergreen branches and candles on the mantel and at the windowsills. Yet as thick, feathery flakes of snow blew across the yard, her heart thudded dully. It wasn't her way to feel so blue, or to feel life was passing her by. But at twenty-two, she heard her clock ticking ever so loudly.

God, have You stopped listenin' to my prayers for a husband and a family? Are You tellin' me I'm fated to remain a maidel?

Rhoda winced at the thought. She gave the horse its head once they were on the county blacktop, and as they rolled across the single-lane bridge that spanned this narrow spot in the Missouri River, she glanced over toward the new gristmill. The huge wooden wheel was in place now, churning slowly as the current of the water propelled it. The first light of dawn revealed two male figures on the roof. Luke and Ira Hooley, Ben's younger brothers, scrambled like monkeys as they checked their new machinery: The Mill at Willow Ridge would soon be open to tourists, and supplied by local farmers. In addition to regular wheat flour and cornmeal, the Hooley brothers would offer specialty grains that would sell to whole foods stores in Warrensburg and other nearby cities. Mamma was already gathering recipes to bake artisan breads at the Sweet Seasons, as an additional lure for health-conscious tourists.

But Rhoda's one brief date with Ira had proven he was more interested in running the roads with Annie Mae Knepp than in settling down or joining the church any time soon. Ira and Luke were nearing thirty, seemingly happy to live in a state of eternal *rumspringa*. Rhoda considered herself as fun-loving as any young woman, but she'd long ago committed herself to the Amish faith. Was it too much to ask the same sort of maturity of the men she dated?

She pulled up alongside Zook's Market. This grocery and dry goods store wouldn't open for a couple of hours yet, but already Henry and Lydia Zook were preparing for their day. Rhoda put a determined smile on her face as the bell above the door jangled. "Happy day after Thanksgivin' to ya!" she called out. "Mamm says you've got a couple turkeys for us today."

"*Jah*, Rhoda, we're packin' your boxes right this minute, too!" Lydia called out from behind the back counter. "Levi! Cyrus! You can be carryin' those big bags of potatoes and carrots out to Rhoda's carriage, please and thank ya."

From an aisle of the store, still shadowy in the low glow of the gas ceiling lights, two of the younger Zook boys stepped away from the shelves they had been restocking. "Hey there, Rhoda," twelve-year-old Levi mumbled.

"Tell your *mamm* we could use more of those fine blackberry pies," his younger brother Cyrus remarked as he hefted a fifty-pound bag of potatoes over his shoulder.

"That's my favorite, and they always sell out. Mamm won't let us buy a pie unless they're a day old—and most of 'em don't stay on the shelf that long."

Rhoda smiled wryly. Cyrus Zook wasn't the only fellow around Willow Ridge with a keen interest in her mother's pies. "I'll pass that along. *Denki* to you boys for loadin' the carriage."

"Levi's fetchin' your turkeys from the fridge," Henry said from behind his meat counter. "Won't be but a minute. Say—it sounds like ya had half of Willow Ridge over to your place for dinner yesterday."

Again Rhoda smiled to herself: word got around fast in a small town. "*Jah*, what with Ben and his two brothers and two aunts—and the fact that those aunts invited Tom Hostetler and Hiram and his whole tribe to join us— we had quite a houseful."

"Awful nice of ya to look after Preacher Tom and the bishop's bunch," Lydia said with an approving nod. "Fellows without wives don't always get to celebrate with a real Thanksgiving dinner when their married kids live at a distance."

"Well, there was no telling Jerusalem and Nazareth Hooley they *couldn't* invite Tom and the Knepps," Rhoda replied with a chuckle. "So there ya have it. They brought half the meal, though, so that wasn't so bad."

"Tell your *mamm* we said hullo." Henry turned back toward the big grinder on the back table, where he was making fresh hamburger.

"*Jah*, I'll do that. And *denki* for havin' things all set to go."

Jonah Zook stood behind his *dat*'s counter trimming roasts, so Rhoda met his eye and nodded, but didn't try to make small talk. Jonah was a couple years younger than she, and had driven her home from a few Sunday night singings, but he had about as much sparkle as a crushed cardboard box. And goodness, but she could use some *sparkle* about now . . .

Rhoda glanced out the store's front window. Levi and Cyrus were taking their sweet time about loading her groceries, so she wandered over to the bulletin board where folks posted notices of upcoming auctions and other announcements. No sense in standing out in that wind while the boys joshed around.

The old corkboard was pitted from years of use, and except for the sale bills for upcoming household auctions in New Haven and Morning Star, the yellowed notices for herbal remedies, fresh eggs, and local fellows' businesses had hung there for months. Rhoda sighed—and then caught sight of a note half-hidden by an auction flyer.

Need a compassionate, patient caretaker for my elderly mother, plus after-school supervision for two kids. New Haven, just a block off the county highway. Call Andy Leitner.

Rhoda snatched the little notice from the board, her heart thumping. She knew nothing about this fellow except his phone number and that he had an ailing mother and two young children—and that he was surely English if he was advertising for help with family members. Yet something about his decisive block printing told her Mr. Leitner was a man who didn't waffle over decisions or accept a half-hearted effort from anyone who would work in his home. He apparently had no wife—

Maybe she works away from home. Happens a lot amongst English families.

—and if he had posted this advertisement in Zook's Market, he surely realized a Plain woman would be most likely to respond. It was common for Amish and Mennonite gals to hire on for housework and caretaking in English homes, so surely no one would object if she gave him a call and started working there, why—as soon as tomorrow!

*How many of these notices has he posted? Plenty of
Plain bulk stores to advertise in around Morning Star,
and the big discount stores out past New Haven.*

Pulse pounding, Rhoda stepped outside to the carriage.
"You fellas got all my stuff loaded, *jah*?" she demanded.
Levi and Cyrus were playing a rousing game of catch
with a huge hard-packed snowball, paying no heed to the
snow that was falling on their green shirt sleeves.

Levi, the older and ornerier of the two, poked his head
around the back of the carriage. "Got a train to catch, do
ya? Big day chasin' after that Ira Hooley fella?" he teased.
"Jonah, he says ya been tryin' to catch yourself some of
that Lancaster County money—"

"And what if I have?" Rhoda shot back. "Your *mamm*
won't take it too well when I tell her you two have been
lolligaggin' out here instead of stockin' your shelves,
ain't so?"

Levi waited until she was stepping into the carriage
before firing the snowball at her backside. But what
would she accomplish by stepping out to confront him?
Rhoda glanced at the two huge turkeys, the mesh sacks of
potatoes, carrots, and onions, and sturdy boxes loaded
with other staples Mamma had ordered, and decided she
was ready to go. She chuckled at the two boys' outcry
when she playfully backed the carriage toward them.
Then she urged the mare into a trot. All sorts of questions
buzzed in her mind as she headed for the Sweet Seasons.
What would Mamma say if she called Andy Leitner?
What if a mild winter meant the breakfast and lunch
shifts would remain busy, especially with Rachel off collecting wedding presents for a few more weekends?
Hannah Brenneman had only been helping them since her
sixteenth birthday last week—

*Jah, but she got her wish, to work in the café. And
Rachel got her wish when she married Micah. And*

*Mamma for sure and for certain got more than she dared
to wish for when Ben Hooley asked to marry her! So it's
about time for me to have a wish come true!*

Was that prideful, self-centered thinking? As Rhoda
pulled up at the café, she didn't much worry about the
complications of religion or the Old Ways. She stepped
into the dining room, spotted her cousins, Nate and Bram
Kanagy, and caught them before they went back to the
buffet for another round of biscuits and gravy. "Could I
get you boys to carry in a couple of turkeys and some big
bags of produce?" she asked sweetly. Then she nodded
toward the kitchen, where Hannah was drizzling white
icing on a fresh pan of Mamma's sticky buns. "Could be
you can talk our new cook out of a mighty *gut* cinnamon
roll, if ya smile at her real nice."

Nate rolled his eyes, but Bram's handsome face lit up.
"*Jah*, I noticed how the scenery in the kitchen had im-
proved, cuz—not that it isn't a treat to watch you and
Rachel workin'," he added quickly.

"*Jah*, sure, ya say that after ya already stepped in it."
Rhoda widened her eyes at him playfully. "Here's your
chance to earn your breakfast—not to mention make a
few points with Hannah."

Rhoda went back outside to grab one of the lighter
boxes. Then, once Nate had followed her in with bags of
onions and carrots, and he was chatting with Naomi,
Hannah, and Mamma, she slipped out to the phone shanty
before she lost her nerve. Common sense told her she
should think out some answers to whatever questions
Andy Leitner might ask, yet excitement overruled her
usual practicality. Chances were good that she'd have to
leave him a voice mail, anyway, so as she sat down in the
phone shanty and her fingers danced over the phone
number, her thoughts raced. Never in her life had she considered working in another family's home, yet this seemed

like the opportunity she'd been hoping for—praying for—
of late. Surely Mamma would understand if—

"Hello?" a male voice came over the phone. He
sounded a little groggy.

Rhoda gripped the receiver. It hadn't occurred to her
that while she'd already worked a couple of hours at the
café, most of the world wasn't out of bed yet. "I—sorry I
called so early, but—"

"Not a problem. Glad for the wake-up call, because it
seems I fell back asleep," he replied with a soft groan.
"How can I help you?"

Rhoda's imagination ran wild. If this was Andy Leitner, he had a deep, mellow voice. Even though she'd
awakened him and he was running late, he spoke pleas-
antly. "I, um, found the notice from an Andy Leitner on
the board in Zook's Market just now, and—" She closed
her eyes, wondering where the words had disappeared to.
She had to sound businesslike, or at least competent, or
this man wouldn't want to talk to her.

"You're interested in the position?" he asked with a
hopeful upturn in his voice. "I was wondering if the store
owners had taken my note down."

Rhoda's heart raced. "Jah, I'd like to talk to you about
it, for sure and for certain," she gushed. "But ya should
understand right out that I don't have a car, on account of
how we Amish don't believe in ownin'—I mean, I'm not
preachin' at ya, or—"

She winced. "This is comin' out all wrong. Sorry," she
rasped. "My name's Rhoda Lantz, and I'm in Willow
Ridge. I sure hope you don't think I'm too *ferhoodled* to
even be considered for the job."

"*Ferhoodled*?" The word rolled melodiously from the
receiver and teased at her.

"Crazy mixed-up," she explained. "Confused, and—

well, I'm keepin' ya from whatever ya need to be doin',
so—"

"Ah, but you're a solution to my problem. The answer
to a prayer," he added quietly. "For that, I have time to
listen, Rhoda. I need to make my shift at the hospital, but
could I come by and chat with you when I get off? Say,
around two this afternoon?"

Rhoda grinned. "That would be wonderful-*gut*, Mr.
Leitner! We'll be closin' up at two—my *mamm* runs the
Sweet Seasons Bakery Café on the county highway—and
we can talk at a back table."

"Sounds perfect. I'll see you then—and thanks so
much for calling, Rhoda."

"*Jah*, for sure and for certain!"

As she placed the receiver back in its cradle, Rhoda
held her breath. What would she tell Mamma? She felt
scared and excited and yes, *ferhoodled*, because she now
had an interview for a job! She had no idea about caring
for that elderly mother . . . or what if the kids ran her so
ragged she got nothing done except keeping them out
of trouble? What if Andy Leitner's family didn't like her
because she wore Plain clothing and kapps?

What have ya gone and done now, Rhoda Lantz?

She inhaled to settle herself, and headed back to the
café's kitchen. There was no going back, no unsaying
what she'd said over the phone. No matter what anyone
else thought, she could only move forward.

And wasn't that exactly what she'd been hoping to do
for weeks now?

Thrilling Suspense from
Beverly Barton

Available Wherever Books Are Sold!

Visit our website at **www.kensingtonbooks.com**

More from Bestselling Author
JANET DAILEY

Calder Storm	0-8217-7543-X	$7.99US/$10.99CAN
Close to You	1-4201-1714-9	$5.99US/$6.99CAN
Crazy in Love	1-4201-0303-2	$4.99US/$5.99CAN
Dance With Me	1-4201-2213-4	$5.99US/$6.99CAN
Everything	1-4201-2214-2	$5.99US/$6.99CAN
Forever	1-4201-2215-0	$5.99US/$6.99CAN
Green Calder Grass	0-8217-7222-8	$7.99US/$10.99CAN
Heiress	1-4201-0002-5	$6.99US/$7.99CAN
Lone Calder Star	0-8217-7542-1	$7.99US/$10.99CAN
Lover Man	1-4201-0666-X	$4.99US/$5.99CAN
Masquerade	1-4201-0005-X	$6.99US/$8.99CAN
Mistletoe and Molly	1-4201-0041-6	$6.99US/$9.99CAN
Rivals	1-4201-0003-3	$6.99US/$7.99CAN
Santa in a Stetson	1-4201-0664-3	$6.99US/$9.99CAN
Santa in Montana	1-4201-1474-3	$7.99US/$9.99CAN
Searching for Santa	1-4201-0306-7	$6.99US/$9.99CAN
Something More	0-8217-7544-8	$7.99US/$9.99CAN
Stealing Kisses	1-4201-0304-0	$4.99US/$5.99CAN
Tangled Vines	1-4201-0004-1	$6.99US/$8.99CAN
Texas Kiss	1-4201-0665-1	$4.99US/$5.99CAN
That Loving Feeling	1-4201-1713-0	$5.99US/$6.99CAN
To Santa With Love	1-4201-2073-5	$6.99US/$7.99CAN
When You Kiss Me	1-4201-0667-8	$4.99US/$5.99CAN
Yes, I Do	1-4201-0305-9	$4.99US/$5.99CAN

Available Wherever Books Are Sold!

Check out our website at www.kensingtonbooks.com.

Romantic Suspense from
Lisa Jackson

See How She Dies	0-8217-7605-3	$6.99US/$9.99CAN
Final Scream	0-8217-7712-2	$7.99US/$10.99CAN
Wishes	0-8217-6309-1	$5.99US/$7.99CAN
Whispers	0-8217-7603-7	$6.99US/$9.99CAN
Twice Kissed	0-8217-6038-6	$5.99US/$7.99CAN
Unspoken	0-8217-6402-0	$6.50US/$8.50CAN
If She Only Knew	0-8217-6708-9	$6.50US/$8.50CAN
Hot Blooded	0-8217-6841-7	$6.99US/$9.99CAN
Cold Blooded	0-8217-6934-0	$6.99US/$9.99CAN
The Night Before	0-8217-6936-7	$6.99US/$9.99CAN
The Morning After	0-8217-7295-3	$6.99US/$9.99CAN
Deep Freeze	0-8217-7296-1	$7.99US/$10.99CAN
Fatal Burn	0-8217-7577-4	$7.99US/$10.99CAN
Shiver	0-8217-7578-2	$7.99US/$10.99CAN
Most Likely to Die	0-8217-7576-6	$7.99US/$10.99CAN
Absolute Fear	0-8217-7936-2	$7.99US/$9.49CAN
Almost Dead	0-8217-7579-0	$7.99US/$10.99CAN
Lost Souls	0-8217-7938-9	$7.99US/$10.99CAN
Left to Die	1-4201-0276-1	$7.99US/$10.99CAN
Wicked Game	1-4201-0338-5	$7.99US/$9.99CAN
Malice	0-8217-7940-0	$7.99US/$9.49CAN

Available Wherever Books Are Sold!
Visit our website at **www.kensingtonbooks.com**